WHEN LOVE COMES

A DIAMOND CREEK, ALASKA NOVEL

J.H. CROIX

J.H. CROIX

This is a work of fiction. Names, characters, businesses, places, events and incidents are either the products of the author's imagination or used in a fictitious manner. Any resemblance to actual persons, living or dead, or actual events is purely coincidental.

ISBN: 1500903140

ISBN 13: 9781500903145

Cover design by CT Cover Creations

❀ Created with Vellum

DEDICATION

A shout out to my husband – a man who has the sense to enjoy horror and romance at the same time (only in real life romance), supports every dream great and small, adores our dogs, and loves me in spite of myself.

Sign up for my newsletter for information on new releases & get a FREE copy of one of my books!

http://jhcroixauthor.com/subscribe/

Follow me!
jhcroix@jhcroix.com
https://amazon.com/author/jhcroix
https://www.bookbub.com/authors/j-h-croix
https://www.facebook.com/jhcroix

NOTE TO READERS

Welcome to Diamond Creek, Alaska! Each book in this series can be read as a standalone novel. The Diamond Creek, Alaska Novels are steamy, tender, and poignant contemporary romances set in the beautiful, wild, and quirky community of Diamond Creek.

In When Love Comes, you will meet Hannah and Luke and share their journey. I hope you fall in love with them, just as I have. As for whose heart may be up for grabs next? Well...I hope you'll keep reading as Diamond Creek has many stories, surprises, and sexy escapades to offer, all set in the breathtaking beauty of the Alaskan wilderness. From someone who called Alaska home for over a decade, Alaska might be cold, but its romance is hot!

Happy reading and thanks for joining us in the last frontier!

~J.H. Croix~

PROLOGUE

*H*annah stared at the groceries that had tumbled out of her basket. A smashed tomato rested against a jar of olives, red tomato juice pooling on the floor. A can of soup rolled until it bounced against a display sign for orange juice promising, of all things, to make every day great. Hannah wished a great day could be guaranteed with orange juice. She'd buy it in bulk. She knelt down to clean up the mess. A second ago, she'd collided with someone as she came around the corner of the aisle.

"What the hell?"

She started to apologize, only to be cut off.

"Oh, whatever. Look where you're going, why don't you?" a man said, the words more of a demand than a question.

Hannah stood up, leaving her spilled groceries on the floor, and found herself looking down into the face of an irate man decked out in gym clothes, a matching top and bottom of shiny red fabric. She opened her mouth to speak, only to have his words trample her thoughts.

"Jesus, you're a freakin' giant. Enjoy cleaning up your

mess." He waved a hand toward the groceries on the floor and stalked off, his shoes squeaking with each step.

Hannah watched him walk away. She looked around to catch a few sympathetic glances, but no one said anything or moved to help. She didn't appreciate being called a giant, but she was tall by most standards at six feet. She went through the motions of shopping, feeling alone in the store. Back in her small apartment, she turned on the TV to fill the quiet. While she ate a solitary dinner, her mind rolled back to a place where she didn't feel so alone.

Hannah's memory of the night she first arrived in Alaska was vivid. She was six years old and wide-awake despite having traveled for more than twelve hours from North Carolina with two layovers and three flights. With her forehead pressed against the plane window, glittering lights came into view in the dark sky, their reflections shimmering on the ocean water as the plane descended. Their destination, Diamond Creek, lay along the shores of Kachemak Bay. The lights shaped a town in darkness for her, streets curving up hillsides and winding along the ocean. A few neon signs shone boldly in the darkness.

As they landed, the tiny plane bounced and rumbled. The whir of the motors grew louder. She would forever associate that particular sound with Alaskan nights. It heralded their arrival. Hannah remembered the distinct sound of tires rolling over snow-packed roads, later the feeling of a heavy quilt tucked around her as she was lulled in and out of sleep, and then awakening to bright sun. Twenty-two years later, her first look out the window was still sharp in her memory. Snow-covered peaks stood stark against a bright blue sky. Deep green spruce trees dusted with snow were scattered across the view. Sunlight glinted on the ocean bay with wind whipping waves across the water.

Hannah glanced around her small living room and

sighed, thinking that she was sighing a bit much lately. The nightly news rattled on in the background. She was probably four thousand miles, give or take, away from Alaska. Her view here was of a coffee shop across the street in a small town in Massachusetts. The town's main street was picturesque in its quaint charm, but it lacked the wild sense of Diamond Creek. Her parents remained in Diamond Creek, where she was raised until graduate school led her to Massachusetts.

Just as she was starting classes for her graduate degree in environmental science, the news came that her parents had died in a plane crash in rural Alaska. Their death had ricocheted through her heart. That was two years prior, and she had yet to return to Alaska since the surreal trip for the funeral throughout which she'd been emotionally numb. She thought back to the incident at the grocery store, a small matter really. She lay awake that night, her mind spinning on the wheel of the feeling that had clung to her in the grocery store. *Alone.* She tried to remember if she'd had anyone to share dinner or drinks with in recent memory, or if anyone had visited her apartment in the last year. The fact that she had to think about it offered the answer. Her encounter with the rude stranger at the store marked a high point in human interaction beyond when she was at work or in classes. Her life was solitary, a marked contrast to her life in Diamond Creek where a day didn't go by without someone who mattered being woven into its fabric.

The following morning, Hannah looked across the street to the coffee shop, blinking her eyes at the prick of tears, the wish to be home rushing through her. Visceral memories of Alaska suffused her mind. Cool windy days in summer. Walks along the beach scattered with rocks, the occasional lava stones, seaweed, and starfish. The fuchsia of fireweed come fall, and colors dancing along the ground. The curious quiet of winter, when the snow muffled all sounds. The bite of winter air and breath of wood smoke. Stars bright and bare against the sky. And the tight-knit community of friends—interwoven in such a way that feeling alone was rare.

She stared blindly at the coffee shop across the street and shuttered her memories, shying away from the feelings they elicited. She was one week away from finishing her degree. As she closed her apartment door and listened to the echo of the lock in the hallway of hardwood floors, the yearning to be in Diamond Creek, where they never locked the door, was so acute she swallowed a sob. With no one in the hall to see, she leaned her forehead against the door and let tears slip down her cheeks. Later that morning, she turned in her final papers. It would be one month and almost as many sleepless nights before she found herself on the lone highway that led to Diamond Creek.

CHAPTER 1

*H*annah gripped the steering wheel of her parents' Toyota truck and felt waves of grief alternating with exhilaration flow through her. Her father's friend Frank had offered to drop off the truck for her when she landed in Anchorage. Nostalgia washed through her when she spied the bright red truck in the airport parking lot. When she opened the back of the cab, she found herself looking at odds and ends that had traveled with her parents in any of the trucks they'd had, her eyes landing on two pairs of brown XtraTufs. XtraTufs were the favored heavy-duty rubber boot in Alaska—her parents never went anywhere without them. Knowing that they had probably last been touched by her parents brought a flash of grief.

For God's sake, they're just boots. With her chest tight, Hannah tossed her bags into the back of the truck.

It was late spring in Alaska with lupine starting to bloom in small clusters in the tall grass along the highway. The landscape varied, fields of grass alternating with spruce forests and ocean views. Exhilaration rose through the grief and came from being back in a place where she belonged. She had missed the feeling so much that she hadn't known how empty she felt away from here. At the same time, the loss of her parents was so sharp; she could barely tolerate it at times.

Hannah's recollection of her mother, Janet, was one of steadiness and warmth. To those in the lower forty-eight (as the rest of the United States was known to Alaskans), her mother's beauty would likely have been considered at odds with her willingness to get dirty. She could change the oil on a truck, fillet a fish, chase off moose, and head out for dinner looking beautiful. As for her father, John, he'd loved his wife, his daughter, and his work. His love of biology led them to Alaska and kept him intellectually immersed.

Hannah grinned as she caught sight of a moose along the side of the road, calmly nibbling at an alder tree. They were so common in Alaska that drivers had to be careful in the winter months to avoid them on roads. They were often seen ambling about town and in backyards. Diamond Creek was south of Anchorage toward the lower end of the Kenai Peninsula. There was only one route there, south along Seward Highway and then farther south on the Sterling Highway. This had been the last road she'd traveled in Alaska with her mother –almost two and a half years ago when her mother drove her to Anchorage for her flight out to Massachusetts when she moved away. Hannah blinked when she recalled that she and her mother had argued on that drive, the last time she'd seen her mother. Her mother had tried to bring up her concern about Hannah's most recent impulsive choice—that she'd blown her meager savings on a trip to Costa Rica with a man she'd barely known. Hannah had reacted as usual—she'd dismissed her mother's concern and changed the subject. She'd tried to hide what it felt like to let them down time and again and shoved her battered self-respect out of the way with bravado.

The recollection made her cringe. The argument between her and her mother could have been a record she played over and over, the only variations related to where she was running off to and with whom. She didn't like to think much about it, but she used to drive her parents nuts. In some ways, she had it together in that she had high grades and usually had a job. Before college in Anchorage, she had been less wild, but then she had her heart broken in the worst way. Or that's how it felt. She'd fallen hard for Damon, a charming, rugged, handsome guy from Juneau.

Damon was everything Hannah thought she wanted—funny, smart, and an avid outdoorsman. She fell hard and along the way ignored all the obvious red flags, such as that he was a tad too familiar with lots of women and tended to be vague if she asked too many questions. But he was so much of what she thought she wanted that she dove right in, convinced they would be together for good. Her fantasy was blown up about a year into their relationship when she and Susie, her best friend, had gone for coffee at a new place in Anchorage. Lo and behold, Damon was there, cozied up to another woman. Susie had walked right up to Damon and called him out. Hannah had slunk back to the car. She'd actually let him persuade her it was a fluke and a huge mistake. Take two was when she ran into him with yet another woman when she was out for dinner with Susie and a few friends.

She'd had enough sense to break it off for good then. But the damage was done, and she spent the next few years running away from how she felt. She kept her relationships shallow and let the taste of adventure tug her just about anywhere, her heart shielded all the while. She'd convinced herself she could play it just as cool as the men who kept things casual. Her parents worried about her and didn't like seeing their only child running off on trips around the world with men she barely knew. The consequences of her superficial, flighty choices were the incremental loss of her self-respect and her parents' disappointment. She also had no savings to speak of and was often scrounging for money to cover bills.

Hannah wished her parents knew she'd stopped being so impulsive after they died. It was as if a switch turned off. She'd become almost rigidly responsible. Actually, the last trip she'd chased after a man had been the trip to Costa Rica, which had been the source of conflict with her mother. The man in question had ended up leaving her stranded in a hotel with no money to pay the bill while he took off with a lovely young woman he met there. Hannah had been forced to sneak out of the hotel, using what little money she had left to pay for the cab to take her to the airport. She'd been wise enough to purchase a round-trip ticket. After her parents died and she'd built up a teensy amount of savings, she'd paid off that hotel bill.

As she approached Diamond Creek, she pulled over to a viewing spot. Parts of Diamond Creek along the shoreline sat high on a bluff that flanked the ocean below. She leaned against a railing along the edge of the bluff. In a few weeks, the area would be filled with campers and RVs, drivers stopping to snap photos of the view. For now, it was blessedly empty. Looking out over Kachemak Bay, Hannah breathed deep. It was early afternoon, and the wind was light. The mountains stood silently across the water, mostly green with patches of snow left in the shady areas. Tears slid down her cheeks, and her chest loosened for the first time in years. A raven flew past her and called to another in the distance. An eagle glided low along the shoreline.

Gathering herself, she went into the rest-stop bathroom. Wiping her face with a damp paper towel, she looked in the mirror. Her long brown hair hung in tangled waves around her shoulders. Sky-blue eyes looked back at her, eyes she'd inherited from her mother. Her mouth was wide with full lips. She was too tall for the mirror, which cut her reflection off at the forehead if she stood up straight. Tugging her hair back, she twisted it into a knot and returned to her truck.

The sign for Emerald Road sat crookedly at the base of a small hill. She remembered when the city had installed new street signs years ago. The Emerald Road sign had tilted drunkenly after the first spring of frost heaves and mud, remaining in that state since. Her childhood home was the last on the road, which ended in a gravel cul-de-sac. The house was a two-story barn-shaped home with cedar siding. Blue spruce trees stood sentry at the entrance of the short driveway. She came to a stop and turned the engine off. Silence seeped through her for a moment before being interrupted by magpies chattering in the trees. Her gaze traveled around the yard. The spruce trees opened up to a small grassy area with the house sitting to one side. A field of fireweed, not yet blooming, flanked the left of the house with trees filling the rest of the area. Her mother's raised flower beds were overgrown with weeds.

Hannah imagined the family's old dog, Grayson, running out to greet her. Grayson had died peacefully in his sleep shortly before she'd left for graduate school. She felt his absence sharply. He'd been a fixture of her life with her parents in Alaska, a quiet, steady presence.

Aside from the funeral, which Hannah barely recalled, the last time she'd been here, her parents had been vibrant and well. The house had usually buzzed with activity, holding a sense of motion and purpose. Now it lacked any sense of presence within. The house looked out over the road, which afforded an open view of the bay and mountains. Turning away from the view, Hannah stepped to the deep purple door that stood out against the wood-frame house, reflecting her mother's whimsical touch. When she entered the house, a soft quiet enveloped her. Despite two years of absence, the house held echoes of her parents' presence.

Hannah's heartbeat kicked up as she began to move through the house. The first floor of the house consisted of an expansive living room that opened onto the kitchen, exposed wooden beams angling across the rooms. A bathroom and laundry room were situated behind the kitchen. A deep green soapstone woodstove anchored the living room. Walking upstairs, she stepped onto the landing and into a loftlike space with a railing on one side from which the living room could be seen. It had morphed throughout the years from a playroom to a television area to her mother's office and sewing area. Her parents' old bedroom was down a short hallway to the front of the house with the other two bedrooms on the back end.

Her parents' bedroom looked as it would have had they gone on vacation, clean and quiet with the bed made. Their clothing still hung in the closet. Hannah's bedroom was as she'd left it last. In here, at least, she felt less of her parents' lingering presence. Though few of her belongings remained, her bed was covered with the quilt she'd had throughout high school, a spiral of bright colors with a swirling star in the center sewn by her mother. Her chest started to loosen. In spite of two years of fear, she'd gotten through what she had been most afraid of: being here, in the place that held the memory of her parents. Back downstairs, she looked at the empty refrigerator. She needed to go to the store, which while maybe not as difficult as coming to her old home, would actually involve speaking to people.

Hannah left her bags in her old room since it felt the most comfortable for now. Her choice now was to wander around the empty house or take her hungry self to town. She had one granola bar left. She wished Grayson were here to give her courage. He'd loved car rides and often tagged along on errands. But no Grayson, just herself. For a flicker, she felt swamped by the cold emptiness that she'd tried to keep at bay since her parents died. She took a deep breath, shored her feelings into a corner, and hopped back into the truck.

CHAPTER 2

*T*he house sat atop one of the hills overlooking town. As Hannah drove down, she saw familiar names on mailboxes and an old friend's car parked in a drive. Once on the main road that led into town, she passed the post office, its parking lot busy. In rural towns like Diamond Creek, the post office served as a central gathering point. She caught sight of Frank's wife, June, walking across the lot. Her throat tightened as she worried over whom she might encounter first, desperately wanting to see old friends yet anxious about it.

Entering the grocery store, she went on autopilot and grabbed a cart. In a scant minute, she felt her friend Susie before she heard her squeal. Susie had a forceful presence. As Hannah turned with anxiety beating like wings in her chest, Susie threw her arms around her. She returned the hug, dropping her purse in the process.

"It's you, you, you, you! I knew you'd be here soon. I felt it," Susie said in between bouncing on her feet, hugging Hannah, and patting her on the shoulder.

Hannah was so relieved to be in Susie's presence, the

wings of anxiety settled, and she felt almost giddy. Bending to retrieve her purse, she looked up into Susie's warm brown eyes and took in her matching brown curls, which tumbled as wildly as ever about her shoulders. Susie tended to dress colorfully and held true to that today in a purple blouse paired with green leggings.

Hannah plowed through her anxiety. "Yup, I'm here. Finally…" She stumbled on. "I'm sorry I didn't call or text or e-mail or write or whatever much. I don't know what to say. Other than that I missed my parents and anyone connected to them—that meant you…and, well…I wasn't ready." She caught herself, startled that the words had poured out so fast. She'd thought for hours over what she'd say to explain her silence and hadn't come up with anything that made sense. Her words were bald and bare, but they were the truth.

Susie didn't blink or hesitate. "Of course you weren't ready. I've been waiting—safe to say lots of us have." Susie reached over for another hug and just held Hannah close. If it were any grocery store other than this one, Hannah might have wondered what other shoppers thought, but here she felt safe to just be hugged by her best friend.

Susie pulled back again. "You must have just gotten in. Frank mentioned you'd be arriving soon. Have to admit I didn't just 'feel' you'd be here. Frank clued me in," she said with a smile. "Have you even been to the house?"

Hannah nodded. "It was weird, but I'm okay. I wish Grayson were still around. I knew it'd feel empty without Mom and Dad; I just didn't think how strange it would be without him too. I'm here to stay, you know. Can't tell you how relieved I am that you're okay with me being…well… such a mess about staying in touch while I was gone." She felt tears well up and paused to take a breath.

Susie touched her on the shoulder. "Look, I won't pretend I didn't have my moments of being cranky about it.

But you're my best friend and...your parents...to have them go like that, it must have been hell—probably still is. I was worried and pissed off sometimes, but I knew you'd come home. Just didn't know when. Glad it wasn't much longer because it's hard to replace your best friend since first grade."

At that, Susie's eyes welled up. "I don't know if you want my help, but you're getting it," Susie said, lifting her chin and looping her arm through Hannah's. "You need to get situated, so let's make it happen."

Despite two years with only a few calls, Susie was the closest thing to family Hannah had left. Being in her presence felt like coming home. She squeezed Susie's arm. "I'd love your help. You can boss me around."

In short order, they were back at the house unloading groceries. As Susie looked around the house, Hannah wondered if she'd been by to check on the house since her parents died. Instead of burying the question, she asked and learned that Susie, along with Frank, June, and a few other family friends, had emptied the refrigerator and cleaned the house in the weeks following the plane crash and funeral. Susie explained how they had decided to leave her parents' belongings for her to deal with because they didn't want to get rid of anything sentimental. Hannah was relieved to know that someone had taken care of the house since she hadn't been able. Her parents had loved their home, and when she had allowed thoughts to surface about it while she was gone, she had fretted about leaving the house alone.

Susie stayed late into evening. As it was early summer, she and Susie sat on the deck for a few hours, drinking wine that Susie had insisted on buying and nibbling on remnants of dinner. Over the course of the evening, Susie gently asked when Hannah wanted it to be known she was back in town. She reminded her Frank and June had mentioned it to a few and that word always traveled. Hannah appreciated

Susie's respect about not pushing her but knew she needed to dive in. She'd mastered the art of isolation during the past two years, and if she carried that over here, it might become a safety blanket she couldn't release.

Summer in Alaska meant endless sunsets. It was well past midnight when Susie left, and the sky was still wispy gray. Hannah took a long shower in her parents' bathroom. The bathroom remodel had been one of her mother's pet projects. It was tiled floor to ceiling in a soft green tile. There were wall jets and an overhead rainfall shower. It was bliss and helped her wash away her trip and the surreal feeling of being in the house and seeing Susie again. The quiet of the house offered a comfort she hadn't expected. She fell asleep within moments of tugging up her old quilt.

CHAPTER 3

*S*alty ocean water sprayed Hannah's cheek when the salmon bounced against her shoulder. The salmon in question splashed back into the water, disappearing from sight with a flick of silver. She heard a laugh and turned to glance at Susie, who stood in the water alongside her, the strong current flowing around them.

"Close, but not close enough. Needs to be in your net," Susie commented, her smile wide.

Hannah shrugged. "We already have plenty; I don't mind missing a few. Just glad it didn't hit my face."

She adjusted her grip on the dip net and glanced back toward the water. They stood waist-deep in waders in water where the ocean surged into the mouth of the Kenai River, engaging in a yearly ritual for most Alaskans: salmon dipnetting. This occurred midsummer and involved standing in icy ocean water flowing upriver with salmon fiercely following the current on their way to yearly spawning grounds. Those who braved the water held tight to large nets and hoped for salmon to swim into them as they made their way up the river.

Hannah had been home a few days, dipnetting the last thing on her mind. Susie called the day before and insisted Hannah accompany her today, cajoling her into coming by reminding her that they used to go together every year. Now that they were there, Hannah couldn't believe she'd hesitated. She'd forgotten how invigorating it was to be in the midst of the thrum of activity. A wall of salmon seemed to be entering the river today, riding the momentum of the tide. Within an hour, they had caught close to thirty salmon. Hannah felt the cold water through her waders. Though perfectly dry, her legs were beginning to tire from the cold surrounding them. Salmon bumped against her legs as they swam past. Her net abruptly surged, the weight of a salmon almost pulling it out of her hands. After a quick tug to pull the net under her control, she turned to drag it to shore.

As she reached the sandy beach, she looked back to make sure the salmon remained in the net. Its silvery skin gleamed in the bright sun. She stumbled when she ran straight into someone. Turning forward, she found herself looking into bright green eyes. She straightened and looked at the tall man she'd barreled into. At six feet, she rarely had to look up at men, but she found herself tipping her head back slightly. She took in windblown, shaggy black curls, a wide sensual mouth, chiseled masculine features, and a loose-limbed, athletic body.

"Oh, sorry," she said.

"No need to apologize. Wasn't paying attention," the man said, dimples joining a smile to cause a flutter in Hannah's belly. For a moment, she wished she wasn't garbed in fishing waders and rubber boots. She guessed her hair was a mess, not to mention that she had fish slime smeared on her shoulder.

"Just coming by to say hey to Susie. She's a friend. Don't think I know you, though. I'm Luke...Luke Winters," the man said with a question in his eyes. He lifted a hand to brush curls away from his eyes. There didn't seem much point to it, as the wind blew his curls wild again.

Hannah realized she was staring at the same time she felt the salmon in her net make a leap. She turned back to see the salmon had managed to untangle itself from the gill net and was flopping its way out of her net. With a lunge, she moved to grab the salmon at the same time Luke did. Their shoulders collided as Hannah reached for the errant salmon. Needless to say, her hold on the fish was poor, and she ended up flinging it into Luke's chest just as she stumbled and fell in the sand. She looked up at him and sighed inside. He appeared to be the quintessential rugged outdoorsman and had quickly gotten hold of the salmon she'd flung at him. With a lifted eyebrow, he unhooked a small, bright orange fish whacker from his belt and proceeded to stun the fish. He took two quick strides and dipped the fish in and out of the water, rinsing the sand off.

"Are those coolers yours?" he asked, gesturing toward two coolers nearby as he stepped back.

At her nod, he tossed the salmon into the cooler closest to him. Hannah remained in the sand, where she'd fallen with her legs splayed in both directions. Her dark brown hair had come loose from its ponytail and blew in long strands across her face. She pushed them away and then realized her gloves were wet and sandy, leaving sand in her hair and streaked across her face.

"Need a hand?" he asked, extending one toward her.

She silently reached up and grasped his hand. She got her feet under her and felt a strong pull bring her up effortlessly. Once standing, she felt a little less clumsy and pulled her gloves off. She quickly brushed the sand off her cheeks and tucked her hair behind her ears. She looked back into Luke's eyes and took a deep breath.

"I'm Hannah...Gray," she belatedly said. "And no, I don't

think we've met before. I'm an old friend of Susie's, but I was away at school for the last two years."

"You caught that I'm Luke, right?" he asked.

"You mean before I threw a fish at you? I caught your name, but got a little sidetracked there. How do you know Susie?" she asked, glancing out to the water where Susie remained, her back to them as she spoke to someone else standing nearby in the water.

"She does the accounting for the fishing business I have with my brothers, The One that Didn't Get Away. We live about an hour south of here in Diamond Creek," he said.

"Oh, that's where I'm from. Love the name of your business," she said and paused, not wanting to explain just yet that she'd spent most of her childhood there and that her parents had died in a plane crash while she was away at graduate school.

Luke's green eyes held a questioning look. At her silence, he remarked, "Well, I just came over to say hi to Susie." He cupped his hands around his mouth to call to Susie.

Susie turned with a wave and hollered a return greeting to Luke but remained in the water.

Luke turned back to Hannah. "How long have you been here? Looks like you're close to your limit already," he said with a nod toward the coolers.

"We've only been here about an hour. Seems our timing was good. With the tide coming in, there's a ton of salmon passing through. I think I'm about done for now."

She usually managed polite conversation perfectly well, but something about this man muddled her. If she were feeling cliché, she'd blame it on his handsome, manly appearance, but growing up in Alaska had exposed her to reams of men who looked and lived the modern version of frontiersmen. She thought perhaps it was her, seeing as she felt like a giant bumbling mess at the moment. Between her waders and rubber boots and the fact that she had managed to cover herself with sand when she fell, she wanted to hide. The wind coming in from the ocean kept blowing her hair in her eyes.

The silence started to drag, at which point Luke spoke again. "Well, it was nice meeting you. Are you back from school to stay?"

Wonders didn't cease, and she managed to respond. "Yeah, I am. Back to stay. I just got back a few days ago. I'm still settling in, but Susie got me here today." She glanced to Susie again, who was chatting away with the nearby net holder. "She's one of my best friends. I forgot how much fun dipnetting is." She paused, again running out of words, and then pushed forward, taking the focus off herself. "How long have you been in Diamond Creek? I don't remember you from before."

Luke seemed unaware of her internal struggle, both the effect he had on her and the constant bubble of her parents' memories in her consciousness. Trying to explain what it was like to return to Alaska involved boulders of memories that she wasn't ready to roll out of the way.

"Moved here about two years ago with my two brothers. Before that, fished in Alaska for a few years, commercially that is, and decided we'd rather live here instead of coming up from Seattle. We love it. Sounds like we moved to Diamond Creek right about when you left for school," he said.

Just as she started to respond, someone called Luke's name. Hannah followed Luke's gaze and saw another black-haired man at a distance waving at the base of one of the paths toward the parking area. Luke returned the wave and turned back to her.

"That's my younger brother, Nathan. Time to go," he said. Despite his parting words, he took a speculative look at her, not yet moving to leave. Hannah swore her toes curled in her boots. She thought for a split second that he saw right past her waders, boots, and messy hair. His green eyes seemed to darken for a moment that passed in a flash, and she wondered if she were tricking herself.

"Well, with you back to stay, I'll see you around. Diamond Creek isn't too big. Not to mention that Susie's a friend," Luke said.

Hannah realized she was staring and silent, *again*. "Oh yeah, I'm sure we'll see each other again. Nice to meet you," she said.

"Ditto," he said, dimples winking again. At that, he turned and walked across the beach toward his brother, weaving his way through stations of coolers, people cleaning fish, and areas where seagulls were gathered, feasting on the easy meal offered from the scraps of cleaned and gutted fish.

His stride was long and loose. His shoulders were broad and muscled, the cotton jersey he wore pulled tight across them. He met his brother at the path, and they disappeared from sight as they crested the small slope that led to the parking lot. She looked around and saw Susie turning to head into shore. Glancing down, she groaned. There was so much sand on her, she might as well have laid down and rolled in it. Sand stuck in sheets on her damp waders from her brief tumble when she ran into Luke. She blushed when she realized she had actually thrown a fish against him by accident. She swatted her gloves against her legs, knocking some of the sand loose.

CHAPTER 4

A flash of black and gold caught Hannah's eye. She turned to look out the window and saw a dog in motion come to a quick stop and start sniffing madly along the edge of the deck. The dog was mostly black with gold accents on its feet, eyes, and chest. The dog's fur was long and glossy, its tail a waving flag of black and gold. The dog lost interest in that particular spot on the deck and turned toward the window. She caught the dog's eye, at which point the dog sat down and stared intently at her through the window. With a shrug, she walked to the door and stepped outside.

The boards on the deck were cool on the soles of her bare feet. It was early morning, just past seven. The sun was slowly climbing above the horizon, and a damp mist coated the grass. Drops of dew glinted on the grass where the sun touched. As she stepped out, the dog immediately walked over and circled around her legs, a bundle of softness and friendliness. After a brief inspection, she determined the dog was a female. She was lovely and sweet, her fur silky and luxurious against Hannah's hands.

Hannah heard the sound of footsteps on the gravel road, moving in the rhythmic pace of a run. The dog's ears perked, and she turned to face the road. Hannah guessed that the dog's owner was running up the road. A tall, lean man crested the hill of the road, jogging at a fast pace toward the house. She waited on the deck while he ran toward them. As he got closer, Hannah realized it was Luke, the man she'd thrown a fish at a few days prior. The dog started to wag her tail wildly and ran off the deck to greet Luke when he reached the steps. Hannah bit her lip and sighed to herself. While she was perhaps in better shape than she had been when she ran into him at the beach, she hadn't showered yet and had thrown on sweatpants and a cotton top. He came to a stop and tugged at the edge of his sleeve to wipe sweat off his brow, exposing a flash of a muscled abdomen. Despite the cool morning, he was dressed only in running shorts and a lightweight shirt. She guessed he'd been running for some time to work up a sweat in this temperature.

"Well, hey there, Jessie," Luke said, reaching to pet the dog who came to his side. He looked up at Hannah with those deep green eyes. His gaze unnerved her. Her belly felt hollow for a moment.

"Hey, sorry about this one here," he said, gesturing to the dog. "Jessie sometimes does her own thing when I take her running. She's not actually my dog, but a stray that showed up a few weeks ago. Been keeping her until we can find her a home."

Luke took a glance around the yard and brought his gaze back to Hannah. "Didn't know this is where you lived. I live down the road a bit and usually run by here a few times a week. It's been empty for the last two years," he said.

Hannah wanted a chance to gather herself before responding. Luke brought flares to life in her, and she wasn't ready to deal with it at this hour. She couldn't simply not respond though. She took a breath. "Right. It's my parents' house, but they haven't been here."

She thought of what to say next. Two years and she still hadn't figured out how to talk about her parents dying. Saying they hadn't been here didn't seem to capture why the house had sat empty. She forged on. "It's not just that they haven't been here. They passed away while I was away at grad school." She stopped and looked down into Luke's eyes. He strode forward just as she moved to walk down the two steps that led to the ground.

Something flickered in his green eyes, and then a rueful smile touched his lips. "Heard about your parents. Didn't connect the dots just now. I'm really sorry."

Hannah felt his warm hand engulf hers. Even when she was standing a step above him, Luke was almost eye to eye with her. She was used to being as tall, if not taller, than most men. She'd been relieved when she'd finally stopped growing at seventeen. When she'd started to sprout in junior high, it had seemed like she grew overnight and towered over her female friends. Truth be told, she did tower over them. Susie was a contrast, petite and barely five feet tall. The two of them had made an odd pair in high school—Susie, the tiny dynamo, with Hannah, the tall, not too elegant one.

Her hand warmed in Luke's grasp. She wanted him to hold on and then thought it was crazy to wish for a strange man to just hold her hand. Her toes curled against the bottom step. The sun pushed past the tops of the spruce trees that had been shading the spot where she stood. A warm beam of sun streamed across them. She pulled her hand from his grip, feeling awkward.

"I mostly grew up here, but I stayed away to finish school after my parents died," she said.

"My brothers and I bought a house just down the hill on Bay Ridge Road. I usually run up here most mornings. Nice spot here." He caught her gaze. "Diamond Creek's a small town. That's how I heard about your parents. Again...I'm sorry."

She searched his eyes, almost mesmerized by the green. She looked away, but not before she caught a sense of curiosity in his gaze. "It's small, that's for sure...and thanks...for understanding about my parents. It's not easy to talk about," she said. She looked down at Jessie, who'd moved closer to her and was rubbing against her legs.

Luke followed Hannah's eyes to Jessie. "Don't know where she came from. Started following me in the mornings when I went running and ended up camping out on our deck a few weeks ago. No one seems to know if anyone local had her before, and no one's claiming her. She's a sweetie, though. Been calling her Jessie. We're scouting around for a home for her—not the best plan for us to have a dog when we spend so much time away fishing in the summers. Sorry she interrupted your morning. Every so often she wanders off."

"It's okay. I'm up early anyway. She seems like a sweet dog," Hannah said and reached to pet Jessie again, her fingers slipping through the glossy fur. She looked over at Luke again. "I guess you'd probably like to keep running, huh?"

He nodded, his eyes holding hers, the green darkening. "Figured I'd see you around and probably will again," he said. His eyes lingered for another moment before he turned to walk back toward the road. Jessie remained at her side. Luke whistled and Jessie took off, running to his side. She watched them go as he began to jog, silhouettes against the rising sun in the sky as it curved up along the hillside.

* * *

LUKE JOGGED BACK DOWN the hill that had led to the Grays'

old house. He'd been surprised to see someone there, although he had heard a few rumors that their daughter was moving back. He hadn't realized that she was the friend that had been with Susie the other day. He glanced down at Jessie and smiled. She trotted alongside him, her tongue hanging out to one side, black and golden tail swaying with her gait. He hadn't wanted to admit to Hannah that he'd let Jessie run around in the yard there a few times. The place where her parents' house sat was about the halfway mark of one of his five-mile running routes. He sometimes took a brief walking break after he got to the top of that hill. Jessie would meander about the yard for a few minutes. He hadn't thought much of it since the house had sat empty the entire time he'd lived in Diamond Creek.

He thought back to Hannah. He'd been startled to see her when he'd crested the hill. She was tall and lovely in an unconscious way, which he'd noticed at the beach the other day. When she'd stepped down to shake his hand, he'd realized she was only a few inches shorter than he was. At six foot four, he was used to feeling larger than he wanted to around most women. She'd looked slightly disheveled this morning, as if she'd had just enough time to toss on some clothes. She'd been barefoot, wearing thin gray sweatpants that clung to the curves of her long legs and flared at the bottom, swinging around her calves. A worn blue cotton shirt had hung softly from her shoulders. Her hair was a rich brown, long with curls at the tips, bangs brushed carelessly away from her eyes. And those eyes. A sky blue, almost ethereal. Luke sensed her to be a little shy, but then he didn't know if he could get a sense of her from that moment in time—an unexpected encounter, at seven in the morning no less, and her just home after being away for two years.

He'd liked her feet, of all things. He laughed aloud, and Jessie looked up at the sound. He smiled down at her and kept on running. Hannah's feet were long and slender, the arches high against the wood on the deck. Her toenails were painted a deep blue, adding a touch of whimsy to her overall appearance. He'd hoped he'd see her again after meeting her at the beach, and now wished he could have more than a passing encounter. He kept jogging toward home, the road curving in front of him. As he rounded a corner, a view of the bay opened up. The water looked calm this morning. A few clouds billowed in the sky.

Luke thought of his day ahead, which included a trip to the harbor to check on their boats. Another turn in the road, and the house he shared with his brothers came into sight. It sat back from the road at the base of a sloping hill. Spruce trees stood tall behind the house with a small stand of birch to one side and wildflowers along the edge of the small lawn in the front yard. He slowed to a walk when he reached their driveway, looking up when he heard his older brother's voice.

"Where are those damn keys?"

Jared appeared to be talking to himself and hadn't yet noticed that Luke and Jessie were coming down the drive. Jared stood in the garage. Their younger brother, Nathan, had left his truck parked halfway in the garage with the back end far enough out that the garage door couldn't close. When Luke had noticed it on his way out for his run, he'd shrugged and figured Jared would be pissed when he got up. At twenty-eight, Nathan was careless. He was prone to haphazard parking on late nights. Of the three brothers, Luke was in the middle and often played to stereotype, functioning as the middleman between his younger and older brothers. Jared was a full seven years older than Nathan, with Luke in the middle—three years younger than Jared and four years older than Nathan.

Jared finally noticed him when Jessie ran up to his side as he leaned into Nathan's truck. She licked his hand, Jared petting her head in return. He gestured to Nathan's red truck. "Our little brother has managed another marvelous parking job. Just crooked enough that I can't back out."

Luke followed Jared's eyes to the back of Nathan's truck. He shrugged. "Not much to do about it unless we find the keys or drag his sorry ass out of bed. You try the house for his keys?" he asked.

"Yup. And everywhere else but his bedroom. Thought about waking him up, but honestly, he's like molasses after a late night. Waking him up is more annoying than dealing with it myself. But if I don't find the keys soon, I'll have to." He gestured to Luke. "Good run?"

"Yeah. My favorite time of day. Was up by the Grays' old place. You know...the couple that we heard about that died in that plane crash on the way to Barrow not long before we moved here? Their old house has just been empty the whole time we've been here."

At Jared's nod, he continued, "Ran into their daughter by chance. Jessie took off ahead and was nosing around the deck. I actually met her the other day when we went dipnetting. Was interesting to meet her. Name's Hannah."

Jared lifted an eyebrow. "Old friend of Susie's, right?"

Luke nodded. "Just interesting to meet her."

Jared lifted his other eyebrow.

"What?" Luke asked.

The eyebrows stayed up. "Just curious that you find the need to tell me this now."

Luke rolled his eyes. "Around here, meeting someone new is news. Whatever."

He shook his head and walked toward the door that led from the garage to the kitchen. He heard the door to Nathan's truck close as he stepped into the kitchen. Jessie followed him in and immediately went to the water bowl they'd set out for her. Thirsty himself, Luke gulped down a full glass of tap water, then stared at the empty glass and thought of Hannah. His mind seemed to be on a pull chain to her. He wasn't sure what it was about her, but he was drawn to her in a way that he hadn't experienced before. He couldn't deny that she was easy on the eyes. He could have looked at her all day. She had a soft beauty that she didn't seem to notice. He was unfortunately aware of how many women thoroughly understood the superficial attributes they had and used them to their advantage. He'd been burned one time too many with women who seemed to think they could access his parents' money through him.

He and his brothers had grown up in and around Seattle. While their mother had been a teacher, their father had run a successful engineering business that designed and manu- factured parts for the aviation and aerospace industry. He had sold it at the height of its success. Their family wasn't world-famous for their money, but they were well known in Seattle. Luke and his brothers were accustomed to plenty of attention from women. Hannah held herself at a distance, which was a change for him. His parents had a solid, down- to-earth marriage. They'd met long before his father started making good money and didn't emphasize the material side of life. When Jared had started talking about moving their fishing business to Alaska since they often fished there anyway, Luke had jumped at the chance to live somewhere more grounded and less pretentious. He also thrived on the challenge of outdoor sports, skiing, hiking, and the like. Alaska offered that in spades.

Diamond Creek had turned out to be what he wanted. The starkness of the seasons in Alaska, coupled with the small community and distance from the rest of the world, brought most everyone down to earth. There were few, if any, class distinctions here. The range of connections and friendships crossed financial lines, political lines, and more. The small world of Diamond Creek was how he'd heard rumors that the Grays' daughter might return. He knew she'd been a good friend of their accountant, Susie. He hadn't heard much else about her, other than that her parents were deeply missed in the community, and their deaths rippled in the tiny town where friends still mourned them.

Luke looked out the windows that faced the bay. Their kitchen opened onto a living room and a wall of windows, floor to ceiling, that offered a view of Kachemak Bay, one of Alaska's coastal jewels. Kachemak Bay was a bay off the Cook Inlet, which extended from the Gulf of Alaska in the Pacific Ocean to Anchorage, the largest city in Alaska. A winding highway traversed a branch of the inlet, Turnagain Arm, and led to the Kenai Peninsula. Diamond Creek was situated toward the southern end of the peninsula. The views along the highway were breathtaking. At points, it felt like one could touch the mountains that stood tall across the water while the road hugged the bottom of the mountains. A few glaciers were visible along the way, their eerie translucent blue ice an alluring beauty.

Diamond Creek and a few other communities were interspersed on the shores of the bay, which was a popular area for sportfishing, in addition to many commercial fishing businesses using the towns as launching points into Alaskan waters. Luke and his brothers had initially started their fishing business in Seattle. After a few ventures to Alaska and obtaining the necessary commercial permits to fish there, they decided to relocate since they collectively fell in love with the area.

The calm of the morning was gradually fading as the wind picked up, ruffling the surface of the water. Luke dimly heard Jared rummaging around in the garage and wondered when he'd give it up and go wake Nathan. For the most part, the brothers got along well and managed to play off one another's strengths to handle their business. Despite Nathan's careless attitude at times and his penchant for late nights in the summer, he was a hard worker and didn't shy away from the less savory tasks of fishing. Jared's patience with his bad parking was limited. But then, Jared tended to be impatient with anyone who didn't take his methodical, organized approach to life. Luke heard a burst of profanity from the garage and then the distinct sound of an engine starting—the keys had been located. In a few moments, Jared came through the door that led to the garage.

Luke switched on the coffeemaker as Jared stepped into the kitchen. "Guessing you found those keys."

Jared nodded. "Looked all over only to find them sitting on the seat of my truck. Think I might hide the keys from him one of these days."

"Not a bad idea. When are you headed out?" Luke asked.

"Soon," Jared said. "Thanks for the coffee. Got side-tracked looking for Nathan's keys. What's your plan for the day?"

"Planning to head to the harbor to check on the boats and make sure we're geared up for our trip in three weeks. Did you get the list ready for shopping?"

"Yup, ready to go. Headed to town in a bit here to go to the bank and check in with Susie. Then parking myself in the office downstairs to go over our finances before next week."

Luke nodded and checked how close the coffee was to being ready. "Have to see if we can find a place for Jessie here. She's great to have around, but we'll be gone for three weeks on this trip. Any ideas?" he asked.

Jared shook his head. "Not off the top of my head. I'll ask Susie, though. You know her. Knows everyone and their business."

"That she does. I'll ask around at the harbor again too."

Seeing that there was enough coffee, Luke grabbed a mug to fill. A dash of cream, and he took a welcome swallow of coffee. "Well, I'm headed for the shower. If you're gone before I'm done, leave that list for me. I'll rouse Nathan and send him off to take care of it," Luke said.

"Got it. Better you than me. I'm too annoyed with him right now," Jared said.

At that, Luke walked out of the kitchen down the hallway that led to the bedrooms.

CHAPTER 5

A week later, Hannah woke with the sky barely light. Waking up in her old room was still soothing and strange. She took a shower and rummaged for breakfast. Seated at the kitchen counter that faced into the living room, she took in the view of the bay and mountains and soaked in the familiar sight of the yard. She pondered Luke and his green eyes. She said his name aloud and caught herself glancing sheepishly about the kitchen, as if anyone could hear her. As she was washing dishes, she heard the sound of a vehicle rumble into the drive. Looking out the window, she saw an unfamiliar green Toyota truck and watched as Luke climbed out. She was surprised to see him and curious, taking in details as he went to the passenger side of the truck to check on something. His wavy and careless almost-black hair curled along the edge of his collar. He wore faded jeans, worn leather boots, and a red windbreaker. He turned to look at the house and shrugged to himself before walking up the deck stairs to the kitchen door. She stepped out just as he reached the top of the stairs. She caught the flash of a dimple and his warm green eyes.

Luke gave a small wave. "Sorry to show up unannounced, but I didn't have your number. Susie sent me your way." He hesitated. "Remember Jessie, the dog that I had with me yesterday? Well, Susie seems to think you're the person I should ask about taking her. Thought I'd just stop by." Luke looked to Hannah. When she didn't respond just yet, he said, "Would love to keep her, but we commercial fish, so we're gone for weeks at a time. Susie was pretty insistent about asking you, so here I am."

A tumble of thoughts and feelings raced through Hannah. She laughed to herself when she thought of Susie sending Luke with the dog. Knowing Susie, she'd likely hatched this plan as soon as she knew Hannah was home, but decided ambush was the best option. She looked back over at Luke who was politely waiting. They both spoke at once. "I, well, I...." from Hannah. "This may seem crazy..." from Luke. They both stopped. Hannah gestured to Luke. "You first."

"May seem crazy, but Susie seemed pretty confident you'd want Jessie. She promised me you'd be a good home too. Been putting off finding Jessie a home, but soon we head out for almost three weeks. Much as I'd like to keep her, she needs to be with someone who's around more than me. Most summers, I'm out for work at least a week or two every month. She's a good dog. Trust me, she's a keeper. Do you want to see her again?" he asked, gesturing to his truck.

Hannah looked over. "Well, it may be crazy, but I've known Susie long enough to know that sometimes what's crazy is the right thing. I would love to have a dog again. I just hadn't thought it would happen so fast."

She wondered what Luke knew of her. If Susie sent him with Jessie, Susie trusted him, so by extension Hannah would. She thought about trying to explain to this man with deep green eyes that she would give anything for the unconditional love of a dog just this moment. Because while she hadn't been thinking about a dog precisely, she craved the presence of anyone other than just herself in the house. The echoes of her parents and Grayson were too keen at some moments. Just the idea of having a dog to get to know almost brought her to tears. She also thought it would be a good way to help her link to the present instead of being bound too deeply to her memories. As these thoughts circled through her mind, she wanted to reach up and brush Luke's unruly curls away from his eyes. He had a tendency to shake them back.

She followed Luke's gaze and found him looking quietly at the field to the side of the house. He seemed content to wait for her to continue.

"I'd like to see her again if that's okay," she said.

Luke's response was to walk down the stairs. As they approached the truck, Hannah saw Jessie sitting in the passenger seat of the truck. Jessie's wagging tail turned into a blur as Luke opened the door. Jessie flew out of the truck, ran in tight circles around them, and rubbed against Hannah's legs. She quickly calmed, sat at Luke's feet, and watched him expectantly.

"She wants me to throw her a ball. She'll fetch all day if you'll let her. Do you mind if she runs around here for a few minutes?" he asked.

"No, no, of course not."

Luke grabbed a ball from the glove compartment. He began a game of fetch with Jessie who raced back and forth. Her fur was long, silky, and wavy, and her tail flew like a flag behind her. She was a medium-size dog on the leggy side.

Hannah asked Luke what he knew about Jessie. In explanation, he offered, "Not much really. Hung out on our road for a few days. None of the neighbors knew where she came from. We started feeding her, and after a day or two of her camping on our deck, she was staying with us. She likes to play outside, but inside she's pretty mellow. We let her on the couch, so if you want to keep her off, you might have some work to do there. She's affectionate and seems easy to train. Took her to the vet to get her checked out. Did the shots and got her spayed about two weeks ago. She's healed up, but you can still see where the incision was. The vet guessed she was maybe a Lab-Gordon setter mix. They say her coat is like a Gordon setter's. That's about all I can tell you, other than that she's a sweetie."

Jessie had been exploring the weed-filled flower beds. Luke called her over and asked her to sit. Hannah reached to pet her, her hand sinking into soft, silky fur. Jessie immediately leaned into her hand and rubbed against her legs again. She looked up with her tongue dangling and a smile. Hannah would usually wait on a decision like this, but she found herself telling Luke she'd be glad to keep Jessie.

Luke looked relieved with a simultaneous glimmer of sadness. He caught her watching him. "Part of me wishes I could keep her, but being out of town for weeks at a time isn't a good situation for a dog."

Yet again, the instinct to withdraw and politely send Luke on his way rose. But before she'd come home, Hannah had promised herself she'd try not to wall the world away. So she invited him in for a cup of coffee. Jessie followed them in and immediately began exploring the house. Hannah realized that she hadn't clarified when Luke wanted to officially leave Jessie with her, and that she needed to handle logistical details, like getting her vet records and food and water bowls. She hurriedly asked Luke when he wanted to leave Jessie.

"Honestly, whenever you're ready to have her. Figured if

you were a friend of Susie's, you'd probably put up with me asking you how Jessie's doing and maybe even let me see her every so often," Luke said with a laugh. "Might be ridiculous, but I feel kind of responsible for her since I found her. And she's an awesome dog."

Hannah poured Luke a cup of coffee and got her own ready. "That's not ridiculous. You can check in with me anytime about Jessie and even visit. As for when I can take her, I just need to get some things for her. Dog bowls, food, that kind of stuff."

"Oh, you can have what we've been using. We've got it all, even food. Should be enough to get her through a week or so. I'll also make sure you have a few tennis balls for her. Didn't get her any of those though. She has a knack for finding them."

"Well, in that case, she can stay today. Or is that too soon?" she asked.

"I'll miss her, but she should be where she can stay. Didn't bring her stuff with me though. Spur of the moment thing after I ran into Susie at the gas station. Hope it's okay that I dropped in." Luke took a sip of his coffee and looked across the counter at Hannah.

Hannah laughed. "Well, Susie's never been known to hesitate. She knew I missed our old dog. I hadn't really thought about getting another dog just now, but it seems meant to be. If that makes any sense."

"Sense or not, it's probably best for Jessie to get to know you sooner rather than later," Luke said with a shrug.

She felt caught in his green eyes and quickly looked away. She was out of sorts, drawn to Luke's eyes and comfortable masculinity. He carried a warmth combined with a down-to-earth feeling that simultaneously lulled her into feeling at home with him and kicked up her heart rate. Jessie was sniffing her way around the living room. Hannah called her over as a distraction. Jessie came quickly and flung herself on the floor by the counter where they were seated. Hannah shifted into small talk, asking Luke what he thought of Diamond Creek and what type of fishing he did. He filled in a few more details about their decision to move from Seattle to Alaska.

He joked about the feeling of being under the social microscope of a small town. "You'd have thought we were aliens for the first few months with all the curiosity, but that's gone now. We love it here. Keep saying we need to spread out, but we all still live together in the house we bought as a starter property when we got here. Works for now."

Hannah realized that at some point Luke would ask more about her and wondered what he might know from Susie or anyone else in town. She reached to pet Jessie, realizing Jessie was quickly becoming a way to take her mind off things. As she rubbed Jessie's neck, she decided that rather than waiting for the questions to come, she'd take the lead. With a deep breath, Hannah succinctly explained that she'd spent most of her childhood in Diamond Creek and stayed in Alaska through college, and that her parents' unexpected death had happened just when she started graduate school.

"I knew that I wanted to come back because Diamond Creek is home to me. My closest friends are here. But..." She paused for a moment. "I don't know if you've lost anyone important, but it kind of threw my world into... well, I was about to say chaos, but it's more like being frozen on the outside and a mess on the inside. Being in school seemed to help because it gave me something to focus on." She looked to Luke as she finished and again felt pulled into his eyes. They were dangerously green; it was too much really.

"Can't say that I've lost someone like that. But I know how much my family means to me. Probably don't need to tell you this, but Susie is beside herself to have you back here." Luke looked at her intently for a moment when he stopped speaking, and when she looked away, he turned to look out the window.

Hannah thought she should say something. "The whole thing is awkward to try to talk about. Being away when it happened was good and bad. It's like I could pretend I had another life, which in a way, I did. I'm relieved to be back though. I missed it more than I let myself know." She took a breath. "Moving on though, Susie's a good friend...the best really. Not to mention a damn good accountant."

She followed Luke's gaze out the window, taking in the spruce, the mountains, and the bay. Luke turned to look back. "Well, you're here now. And now you'll have Jessie too. She deserves a good home. Susie assured me you couldn't be better. Glad I took the chance to ask." Luke searched out Jessie who had remained cozied against Hannah's legs while she stroked her. "Sweetheart, right?" he asked.

"Oh, hard to miss that. She's an easygoing girl. I think we'll do just fine. How much longer are you in town before you head out for fishing?"

"About two weeks. Still sorting out the final details of when we'll leave and who will be on the crew. Then the usual guiding trips for most of the summer."

"Well, maybe before you go, we can plan to get together for a Jessie visit. Do you want to keep her for the day until I can arrange to pick up her stuff from you? I have to head into town in a bit anyway."

"That'll work. We live a little farther up the hill, not far from here. Jessie usually tags along with me whenever I'm out and about. Let me give you my cell number, and you can call when you think you'll head our way. I'll give you directions."

They exchanged numbers, and Luke gulped the last of

his coffee. "Good coffee, by the way. Might beat Misty Mountain." He winked as he got up to leave. She walked Luke and Jessie to the door. Jessie leaped into the truck, and they drove off. The house felt quiet in their absence. She thought having Jessie here would take the edges away from some of the emptiness that the house held.

CHAPTER 6

*L*uke cracked the windows for Jessie as he drove away from Hannah's house. Jessie immediately nosed her head out and leaned into the breeze. He thought back to the last half hour and wondered about Hannah and if Susie had an agenda in sending him Hannah's way. He didn't doubt Hannah would be a good owner for Jessie; in fact, he was relieved Susie suggested it.

In the days since he'd collided with Hannah at the beach, he'd forgotten how beautiful she was. He had taken every chance he got to look at the view outside just so she wouldn't think he was staring. Her sky-blue eyes were hard to look away from. She carried herself unself-consciously. He doubted she knew how beautiful she was. She had an air of sadness about her. Diamond Creek was small, and from what he could tell, her family had been woven into the community. Their deaths on a flight to Barrow had saddened the many friends they'd left behind. Given how many friends he and his brothers had in common with them, Luke figured he would have come to know her parents had they still been alive when he moved to town.

Over time, he'd heard people wondering when Hannah would come home. Susie had worried about her often. When he had run into Susie this morning, she'd been ecstatic that Hannah was home. As soon as she saw Jessie, she immediately began trying to convince him that he should see if Hannah would take Jessie.

Luke wondered more about what Hannah was like aside from being one of Susie's best friends. He had only a sketch of her life—that she'd been her parents' only child, and she'd left town for graduate school in environmental science. What he had sensed, she had confirmed when she talked about her parents' death and the struggle of being away. It was obvious she was still grieving in some ways. Beyond getting a gauge on her loss, he hadn't had many blanks filled in today. He knew she was an avid hiker and runner because Susie had mentioned it last year when he and Jared had participated in a local race. Luke found himself wishing to know more and circling back to those blue eyes and silky hair. Aside from how pleased he was to have found a good home for Jessie, he couldn't deny that Jessie gave him an excuse to see her again.

Moments later, he walked into the house with Jessie at his heels. He found Jared downstairs in the office reviewing details for their upcoming trip, and Nathan on the phone with what sounded like a potential crew member.

Jared looked up. "Longest gas run I've known you to take."

"Yeah, yeah. Ran into Susie. You remember the woman I mentioned the other morning, Hannah? Susie seemed to think she needs a dog."

Jared smiled slowly. "You just jumped on that chance, huh?"

Luke rolled his eyes. "Well, seeing as we're headed out in a few weeks, I thought I should follow Susie's lead. May have caught her off guard, but she said she'll take Jessie. She's coming by later today to get her."

Jared laughed. "Well, all right then. Hope you don't think Nathan and I were pressuring you to get rid of Jessie. We love having her around too, you know. It's just…"

"No need to explain. It won't work for us to keep her; we're gone too much in the summers and sometimes in the winter."

Nathan hung up the phone and jumped in. "So, did I just hear you met Susie's long lost friend and found Jessie a home?"

Luke nodded. "Hannah's nice. Don't think we could have found a much better place for Jessie. You'll meet her later if you're around," Luke said. He shifted focus. "What's the status on whomever you were just talking to for the crew? We still need, what, about three more for the run?"

Nathan filled them in while Jared kept checking notes and filled out a shopping list for Luke. Luke's mind remained half on Hannah and half on what he needed to do for the upcoming trip. Part of him hoped his brothers wouldn't be around this afternoon because they were attuned to him and would likely pick up on his attraction to her. The last thing he needed was weeks of teasing from them with Jared already starting. He mentally swatted the thought away as he realized he might be thinking a little too much about Hannah.

He focused on Jared, who was asking him questions about what he thought they needed from the store. As usual, Jared was weeks ahead of the game in organizing for the trip. He already had dry goods listed for Luke to pick up for the boat. When Luke and his brothers had started their fishing business, they had naturally fallen into different roles. Jared handled most of the planning while Nathan handled most of the contacts they needed to make and the grunt work. Luke fell somewhere in the middle, doing a bit of everything.

Luke headed back toward town. The next few hours kept him busy with various errands. He stopped by the harbor before going back home. The Diamond Creek Boat Harbor was tucked in Otter Cove, a small cove within Kachemak Bay. It was sheltered from the wind and higher waves by high bluffs on both sides. The harbor was filled with boats every summer, ranging from large commercial vessels to small motorboats used for recreation. He loved coming to the harbor, even just to stop by. During summer months, it was usually busy; yet he felt grounded by the sound of water lapping against boats, gull calls, and the occasional eagle call. There was a resident otter, Howard, who swam about and entertained everyone with his antics. In the winter, it was much quieter, yet the brace of cold ocean winds refreshed Luke. He loved the sounds and smells of the ocean.

The brothers owned one commercial fishing boat, *Iris*, named after their mother. She was alive and well in Bellingham, Washington, where she and their father, Matthew, had retired after years of living and working in Seattle. She'd been an elementary schoolteacher, and their father had started an aerospace engineering company that became successful enough that they could retire early in comfort. Matthew's serious hobby was fishing. The brothers got their love of the ocean from their father. He'd taken them out every chance he could. He'd been thrilled when they decided to try to fish for a living. While their parents missed them being nearby, they visited Alaska several times a year. Iris and Matthew were both still healthy, but Luke and his brothers had a few discussions about planning to get them to Alaska, so they'd be closer if their parents needed support. For now, their parents were enjoying retirement and showed few signs of slowing down.

Luke thought about his parents as he tucked canned goods away in the storage area of the boat. He wondered what they'd think of Hannah and shook his head at himself. He'd spent maybe thirty minutes in her company and was already imagining her meeting his parents. For him, that was quite a leap and one that wasn't particularly comfortable. While he might not be quite the playboy that Nathan was, he wasn't interested in anything serious. He was more focused on his next adventure, which usually entailed something risky. Whether it be telemark skiing in the backcountry, a grueling hike through Resurrection Pass, known for its frequent grizzly bear encounters, or white-water kayaking, that was when he felt invigorated. Romantic relationships were secondary and best kept casual.

While he finished organizing the storage area, he considered his draw to Hannah. He hadn't had a serious relationship since just before they moved to Diamond Creek, and he had learned his lesson in that relationship. His father's successful business kept the family name in the public eye when they lived in Seattle. The business made enough money that plenty of people tried to make connections through Luke and his brothers, including women. His ex-girlfriend, Cristina, had been livid when Luke had broken up with her when he'd tired of her constant focus on how much he'd inherit from his father and her frustration that he wasn't planning to work for his father. The day after Luke broke up with her, she'd tried to seduce Nathan, so committed she was to worming her way into their family's money. He and his brothers may have had many flaws, but lack of loyalty wasn't one of them. Not only had Nathan turned her down, but he'd told Luke immediately. As much as he'd like to say Cristina had shown her true colors by then, little did he know how far she'd go. She harassed him constantly after the breakup and Nathan turning her down. Even after they moved to Alaska, he occasionally had to field calls from her and heard from friends that she still asked about him.

His experience with Cristina had given him a cynical view of relationships. The person he'd thought he'd fallen in love with was not who she was at all. He'd kept his distance from women since then and had been relieved to move away from Seattle. At thirty-two, he sometimes thought maybe he wanted what his parents had. While they'd be the first to say their marriage wasn't perfect, their acceptance of each other, love beyond the surface, and sustained commitment was what he looked toward. That said, he wasn't sure it was for him. He was pretty comfortable with his life as it was—light, easy relationships without the risk of making another miscalculation about a woman.

Luke locked up the boat's cabin and checked the moorings by habit before leaving. As he walked back to his truck with Jessie trotting at his heels, his phone rang. Hannah was on the other end, letting him know she could meet him to pick up Jessie. Through the brief drive home, he stroked Jessie. He'd miss her presence, despite the fact that she'd only been with him for a few weeks. He trusted Susie's opinion, which is why he'd driven straight to Hannah's after Susie suggested he ask Hannah about Jessie. Now, he kept wondering more about Hannah. He wanted a chance to get to know her despite his misgivings about why.

When he arrived back at the house, Jared was still downstairs in the office. Jared explained that Nathan had gone on a coffee run because he'd been too impatient to wait for Luke to return. Jared shrugged. "You know Nathan—if he thinks he needs coffee, or anything else, it's gotta be right then. So did you have a chance to drop things off at *Iris*?"

"Yeah. Just came from the harbor. Hannah's on her way over in a bit to pick up Jessie. Gonna miss this girl," Luke said and knelt beside Jessie to hold her close for a moment. "But glad Susie found her a good home. Hannah's up at her parents' old house by herself. Jessie will be good company. Nice place for Jessie too. Plenty of room to run around and off the busy roads."

A car door slammed outside. Through the window, Luke saw Hannah climbing out of the red truck he'd seen in her driveway.

Jared had followed him to the window. "So that's Susie's long lost friend. Hmm."

Luke didn't respond and started walking upstairs. He met Hannah at the door, just as she was about to knock. Jessie slipped past him and circled Hannah excitedly with yips and barks of greeting. Hannah looked up while petting Jessie. "Well, she seems happy to see me. How are you?" she asked.

"Just fine. Been running errands. How about you?" he asked.

"Fine as well. Also running errands. I'm excited about Jessie. I can take her on some of my favorite walks."

Luke gestured for Hannah to come in. The home he shared with his brothers was a timber-frame house with exposed beams and wide-open common spaces. The main entrance had a small curved deck reached with a set of stairs. The house was built into a hill with the main entrance on the upper floor. There was a larger deck that ran the length of the house on the back. The entire back of the upper floor was a wall of windows and sliding glass doors looking out over the bay and mountains. The upper floor contained most of the common spaces with a living room, dining room, and kitchen area. The living room had a beautiful gray soapstone fireplace. The stone retained heat for hours and kept the house warm in the winters. There were three bedrooms upstairs off a hallway to one side. The stairs that led downstairs were off to the opposite side of the living room. What was intended to be another family room downstairs was their office. There was one actual desk with tables and file cabinets lining the walls. Jared used the desk while Luke and Nathan had their laptops placed haphazardly on the tables. Luke headed toward the kitchen area and looked to see if there was anything to offer Hannah.

Hannah had stopped by the kitchen counter and was taking in the view of the bay. "I missed this view so much. I can't believe I forgot what it was like to see this every day. You have a great view here—wide-open. We have more trees at my parents' place." She flinched. "Well, there's no 'we' to speak of. I hate it that little things like that trip me up every day." She shook her head. "I keep trying to get used to it. Anyway, my point was that the view is lovely here. You and your brothers have a nice place."

"We like it. Plenty of space for the three of us, and our office is downstairs. And there is that view."

As he spoke, Jared came up the stairs. "Here's my older brother." He gestured to Jared. "Jared, this is Hannah, and Hannah...Jared. Hannah's here for Jessie." Turning back to Hannah, he said, "Let me get Jessie's stuff. Haven't had a chance to do that."

While he grabbed the few items they had for Jessie, Jared and Hannah chatted in the kitchen. Luke returned to the kitchen area with Jessie's stuff in a bag and joined them at the kitchen table as they bemoaned the traffic that came with the explosion of summer tourists. Jared asked Hannah what she planned to do now that she was back, which Luke had been wondering himself.

"When I left, it was for graduate school. Before that, all I'd ever done were after-school jobs at a few stores in town and waiting tables in the summer. I worked throughout college, but also just waiting tables. While I was getting my graduate degree in environmental science, I took a job with a nonprofit that advocated for preservation. They focused on wetlands mostly. My plan for here was to feel out my options with the state and fed jobs. With my degree, it's possible to hook up with one of the environmental management agencies. Since my parents' house is paid off and I inherited a little money, I have a grace period before I have to get too worried about finances."

"That'll buy you some time," Jared said. "Since you grew up here, you know how it is. So many people have several jobs going all at once or at different times of the year. We do guiding trips for recreational fishing in between our commercial runs. Come winter, snow removal to keep the cash flowing."

She nodded and caught Luke's eyes. "Yeah, that's how it's always been here. There's a seasonal nature to some of the work, so people have hodgepodge jobs. My dad was an exception because he was a biologist and was busy year-round. My mother was a teacher at the high school and ran a small landscaping business in the summer. I'm flexible, so I'll play it by ear."

Hannah remained for another half hour. Luke found himself quieter than usual, caught up in watching her. She had subtle expressions and a soft warmth. He wanted to break through that wall of reserve around her, wanted to know if she felt the same spark he did, and then wondered what the hell he was thinking. He caught Jared looking at him with a knowing expression and looked away. He didn't know that he wanted to think too much about the fact that for the first time in years, he was more than just casually interested in someone, nor did he want to suffer through Jared's teasing about it. As Hannah got ready to go, she asked if he was sure he wanted Jessie to go with her now.

Jessie lay sprawled on the kitchen floor. "Much as I'd love for her to stay, she'd be abandoned for weeks at a time."

With that, he walked Hannah to the door and outside with Jessie. Jared followed them to the door and said good-bye. Luke walked to Hannah's truck and encouraged Jessie to hop in, which she did without hesitation.

"Your canine copilot now—a good one." He couldn't look away from the blue of Hannah's eyes for a moment. He spoke again without thinking. "Maybe we could get together for dinner before I head out on this trip?"

She looked surprised, her blue eyes widening. She held his gaze, a question and a shade of wariness in her eyes. "Maybe we could," she said slowly. "You have my number. Plus, I'm counting on visits for Jessie." With that, she stepped into her truck, started it, and put it into gear with a quick wave when the truck started to move. The dust from the driveway lifted around Luke as he stood watching her drive away. He heard the crunch of gravel behind him and then Jared's voice.

"My hunch was correct. You like her," Jared said and started to laugh when Luke pretended to cuff him on the chin.

"Maybe I think she's interesting. Cut me some slack. I don't hound you about women even though every single woman in this town and then some has been slobbering over you while you play it cool and distant," he said.

Jared clapped him on the back and followed him back in the house. "I'll cut you some slack for now. In the meantime, while you were starry-eyed with Hannah, I took a call about a small guiding trip in two days. Think you can take the trip with me?"

Luke spent the rest of the afternoon working around the yard and contemplated when the timing was right to call Hannah for dinner. This thought was repeatedly interrupted with wondering what the hell he was thinking. The last time he'd been this interested in someone, it had been Cristina, who'd shown him clearly that his judgment was poor when he let his hormones have a say.

CHAPTER 7

*H*annah sat with Susie at Misty Mountain and sipped a cup of coffee. They had taken to meeting for coffee every few days. With two years to catch up on, she savored the time. Jessie had been with her for a week, and now she couldn't imagine not having her. It was early, but the sun was already well above the horizon, full into another long Alaskan summer day. She thanked Susie for sending Luke her way with Jessie, which elicited a wide grin.

"What's that for?" she asked.

"Well, I thought you might like Jessie since you mentioned missing Grayson, but…Luke's a friend, and I had a sense you two might click," Susie said with a laugh.

"Cut it out, will you? I just got back here, you know. I haven't exactly been thinking about men lately."

"My point precisely. Maybe you should think about them. When's the last time you went on a date?" Susie asked.

Hannah wrinkled her nose and eyed Susie. "Last time I went on a date, if you want to call it that, I chased Paul, that guy I met in Boston, to Costa Rica. Costa Rica was lovely, but he wasn't. A few days into our trip, he was shacking up with someone else at the resort. Left me with a hotel bill I couldn't afford."

Susie gave her a considering look. "Forgot about that little jaunt. It was hard to keep up with you for a few years there."

Silence fell between them. Hannah knew that while Susie may have been more tolerant of her wild streak than her parents had, Susie had also worried about her choices when it came to men after what happened with Damon. They'd been right to question, but she couldn't admit it at the time. She'd tried to convince herself she could heal her broken heart and shattered confidence by skating on the edge of risk and almost purposefully choosing men that she knew from the outset didn't care. Then she couldn't be surprised. Her parents' death had catapulted her in the opposite direction. Since then, she'd walked a tightrope of responsibility, completing her graduate program with honors, holding down a job at the same time, and saving every penny she made beyond what she needed for bills. Men were not on her radar.

Susie studied her with concern. "If that was your last date, that was right before your parents died. I'm sure you hate me pointing out the obvious, but…you've pretty much shut down since they died."

Hannah held her silence. She knew Susie was right, but she didn't want to talk about it now for fear she'd end up in tears in the middle of Misty Mountain.

Susie let her off the hook. "Luke's nice. That's all. Even if you're just friends, he's a good friend to have. His brothers are nice too. Well, Nathan's nice enough. Jared, the older one, is kind of a tight ass, seriously detail oriented. But that doesn't matter because you like Luke even if you won't admit it. I was thinking of having a dinner party this weekend. It's time for you to see a few more friends. The Winters brothers will come, and you can bring Jessie. What do you think?" Susie asked.

Hannah hesitated before answering. "Well...I don't know. It's been nice to ease back in town slowly. And now you have me nervous about Luke. I hate being set up. You tried that several times in high school. Did it ever work out?"

"Well, that's only because they weren't the right guys. My judgment has improved. Just relax if you can. I know it's been a rough patch since your parents died, but every time I turn around, someone's asking me about you. Everyone knows you're home now. If it's not my party, someone else will expect you to show up at theirs. This way, it's on your terms."

"You mean, your terms," Hannah said with a laugh. "If it were anyone other than you, I'd say back off. But you might be right. I've been holing up at the house too much except for when I see you and take Jessie for walks. Name the date, and I'll be there. But you'd better not push this Luke idea of yours."

Susie just grinned. After Susie left for the office, Hannah took Jessie for a walk on the beach. Gulls circled overhead, and the occasional eagle passed by. Boats pulled out of the harbor, the low rumble of motors carrying across the water. Jessie raced in and out of the water fetching sticks. The walks anchored Hannah back to Alaska and to Diamond Creek. She took in the salty tang of the air and the rush of ocean breezes with hints of fish and seaweed.

Jessie had fit into Hannah's life seamlessly. While it had been over two years since she'd been here, she quickly found herself readjusting to rhythms that echoed from the past. Rising early in the cool gray dawn, she went for walks along her road and a few nearby trails. It was coffee and breakfast either at home or with Susie in town. She had gradually encountered other old friends, some warmer than others. She had a few bridges to mend, but figured she had time. It was unsettling at times to be home without her parents there, but not as painful as she'd feared. Her distance had helped her accept their absence on some level. There were moments when she was pierced with the loss, particularly as she made her way through the house and tried to make sense of what was there. Some of their belongings were easy to discard, but others were wrenching. She couldn't bring herself to empty the coat closet yet. Perhaps because she had been so used to what was held there—a jumble of jackets, boots, and the odds and ends of daily life. One of her father's favorite baseball caps sat on the shelf, faded and worn. Susie had come by a few times to help lug bags and boxes to the local thrift store. Hannah had rearranged the office area upstairs and made it her own. She still slept in her old bedroom, as it felt the most comfortable for now.

Hannah watched Jessie race along the shore, yipping at gulls swooping above her. At Hannah's whistle, Jessie quickly ran over to her, following her back to her truck. The beach she'd chosen today was reached by a trail off the harbor parking lot. As she entered the lot, Luke was walking into the lot from the harbor side. Jessie ran over to him and leaped in the air. He laughed and allowed Jessie to circle and rub against him. Hannah followed Jessie over to say hello. One look into Luke's green eyes, and she thought maybe Susie had a point. She again noticed she was almost eye-to-eye with Luke. She was used to being taller than many men. He was actually taller than she was, which was a nice change.

"Nice to see you. Jessie looks happy. How is she settling in?" Luke asked.

"Oh, she's been great. I can't imagine life without her now. She goes with me everywhere. I'm sorry for your sake that you couldn't keep her," she said.

Luke knelt down and ruffled Jessie's neck, Jessie leaning into his hands. His dark hair was tousled, and Hannah once again felt the urge to brush the hair out of his eyes. He had a rangy, athletic build. He didn't look like someone who went to a gym, but rather someone whose daily life kept him fit. She pegged him to be in his early thirties. He had laugh lines around his eyes, and his dimples winked with every smile. She watched his hands stroking Jessie. They were long and lean, like the rest of him. Luke gave Jessie a final pet and stood again. Jessie sat at Hannah's feet and looked up at both of them.

"No need to be sorry. You're glad to have Jessie, and I can feel good knowing she's in a good home. How have you been settling in?" he asked.

Hannah shrugged. "Okay. I've had my moments, but mostly I'm just so glad to be back. Jessie's great company. It's about time I started figuring out the work situation. How have you been? Aren't you and your brothers headed out soon?"

He nodded. "Another week and a half. Just busy getting organized. What do you think about grabbing some dinner tonight? Can't say I didn't warn you I'd ask," he said.

She froze for a moment. A voice inside cautioned her to take it slow. But she knew circumstances would force things to go slowly with Luke leaving for a few weeks. She said yes before she allowed herself to think more.

The yes sat there all by itself for a moment, and Hannah wondered if she'd sounded strange. Then she braved a glance at Luke again and saw a vanishing dimple.

"Any preferences? May be one or two new places that came on the scene while you were gone. If there is such a thing as a scene here. Any old favorites?" he asked.

"I like just about anything. Now that I'm here, I'll have time for old favorites. Take your pick. Should I meet you there? I could bring Jessie. It's cool enough for her to wait in the truck while we eat. Maybe we could walk her after dinner," she said.

"Sounds good. How about we meet at six at the Boathouse Café? They just opened last summer and close up shop during the winter. Great seafood and a ton of other stuff. It's on the other end of Harbor Drive, right by the bay where the old Pat's Diner was," he said.

Hannah agreed and watched Luke depart before she loaded Jessie into her truck. She thought about calling Susie, but wasn't ready for the teasing just yet. While she drove home, she began to dwell on whether or not dinner with Luke was a good idea. By the time she got to the house, she had to order herself to stop worrying. It was just a dinner. Going from the extreme of casual flings to nothing had left her in a state of confusion about how to navigate this.

Though she didn't want to, she had to admit that Luke was certainly compelling. Just thinking about him now kick-started her heart rate and flushed her face. She knew if Luke saw her now, her blush would only deepen. She hated the fact that she was a blusher. Always had been and figured she always would be. She shook her head and walked with Jessie into the house. In the week and a half that she'd been here, she had stopped feeling like she was entering a place frozen in time. She wasn't the neatest person, and her left-over dishes in the kitchen and scattered books and clothes in other areas made the home feel alive again. She looked at her watch. Only three hours until dinner.

While Jessie napped in the sunny part of the kitchen, Hannah busied herself with cleaning and doing laundry. The time passed quickly, and she ended up rushing to get ready with a quick shower and fortunately not enough time to obsess over what to wear. She wore loose gauzy pants, a dark cream color, which swung softly around her ankles. Her top was a fitted royal blue blouse, and she slipped a green scarf around her neck. She loved bold jewelry and wore large silver hoops earrings, a cluster of silver bracelets on one wrist, and a wide hammered silver band on the other. She added one of her mother's necklaces, a teardrop jade necklace. It gave her something to touch when she felt restless and anxious. Hannah fed Jessie and got her situated in the truck again. Jessie leaned her head out the window, ears flapping in the wind, as Hannah drove down the hill to town. She pulled up at the Boathouse Café, which had previously been Pat's Diner, owned by Pat and Patty Dunlop. When the husband of the couple had developed health problems, they had decided to retire. They still lived in town from what she had heard. She wondered what they thought of the new place.

Hannah made sure Jessie was comfortable for the time they'd be eating and looked to see if Luke's truck was here yet. Spying it parked in the far corner, she headed inside. When she walked in, it occurred to her that for the first time since she'd moved back, she hadn't entered a place wondering whom she might see and if they might bring up memories of her parents. She laughed to herself and thought that perhaps obsessing over a man would keep her occupied, at least for now.

The space had been updated from its former basic diner look with booths and vinyl-covered stools at a long counter. The grill area was still visible, but the new owners had updated the rest. The counter was dark mahogany wood, and the wall behind the grills alternated mirrors and sections of dark wood shelving with spices, stainless steel cooking utensils, and wines. Shiny copper cookware hung above the grilling area. Diamond Creek was well-known for its restaurants, within Alaska and beyond, so it wasn't a surprise to Hannah that the place would have fit in Seattle just as easily as here. The booths remained, but the tabletops had been replaced and were also shiny mahogany with crisp white place mats. The windows were hung with a variety of brightly colored curtains, giving the restaurant a cheerful warmth.

Luke was seated in a corner booth talking with a couple seated nearby. Hannah didn't recognize them and was relieved. As nervous as she was to be on a date, she didn't need the speculation of others. In a town the size of Diamond Creek, social curiosity and gossip were rampant. As much as she'd wanted to, she hadn't called Susie to pry for more details about Luke. She had no idea if he'd dated anyone else they knew or what his history was. All she knew was what he'd told her and that Susie wanted to set them up. While Susie may have been off her mark in past efforts at matchmaking, she had good judgment about who was decent and who wasn't.

Luke caught her eye and stood up to greet her. He introduced her to the couple he'd been talking with. They were tourists he'd taken out on a guiding trip the week before. Once they got seated, Hannah turned to look at the window. The café had a clear view of the bay and mountains. She savored the familiar sight. This area was just off the beach, so she felt like she was sitting beside the water.

Luke watched her and followed her eyes out the window. "Can't get enough of it myself. Been here over two years now and could look all day every day. Pretty sure it doesn't wear out."

"No, I don't think it does. I missed it," Hannah said as she turned back to Luke. She took in his green eyes and tousled hair. She guessed that even just washed and brushed, which it looked at the moment, his hair tended to be just shy of unruly. Her stomach fluttered when he smiled at her.

"So what do you think of this place so far? Never saw the old diner myself, but heard they made a lot of changes," he said.

"Oh, they have. Pat's was a pretty typical-looking diner.

Basic and simple. The food was delicious. I like this, though. It's nice to have something different here. I'd rather they didn't try to make it what it was before."

They made small talk, which didn't keep Hannah's mind off Luke's eyes and hands. She had a thing for a man's hands, and Luke's were about perfect. They were strong without looking too rugged. They were also expressive. He gestured often in an unconscious way. As he was relating a story about a recent guiding trip, she heard a squeal and looked up to see her old friend Cammi. Cammi had run in the same circle as Hannah and Susie, and was known for being overly sentimental and just plain good to have as a friend. She was as loyal as they came. She looked much the same as she had before. Her straight honey-brown hair was in a short pixie cut. She wore a long cotton skirt of bright purple with a peasant-style white blouse. She carried herself with a sweet air and brought to mind flowers, herbs, and warmth.

Cammi made it to their booth as Hannah stood. Cammi engulfed her in a hug. Cammi stepped back, held her shoulders, and just smiled. She turned to greet Luke. They appeared friendly.

"I'd heard you were back," Cammi said. "I just asked Susie for your number today. Was planning to call tomorrow. So, so, so glad you're home. We missed you. I have a thousand questions, but I see you're actually having dinner. Let me introduce you to my friend." Cammi grabbed the arm of an unfamiliar woman who'd been standing nearby waiting. She was tall with straight blond hair that hung halfway down her back. She had an unadorned beauty with a tomboyish quality to her.

"This is Dara. She's a friend I met in college. She came to visit last summer and couldn't leave." Cammi gestured back to Hannah. "Dara, this is Hannah. You know Luke. Hannah's our old friend who was away for a couple years. Rumor has it she's back to stay."

Cammi's joy was infectious. "It's so good to see you, Cammi! And nice to meet you, Dara," Hannah said. "The rumors are true—I'm back to stay. Susie sent Luke to me with a dog. Only a few days after I got back." She paused to look around the café. "This place has had a makeover. So much has changed since I left, but there's plenty that's the same. Susie told me you had moved back after you stayed in Oregon for a bit. When do you want to get together?" she asked.

They made plans to meet for lunch the day after tomorrow. Luke exchanged pleasantries with Cammi and Dara before the hostess signaled them. Cammi looped her arm through Dara's as they were led to a booth on the opposite side of the restaurant. Hannah sat back down and took a deep breath, noticing that Luke was watching her.

"It's great to reconnect with old friends, but it brings up a lot. Cammi's parents were close to mine. It's hard to not think about them being gone." Hannah shook her head and looked back out at the bay for a moment.

"Cammi's one of the first people we got to know when we moved here. Her little coffee truck was where we went for coffee on the way out to fish," Luke said, holding Hannah's gaze, appearing to gauge her reaction. "Being home brings up a lot of memories, I'm sure. You seem to be getting through it okay."

She thought for a moment. "I am...getting through it, that is. Instead of dwelling on the past—that's my motto these days. Tell me what's good for dinner here," she said.

Luke obliged with his suggestions, and dinner passed quickly. He was a polite dinner partner, patiently answering questions. He discussed growing up in Seattle, and his parents frequent visits to Alaska since they retired. When he spoke of his family, there were glimmers of a soft side to him. He joked about whether it was the best idea that he and his brothers worked together, chuckling about how most of the conflicts ended up between Nathan and Jared while he played referee.

As Hannah shared some of her own stories, she realized she'd lost touch with the silly side of herself since the plane crash. Seeing Cammi reminded her of things they used to do, including late night bonfires on the beach and costume parties to liven up long winters. She'd forgotten that she wasn't just a serious graduate student and a lonely woman who felt lost without her parents. She was beginning to realize the fear that kept her from staying in touch with friends in Diamond Creek may have taken her further away from herself. Despite the memories and how fresh they felt, the people here were the ones who knew her before her parents died and could help her find her way back.

CHAPTER 8

*L*uke looked across the table at Hannah. She had relaxed during dinner, or so he thought. She was sipping on a glass of wine. The encounter with Cammi and Dara seemed to take an edge off. He couldn't have planned it that way, but many of her friends were friends he'd made since they moved here. While Diamond Creek was small, there were circles of friends, many overlapping. He took advantage of her gazing out the window to take in the sight of her again. He wanted to touch her hair; it fell in glossy waves past her shoulders. The rich brown of her hair brought out the blue of her eyes. Her fingers toyed with the jade teardrop at her throat.

Luke had an internal tug-of-war going on. He was more interested in Hannah than was comfortable for him. This was the first time in years that he wondered what a woman thought about him. Not that he hadn't been interested in other women since the crash and burn of his relationship with Cristina, but they'd all been shallow relationships, good for a little fun, but not much more. He sensed himself drawn to the challenge of Hannah's reserve. He also thought he understood something about her. She had been so wrapped up in losing her parents, she forgot to take care of herself. Thinking these kinds of thoughts made him shake his head—not a place he wanted to go, thinking he understood her.

Hannah finally turned away from the view and caught him watching her. He didn't look away. For the moment, the draw was worth it. He told himself he'd worry later if he found himself in too deep. She blushed but held his eyes and smiled. "We should check on Jessie. Do you still want to go for a walk? We could just go on the beach right here for a few minutes."

He didn't hesitate. "Let's do it."

He signaled their waitress for the bill. As they left the café, he placed his hand on her back. It was warm to the touch. Hannah didn't move away. Opening the back of her truck, she produced a pair of rubber boots and changed out of her sandals for the walk. She was ever practical, not surprising since she'd been raised mostly in Alaska. While she changed into her boots, he let Jessie out and got her leash in case they needed it.

As they walked along the water, he took in the smell of the ocean, his favorite smell. It didn't matter where he was, what beach, what state, or what ocean. He loved the salty scent of the air, the earthy tang from seaweed, rocks, and shells. Jessie ran ahead and circled back to them while they walked. Hannah had a long stride and kicked at small rocks with her boots as she walked. The breeze tousled her hair. Her arms swung loosely. He caught her hand as it swung past his. Her stride faltered for a split second, but her hand curled into his. It was becoming chilly, so they turned back. The sun was slowly setting, the sky fading into rose and streaks of yellow. Sunset in the summer in Alaska didn't mean darkness was coming anytime soon—just a long dusky evening with darkness falling for a few brief hours and the sun rising not long after.

* * *

HANNAH ENCOURAGED Jessie to hop into her truck when they got back to the parking lot. She gave her water and then softly closed the truck door. Turning to face Luke, she dusted sand off her hands. She turned more quickly than she intended and lost her balance when her boot caught on the edge of the truck tire. With a squeak, she tumbled into Luke. As she tried to right herself, he steadied her with his hands on her arms. Catching her balance, she tilted her head, just barely, to look at him. His eyes were bright, and when she opened her mouth to speak, he leaned in and sealed his lips over hers. Her mind went blank, and her world narrowed to the point where their lips joined. He softly nipped at her lower lip. A rush of heat coursed through her. Her mouth opened, and his tongue slipped inside. She could have kissed him forever—he knew how to take his time. It was a soft, slow tangle of lips and tongues, nips and strokes. His hands stroked from her shoulders down her back. She circled a hand around his neck and slipped her fingers through the dark curls. She gulped in a breath of air when he pulled away from her.

Hannah looked into Luke's green eyes, just looked. He looked back without speaking for a moment.

"Wanted to do that since the day I met you," he said bluntly.

She blushed, but managed a laugh. "Fair enough. If you didn't notice, I wanted to do that too," she said. She was rewarded with his dimples. His arms were still around her, but he loosened them and stepped back.

"As much as I'd be happy to take this further, I don't want to rush…" he said and then looked away for a moment

67

before turning back. "Starting to think I'm lucky you ran into me at the beach and then Susie sent me your way with Jessie."

She took his words in and felt her heart dance a little jig. "Should we try dinner again soon? Maybe you could come to my place. Jessie would love that. I'm a pretty good cook too."

"Sounds good...but before I let you go..." Luke pulled her right back against him, and they spiraled to the heated place they'd been. Hannah leaned into him and let her tongue get caught in a wild tangle with his. He cupped one cheek and slipped his thumb down the center of her chin, angling to slide it softly down the side of her throat and tracing one of her collarbones. His touch left sparks and tingles in its wake, bringing her to a heated shiver. He drew her closer and ran his hands down her back, pulling her hips against his. Their kiss became frantic with Hannah pressing into him, gripping his shirt. She could feel his erection low against her belly. Slick heat built between her legs with the rest of her burning. Anything that passed for thought was long gone.

A car door slammed, and reality intruded. She realized she would have happily rushed Luke far past a kiss right there in the parking lot in her hometown in full view of anyone and thought nothing of it. He appeared to have heard the door as he pulled slowly away and lifted his head. He turned to look over his shoulder and then back at her.

She smiled sheepishly and shrugged. "I guess a parking lot isn't the best place for a kiss for us."

"No, I guess not," he said with a soft laugh. He pulled back farther and let his hands slide away from her. "I don't usually make a scene like that."

"Neither do I. That one got away from me."

"Should I say maybe I'll call you, or not bother

pretending that I don't want to go ahead and make plans to see you again?" he asked.

Hannah looked back into his green eyes and saw a hint of vulnerability. She sensed this wasn't easy for him and knew it wasn't for her. But if there was one thing the last two years had taught her, it was that it wasn't worth hiding.

"Let's not pretend. How about we meet at the dinner party Susie's having this weekend?" she asked.

"First I've heard of it, but if you're going, I'll be happy to meet you," he said.

She had begun to crave his smiles and accompanying dimples. Just as he turned to go, he leaned over and gave her a lingering kiss. It felt chaste compared to the conflagration they'd just experienced, but it was sweet. It left her tingling. She drove home, absentmindedly petting Jessie and occasionally touching her fingers to her lips as if to try to hold on to his touch.

CHAPTER 9

The next morning dawned clear and cool. Luke stood by the windows after returning from his run and looked out over the bay. The day was calm with the bay smooth in the stillness. He loved this quiet time of day when much of the world was still asleep. Jared had gone for a run. Occasionally they ran together, although Luke had been up earlier than usual today. He had slept restlessly last night after dinner with Hannah. He couldn't keep thoughts of her out of his mind. He'd actually had to take a cold shower to douse the fire she'd left burning. He felt like a teenager again.

He was thankful for the car door that slammed and shook him out of the kiss. He had been about to push Hannah against the truck and take her right there. As much as he wanted her, he didn't want to make a public spectacle of them. He'd driven home picturing her long legs wrapped around his waist. Both Jared and Nathan had been out when he'd gotten home, so he'd avoided questions and had time to compose himself. Off and on through the night, he'd woken thinking about her. He found himself alternately ignoring the warning bells that he was too interested in her and trying to convince himself it was just lust. Lust was harmless. Considering anything more only revived memories of how stupid he'd been over Cristina. He couldn't imagine Hannah being that shallow and superficial, but then he hadn't envisioned that with Cristina either. He wasn't interested in emotional risks, just those that came with testing himself outdoors, like heli-skiing in the Chugach Mountains.

He was relieved and frustrated that he had a guide trip today. He would be busy, and busy was good for his frame of mind. He also wanted to see Hannah again as soon as possible, and the weekend couldn't come quickly enough. Knowing that he'd be out fishing for a few weeks, he didn't want to miss what time he had. But that was the reality of fishing for a living. He finished his coffee and went downstairs to get ready for the day. Not long after, Jared joined him, and they set out for the harbor.

He sensed Jared glancing at him as he drove.

"Well?" Jared asked.

"Well, what?" he asked in return.

"You're a little out of it this morning. Heard from Cammi that you were at dinner with Hannah at the Boathouse last night. Ran into her when I went by the store last night. Funny you didn't mention it," Jared said.

Luke looked over at Jared and caught him grinning. "So I had dinner with Hannah. That supposed to mean something?"

"Only when you keep it to yourself," Jared said with a chuckle.

Luke rolled his eyes. "Just remember I can give as good as I get and the tables always turn."

"Just thought I'd point out that you've been working on a long spell of dating lightweights. Hannah seems a little... well, like she might be beyond your type."

Luke shifted down, rolling to a stop at a corner, and turned to Jared. "Lightweights, huh?"

Jared nodded. "Exactly. Pretty women that fall for you but don't mind that all you want is a few dates and a tumble between the sheets. Not that I know Hannah much, but that's not the vibe she gives off. Maybe you should think about something other than a little fun."

Luke shifted the focus as he turned onto the main road that led into town. "Let's talk about pots calling kettles black. You're the master of casual dating. Half the women in this town pine after you. Find it interesting that you think it's time for *me* to think about something other than a little fun."

"Fair enough, fair enough," Jared said with a shrug, unperturbed. "Relationships aren't my thing. Too messy. Up to you and Nathan to produce the grandkids that Mom and Dad want. The sooner you do, the less pressure on me."

Luke choked on a laugh. "Already planning children for Nathan and me? Is there anything you don't plan? Never mind. Cut me some slack, or I'll recruit Mom and Dad to harass you more about those grandkids."

Jared looked horrified. Luke pulled into the parking lot at the harbor. The early morning sunlight glinted across the surface of the water, smooth and glassy in Otter Cove. Despite the fact that it was not yet six o'clock, the parking lot was filling up. Summer in Alaskan communities was short and intense; the long days crammed into a few short months were filled with activity from early dawn to late dusk. Some of the larger fishing boats were being readied for fishing runs, while smaller guide boats would be filling with tourists and heading out to the bay within the hour for a full day of fishing. Luke looked toward *Iris*, their commercial boat. The boat sat quietly in her slip. Just beside *Iris* sat their smaller guide boat—basically a large utilitarian motorboat. They didn't do guiding full-time, but it brought in extra cash in between commercial runs and kept them from having to worry too much during years when the commercial runs weren't as profitable.

They quickly got to work. Luke sorted fishing gear, while Jared did a quick run-through of the mechanicals and electronics to make sure the motor and all else was running smoothly for the day. By the time they were ready, they had about fifteen minutes to spare. Luke offered to make a quick coffee and food run, to which Jared quickly agreed.

* * *

LUKE WALKED into Misty Mountain Café and ordered two large shots in the dark, the house coffee dosed with a shot of espresso. He grabbed some savory rolls and two hearty sandwiches. While he waited for the coffees to be ready, he felt a tap on his shoulder and turned to find Susie smiling at him.

"Good morning there, Luke," Susie said.

"And to you," he said with a nod. He wondered if Susie knew he'd had dinner with Hannah. The rumor mill was like a brush fire in Diamond Creek. He braced himself for questions, teasing, and the like.

Susie didn't hesitate. "Heard you had dinner with Hannah last night. I'm trying to decide if I should be offended that neither one of you said a word to me about it."

He sighed and met Susie's gaze head-on. "Just dinner, Susie. When did I have to start reporting to you when I have dinner with someone?" he asked.

"When you have dinner with my best friend who just moved back home, that's when," she said with a flash of protectiveness in her eyes.

He felt caught between wanting to get out of the conversation and wanting to ask Susie about Hannah. Of the long list of things he loved about living in a small town, the sense of community was high on that list. That said, he barely tolerated how that sense of community could feel as if it were turned against one when friends wanted to know what was going on and when rumors raced in tight circles. In larger communities, it was much easier to lay low and wait to show one's hand. It was nearly impossible, if not completely impossible, to do so in a community the size of Diamond Creek. He tried to remind himself that Susie was curious because she cared, not because she was nosy. He knew she'd missed Hannah while she was gone and considered her as close as family.

"Okay, here's the thing. I like Hannah, so I asked her out to dinner. Not much else to say."

Susie looked at him for a long moment, and her eyes softened. She tended to be brash and assertive, but she had a softer side that occasionally surfaced. "Got it. Here's my thing. I'm glad you asked Hannah out to dinner. I have a hunch about you two," she said and paused when Luke raised his eyebrows at that. She wagged her finger at him with a shake of her head, her brown curls bouncing. "Of course, now I'm feeling protective and want to make sure you're not planning to treat her as casually as everyone else you've dated around here."

She held up a hand when he started to respond. "Not that I'm saying you were anything other than aboveboard with everyone. You made it pretty clear you just wanted casual, and that's what you've gotten. I realize you can't promise me you'll marry her and live happily ever after with only one date under your belt, but maybe you can think about the fact that she's a pretty awesome woman who hit a rough patch the last few years. I don't know why I thought you'd be good for her given your dating history of nothing but casual. I think there's more to you than that," Susie said with a pointed look.

Luke took in her words and tried to ignore the defensive

feeling that rose. Just then, his name was called, indicating that his order was ready. Susie followed him while he picked up his order. In tacit agreement, they made small talk while they were near others waiting in line.

When Luke was adding cream to his coffee, he continued, "Maybe I keep things casual, but it doesn't mean I'm a jerk." As he spoke, he realized that from Susie's view, he might be one if he unintentionally hurt Hannah. A wave of discomfort rose when he realized he felt protective toward Hannah as well.

Susie gave him a speculative look before speaking. "You're a decent guy, so I hope you act like one. You'll hear about it from me if not. Before you take off, though...I'm having a dinner party this weekend, kind of a welcome-Hannah-back-to-town gathering. Can you and your brothers make it? I was thinking of Saturday."

"I'll be there," he said and decided against mentioning that Hannah had already told him about the dinner party. "Jared and Nathan should make it, but I don't know offhand if they have plans." Luke looked at the clock. "Gotta run. See you Saturday if not sooner."

He lifted a coffee in good-bye and headed back to the harbor. By the time he got there, about half of their customers for the day had arrived. Within a half hour, the boat was full, and they were ready to leave the harbor.

The day alternated between passing in a blur and stalling while they sat and waited for the halibut to bite. Luke was thankful that they had a chatty group for the day. Making conversation with the tourists about Alaska and learning about their various lives kept his mind from dwelling on Hannah. They returned to the harbor with everyone on board catching their limit. The day ended with him and Jared helping customers fillet their fish or sending them over to Fish Factory, the local business that provided full services for freshly caught fish, including filleting, slicing fillets to selected weights, flash freezing, and vacuum-packing the fish. Once they had sent off their happy customers and their fish, he and Jared hosed down the boat.

As Luke drove home, he felt tired to his bones. A long day on the water did that, even when he loved what he was doing. He caught sight of Hannah's truck at the grocery store and thought about coming up with an excuse to stop. He elected not to when he considered the teasing he might have to endure from Jared. By the time Luke and Jared got home, they both headed for showers and tried to beat each other to the kitchen for whatever food could be found. They were saved when Nathan showed up with pizza.

Nathan held it aloft as he came through the front door. "Here you go, guys. Meant to call, but figured you'd eat whatever I brought home."

Jared sighed. "Thanks, man. Was about to arm wrestle Luke here for the last of the chips. How is it that Luke just went to the store the other day and there's hardly anything left?"

Nathan rolled his eyes as he set the pizza on the kitchen counter. "We eat a lot. Maybe we should get a bigger fridge."

Luke laughed. "Not a bad idea, not at all. Hand me that pizza." He hooked his finger over the edge of the pizza box and dragged it closer. "By the way, ran into Susie this morning when I went for our coffee and food. We're invited to a dinner party at her place on Saturday. Told her I couldn't make promises for you two, but I'll be there," he said.

With a wink to Nathan, Jared asked, "Wonder if Susie's friend Hannah will be there?"

"I'd bet on it. Heard you had dinner with Hannah. Trying to keep secrets?" Nathan asked.

Luke took a bite of pizza and shook his head. "So this is how it's gonna be? Just dinner, dude. Since when is that a big deal?"

"Just a hunch," Nathan said with a grin and a shrug, catching Jared's eye.

Luke looked at his brothers, both looking back at him with grins. He sighed, shook his head again, and focused on eating his pizza. He knew the more he reacted to their teasing, the more he'd hear. That's how it was in their family. He also knew if the tables were turned, he'd be enjoying either brother's discomfort. Jared and Nathan spent the rest of the night occasionally trying to get a rise out of Luke. They spread out in the living room to watch the late night news and shows.

CHAPTER 10

*H*annah pulled at the weeds in her mother's old flower beds. They were choked with weeds, mostly chickweed and horsetail. The chickweed was easy to break free, but the horsetail was another matter. Bright green with the appearance of a horsetail poking out of the ground, horsetail grew in swaths and took over if unchecked. She had learned from her father that the weed was ancient, the plant's eons on earth evidence of its hardiness. The roots ran deep and were strong and interconnected. She cursed its strength. She'd been weeding for about an hour, and her arms were wearing out.

She heard the sound of a car and looked up to see Susie's faded blue Subaru pulling into the drive. Pushing up from her knees, she stood and pulled off her gardening gloves. Knocking them together to shake the dirt free, she walked over to greet Susie. Jessie came running from where she'd been napping in the yard nearby.

As Hannah approached the car, she saw that Susie wasn't alone. Cammi climbed out of the passenger side. Jessie raced to Cammi's side, and Cammi leaned over to pet her.

Susie called out, "Hope it's okay that we just stopped by. We're headed to Anchorage for a one-day marathon shopping run tomorrow and thought we'd stop to see if you needed anything."

"I'm more inclined to just admit we needed an excuse to stop by," Cammi said. "Seeing as I've seen you only once since you came home after over two years *and* you happened to be on a date with Luke Winters last night, I'm feeling nosy."

Hannah paused as she reached the car. "Nice to see you too, Cammi. Am I going to get the third degree here?" she asked. It had been two years since she'd had to put up with friends who paid attention to what she was doing and asked nosy questions. As annoying as that could be, it was nice to know she mattered.

Susie leaned over to check one of her tires. "Yes, you will get the third degree. I admitted I sent Luke and Jessie to you with more than one agenda in mind, so now you have to tell us how dinner went." She stood back up, her brown curls falling in their usual disarray around her face. Her eyes twinkled when she spoke again. "We haven't had a chance to gossip about your love life, or lack thereof, for two years, so we're making up for lost time. This is the point where you invite us in for coffee."

Hannah sighed and smiled simultaneously. "I don't see how I can escape, so I might as well as invite you in."

She walked over, gave them both hugs and gestured for them to follow her inside while Jessie ran ahead to the house. Susie and Cammi made themselves comfortable at the kitchen counter, complaining about the summer tourist traffic and the slow start to warmer summer weather while Hannah got coffee going.

Once Hannah turned on the coffeepot, Susie jumped in. "So, you went to dinner with Luke? What does that mean?"

"It means I went to dinner with him," Hannah retorted.

"Oh, don't be all mysterious about it. I like Luke, and like I said, I have a feeling about you two," Susie said.

"Fine. I like him, so when he asked me out for dinner, I said yes, and we had dinner. That's about all there is to tell right now."

Cammi piped up. "Just dinner? We want more than that."

"Not much to say when we've only had one date. I should be the one pumping you two for information, not the other way around," Hannah replied.

Susie looked at Cammi. "We don't have a ton to tell you about Luke. He and his brothers, Jared and Nathan, moved here about two years ago, not long after you moved to Massachusetts. They had already started their commercial fishing business in Seattle and moved the business up here when they came to Diamond Creek. Luke's the middle brother. Of course, if you've met them all, you've noticed they're handsome as all get-out, so they've been drooled over since they've been here. The local joke about their business, The One that Didn't Get Away, is that it applies only to fish because none of the women here can catch any of them." Susie said with a grin.

Cammi picked up where Susie paused. "Well, we didn't drool over them, but most everybody else did. All three have kept it casual. Jared's probably dated the least, only once in a while have I heard he was seeing anyone. They're all outdoorsy types, but that's not exactly news in Alaska. Luke could probably give you a run for your money with hiking and skiing. He's known for pushing limits—he ran Mount Marathon last year, and you know how grueling that is. Jared seems to run the show as far as what happens with the business. Nathan is the wildest. He's always seeing someone and can be found at the bar a few times a week, but he's known as a nice guy too."

Susie chimed in again. "We got to know them when they hired me to do their books. Aside from you and a few others, you know I pretend to avoid the rumor mill, so I can't give you much more than Cammi did. As for business, they run a tight ship. Their business is sound. I met their parents last summer when they were up for a month or so. Nice people. Seem like a close family."

Hannah looked over at Susie and Cammi and felt tears well. Silly as it seemed, it was heaven to sit here, drink coffee, and be nosy about some guy she had dinner with. She hadn't allowed herself this luxury while she was away. "I won't pretend it isn't annoying to have you two show up at my door asking about a date I had just last night. But it's nice to be back with my friends who care enough to be that nosy." She brushed an errant lock of hair off her forehead.

Susie came around the counter and hugged Hannah. "We're damn glad to have you home. And it's fun to drop in and be nosy. We probably wouldn't have bothered if you hadn't been gone so long. I'll take every excuse I can manufacture to see you."

Cammi squealed, ever sentimental, and walked over for another hug too. "We missed you, sweetie." She turned to look at Susie. "Did you mention your dinner party for Saturday?" she asked.

"Yup, told her about it the other day," Susie said, picking up her coffee cup again. "Luke already told me he'd be there," she said with a wink.

Hannah looked down at Susie, who was close to five feet tall, a good foot shorter than Hannah. She'd always been amazed at the contrast between Susie's petite physical size and outsized bold personality. Susie barreled toward life and tended to pull others along in her wake. Hannah was realizing how much it would have helped her to have Susie by her side during the darkest days after her parents died. She could have used her forceful personality and unwavering support. She was grateful to be back in Diamond Creek with Susie back in her life.

"I'll be there Saturday. Anything I should bring?" Hannah asked.

"Just yourself and maybe a bottle of wine," Susie said.

They spent another hour over coffee. Susie and Cammi filled her in on the status of other friends she hadn't seen yet. They teased her lightly about Luke, but didn't push. Hannah soaked in her time with them, while Jessie sacked out on the kitchen floor. She brought up her possible plans for work and bounced ideas off them for feedback. At one point, she looked around the kitchen and into the living room and thought back to how empty and lonely the house had felt when she arrived almost two weeks ago. Her mind wandered further back to the two years of isolation thousands of miles away. It had been a long path to get back home and to feel her soul coming to life again. Looking around, the house felt like a place of home and community again. The feeling was different from how the house had felt when her parents were here, but it was healthy and solid and carried a sense of hope.

Eventually, Susie and Cammi left with hugs and promises to see each other in a few days, if not sooner. Hannah waited with Jessie on the front deck and watched the dust lift on the road behind Susie's car, remaining on the deck for a while after they left. She thought of her conversation with Luke about how the view never got old. She counted the peaks of the mountains across the bay, an old childhood habit that had started the day she arrived. She'd never seen mountains that big, so she'd counted them and proudly reported to her mother that she could see seven peaks from the house. Today as she counted, she found herself whispering aloud, as if her mother could hear. A quiet joy mixed with sadness rose in her heart. She missed her parents deeply. Their presence was still a void in her heart and world. She didn't know if she could ever fill it, but she was starting to feel a sense of hope that she could move through her grief.

* * *

THE NEXT FEW days passed quickly. Hannah kept busy working on the yard and slowly sorting through the house. She walked daily with Jessie, exploring just about every trail she remembered and a few new ones. Frank and June had finally stopped by the house after a call to check on her. Frank was as steady as Hannah remembered him. He was a few years older than her father had been, his hair graying, his hands roughened from work, but his brown eyes as kind as ever. June tended to mother-hen Hannah. She was round and soft, her blond hair always worn in a long braid that hung over one shoulder. If she was graying, you couldn't tell. She had a timeless quality to her. June was one of her mother's closest friends and had known how worried Hannah's parents had been about her those last few years when Hannah was running amuck. Hannah felt a prick of embarrassment, wondering what June had known about how impulsive Hannah had been and how much her mother had worried over it. She wanted to tell June she'd become what her parents had hoped for—responsible and not chasing one man after another on the latest adventure. For a moment, it occurred to her that they likely hadn't wanted her to live like a nun.

As they were leaving, June mentioned that she had a few file boxes of papers from Hannah's mother. "Your mother gave them to me years ago actually. Your parents were in the midst of the master bedroom and bath remodel. She said she wanted these boxes in a safe place, so she gave them to me. She kept saying she'd come by and pick them up, but you know how that goes. It never happened. I can drop them off here, or you can swing by to get them. Whatever's easier for you," June said.

Hannah agreed to pick them up and had gone over the next morning. She was puzzled about the boxes. She remembered when the remodeling project was happening and tried to remember if she'd seen the boxes before. They were nondescript paper filing boxes. She had no recollection of seeing them and wondered where her mother had stored them before the remodel. Carting them into the living room, she left them by the couch to look through later.

Before she knew it, Saturday was upon her. When she woke in the cool dawn, she lay in bed and wondered about Luke. She was anxious to see him again and anxious in a different way about seeing the other friends who would be at Susie's. Her thoughts also kept circling back to the file boxes. She couldn't pin down why, but she had a strange feeling about them. Jessie's cool nose nudged her hand, and she turned her head to see Jessie standing beside the bed wagging her tail. Pushing her questions and anxiety away, Hannah tossed the covers back.

Later that afternoon, Hannah went over to Susie's early to help. She brought two bottles of wine, a red and a white. This was the first time she'd been to Susie's place since she'd moved back. Susie had moved out of her parents' home after she graduated from college and purchased a small home nearby. She lived on the other side of the hill from Hannah above town. Rather than driving down into town, only to drive back up the other side of the hill, Hannah took a back road across the top of the hill. Pulling into Susie's driveway, her heart warmed at the sight of Susie's house. It was quintessential Susie, small and colorful with a touch of whimsy. It was a small cottage-style timber home with a deck that wrapped around the entire house and purple trim on the windows. A small purple Jolly Roger flag flew from one corner of the house.

Susie came out and waved at her from the deck by the door. Hannah walked up the stairs to the deck. "I meant to get here a little earlier to help, but I got caught up working on the yard. It's been a mess really." She set the wine bottles on the deck railing and gave Susie a quick hug.

"You didn't even have to come early to help. I just wanted you here so I'd have some time with you to myself. I'm selfish that way," Susie said as she stepped back from returning Hannah's hug.

"Just how many people did you invite?" Hannah asked.

"Not that many actually. If everyone shows up, it's not more than twelve people. Don't worry about it. You've seen most of them. You haven't seen Maggie and Jason though. Maggie can't wait to see you," Susie said as she put the white wine in the refrigerator.

"I thought they broke up before I moved away."

"They did. Then they were both living in Anchorage. When they both moved back to Diamond Creek, it was this big drama because Jason dumped the girlfriend he'd brought with him. Maggie said she forgot that Jason was her soul mate. The girlfriend he brought with him ended up staying in town too. Name's Callie. She's nice enough, but I don't know her well. For a while, she dated Luke's younger brother, Nathan. Not sure what came of that," Susie said.

For the next half hour or so, Susie filled Hannah in on other happenings over the past two years. While some things had changed, many stayed the same. If anything, one thing Hannah could count on was that the gossip channels in Diamond Creek were alive and well. For now, she was soaking it in. She loved being back in town and feeling like she knew who was who and what was what. She helped Susie assemble a tray of cheese and crackers. Susie then assigned her to put together a tray of vegetables and dips.

"This isn't really a dinner party by the way. It's an appetizer party," Susie said with a laugh.

As Hannah finished slicing vegetables, there was a call from the screen door that led onto the deck. She turned to see Cammi and Dara. Susie gestured for them to come in. Cammi and Dara came with hugs and chips and salsa. Not long after they arrived, Maggie and Jason showed up. They looked much the same as they had when Hannah last saw them. Maggie had shiny black hair that hugged her scalp in a short cap. Jason had retained the rugged outdoorsy look he'd had all through high school. His blond hair was a shaggy contrast to Maggie's sleek locks.

Hannah was surprised to find how quickly it felt like she hadn't been gone. Maggie and Jason had opened a construction business. Maggie handled the office side of it while Jason handled the building. Hannah was busy talking with them while Susie persuaded Cammi and Dara to help her rearrange the chairs away from the table. She looked up from her conversation to see Luke entering the kitchen with Jared and who she assumed to be Nathan behind him. They came with more wine, in addition to beer from the local brewery, Diamond Creek Brewery. She lost focus on what Maggie was saying for a moment. Her heart stepped up a beat, and her stomach had the hollow, fluttery feeling that seemed inevitable when Luke was nearby. She forced herself to pay attention to Maggie.

After Luke greeted Susie and the others, he came in her direction, tugging Nathan with him. Nathan was clearly Luke's brother. They shared the same black curly hair. Nathan's was longer and messier and paired with sharp blue eyes. He was a shade taller than Luke.

Luke introduced them, and Nathan graced her with a lopsided smile. "Hello there. Heard about you. Hope it's good to be back in Diamond Creek."

Nathan's easy warmth relaxed her. "Hello to you too. It's

great to be home and nice to meet you. Luke's mentioned both you and Jared. It sounds like the three of you have a good gig going with your fishing and guiding."

"That we do. Me being the youngest, Luke and Jared think they're my bosses, but they couldn't do it without me," Nathan said in return, his eyes taking on a mischievous glint. "So what did you think of the Boathouse? Heard Luke took you there."

Luke shook his head. "He just can't resist commenting on the fact that we had dinner the other night. Ignore him."

Nathan's eyes twinkled, but he stayed silent.

"It was great," she replied. "I'm glad something good opened there since Pat's closed. Diamond Creek has plenty of good restaurants, but we've also had some that just didn't take. It's nice to have another good place."

Nathan nodded politely and appeared to be holding back a laugh. Jared approached them then. The three brothers shared variations of black curls with Luke and Jared sharing green eyes, and Nathan the odd one out, his eyes bright blue. They were rugged and just plain handsome with strong, sculpted features and lanky, muscled builds. Jared and Luke were level in height while Nathan was slightly taller. Jared had the sharpest features of the three and a coiled presence. Nathan's slouch and teasing manner almost seemed a reaction to Jared. Luke appeared somewhere in the middle, not keyed up like Jared, but not loose with the wild edge that Nathan held. Seeing the three of them together, Hannah easily understood why they'd set hearts aflutter and gossip abounding when they'd moved to town. Three handsome, rugged men new in a tiny town like Diamond Creek—she could only imagine the first year they'd been here.

Hannah shook her head when she caught her mind wandering and brought her thoughts back to the room. Jared was asking Nathan about confirming the dates for their upcoming trip with the crew. Luke was casually chatting with Maggie and Jason. He nodded toward the couch where Hannah was seated. "Can I join you?" At her nod, he sat and turned toward Maggie and Jason. "Had the pleasure of meeting Hannah and then Susie convinced me to ask her to take Jessie." He reached over to set a bottle of beer on the coffee table.

She looked away for a moment, but was pulled back by Luke's voice. "So, how have you been?" he asked.

She turned to find his green eyes looking directly at her. Laughter lurked in them. The heat of his body permeated her, as he'd seated himself fairly close to her on the couch. When she looked into his eyes, she couldn't look away. She bit her lip. "I'm doing okay. How about you?" Hannah asked. Silently, she wondered if she was being stupid about Luke. She worried that she was drawn to him for all the wrong reasons—just another handsome, charming guy who loved the outdoors as much as she did. She mentally batted that thought away.

"I'm okay. Glad to see you here. Been busy between day trips and getting ready to leave in about a week. Not much left to do at this point, so I have some extra time on my hands. Hoping you'll let me join you for a few of your walks with Jessie."

"Oh, of course. I don't plan them really. I could just call you maybe before one of our afternoon walks."

Luke nodded and then responded to something Jason said. Jared and Nathan tugged chairs across from the coffee table. Susie, Cammi, and Dara came in from the kitchen area. Dara situated one of the food trays on the coffee table. The next few hours were spent with casual visiting, nibbling on snacks, and sipping wine. A few other friends showed up. Hannah found herself distracted by Luke's presence. He stayed beside her on the couch and ended up sitting almost flush against her when the couch filled with others looking for somewhere to sit.

Maggie, as she'd been prone to doing since they were kids, managed to bring up an awkward topic; in this case, it was Hannah's prior penchant for impulsive trips. "So Hannah, any of your crazy trips lately? Last one I heard about, you'd taken off to Costa Rica to hike some mountain there."

Hannah sighed internally. She definitely didn't want to get into that in front of Luke, but it didn't seem she had much choice with Maggie waiting expectantly.

"Oh not recently," she said, hoping Maggie would let the topic drop.

But no, Maggie carried on. Sweet as she was, she had a flaky side to her and rarely picked up on cues until after the fact. "Well, after college, Hannah drove her parents crazy," Maggie said, directing her comments to Luke. "She was either off to hike or ski some mountain nowhere near home, or whitewater rafting or something like that. Didn't you do the rafting thing all summer once?"

Hannah just nodded, keeping her gaze focused on the coffee table with a quick pleading look to Susie. Susie didn't seem inclined to help her out, as she returned Hannah's look with a quirk of her lips. Hannah sensed Luke's gaze and gave him a tight smile.

"Well, anyway, Hannah's about as tough as it gets for a woman when it comes to the outdoors," Maggie said, content to continue without Hannah's response. "She beat half the men in Mount Marathon one year. God, remember how mad that made Damon?"

Just as Hannah thought she'd have to respond, Cammi saved her. "That's why we girls are all glad Hannah's home —she represents us when we need to show the men we can keep up. Of course Damon got mad when she beat his time!" Cammi said, her sweet voice belying her protective nature. Cammi turned toward Luke. "Damon was just a college boyfriend. You know, nothing too serious. He couldn't handle that Hannah could beat him at some sports. She's a hell of a runner." Hannah sent a silent thanks to Cammi.

Jared cocked one eyebrow. "Mount Marathon is no easy feat. Ran it one year, and that was enough. Kicked my ass. Impressed that you beat half the men. You'd probably have beat Luke and me. We were in the middle of the pack."

Luke nodded. "Probably. We only got through by harassing each other after the first half," he said with a chuckle.

The awkward moment passed, and conversation shifted. Hannah had forgotten that Damon had been so intimidated that she could keep up with him when it came to running, hiking, and skiing. She'd avoided admitting it to herself at the time, but Damon wanted a girlfriend who was constantly impressed by him. She thought back to the hours after the Mount Marathon race that she'd finished only a few minutes ahead of Damon. The race was a run up and down a mountain in Seward, Alaska, and had been run for over a hundred years, allegedly on a bet the first time. It was just over three miles, but the terrain was rough. Runners climbed almost one thousand feet in a short distance and then barreled down the other side of the mountain. The year she ran it with Damon was the second time she'd done it. He'd barely spoken to her the rest of the day. The following week was when she'd first found him with another woman.

She surreptitiously looked at Luke. He and Jared appeared to have little need to impress. In other ways, he had an unfortunate amount in common with Damon—handsome, charming, rugged, and appeared to share her love of outdoor activities. With a mental shake, she pushed thoughts of Damon away and focused on the present.

Cammi was teasing Susie about something. While Jason explained his preference for building timber frame homes to Luke and his brothers, Maggie had her head on his shoulder, looking sleepy. Hannah's heart settled as she looked around the room. Her parents weren't here and wouldn't be here with her again. Gatherings like this with them were commonplace when they'd been alive. They'd taught her about the gift of friendship and community. When she'd been away, she hadn't forgotten that, but she'd built a cocoon around herself to manage her grief and had stayed there perhaps too long.

She took a swallow of wine and felt Luke shift beside her. His thigh was against hers. She'd tucked her other foot under her knee and sat at a slight angle facing him. She pushed a lock of hair behind her ear. She felt Susie watching them. Susie winked. Hannah shook her head and turned back to Luke.

"How long are you staying?" he asked.

"Probably not much longer. No matter how much I fight against it, I'm a morning person. Even if I stay up late, I'm up early whether I want to be or not. How about you?"

"Wondering if I could catch a ride. I'm not up for tagging along with Jared and Nathan. They're off to Sally's for whatever band is playing."

She answered without thinking. "Oh sure. I'll probably leave soon. Before we go though, I need to check in with Susie." She got up and walked into the kitchen where Susie had gone after her wink. She found her scraping off plates and starting to clean up. Hannah silently began to help.

Susie didn't let the silence last. "If you were hoping no one would notice that you and Luke are into each other, you didn't try very hard tonight," she said with a chuckle.

Hannah turned from filling the dishwasher. "That obvious?"

"Um...let's see, he showed up and pretty much walked

right over to you after he said hi. I don't think I've seen the two of you move, except to go to the bathroom or get some food. He's trying to play his cards close, but it's not hard to see that he likes you. He can barely keep his eyes off you. The only thing helping him is good manners. He's too polite to just ignore everyone else."

"Oh," Hannah said with a sigh. "It's next to impossible to lie low in this town."

Susie just looked back at her, a dishcloth and plates in her hands.

"I don't know if this is a good idea," Hannah said, the words coming out in a rush. "My track record with men is not good. Not at all. I know you think Luke is nice, but he's a lot like half the guys I chased around on all those trips. I don't need more of that."

Susie put down the plates she held and stepped over to face Hannah. "Look, I'm not going to pretend I know what it's been like for you. You had a few years there after Damon did his number on you when all you did was run from one thing to the next, men included. You barely talked to me about it, but I know damn well you hated that your parents worried about you. From what I can tell, you've gone in the opposite direction since they died. You're practically living like a nun. You know they wouldn't want that."

Susie held a hand up when Hannah opened her mouth. "I'm not saying this as a judgment, but just an observation. I've known you for a long time, and while I may have missed two years of time with you, I still know you. You seem to have forgotten a part of yourself, the fearless part. Do you remember the time we hiked the trail over on Paradise Hill and got chased by that wild mama moose?"

At Hannah's nod, Susie continued, "Maggie and I were freaking out, trying to hide behind trees while you hollered and chased that damn moose and her calves off. I thought you were crazy, and that's saying something because people are always telling me I'm crazy. Then there was the time that Tommy dared you to dive into Otter Cove one night and you did it!" Susie threw back her head and laughed. "Even though he was your boyfriend at the time, I don't think he realized you'd do it, much less in front of four people. You didn't hesitate—just stripped to your underwear and dove right in. Froze your tail off, but it looked like fun for a minute. Good thing you two didn't stay together; I thought he was a little too tame for you. Now Luke may be on the quiet side, but I don't think he'd blink if you did something like that."

Hannah interrupted, "Whatever happened to Tommy? We lost touch before I even went to graduate school."

Susie lifted her eyebrows. "Nice try at changing the subject. I'll bite, but only for a second. Tommy went to UW in Seattle. While he was there, his dad retired, and next thing we heard, they were moving to be closer to other family. I don't think Tommy came back after that. Back to my point though…it wouldn't hurt you to channel that girl who wasn't afraid to chase off an angry mama moose or dive almost naked into Otter Cove in the dark when the water's freezing all year-round," Susie said before turning back to continue cleaning up.

Hannah took Susie's words in and cleaned quietly for a few minutes. Susie's voice cut into the quiet. "You can find something between that girl and the one who ran so far, so fast that we all got worried. That's all I'm saying. As for Luke…I don't have a crystal ball, but he's not a jerk. I know that much."

Hannah wasn't thinking about Luke, but rather about the girl that Susie mentioned. It wasn't that she'd forgotten doing those things; it was more that she had a hard time feeling like the girl that she'd felt like then. She'd pushed too far in that direction, and then her parents' death had swung the pendulum to the point that she forgot what it was like to have fun. She paused from wiping down the counter. "I had a lot more fun back then. Wouldn't be a bad idea to dive into Otter Cove again," she said with a wry smile.

"I wasn't being literal, but I'm with you there on Otter Cove. Maybe wait a bit before you strip in front of Luke like that. I don't think he'd blink—in fact, he'd probably take a good look. But you haven't known him that long just yet," Susie said with a wink. She put away some leftovers before speaking again. "Just one more thing. If you don't even try, you lose from the start. You lose the chance, and you lose what might have been. Now go back out there and flirt with the man." Susie snapped a dish towel in Hannah's direction.

Hannah dodged the towel. "Well, I was going to give him a ride home. I came in here to tell you I'd be going soon. Before I do, though...thanks for having this tonight. It gave me a chance to visit friends and just...well...just be here."

Susie wanted to bet breakfast at Misty Mountain on whether Hannah could manage to leave with Luke without sparking gossip. Knowing she'd lose, Hannah ignored Susie and made her way back into the living room. Fortunately, Luke and his brothers were standing when she entered the room. Jared was explaining that they were headed to Sally's. She just stood back and followed the tide. She gave hugs and said her good-byes with promises to see more of everyone there soon. The shifting of the group led to others starting to help Susie clean up and allowed her to slip out casually with Luke and his brothers.

Despite the late hour, the sky was still faintly light, a soft slate gray with wisps of sun streaks left. The moon was rising above the mountains through the faded pink and gray. The mountains were a dark outline against the backdrop of the sky. Just as she was wondering if Luke changed his mind about needing a ride, she heard him tell Jared and Nathan he was catching a ride with her and taking a pass on Sally's. Their laughter floated across the yard. Luke grabbed something out of Jared's truck and met her at the steps, a jacket in his hand. The air was quickly cooling off. Alaska was an environment of contrasts. Summer days could be hot with blinding sun. Within hours of the slow sunset, the temperature could drop twenty, and even sometimes thirty, degrees.

Hannah sensed Luke watching her and turned toward him. "Just enjoying the endless dusk here. I missed summer evenings here. Such a quiet time. We should get going. Might be quicker to get to your house through town, but I'd rather drive across the hill if that's okay—much better view."

"You're in charge," he said, gesturing to her truck. "Not a long drive either way."

Luke followed her over to her truck. She'd started to think of it as hers rather than her parents'. As she drove toward Luke's house, they talked about his upcoming fishing trip. She was tense but managed to make polite comments. A few hours sitting beside Luke had stoked her nerves. Being alone with him in the deepening dusk put her senses on high. She couldn't deny that she was drawn to him physically. He definitely had the flint to make her spark. It wasn't just his dark curls and bright green eyes; it was the heat she felt whenever he was near. She thought back to what Susie said in the kitchen. The girl Susie mentioned, the Hannah who didn't stop to think before chasing away moose, or diving into a cold harbor in the dark, seemed a distant memory. She'd pushed that part of her into a corner after almost burning herself out with her wild choices. Luke kindled the wish to be daring again. That feeling ran into the wall of protection she'd built around her heart after her parents died.

Luke was quiet for the last part of the drive. Hannah pulled into his driveway and turned the engine off. The quiet was punctuated by the sound of a distant raven call.

Luke stepped out of the truck before she had a chance to speak and walked around to the driver's side. She rolled down her window and looked into his eyes in the gloaming. Despite the rapidly fading light, she could still see the green of his eyes. She shivered from the chilly air.

Luke took a long look and then leaned toward her. He moved slowly enough that she had time to turn her cheek or say something. She felt like he was giving her time to say no if she wanted to. She wondered if he sensed her hesitance. She wanted to tell him that it had nothing to do with him and everything to do with her. She didn't break from his gaze or speak. She watched as his lips came to hers. Her eyelids fell as his lips landed softly and purposefully on hers. She let herself lean into his kiss. She opened her mouth, and his tongue stroked inside.

In seconds, Hannah felt like she was on fire. Her breathing was labored, and she felt perspiration slide between her breasts despite the cool air. As she pulled back to take a breath, Luke quickly stepped back and swung the door open. Before she had a chance for another breath, he captured her lips again. She turned into him, so that she was sitting on the side of the seat facing toward him with her feet propped on the edge of the truck. He stepped between her knees and brushed her hair back from her face with one hand. She leaned farther into him until she was almost flush against him. She felt his erection press in between her legs and liquid pool in her center.

Luke's hand tangled in her hair as their kiss went wild. His lips traveled down one side of her neck. Goose bumps rose in a trail behind his lips. He traced her ear and collarbone with the tip of his tongue. Tearing at the buttons on his soft flannel shirt, she pulled it apart. She thought she might expire if she couldn't feel his skin. She slid her palms up his abdomen and chest and nipped at the lower part of his neck. He inhaled sharply. He paused for a second, and then she felt his hands moving down her back, walking his fingers slowly down her spine.

Hannah didn't know how sensitive her spine was until that moment. Each point Luke touched along her spine came alive. One hand slipped under the hem of her shirt and caressed her side coming around to the front. He deftly unhooked her bra with his free hand. He found her lips again just as his warm hand slipped up to cup the breast he bared. Her nipples tightened unbearably. She sighed into his mouth. He didn't remove the hand cupping her breast while he used his other hand to swiftly unbutton her blouse. He pushed it off her shoulders, and her bra slid off with it. Her head fell back as his lips traveled down her neck again. He dallied at her collarbone and made a trail of soft wet kisses down the center of her chest. Her nipples almost hurt. He licked his way to the soft underside of her breasts and outlined them with his tongue, all the while softly playing with her nipples with his fingers. Just when she thought she might lose her mind, his lips closed over one nipple. The relief was so sweet, she gasped. She looked down for a moment, seeing Luke's dark head bent over one breast and his large hand caressing the other. She saw the wet outlines he'd made on her chest and felt the area between her legs dampen even more.

Luke pulled back and looked at her. Hannah stared back, taking in the view of his upper body. He was fit and sleek, not like an athlete, but like a man who used his body for work. His muscles were defined and sinewy. He had a scar that started below his bottom left rib and curled around part of his waist. She traced it with her fingers. She reached up to push his shirt off his shoulders, not breaking eye contact. As she did so, he dragged one fingertip slowly down the center of her abdomen. He paused to suck on the same fingertip and then continued tracing a moist line down her belly. He used his other hand to unbutton her jeans and slowly slide the zipper down as his wet fingertip reached the top of her panties. He watched her watching him.

"I think we need to stop soon, but I need to take care of something first," Luke said softly. Hannah's breath was coming in fitful gasps. He kept watching her as he slipped his finger down, directly into the dripping heat between her legs. She instinctively opened her legs. He delved into her slick heat. Her head fell back again, and he leaned to nip at her neck. He stroked softly and deeply into her. A second finger joined the first. Her heart beat wildly, and her body felt like liquid fire.

Luke brought one hand up to cup the back of her head and brought his lips to hers again. He began stroking her with his thumb above where he was diving into her with his fingers. She clenched her fists around the edges of his shirt and pulled him as close as she could. She gasped into his mouth and came apart in waves. Her body clenched and convulsed around his fingers. She became boneless and felt her body shudder. His hand went still, and he slowly slid his fingers out. He softened their kiss and pulled back a fraction to look into her eyes. Their lips were no more than an inch apart.

"I don't think you realize what you do to me," Luke said.

Hannah felt the motion of his lips against hers and spoke. "I don't know. I don't want to stop, but I think we should. I feel like I'm not being fair, though."

He shook his head. "More than fair. I got to watch you fall apart in my arms. That's enough for now."

She just looked at him for a long moment. He pulled farther back until he had moved out from the cradle of her legs. She felt cool air wash against her bare breasts and abdomen and shivered at the contrast. Uncurling her hands, she let go of his shirt. The moon was high in the sky, and what light was left was residual. She was relieved for the mask of fading light. She looked up at Luke and down again as she felt his hands return to gently pull her zipper up and button her jeans. He quietly helped her fasten her bra and button her shirt. She reached up and buttoned his shirt, smoothing her hand down the center when she was finished. They remained there in the quiet night for a few more moments. Another raven call pierced through the silence.

Luke cupped his hand under her chin. "I want to see you again before we leave for our trip. When can that happen?"

Hannah fought the urge to look away from his intense gaze. She wanted to stare at him for hours and was frightened by the strength of her feelings. It took her a moment to respond. When she did, her voice came out roughly. "Well, I'd say the weekend, but it is the weekend. You have more of a schedule than me right now. Just pick a night."

He held her gaze. "How about Wednesday? We have two guiding trips in a row. Group of tourists that want to fish for silver salmon. Wednesday at seven?" he asked.

She nodded her ascent. Stepping away, he gestured for her to tuck her knees back inside the truck. "Don't forget to buckle up," he said, carefully shutting the door before he leaned forward for a brief kiss.

Luke turned away and walked to the front stairs of the house. He stood on the stairs with one hand tucked in a pocket, the other hand lifted in a wave. She watched him in the rearview mirror for a moment, illuminated by a soft light over the front door that cast a circle around the stairs.

CHAPTER 11

*H*annah walked Jessie through the drizzle the following morning, returning from the walk damp and chilled. After drying Jessie off with a towel, she took a long, hot shower. Eager to get her mind off of the treadmill of thoughts about Luke, she ducked the odd feeling she had about the file boxes she'd picked up from June and started going through them. She quickly realized the boxes were filled with her parents' personal papers, encountering birth certificates, social security cards, and the like. She also found letters from before their marriage when her father was out of state. It was strange to read their words to each other in the younger part of their relationship. Her mother's letters were filled with informative, practical details with occasional comments about how she missed him. Her father's were more sentimental, scattered with endearments. His longing to be with her mother was the thread that wove through all of his letters. Her throat tightened as she read their words. They'd loved each other and had nurtured that love for many years beyond its beginning. She missed being a part of the circle that they cast around themselves and her.

Despite the passing thought that maybe she should slow down, she pushed herself to keep going. In the second box, she encountered many of her personal items saved by her parents—a copy of her birth certificate, art projects from school, report cards, and more. She was about to take a break when a sealed manila envelope toward the back of the box caught her eye. She pulled it out, thinking there would be a label on it. Thus far, everything had been labeled in her mother's small, tidy handwriting. This envelope was blank and looked old and faded. The edges were worn and bent from being in the box. She smoothed it out on the floor. She looked over at Jessie, who was curled up nearby sleeping on a dog bed Hannah had gotten her. Returning to the envelope in her hand, she had to fetch an envelope opener when the seal didn't give easily.

With a tilt of the envelope, the papers slid onto the floor. They appeared to be legal documents. As Hannah began to read, her stomach started to feel hollow, as though she were falling. The papers indicated that her parents had given a child up for adoption five years before Hannah had been born. She couldn't read for a moment. Nausea welled, and she swallowed against the lump in her throat.

Jessie woke and came over to sit beside her. Her hands buried in Jessie's soft dark fur, she rested her forehead on the top of Jessie's head. She took deep breaths and tried to calm the hammering of her heart.

She finally lifted her head and looked back at the papers. Jessie settled just beside her on the floor with her head on one of Hannah's knees. Hannah carefully picked up the papers again and shuffled through them. The first section was titled "Relinquishment of Parental Rights," which outlined her parents' relinquishment of their parental rights of a daughter named Emma. No last name was listed. The date of birth was five years and ten days prior to Hannah's birth. Based on her estimate, her sister was born while her father was getting his doctorate in biology out of state. She quickly calculated, realizing that likely meant her mother had gotten pregnant when he was home for a visit. She sifted through the rest of the papers. She read through the legal papers several times, trying to find the names of whoever adopted Emma. She found nothing.

Hannah sat still for what felt like hours. She stroked Jessie while anger and confusion welled inside. Had anyone asked her if she ever thought her parents would keep a secret like this from her, she would have confidently said no, absolutely not. She didn't know what to think. She could see that it would have been very difficult for her mother to have a child out of wedlock at seventeen in the conservative South with a lover out of state. Yet even with that sketch of understanding, she was furious that they hadn't told her.

She got up and began to pace in the living room, restless, agitated, and numb all at once. Jessie sat and watched her. Hannah finally called Susie. All she got was Susie's voice mail. She left a quick message asking her to call as soon as she could.

Out of sorts and not ready to look through the rest of the files, she changed into her running clothes and headed for the closest trail. The damp cold seemed fitting now; it braced her. She didn't have the hope that a good, hard run would take her mind off the emotional bomb she'd just found, but running had been a refuge for her for years. The rhythm settled her body and grounded her. In the weeks she'd had Jessie, she'd found Jessie to be the perfect running companion. Hannah ran for close to an hour in the cool, misty rain with Jessie jogging quietly alongside. One stretch of the trail nearby offered a clear view of Mount Augustine, standing tall in the gray mist of the bay. Clouds hung low above the volcano. She breathed in the earthy scents of rain and spruce. When she and Jessie finally returned home, they were both soaked through. She toweled Jessie dry, turned up the heat, and took another steaming hot shower.

Arming herself with a glass of wine, Hannah sat on one of the stools by the kitchen counter. She'd dressed in warm, soft clothes after her shower, aiming for comfort however she could find it. Across the room, the papers were scattered on the sofa where she'd tossed them before her run. She sighed and glanced at her cell phone. Just as she looked away, it rang, Susie's number flashing on the screen.

Susie spoke immediately. "What's up? You sounded weird in your message."

"I sounded weird because I feel weird. Can you come over?" she asked. "It'll be easier to show you than try to explain."

Susie agreed, explaining she just needed to close up her office. When Susie asked about dinner, Hannah realized she hadn't thought about it. Susie, ever practical, reported she'd pick up pizza on the way over.

Hannah turned on the television while she waited. Jessie came over and nuzzled one of her hands. Despite her feelings, the run had done what she'd hoped. It had grounded her and brought her into her body, out of the wild feeling she'd had inside. She picked the papers up from the sofa and brought them to the counter, sorting and smoothing them out before reading again. The only sounds were Jessie's soft breathing from where she lay on the floor, the sound of papers being turned as she read, and the rhythmic patter of rain on the roof.

Susie pulled up shortly and came in without knocking, one hand balancing a pizza box. She set the pizza on the counter and tossed her purse on an empty stool before pulling another one out and sitting down beside Hannah.

"Okay, cut to it. You know I hate waiting to know when

something's going on. Did you forget that in the last few years? The only reason I let it slide was because you sounded so off in your message," Susie said.

Hannah started to smile and felt her mouth wobble. Rather than trying to explain, she simply picked up the papers and handed them to Susie. She took a swallow of wine and went to get plates and another wineglass for Susie.

Susie only took a moment to read. "What! I'm assuming this is the first you've heard of this because I can't imagine you keeping this a secret from me all these years. But then I can't imagine your parents keeping it a secret from you, so I don't know what to think."

Susie slapped the papers down. She grabbed the bottle of wine and filled the glass Hannah had set in front of her. She took a gulp before looking directly at Hannah. "Look, I'm in shock, so I'm guessing you are too. But I don't know what you need from me at the moment. You know me, I'm ready to rage and wish I could tell your parents off. But I don't know if that would help in any way." She paused and smiled. "Actually, I think I'm starting to realize that my attack mode often isn't helpful. I'm working on that."

Hannah felt the tears on her cheeks before she realized she'd started to cry. She wiped them away and looked back at Susie. "I'm just glad I'm home, so that I had someone to call. I have no idea how I feel really. Mostly angry, but I'm confused. I can't even get to the part about how I feel that I have a sister out there somewhere because I'm so confused and angry that my parents never told me this. It doesn't fit what I thought I knew about them. You know? I don't know. It's so...strange. Then there's this part of me that wants to find her, find her now, sooner than now. But that's terrifying, to say the least. Oh God, I just don't know. As for what I need from you, well...just you being my friend...you can be in attack mode if you need to," Hannah said wryly.

Susie leaned over and hugged her briefly. She took a sip

of wine and picked the papers up again. Hannah felt a ghost of that hollow feeling she'd had earlier. She ignored it and busied herself getting a slice of pizza for herself and another for Susie. She pushed the plate in front of Susie and took a bite of her own slice as she sat down.

Susie scanned through the papers again and put them down to take a bite of her pizza. Hannah leaned in and read over Susie's shoulder, again looking to see if anything other than a first name was mentioned.

Susie shook her head. "This is just, well...a shock. I don't know what to say. Now I know why you sounded so off in your message. How are you? I mean, really?"

Hannah shrugged. "Ugh...not so good. I'm just floored. I can understand why they wouldn't tell me this when I was younger. I get that. Kind of hard to explain to a little kid. But the people I thought they were...well...I thought they would have told me when I was older. And I can't ask them about it now. So there's all that, and then I have a sister somewhere."

Susie sat quietly for a moment. Hannah kept eating since her first bite had reminded her that she was starving.

Susie looked back at the papers and then at Hannah. "I'll do whatever I can to help. I know you're in shock because I am. It's just...I don't know. Here's the thing, though. There are plenty of places to start. I know you aren't too close to your extended family in North Carolina, but that's one place to start. Knowing when this happened, your mom's side of the family has to have some clues. Maybe your mom kept it from them, but a pregnancy is hard to hide all the way to the end. I say let's start there. If you're uncomfortable making calls, I'll do it. I don't care who thinks I'm nosy."

Hannah smiled, and it didn't fall apart this time. "You're right. It's not like there's nowhere to start. What do you think our chances are of finding my sister? I don't know if I'm ready, but I'm definitely curious."

"Hard to know those chances. But it's the age of the Internet. It's amazing what people can find these days."

Susie stayed for a few hours. They talked more about what Hannah had discovered, but Susie also helped take her mind off it by prodding her about Luke and insisting that they watch the latest reality dating show together.

"You seriously want me to watch this?" Hannah asked.

"Yes, yes, I do. It's complete madness, but it's a mind suck. Whatever worries you have will fade, at least for the time the show's on. I guarantee. It's just ridiculousness, but strangely fascinating," Susie said.

* * *

HANNAH DRIFTED through the next few days, detached and unfocused. She'd told Susie she'd find phone numbers and e-mail addresses for family in North Carolina, but she didn't have the heart to look. Instead, she took long runs in the cool mornings and threw herself into yard work. Her mother's neglected flower beds gave her plenty to do, not to mention the sad state of the rest of the yard. By the time late afternoon rolled around on Wednesday, she realized she had completely forgotten that she had dinner plans with Luke for that evening. As tempting as it was to cancel, the pull to see Luke again was more tempting. She didn't want to be alone tonight; she craved anything to keep her mind occupied and away from the anger she felt toward her parents and from her unanswered questions.

She raced to get ready on time and was in the kitchen feeding Jessie when she heard a knock on the door. Luke came in at her call. She stood up from scooping Jessie's food, her heart skipping at the sight of him. He looked as if he'd been in the sun for the last few days. The green of his eyes stood out against his sun-burnished skin. His dark hair was tousled, which she'd come to learn was its typical state. She loved the disorderly curls that tended to fall across his forehead. Her hair was still damp from the shower and her feet bare. She'd left herself no time to spare. She'd forgotten how the long Alaskan summer days didn't offer a reminder of the time because the sun stayed up long past when dinner would usually occur. Luke reached down to pet Jessie who'd run to his side.

"Well, hello there. Looks like you might have had a busy day. Did I come too early? Thought we agreed on seven."

Hannah shrugged sheepishly. "We did. I was working in the yard and lost track of time. Seeing as the sun doesn't set for hours yet, I didn't notice the time. I also forgot that I said I'd cook dinner." She gestured to her damp hair. "Just got out of the shower."

"No problem. Took me a while to adjust to the long days here. If cooking here is out, we can go to town for dinner if you'd like."

"What about ordering pizza? I had some last night, but it wasn't Glacier Pizza, which used to be my favorite. Do they still deliver?" she asked.

"They do," Luke replied and pulled out his phone. "Have their number in my phone because they happen to be my favorite too. Want me to call?"

"Sure. Order whatever you want. I'll eat anything they have."

Luke lifted his eyebrows. "Are you sure?" he asked.

She nodded. "I mean it. I like about every kind of pizza, and I've probably had everything they make."

While Luke called, Hannah went to the wine rack, which was tucked under the edge of the counter. She had bought a few bottles since she'd gotten here, in addition to some that Susie brought over on one of the days she came to help with organizing. She selected a bottle of red wine and grabbed a glass out of the cabinet. She quickly uncorked the wine and poured a glass for herself while Luke waited on the phone. Catching his eyes, she held up the wine bottle and opened the refrigerator, pointing to some bottles of beer. He waved toward the beer. After opening a bottle, she slid it across the counter to where he could reach.

She sipped her wine and looked out toward the bay. Luke sat with his boots hooked around the stool legs. His large frame barely fit on the stool. Jessie had finished eating and was napping on the floor beside Luke. To live the life of Jessie seemed fairly simple. She sought and gave love and affection freely. She ate, napped, and ran around otherwise. Hannah needed to thank Susie for sending Luke her way with Jessie. Although she wasn't about to admit to Susie how alluring Luke was, her nerves were high when it came to him. As for Jessie, though, she was thrilled to have her as part of her life. She never felt alone in the house, which had been one of her greatest fears when she'd considered moving home. Jessie had fit into her world so easily and comfortably, and she needed that ease and comfort at this stage. Her thoughts flitted toward her unknown sister for a moment and shied away.

While they waited for the pizza, Hannah gave Luke a tour of the house. Just as she finished showing him the upstairs, their pizza arrived. They started eating immediately. After a few minutes, Luke looked over at Hannah and laughed. "Must have both been starving. I'd apologize for being rude, but I'm not sure who's eating faster, me or you."

"Probably me. I haven't eaten since breakfast. I tend to do that when I'm busy. Forget to eat, that is," she said and grabbed a napkin to wipe her hands.

With the pizza almost gone, they relocated to the living room. Jessie immediately claimed one of the chairs, a mission-style reading chair with a soft, deep seat. The sun was setting over the bay with an early moon rising in the sky. Luke was a polite guest, keeping most of his questions superficial. Hannah felt caught between wanting to lose herself in anything other than her thoughts about what she'd learned yesterday and sensing her well-honed defenses rise against the draw she felt toward Luke.

As they talked, she took in Luke's presence: sexy, handsome, easygoing, and strong. She had a hard time keeping her eyes off his and felt flushed with wine and being near him. She was annoyed with herself for being so drawn to him and didn't trust the wish that she could let her guard down. She couldn't think of a man that held this much appeal for her. She'd had glimmers in the past of the feelings Luke elicited, but nothing quite like it. Her senses were on high alert. Her body remembered the feelings from the other night and craved more. Just sitting near him on the couch, she felt a slick heat between her legs, and her skin felt hot all over. She itched to lean over and kiss him.

Just when she'd almost convinced herself to kiss Luke anyway, Hannah heard a car in the drive. She could just make out Susie and Cammi as they stepped out of the car in the fading light. Luke's eyes held a question.

"Oh, looks like Susie and Cammi came by," she said with a shrug. "I didn't know they planned to."

She met Susie and Cammi at the door. Her body was irritated with the interruption, but another part of her was relieved. She wasn't thinking clearly since yesterday, not to mention her own doubts. She pulled the door open just as Susie and Cammi reached the top of the stairs. Susie was attempting to wrestle her hair into a ponytail. Curls spilled over her hands.

"Did we interrupt?" Susie asked. "We would have called, but I had to bring Cammi home because she got a flat tire, and her spare was also flat. In case you didn't know, she lives less than a mile from you now."

Susie turned to Cammi. "Did you mention that to

Hannah yet?" She brought her gaze back to Hannah. "Cammi rents the old Peters house. Their grandkids fixed it up a while back and started renting it. Anyway, we were driving past your road, and I turned in out of reflex and decided it must mean we needed to see you."

Hannah waved them in. As they entered, Susie tugged on Hannah's sleeve. Hannah turned to look at Susie with a question in her eyes. "How are you today?"

Hannah knew Susie meant more than just how she was doing. She wasn't ready to talk about it in front of Cammi and certainly not Luke. She responded quietly as she heard Cammi greeting Luke. "Just okay. It's not something I'm ready to tell the world. Okay?"

Susie nodded. "I figured. Just wanted to check on you. Should we gracefully bow out pretty quick here? As soon as I pulled up, I realized that was Luke's truck. Aside from everything else, can't say I'm not happy that you're seeing him again." She smiled slyly and dodged when Hannah reached out to swat her shoulder.

Hannah responded just as they entered the living room. "It's okay you're here. No rush to leave."

Cammi and Luke were chatting in the living room. Susie plopped on the chair beside Jessie and began petting her. Jessie soaked it up and rolled over to rest her head on Susie's leg.

Luke looked over at Hannah. "I was telling Cammi that you've granted me visiting privileges with Jessie," he said.

"It's only fair. He brought Jessie to me, and it wouldn't be fair if I didn't let him visit. Do you two want something to drink?" she asked.

Susie answered, "Maybe some water, but nothing else. The yard looks like it's coming along by the way."

Hannah looked out through the soft fading light into the yard. She'd been working so close to the ground, she hadn't taken time to look at the yard from a distance. Her mother's flower beds were beginning to look like something other than piles of cultivated weeds. The stone pathways that wound through the yard were visible again. As Hannah fetched Susie's water, Cammi called out for her to bring a glass of wine.

Cammi and Susie stayed for a little while with Cammi regaling them with stories of tourist encounters at her coffee truck, Red Truck Coffee, one of the busiest tourist stops in town in the summer, situated as it was just by the harbor. Those who lived in Alaska year-round appreciated tourists for what they brought to the economy, but they also often had to bail unsuspecting and misguided tourists out of random pitfalls. Moose and their calves made for endearing photo opportunities unless people came too close, at which point the would-be photographers found themselves in a dangerous situation within seconds. There were the famed Turnagain Arm mudflats as well. Turnagain Arm was the name of a stretch of the Sterling Highway just south of Anchorage. It offered turn after turn after turn of beautiful vistas of mountains and ocean with the road traveling along the winding shoreline through a narrow section of Cook Inlet, hugging the edge of the mountains. When the tide was out, the mudflats looked inviting to walk upon. Unfortunately, the mud in those areas was dangerously difficult to free oneself from, and locals and tourists alike often needed shouts and reminders to keep away from the tempting tide pool walks. Of course, bear stories also abounded.

Despite what Hannah had learned yesterday and her mixed feelings about Luke, she felt a sense of comfort steal over her. The idea of learning about her parents' secret while she'd been in graduate school and away from Diamond Creek was frightening. She reached up to turn on a lamp by the couch and looked around the room. Luke was comfortably talking with Cammi and Susie and didn't seem bothered by the interruption of their dinner. She wanted to reach over and hold one of his hands, which interrupted her moment of comfort, as she wasn't sure she liked the fact that he made her forget her defenses.

Susie and Cammi left not long after, by which point it was late enough that Hannah was yawning. She and Luke had followed Susie and Cammi out to the deck as they said their good-byes. The sky had a purple, grayish tint with faint streaks of pink as darkness took over. The sound of the car motor faded as Susie drove away. Hannah yawned again.

"You're tired. My cue to head out," Luke said.

She started to protest, but he stepped close to her and put his index finger to her lips. "You've been yawning for the last half hour. I have to be up early tomorrow, so let's call it a night. We head out this weekend though, so can I get one more night before I go...Friday?" he asked.

She smiled against his finger, which still rested against her lips. He let his hand fall with a quirk of his lips, his dimples winking briefly.

"You're right. I'm exhausted. Friday would be great," she said.

"How about you come to my place? Jared and Nathan will be in Anchorage on a shopping run, so the house will be quiet."

"Sounds good to me. Can I bring Jessie?"

"Of course! That's a given. Anytime you come to my place, you don't have to ask if you can bring Jessie." He looked toward the moon, which sat low and fat above the horizon, bright against the almost dark sky. "Before I go though..."

His lips landed softly against hers. As tired as she was, her defenses were down. She sank into the kiss and stepped closer to him. She loved being almost as tall as he was. He brought his hands up to cup her face and moved his body against hers. Her head fell back as he lightly traced his thumb along her cheek and up behind her ear, his hand tangling in her hair. She sighed into his mouth and invited him in with strokes of her tongue. Her body came alive with their kiss. She didn't want it to end. He ran his tongue along her lower lip and softly nipped. A liquid heat built in her. She wanted more and wanted it *now*, only to feel him slow down and gently pull back.

Hannah looked into his eyes, bright green in the almost dark, through the mental haze their kiss had created. Luke looked directly back at her, holding her gaze.

"Much as I want to keep going, you're too tired," he said. He let his hands drop from where they'd held her face and stepped back. "See you Friday." With that, he turned and quickly walked down the stairs to his truck.

She watched him drive away, standing in the softly falling dark. Jessie whined, so she let her out. Jessie ran into the yard and began sniffing around. Hannah took in the cooling air and early night sounds. An owl called in the distance. Soft rustles came from Jessie padding about the yard. Hannah allowed herself to just *be* for a few minutes.

Another yawn and she realized she could fall asleep where she stood. A whistle to Jessie, and she turned to go inside with Jessie following. She took a few minutes to put empty glasses and plates in the dishwasher and wipe down the counter. The dishwasher was full, so she turned it on and listened for a moment to the hum as it started running. The sound was comforting and reminded her of peaceful nights at home when she was a child. Her mother had usually turned the dishwasher on just before she went to bed. The distant hum was a sound Hannah associated with falling asleep and feeling safe. For a moment, she forgot that she was confused and even angry with her parents. She thought only of the safety and comfort they had created for her during childhood. As that thought sank in, she remembered what she'd learned and felt a twist in her heart. She had to find a way to incorporate what she now knew with what she knew of her parents before. Their actions did not cancel each other out.

Hannah sighed and walked upstairs. She slipped out of her clothes and tossed them into the hamper in the bathroom. Changing into an old T-shirt and flannel pajama bottoms, she climbed into bed. Still in the dark, she listened to the now-distant hum of the dishwasher. Jessie followed her into the bedroom. She usually settled on the floor beside the bed. Tonight, she sidled up to the bed for a moment and then softly jumped up. Hannah started to tell her to get down, but stopped herself. She needed the comfort tonight. Jessie nestled against her side. Hannah fell asleep, her hand stilling in midstroke on Jessie's back.

CHAPTER 12

"What the hell are you doing?" called Susie.

Hannah leaned her head out of the truck. "I'm backing up. What does it look like I'm doing?"

"Uh...you're about to hit a tree," came Susie's response with a snort.

Hannah hit the brakes and put the gearshift in neutral. She leaned back out the window and looked at Susie who was grinning.

"You forgot that there's a reason you have me back here. You can't see enough through that truck cap. Not to mention that you're not so good at backing up slowly. You back up too fast. It's not a good spot, though. The boat's tucked a little too close to the trees here."

"Which way should I go?" Hannah asked.

"You need to pull forward a bit. Then turn your wheels sharp to the left before you start backing up again. And try going a little slower. I'll holler when you need to stop," Susie said.

Hannah did as Susie instructed and came to a clean stop

at Susie's call. She walked to the back of the truck and stood beside Susie. Looking down, she saw that Susie had guided her to a perfect lineup with the trailer hitch. Without needing to speak, she and Susie reached together and carefully lifted the trailer hitch onto the hitch ball on the truck. They let go slowly as it settled into place. Hannah quickly hooked up the wiring while Susie finished getting the hitch locked in place. Hannah looked down at her boots, which were covered in mud. She pulled the hood on her raincoat up further as rain fell steadily. Susie was also wearing boots, paired with a skirt and blouse and a bright blue raincoat. She'd come straight from work at the office to help Hannah move her parents' old boat from the storage yard where it had been sitting idle for the past two years. Hannah planned to take it up to the house to clean it and make sure everything was working.

At the moment, she was ready for a shower. It had been raining for most of the day. She had wanted to put this off, but the storage yard fee would be charged for another month if she didn't move the boat today. True to the good friend she was, Susie gamely came along to help despite the rain and mud. Hannah had picked her up from her office before driving out to the storage yard. Susie's car was in the shop for a few days, so she was hitching rides. Once they climbed into Hannah's truck, the windows fogged quickly due to the cool mist. Hannah started the truck and turned on the heat.

"I forgot that in Alaska it makes sense to use heat smack in the middle of summer if it's cool and rainy. Damn, I'm soaked," Hannah said as she wiped damp tendrils of hair off her forehead and swiped a hand around the back of her neck to push the damp hair away.

Susie wrestled with her brown curls, which were wild to begin with and went crazy in damp weather. She finally grabbed a baseball cap sitting on Hannah's dashboard and ruthlessly stuffed her curls underneath.

"There!" she commented with relish. "Someday I'll learn to love my curls, but most days they just annoy me. What now? Are you going straight home? Just take me with you. Don't even bother taking me to my house. If you don't mind, I'll stay in the guest room."

Hannah shrugged. "Fine by me. Is there a reason you don't want to go home, though? I don't mind taking you."

"With the boat on the back, it'll kind of be a pain to go out of your way. Plus, I haven't been home all day and never made it to the store for groceries this week. This way, I'll bum off you for the night. Not to mention that I'm still greedy about time with you. This gives me another excuse," Susie said.

"You don't need excuses. Stop by anytime. I mean it."

"Even when Cammi and I barge in on dinner with Luke?" came Susie's sly reply.

"Yes, even then."

"So what's up there? I'm just being my nosy self."

"Nothing you don't already know," Hannah responded as she reached behind her seat for a towel to wipe the fog off the windshield. After wiping quickly across the windshield and driver's side window, she handed the towel to Susie who wiped off the passenger window and tucked it in the back again.

Hannah put the truck in gear, pulling forward slowly to make sure she could sense how the trailer felt. With a brief pause as the truck pulled against the weight of the boat, the truck rolled forward, the trailer smoothly following.

"I'm with you there. Back to Luke...That's it? That's not enough to satisfy me," Susie said.

"Yeah, that's it. What do you expect? I've only known the guy for a few weeks and just got back to town. I know you want grand romance because you usually do, but give me some time here. Not to mention that I just found out the other day that my parents kept a major secret from me and I have a sister somewhere out there."

Susie leaned her head against the seat. "Okay, I'll give you some time. I had a feeling about you and Luke before this whole thing with your parents came out, so I'm impatient. I think you deserve something good. But...I get it. It's only been a few weeks. And damn your parents. I still haven't completely wrapped my head around that. I was thinking that I could do some digging for you if you want me to," she said.

Hannah thought that over for a moment. "You know, my initial thought is to tell you not to. But I need to start somewhere, and you're not afraid to be pushy. Where could we start?" She turned carefully to drive up the hill toward home. She geared down as the truck slowed moving uphill with the weight of the trailer. She glanced over at Susie, who looked thoughtful.

"I'd start with the Internet. My mom has memberships on some of those genealogy websites. She started doing this whole family tree thing a while back. She'll let me use them if I want. But, more important than that..." Susie paused and glanced over at Hannah, "you need to decide if you want to call your extended family too. Stands to reason they may know something, but maybe not."

Hannah thought that over as she turned onto her road. The rain had turned into a soft drizzle, but fog had settled in, and the visibility was poor. "I'll have to think about who to call in my mother's family. She has more family than my dad. He was an only child. Mom had two brothers and a sister."

She pulled into her drive and came to a stop. "I'll back this in tomorrow if the weather's better. For now, let's just get inside," she said, turning off the engine.

They hopped out of the truck and dashed for the door. Jessie came barreling out. Hannah waved Susie to the guest bedroom and bath while she went and took a shower in the master bathroom. After a quick shower, she found a pair of sweats for Susie and tossed them into the guest room. She headed for the kitchen and let Jessie back in. Susie found Hannah rummaging through the pantry and refrigerator for something for dinner. Susie took charge and started spaghetti, putting Hannah to work making salad. While they were waiting for the sauce to heat, Hannah turned on the television and started a fire in the woodstove. After eating and some prompting from Susie, Hannah headed for her mother's desk and tried to find contact numbers for family.

Susie said, "Here's the thing; it's not going to be easy, so I say let's just go for it. I know you—you'll end up putting it off. You've had enough to deal with for the past few years; you don't need this hanging over you. No matter what, it'll be on your mind, so you might as well do something about it."

Hannah sighed. "I know. It's hard not to think about. I'd like to put it off, but it will be just as difficult later as it will be now."

Susie sat cross-legged on the floor in the room upstairs where Hannah's mother's desk was. Jessie sat beside her while Susie absentmindedly petted her. The heat from the fire in the woodstove filtered upstairs, dispelling the damp, cool air. Hannah was seated in the desk chair, sorting through the desk. It didn't take long for her to find her mother's address book. She tossed it to Susie. "There you go."

Susie caught the address book with one hand and began flipping through it. Hannah continued, "Most of my mom's family is under Cotter. That was her maiden name. Now we just have to figure out if I should be the one to call. Seems too much to ask you to do it. Not to mention that they don't know you."

Susie looked up from the address book. "Oh, I'll call. Who cares if they don't know me? But, and here's the part you won't like, you need to be with me. I can break the ice, but they'll want to hear from you. It's only logical. When's the last time you talked to any of them?"

"Last time I saw them face-to-face was at the memorial service they had in North Carolina for my parents. After coming to the one here, I was pretty much out of my mind and couldn't think straight. I don't remember much about it honestly. It's weird. There are chunks of time like that in the first few months after they died. Everything is just fuzzy." Hannah shook her head. "Anyway…back to when I talked to my relatives. We talked on the phone at holidays and such. My parents didn't stay that close with relatives after we moved here. I never thought about it much before, but now I wonder if it had something to do with the whole situation with my sister. Hard to say because it was years after that we moved away."

Susie shrugged. "There's a ton of stuff you'll never know. I know that sucks, but it's reality, even when you don't find out something big like you have. Everyone has secrets," she said.

Hannah slowly twirled in the desk chair and felt a pang in her chest. "I know everyone has their secrets, but this one's a doozy for me."

"It is. I didn't mean to make it seem like it wasn't a big deal. I wish I could make sense of it for you," Susie said.

Hannah looked back at Susie as she spun around to face her. "Let's take a break on this for tonight. I promise I won't put it off for too much longer, but I need a little time." She stood up and headed back downstairs.

Susie and Jessie followed her back to the living room.

Susie seemed to sense she wasn't up for much more heavy talking. They settled in on the couch and channel surfed, ending up on HGTV for most of the time. Jessie dozed between them.

CHAPTER 13

*L*uke ducked his head and stepped into the galley of the boat. Samuel, the cook, was busy at the sink, his back to Luke. The galley area was steamy and warm, a respite from the chilly rain outside on deck. They'd had good weather for the first few days and two days of rain since then. Luke stepped over to the dining area, which had two booths in addition to an area where crew members could hang wet gear while they dried off, ate, and warmed up. There were hooks on the wall and a drain in the floor. After hanging up his wet rain gear and toweling off, he slid into a booth and poured a cup of coffee from the full coffee pot tucked against the wall. About this time, Samuel finally noticed he was there.

"Hey there, didn't hear you come in. How's it going out there?" Samuel called out while he stirred a pot on the stove.

Luke took a welcome sip of coffee before answering. "Good enough. Rain's making it chilly. If we keep on schedule, should make it back to harbor week after next."

Samuel nodded. "Are you in for now?"

"Yeah. Going to check over some gear and wait. What's for dinner? Better yet, when will it be ready?"

"Dude, you're always hungry," Samuel said. He gestured to the stove. "Beef stew and some leftovers. On top of that, a mac and cheese casserole in about fifteen minutes." He grabbed a loaf of bread and came over to where Luke was seated. "Fresh bread. Nibble on that while you wait."

Luke tore off a piece and sighed as he bit into the bread. Samuel's bread alone was enough reason to schedule their fishing trips for when he could come along. He chased the bread with another swallow of coffee. He'd been working straight through since early this morning and was tired and cold. The coffee, along with the steamy warmth of the galley, was thawing him enough that he felt human again. Hannah passed through his mind. He thought back to the last night he'd seen her. She'd come over to his place for dinner, which unsettled him. Their house was definitely a bachelor pad. Since they'd lived there, he and his brothers occasionally had women over, but they were more likely to spend most of their time elsewhere.

Luke had managed a few more kisses that night, but found himself holding back from going any further. Lord knows, kissing her was hot enough to scald him. And *that* was the problem. He enjoyed women and liked feeling in control. With Hannah, his control was slipping, and he didn't like it. He didn't consider himself scarred by his naiveté with Cristina, but informed. He'd learned it was much wiser to look for a good time and keep it light. That was comfortable for him, while the strength of the chemistry with Hannah was disconcerting. He found his thrills with pushing his limits outdoors and preferred to keep it that way. He also sensed something was off with her, but he didn't know her well enough to know, just a gut feeling that worried him. The flare of protectiveness toward her grated at his sense of control.

The cabin door slammed, and Nathan tossed the hood on his raincoat back and shook his head. Droplets of water flew in an arc. Nathan waved to Samuel and nodded at Luke before heading over to hang up his coat and kick off his boots. He slid into the booth on the opposite side and sank down with a sigh, quickly pouring a cup of coffee.

"Damn. Didn't sleep too well last night, and the rain makes me more tired. I'm getting clumsy in this cold. Could use a little more sun," Nathan said, reaching for the bread.

"Feeling about the same, although some hot coffee and Samuel's bread helps. What's Jared up to?" Luke asked.

Nathan shook his head. "Hell if I know. Last I checked, he was staring at maps and spreadsheets. Hard to get him to take a break."

Nathan tore another piece of bread off. "Damn, this is good." He turned toward Samuel. "What kind of bread is this, Samuel?"

"Nothing fancy. Just an oatmeal bread. Figured you guys would like it," Samuel said.

"That we do. Hope there's more because I could eat what's left of this loaf," Nathan responded.

Luke sipped his coffee and watched the exchange. Nathan loved to tease and started in with Samuel. While they were bantering, most of the crew wandered in. Raincoats were hung, boots piled up, and conversation flowed. Luke loved this part of fishing as much as the time outdoors on the water. Most everyone who fished for a living loved to be on the ocean and basked in the experience of living tied to its rhythms, even if only for a few weeks. They worked hard during the days, sometimes brutally hard, and evenings were filled with camaraderie and good conversation. Luke loved being tired to his bones in the elemental way he was when he worked outdoors on the water. He felt completely in his skin, which relaxed him in a way not much else could. Within minutes, Samuel had the mac and cheese casserole ready, along with the beef stew. The guys gobbled it up. Luke sat back full, and persuaded Jared to play a game of Scrabble after he finally joined them.

* * *

TIME PASSED in a blink for the rest of the fishing trip. They were headed into harbor on a sunny day. Luke looked into the clear sky and saw the outline of Mount Augustine in the distance to one side. The shoreline of Diamond Creek was just becoming visible ahead. The sun struck sparks off the surface of the water. The wind was up, as it so often was when it was sunny anywhere along the Alaska coast. They'd gotten their quota, which was exactly what they'd needed. The trip had been fairly uneventful, which was relative when it was a fishing trip. One of the crew members, Alan, had dislocated his shoulder when helping bring a full bailer up. All three brothers had emergency responder training. In this case, Nathan took the lead and quickly slipped Alan's shoulder back into place. He'd been sore for the rest of the trip, and they'd switched him to lighter duty work. That had been the only hiccup.

The shape of the shoreline became clearer. They had an hour or two to get to the harbor and then another few hours of hard work. He was looking forward to finishing up and getting home. An advantage to working away from home and its comforts was how much he appreciated it when he was there. He wondered how Hannah was doing. It had been a long three weeks to think about her. The work kept him busy, but he had plenty of time to wonder. He had to admit the thought of her liquid blue eyes and those lips of hers practically brought him to his knees. This thought was followed in quick succession with that nagging discomfort she brought up. He was torn between wanting to explore what lay between them and wanting to run the other direction.

Luke was shaken out of his thoughts by Nathan, who hollered, "Hey!"

Nathan leaned in the doorway of the main cabin with a scrap of paper and pen.

"Hey, what?" Luke asked.

"Best guess for how long it will take us to make it to the harbor. Whoever wins gets a free dinner at Sally's after we unload," Nathan said.

Luke thought for a minute. "Two hours. We're headed into the wind and water's choppy."

"We're down to minutes here; too many guesses were one hour or two hours."

"You're serious?"

At Nathan's nod, he clarified, "Okay, two hours and five minutes."

Nathan jotted down Luke's guess and turned away. Luke started to walk toward the cabin just as Jared came out. He strode over to where Luke stood before asking, "What was your guess?"

"Two hours, five minutes. You?"

"One hour, fifty-five minutes," Jared said. "Bet you're hankering to see Hannah," he continued with a wink.

"You think so, huh?"

"You've been mighty quiet about her, which says a lot." Jared stared forward at the water as he spoke. "A relationship wouldn't hurt you. Hannah seems nice, and she's gorgeous."

"Did you really just say that?" Luke asked, his tone laced with sarcasm.

"Yup. You haven't given a woman more than a few weeks since you broke it off with Cristina. I'm just saying…"

"You're just saying? Have you ever, I mean *ever*, had a serious relationship?" he countered.

Jared looked away from the water to Luke for a long moment. "Relationships are messy. My life is just fine. So Cristina was after Dad's money through you—whatever. You were all into being serious and got burned. Just think you've played it cool for reasons different than mine. And… someone needs to get going on those grandkids for Mom and Dad. Not me and not Nathan right now. God knows we don't want him to start popping out kids. We'd be babysitting all the time." Jared flashed a wry smile. "My vote's for you. And you totally have the hots for Hannah." With that, Jared turned and headed back to the cabin. Luke shifted his shoulders, the level of unease he felt about Hannah making him restless. Hearing Jared make his point only increased his unease.

Later that evening, Luke, his brothers, and the rest of the crew were seated at one of the long tables at Sally's. They were on the restaurant side of the place, which had booths lining the walls and wooden tables with benches in the center for larger groups. The restaurant and bar were in a renovated barn, so the area felt spacious with the high ceilings. A narrow walkway ran around the upper floor with a small section of seating for the restaurant in what was once the hayloft. The place retained the name of the original owner, Sally James, who'd passed away many years ago. The bar and restaurant were separated by the kitchen and serving part of the bar, which were situated in the center of the building. The food offered was basic pub fare with the addition of fresh seafood.

Nathan had won the bet and was busy ordering the most costly items on the menu at everyone else's expense. Luke looked around the restaurant. He caught himself hoping to see Hannah and batted the thought away. He was bone-tired and ready for a long night's sleep. The only reason he'd been up for coming to Sally's was that he was starving and knew he didn't have the energy to cobble something together at home, not to mention that the refrigerator was likely bare.

Jared took a swallow of beer. "Good trip this time. We could maybe make another run next month. In the meantime, I lined up a few day trips."

Luke nodded. "Yeah, it was a good run. Checked my messages on the way over here and had a few requests. When's the first trip we already have confirmed?"

"Next week. That'll give us time to clean the boat and all the gear, not to mention a little time to relax. Dad called too. Left me a message right before we got in. They want to come up in a few weeks and stay for a month. He wants us to call back tonight if we can."

Luke leaned back as their waitress arrived and set a plate in front of him. He fell quiet as he dug into his food. He thought about their parents, and much as he wanted to see them, he didn't want to be subject to his mother's current favorite topic: her longing for grandchildren. While his father wasn't as vocal, Luke knew he was just as hopeful one of them would settle down soon. He wasn't ready for the pressure of their hopes to be put on him.

Luke looked up to see Susie walking toward them. Her curls were pulled into a loose ponytail. She had the warm smile that usually graced her face. Luke smiled automatically upon seeing her. Susie strode up to their table quickly. "Hey guys, glad to see you made it back. Did you get your quota?"

Jared responded before Luke could. "That we did. What brings you here?"

Susie quirked an eyebrow. "Well, if it isn't obvious, I came to eat. Since that's what you're doing, not sure why you need to ask."

Luke saw Jared bristle. He bit back a smile and watched the exchange continue. Jared liked Susie, as just about everyone did, and he respected her because she did a damn good job handling the accounting. But Luke knew she also set Jared on edge sometimes. She was brash and assertive and wasn't afraid to say whatever came to her mind. Jared would never admit it, but he tended to get uncomfortable with that. He liked to feel in control in conversations, which was not so easy with Susie. She bantered with Jared a bit and then talked accounts with them for a few minutes. Luke wanted to ask her how Hannah was doing and consciously avoided the urge to ask.

Susie asked, "Any plans to see Hannah yet?"

Jared threw back his head and laughed. Luke rolled his eyes. "Not yet. We just got in this afternoon."

Susie's brown eyes twinkled, and Luke wondered if she'd asked the question only to get a laugh. "Just wondering. She's been busy at the house and has started looking into job options. I told her she should see if you guys could use some extra help when you do your day trips. She knows her way around a boat and can keep up with the fishing. She used to go with her parents all the time. I'm just saying..." she trailed off. With that, Susie winked and walked off, leaving Luke wondering what it would be like to spend the day with Hannah on the ocean.

CHAPTER 14

*H*annah toweled her hair dry after showering. It was late afternoon, and she'd spent most of the day working in the yard. A knock at the door and Jessie's bark fractured the quiet. Tugging on a pair of jeans and a tank top, she walked downstairs into the kitchen and saw Susie leaned against the deck railing looking toward the bay.

"Hey there. What brings you up here?" Hannah asked as she unlatched the screen door and stepped onto the deck.

"The chance to visit you," Susie said. "I called actually, but there was no answer, so I thought I'd swing by to see if you were home. I was up at Cammi's place to help her get her new couch in the house. You'd think she'd call someone other than me, seeing as I'm not the biggest person around. But no, she asked me, and of course I said yes. Needless to say, it took a lot longer than we planned. Thank God it was a sectional."

Hannah leaned beside her on the railing and followed Susie's gaze to the bay. She took a breath and let it out slowly. Today had been clear and calm. The water was smooth and deep blue. She looked sideways at Susie. "Did you want to come in?"

"Oh sure. Hope you don't mind me coming by. I like having you back so much that I worry sometimes that I'm not giving you space."

Hannah shook her head and stepped back, looping her arm through Susie's as she did. "I've had nothing but space for two years! There's no one in this house but Jessie and me. And thank God for Jessie because it would feel too empty without her. I love being home again. Honestly, before I left, I think I saw you almost every day. I missed Alaska. But more than that, I missed my friends. I wouldn't want to be here and have you being too respectful of my space. Whatever that means," Hannah said with a roll of her eyes. She tugged Susie into the kitchen with her where Jessie enthusiastically greeted Susie with wiggles and wags.

Susie knelt down by Jessie. "I know we saw each other all the time back then. It's just different, though. We were in high school, then in Anchorage together for college. Friends are practically glued to each other then. Now we're grownups, so they say." Susie paused and looked up from petting Jessie. "I guess I just wasn't sure because you were away for a while. I may not have known exactly what you were going through, but I got that it was too much for you to talk much after your parents died. I guess I just haven't wanted to seem like I'm pushing myself back into your life. I know I can be pushy and sometimes it isn't appreciated."

Hannah looked at Susie for a long moment before answering. "Susie, you're not pushing yourself into my life. I promise. You have no idea how much it means to me that you just drop by, send Luke with a dog to my door, get nosy about Luke, and help me with the boat in the rain. On top of that, you were the only person I thought to call when I found out my parents kept a whopper of a secret from me. Trust me, it's okay that you come by. Come by every day. I need to work on reaching out more myself." She took a deep breath. "Plus you're the kind of friend that I can tell when I'm starving and need to figure out what to do about that before we talk more."

Susie laughed and stood up. "That you can. Do you want me to help throw something together, or should we go get something in town?"

Hannah stepped over to the pantry and looked inside. "I've got a few things here, but I'm feeling lazy. Want to go to Sally's? I haven't been there yet since I've been back in town."

"Sure. I went by there last night, but I can go anytime. They have enough on the menu that I won't have to repeat. You want to drive or should I?"

"I'll drive. But let me put something other than a tank top on and some shoes before we go."

Hannah ran upstairs and threw on a silky green blouse that she buttoned halfway over the tank top. She took a glance in the mirror, swiped a brush through her damp hair, and put on some lip gloss. As Hannah drove to town, Susie kept up a steady stream of talk about old friends. Hannah felt like it would take years to catch up on what she'd missed.

Just as they pulled up to Sally's, Susie said, "Oh, I forgot to tell you I saw Luke, his brothers, and their crew here last night. They had just gotten in from their trip. He looked exhausted. They all did."

"You're just telling me this now?"

"Well, it wasn't like you missed something big. They were eating. I told him I thought you should look into helping them on day trips," Susie said slyly.

"What? Susie! You missed your life's work. You love meddling and should have been a professional matchmaker. I'm not saying you'd pick the right matches, just that you love to meddle."

"Wait a minute," Susie said. "All I did was plant a seed. You did say you needed to start looking for work. You used to fish all the time with your parents. It'd be something to do while you find other work. As for environmental science, well, your options are limited to three places or the government. There's the land heritage group—I forget what it's called—the Inlet Keeper and the Bay Foundation. You probably will eventually get a job at one of those places. But you know how it is around here. With not many options, it's all about timing, and waiting for something means doing odd jobs."

Hannah just looked back at her and didn't respond for a moment. "I should have known you couldn't resist doing something like this."

"Don't tell me you wouldn't love to spend some days with Luke. You look like you're about to spontaneously combust when you're around him. Might as well take what you can get."

Hannah shook her head and turned off the engine. "Take what I can get, huh? I did say you could be nosy, but it doesn't mean I won't get annoyed."

Entering Sally's brought memories back in a flash for Hannah. Sally's was a central place in town. The restaurant and bar were regularly filled with locals. The kitchen pumped out food quickly, so even when there was a wait, seating was usually available quickly. It was a weeknight, so they were able to snag a booth. Hannah slid in across from Susie and took a long look around the room. She recalled many dinners here with her parents. The food was simple and delicious. It was fairly early in the evening, so the place wasn't filled yet. The waitress that came over was a young woman who'd lived down the road from her growing up, Kate Thomas. She'd been about five years behind Hannah in school.

"Hey, Hannah! I heard you were back in town," Kate said

as she placed menus on the table in front of them. Kate's blond hair was pulled back in a bouncy ponytail. Hannah recalled that she'd been active in sports when she was younger, and she still had an athletic look. She had a lively, bubbly air to her. She was wearing jeans and a T-shirt with the Sally's logo on it, the uniform for staff here.

"I am, been back for over a month now. How are you?" Hannah asked while Kate filled their water glasses and pulled out her order book.

Kate twirled the end of her ponytail with one hand. "Oh, I'm good. Working here for the summer. I just finished college, got my BA in psychology. For now, I'm home with my parents and looking into graduate school. How are you?"

They continued chatting for a few minutes, and then Kate took their drink order. Hannah sat quietly while Susie took a call on her cell phone. She looked around and thought about how odd it felt to be somewhere so familiar. Part of her felt like a distant observer. This place had lived in her memory for the last two years and lost its sense of reality. Susie snapped her phone shut and smiled over at Hannah.

"Well, guess who that was?" Susie asked as she pushed her curls away from her face.

"I have no idea. I wasn't really listening. I try not to eavesdrop, you know."

"Sometimes eavesdropping is okay. Anyway, that was Jared, you know, Luke's brother. He needs me to meet with them tomorrow to go over some accounting stuff. He also said to tell you they could use some help next week on one of their trips. I think you should do it. You've been working on the yard and house enough. Time to do something fun while you figure out what's next."

Hannah looked across the table and took a sip of water. "You really think I should work with them?"

"Yes, why not? More time with Luke is a good thing. It'll give you a chance to get to know him in a more natural way. And you said you were going to look into odd jobs. I'm just putting one in your path."

Hannah didn't want to say it aloud, but she wanted to see more of Luke. And that was the problem. She didn't *want* to want to see Luke the way she did. She didn't trust that she wouldn't make a fool of herself and fall for him. The feelings he stirred up were precisely why she'd almost consciously been involved with men who didn't threaten to make her want more than something superficial. "I'll think about it," she finally said.

Susie gave her a long look. "Okay, now let's move on to something else. Have you decided when you're going to try to call your mother's family?"

Hannah took in the question and sighed. She knew Susie wasn't one to shy away from anything. "I don't know. I won't pretend I don't think about it a lot because I do. It's just that every time I do, I try to change the channel in my brain. I want to call, and I don't want to call. It seems crazy, but part of me wants to forget what I found. I mean, my parents will never be here to explain it to me."

Susie opened her mouth to speak. Hannah held her hand up. "Let me finish. I know you're dying to say something. So there's that part, and then I'm desperate to get all the answers I can, no matter how incomplete they are. What if I can find my sister, if she's even really out there? It's surreal. Part of me keeps wondering if it's all a big mistake and there is no sister anywhere. I don't know." She leaned her elbows on the table and placed her head in her hands. She took a breath and slowly exhaled, air sifting through her fingers.

She met Susie's gaze, which was concerned and had that particular resolve that Susie was wont to have. "What are you thinking?" Hannah asked.

Susie set down the menu she'd been holding. "Honestly, you know me, I say let's just charge forward. Remember the Hannah that wasn't afraid to chase off a moose? Well, we need some of her mojo for now. I'll help all I can. Do you mind if I ask my mom about it? She was pretty tight with your mother. For all we know, your mother talked to someone about it. My mom will keep it quiet. Plus, ever since she retired from teaching, she loves a research project. She'll be on the Internet day and night seeing what she can find out if we let her in on what you found. She's got more time and patience for that type of thing than either one of us. What do you think?"

Hannah sat quietly for a moment and wondered what had happened to the Hannah that Susie spoke of, the one who chased moose off and swam in Otter Cove in the dark. The colors in the place mat blurred. Her throat was hot and tight. She swiped a hand across her eyes. She looked over at Susie and met her friend's eyes. For a beat, she felt embarrassed to be wiping away tears, and then remembered that this was the friend whom she'd cried to when the first boy she liked didn't like her back, when she'd failed her first driving test out of nerves, and when she'd sprained her ankle on the front steps of their high school. In turn, Susie, though typically bold, had cried wildly over similar slights. The embarrassment dissolved.

"What do I think? Just a jumble is what I think. But as much as I want to tell you not to talk to your mom, you're right. She might know something or might know if someone else does. There's the part where I want to know as much as I can about what happened, but as crazy as it is to believe I have a sister out there who's been there all along, I have to try to find her. If your mom's up for helping with that, it would be amazing. There's so much emotion for me about it, I can't even seem to start. I need someone else to help me jump-start this. I should have known you

139

would," Hannah said wryly and felt the tightness in her throat ease.

Susie reached over and squeezed Hannah's hand quickly. "Don't worry about crying. Now that I have your permission, I'm on it. I'll call my mom tomorrow. She'd love to see you anyway. Why don't I talk with her, and we can arrange to go over for coffee or something?"

"Sounds good. Just thinking about getting this ball rolling makes me nervous as hell, but I know it has to happen. For now, I need to eat. I can only think about this in small doses," Hannah said. She picked up the menu and started flipping through it.

Susie followed suit, and their conversation shifted to lighter matters. Kate came with their drinks and took the rest of their order. Hannah asked Susie for an update on the state of some of the places where she might be able to snag a job related to her degree. She needed to know who was running what and if it looked like there might be any opportunities on the horizon. They both dug into their food when it arrived. Hannah had ordered the fresh halibut tacos and savored the succulent halibut. It was rare to find halibut anywhere in the East, and she'd forgotten how delicious it was. It was a gourmet version of flounder, less flaky, richer in flavor, and creamy in texture.

While they ate and sipped drinks, a few more acquaintances Hannah hadn't seen yet came over with greetings. She weathered the questions about being home and realized she was settling in enough that people were no longer surprised to see her.

* * *

A FEW HOURS LATER, Hannah walked onto the deck in the soft, gray dusk. She let Jessie out and sat in one of the chairs on the deck for a few minutes while Jessie rolled in the grass and fruitlessly chased the magpies that chattered above her as they flew by. She looked to the bay and the mountains against a backdrop of faint pink and lavender, the last streaks of sunset. Goose bumps rose on her skin in the rapidly cooling air. She stood and called to Jessie who quickly came running.

The house was almost dark. She switched on a light and looked around the kitchen and living room. The space felt quiet and empty tonight. She felt a pang of grief. She imagined her father sitting in his favorite chair by the woodstove where he often read. She pictured her mother in the kitchen. These were only memories, but they had been built on true experiences that occurred time and time again. The imprint of her parents' presence in her life was stronger than their absence.

She shook her head to break her train of thought. She hated that whenever she started to think of her parents now, her mind skipped to what she thought she knew about them and all she was learning she didn't know. It wasn't that she'd expected to know everything about them. She knew that there was likely much she didn't know, that her parents, along with everyone, held parts of themselves deeply private. She just hadn't expected to not know that she had a sister somewhere.

Another long look around the house before turning the lights off, and she walked upstairs. She got ready for bed and propped the pillows to read. She'd still been sleeping in her old bedroom. Just as she was about to flip the covers back, she grabbed her pillows and a book to carry into the master bedroom. Without giving herself time to ponder, she turned on the bedside lamp, situated the pillows on the master bed, climbed between the covers, and settled in to read. Jessie wandered in and sniffed around the room, eventually settling on the end of the bed. Jessie rested her head between her paws and sighed. Hannah looked around the room and went back to her book. As she slipped gradually into sleep later, Luke passed through her mind and she wondered when she might see him again.

* * *

"HANNAH! It's so nice to see you," Faye exclaimed. Susie's mother reached to hug Hannah and kept talking. "Susie told me you were home. I've been wondering how you were, but she keeps me up to date, you know. I figured with you finally home and planning to stay, I'd have plenty of time to see you." Faye tucked her arm through Hannah's and towed her into the house. Susie, who had arrived a few minutes before Hannah, followed them into the house. Hannah had spent many days and slumber party nights here throughout childhood. Susie's childhood home felt almost like her own, familiar and comforting.

Susie had inherited much of her looks from her mother. Faye had passed on her wild curls to Susie. Faye's brown curls were shot through with silver streaks now, but were just as unruly. She wore a loose ponytail, and curls escaped at random all about her head. Faye's brown eyes held a gentle warmth. Faye was also known to be brash, albeit with a softer touch. Hannah felt a sense of relief to see her, mixed with sadness that her own mother wasn't here to help her sort through the secrets she'd left behind.

Faye led her into the kitchen where Hannah and Susie sat at the familiar round table while Faye busied herself getting coffee for them and pulling fresh blueberry muffins out of the oven. They initially chatted about Hannah's move back and how things were going, and Hannah got an update on Faye's life post retirement.

"You work most of your life to retire comfortably, and then realize you're bored as hell after the first few months of bliss at not having to get up and go to work. After the first year, I became the queen of volunteer work, along with doing substitute teaching here and there. Patrick keeps asking me why I bothered to retire. He said to tell you hello by the way. He's up in Anchorage for the week at a conference for the hospital."

Susie chimed in. "Yeah, I thought Mom was going to lose her mind for a bit there. She was so bored she sent me random chain e-mails all the time. I finally told her to stop after I got fed up."

Hannah smiled as she watched Susie tease her mother for a few minutes. She sobered as Faye waded into more serious waters. "Hannah, I just have to say I can't imagine what it was like for you to lose your mom and dad. Even worse that you were away when it happened. I remember your face the day of the funeral. You looked frozen inside. I wanted to help but didn't know how. I'm relieved you finally came home. Susie's missed you, along with me and half the town."

"I appreciate that. It was hard, crazy hard. I'm relieved to be home. I miss my parents so much it's hard to quantify, but it's good to be here."

Conversation paused as Faye brought coffee and muffins over to the table. Hannah and Susie quickly helped themselves to muffins while Faye filled coffee mugs for all three of them.

Faye finally sat down with a mug of coffee wrapped in her hands. She looked over at Hannah and brushed errant curls away from her eyes. "Well, there's no easy way to start this, so I'm jumping in. Susie told me what you found in your mother's papers. I know it was a shock. As for what I may have known, your mother only told me about a year before the crash about what happened. She was short on details though, so I'm not sure how much I can help on that. All she told me was the bare facts. She got pregnant, unplanned of course, when your father was home on break from graduate school. If I remember right, he was about a year into his doctorate. Before she had the baby, they decided to put her up for adoption. Your mom said they just weren't ready for a baby. I'm not sure of the details, but part of the agreement allowed them to name the baby girl, who was named Emma." Faye paused and looked over at Hannah.

Hannah looked across the table at two pairs of kind brown eyes. She didn't know what to say just yet, so she nodded for Faye to continue.

"I don't know much more. I know it was an excruciating decision for your mother to make. I never spoke to your father about it, but Janet spoke as though it were awful for him too. I think they felt stuck in a way it's hard to imagine these days. Pregnancy out of wedlock in that time was considered shameful. Try to imagine having a baby at seventeen—not easy for anyone. Your mother came to me about it because she was trying to figure out how to tell you. She was very worried about making sure you knew that you had a sister somewhere. I think that was another agony for her. They had agreed as part of the adoption process to never try to contact Emma. That was pretty standard back then. I think she wanted to have been able to contact Emma. Knowing your father, my guess is he would have wanted to as well. But you weren't a part of any agreement, and your mother wanted you to know. I think she just hadn't figured out how to do it. In a way, I think it went against her nature to have waited as long as they did to tell you."

Susie looked from her mother to Hannah. "I hope you know she didn't tell me what she knew," she said, gesturing to her mother. "I'd have told you in a heartbeat." She glanced back to her mother. "Not that I don't understand why you didn't say anything." Susie turned back to Hannah. "She said your mother swore her to secrecy. Then your parents died and she didn't know what to do with what she knew, and you were gone."

Hannah sat quietly for a moment and took a sip of coffee. She set the mug down and hugged it with her hands, the warmth anchoring her. She addressed Susie first. "I'd have guessed your mom wouldn't say anything to you. When it comes to telling me things, you're not the best secret keeper." She turned to Faye. "I'm glad to hear my mom wanted to tell me. I won't lie, part of me is angry with them. But I tried to think about why they didn't tell me, and I can sort of understand that it wasn't easy. I just wish I knew what to do now..." Hannah trailed off.

Faye took a breath and spoke. "I think we try to find Emma. I only had a few conversations with your mother about it, but I got the impression that she hoped you'd want to find Emma, for your sake as much as theirs. Susie spoke to me about helping with Internet searches. I'm here to help however you'll let me. In a way, I think of it as helping your mother finish something she wanted to start. You know me, though; you'd better hold me back if you need to because I've got time on my hands. I'll jump on this if you let me." Faye smiled and sat back in her chair.

Susie spoke up at that point. "You probably bargained on this, but you know I'll jump on this too. Do you want us to just start charging ahead, or do you need more time?"

Hannah took in Susie and Faye, both with almost identical expressions of fierce determination and caring. She started to laugh before she spoke. "Only you two could make me laugh about this."

She took a breath and sobered. "You both have my permission to do whatever you think will help find Emma. I don't know where to start, and as you both know, I tend to be more cautious than the two of you. I don't know that caution is what I need now."

The rest of the morning passed quickly. Faye and Susie

didn't dwell on the details about starting the search for Emma. They seemed to sense that Hannah could only talk so much about it.

By the time Hannah left, she realized it was past noon. Despite the weight of her discovery and talking about trying to find Emma, she felt more comfortable in her skin than she had in years. She felt like she was settling in to being home again. Spending a few hours having coffee and muffins with Susie and her mother was such a familiar experience that she forgot she had taken it for granted the countless times it happened over the years. It had been over a month since she'd been home and her anxieties had faded.

* * *

HANNAH WALKED INTO HER HOUSE, distracted by thoughts about her conversation with Faye and Susie. Her train of thought was broken by Jessie who greeted her enthusiastically at the door. On a whim, she decided to take Jessie to the beach. The day was clear, sunny, and breezy. It brought back memories of flying kites with her father on the beach when she was younger. She'd loved to watch the kite dance in the sky. Her father would get it started and let her hold onto the kite once it was flying. She briefly wondered if she could find any of the old kites they'd used in the shed outside.

She spent the afternoon with Jessie at the beach. She collected rocks while Jessie spent the time sniffing like mad and playing fetch after she brought Hannah a found tennis ball to throw. The wind moved from a soft breeze to harder gusts and clouds rolled in quickly as the afternoon wore on. She lost track of how far they walked and cursed to herself when she realized she had a good half hour to walk to get back to the parking lot. By the time she got to her truck, rain was falling steadily with gusts of wind driving it. The warm morning and early afternoon had blown away with wind and rain.

The dropping temperature and driving rain left her wet and cold. She climbed into the truck, loaded a wet Jessie in beside her and started the drive home. She made it out of the parking lot and halfway down the dirt road to the highway when she felt a drag on her wheels. She initially ignored it and made it to the main road, only to feel it getting worse as she drove. Pulling over, she climbed out to find one of her tires flat; the culprit was a nail protruding from the tire. She called Susie and got her voice mail. She sighed and leaned her head against the headrest. Jessie nuzzled her hand on the gearshift. The rain was falling hard now, pounding against the roof of her truck. She heard a knock on the window and turned, surprised to see Luke's face looming in the gray rain. He had a bright yellow rain jacket on with the hood pulled over his head. She rolled down the window.

"Hey, I was just about to call you in a bit, and then I saw your truck. What's up?

She pointed to the flat tire on the driver's rear side. "Hey to you too. Looks like I drove over a nail."

Luke leaned down to look at the tire. "That would be it. I'd offer to change your tire for you, although I'm sure you could do it yourself. How about a ride? No fun to change a tire in this weather."

"As long as it's okay for Jessie to come along," she said.

"Of course, can't leave her here. Anything you need from the truck?" he asked.

"Just my purse. You think it's okay to leave my truck here?" she asked as she looked over to see if she was pulled far enough off the road.

He glanced both ways on the road. "Maybe pull over there." He gestured to the parking lot of an out-of-business gas station just ahead.

"Good idea. How about you follow me over there, then I'll get Jessie over to your truck?"

He nodded and walked back to his truck. She quickly started the engine and drove slowly to the empty parking lot. She was soaked. There wasn't much she could do about it, so she grabbed her purse and let Jessie out. Luke pulled up just beside her. He leaned over and opened the passenger door from the inside. He pulled the seat forward for Jessie to jump into the cab space behind the front seats. Hannah hopped in once the seat was back.

"Thanks for stopping," Hannah said. She pushed her damp hair away from her face. "I'm soaked and so is Jessie. Your seat's gonna get wet. Sorry about that."

"Not much you can do about that. My truck has handled much worse. A little water won't hurt it. In the few weeks I had Jessie, she was in here no matter how sandy and wet she was. Take you straight home?" he asked.

"If you don't mind. I'm too wet to go anywhere else right now."

He just put the truck in gear and started driving. The sky was slate gray and rain fell steadily. This wasn't how she'd first wanted to see Luke after a few weeks, but there wasn't much she could do about it. She was relieved he'd happened to be driving by.

On the drive home, he filled her in on how the fishing trip went and asked about what she'd been doing over the past few weeks. She wondered when and how to talk with Luke about what she'd discovered about her parents and her maybe sister. She wasn't ready just yet though, and didn't know when she would be. Instead she talked about working on the yard and house and starting to look into an actual job. She shivered in the damp, feeling cold and ragged.

He kept adjusting the temperature and defroster to keep the windows from fogging. As he pulled into her driveway, rain fell in sheets. He looked over at her, and she felt her stomach do a small somersault. She saw a spark of recognition flicker in his eyes and impulsively invited him to stay for dinner.

"You'll have to put up with me drying off and changing first, though," Hannah said. She looked over at Luke and unbuckled her seat belt. "No matter how many times this happens, I forget how fast the weather can change in Alaska."

"It got bad fast," Luke said. He turned his truck off and looked out the window. "The day tricked me. It was so beautiful this morning and now this." Luke gestured toward the bay. "Not letting up anytime soon either. As for dinner, sounds good. I'm not up for more driving in this, and it'll be me and my brothers scrounging anyway."

"Okay, let's get inside then." They both raced for the house with Jessie on their heels. Once inside, Luke shook the rain from his hair.

"No sense in bothering to dry off here. I need to get out of these clothes. Let me get your jacket first, though," Hannah said, taking his yellow rain jacket.

Rain dripped onto the tiled entry floor where she hung his jacket. The wind had picked up and was now steadily blowing straight toward the house off the bay. She glanced toward the bay, which was barely visible in the dark sky made grayer with blowing rain.

She headed straight for the laundry room and got a towel for Luke, as well as an old one to dry Jessie. Jessie stood patiently while Hannah toweled her off and then padded over to the dog bed in the kitchen. Luke rubbed his hair dry with the towel she'd handed him.

"There's wine over there," Hannah said, gesturing to the wine rack. "And beer in the fridge. Help yourself while I get changed. You can also turn on the TV if you want."

Upstairs, she peeled her wet clothes off. Shivering, she quickly dried off with a towel. She rubbed her hair briskly and pulled on sweatpants and a soft blue fleece top, tugging on a pair of fuzzy socks at the last minute. She thought for a moment that she should put more into her appearance, but she was too cold to think much more about what to wear. Pausing in front of the mirror, she brushed her damp hair out and left it at that.

Downstairs, she found Luke in the kitchen with a bottle of beer in hand. He nodded toward the woodstove in the living room. "You might want to start a fire. It's chilly and damp."

She followed his gaze. "Good plan. Want to start one while I figure out what we can have for dinner?" Her parents passed through her mind when she gestured toward the firewood, neatly stacked in the small, decorative cast-iron wood rack by the woodstove. She'd never asked Frank if he'd stacked the wood there. As she watched Luke start to lift pieces of wood from the rack into the woodstove, she wondered if her parents had left them there or not. She gave a quick shake of her head and turned away, walking into the pantry.

Within a half hour, the fire in the woodstove was cranking along, the heat slowly dissipating the damp chill in the air. Hannah had pulled together a salad and gotten chicken stew with dumplings simmering on the stove. In the meantime, she handed Luke a box of crackers and some cheese to slice, so they had something to nibble on while they waited for the stew. She didn't want to wait too long to eat, but the weather called for comfort food, and chicken stew with dumplings was a childhood favorite. It was a southern carryover from her mother. She couldn't help but think of her mother as she made the stew and dumplings. She carefully spooned the dumpling batter into the stew and smiled for a moment when she recalled her mother making a game during her childhood of counting how long the dumplings would sink before they bounced to the top.

She looked over at Luke to catch him slipping Jessie a piece of cheese.

"Hey! I saw that. Jessie's a good beggar, but I try to limit it. If I fed her everything she wanted, she'd hardly be able to walk soon."

His smile was sheepish. "You caught me. I promise that was the first piece. I'm a softie. So tell me what you're thinking about work."

She reached to slide her wineglass over and took a sip. "Well, I figure I'll need to do some of whatever comes along while I see if I can snag a job at one of the local environmental organizations, or maybe through the state at Fish and Game. You've been here long enough to guess how that goes. It's all about timing. I'll need to be patient, but I also like variety. A few different jobs here and there will keep me afloat while I put my feelers out. In the meantime, I'm flexible."

Hannah thought about Susie's comment that she go on some day fishing trips with Luke and his brothers. She didn't have the nerve just yet to ask and then bit her lip when Luke spoke.

"Susie mentioned you used to do fishing trips with your parents. Sometimes we could use extra help on our day trips. If you want, I can let you know when. We don't expect phenomenal fishing skills. Just helps to have someone who knows the ropes on the boat and can help the customers." He held her gaze across the counter.

She had grown accustomed to the sparks that danced along her nerves when she was around him, but it made it hard to focus sometimes. She let her eyes fall and then looked back. "Well, if you guys need help, just give me a call. I probably need a day's notice. On that thought, though, let me make sure I still have all the gear I'd need."

"You don't need fishing gear, if that's what you mean."

"But I need to make sure I have the right clothes, like my

heavy-duty rain gear and gloves. It's around the house—I just have to make sure it's where I think it is. Haven't used anything but my waders since I got back. I'm guessing nothing you guys have would fit me."

Luke's dimples winked at her with his quick smile. "No, definitely not. Well, let me know when you think we could line you up. Usually it's Jared and me who handle those trips. Every so often, Nathan comes along."

Hannah experienced a flash of uneasiness. She found herself wishing they'd need help soon and often, as that would give her excuses to be around Luke. And *that* elicited the restlessness that had prodded her into her impulsive adventures with indifferent men whose common denominators were good looks and a taste for risk. While she couldn't say that Luke was indifferent, he got checks for good looks and a taste for risk from what she'd heard.

"Definitely call if you need an extra hand," she said, surprising herself. She wondered if she was walking into a foolish mess by letting the chemistry between them make her lose hold on the self-control she'd reclaimed after her parents died. She didn't need to make a fool of herself over Luke. She couldn't let herself end up in a space where that restless feeling led her back down an impulsive path.

The dumplings simmered to the top of the stewpot. Hannah distracted herself with getting the stew ladled into bowls. After serving Luke, she tugged a stool to where she stood and sat facing him across the counter. Savoring every bite, she tried to remember the last time she'd made this and realized it had probably been before she moved away. Luke plowed through his first bowl before she finished.

"Want more?" She waved him toward the stove. "Help yourself." She watched while he ladled more stew. His muscles flexed through the cotton jersey shirt he wore. She knew what attracted her to him, but wondered what he saw in her. She didn't feel unattractive necessarily, but tended to think she didn't stand out. She thought again of Susie reminding her of her younger self. While she may have been more daring back then, giving in to intimacy had always been hard for her. After what happened with Damon, she'd decided it wasn't worth it.

Luke sat back down and immediately began eating again. He caught her watching him. "Did I forget to mention that I was starving? When you offered dinner, I was relieved I didn't have to go home and figure out what to eat."

"You gave me a ride in the rain, the least I could do was offer you dinner."

She stood and carried her bowl over to the sink. "So do you have any other major fishing trips scheduled for the summer?"

"Not sure yet. We're thinking about one more. We'll be busy straight through September with guiding trips. Then we break for the winter. Nathan keeps hounding Jared and me to consider crab fishing, but I'm not up for that. Damn cold and risky. If you luck out, payoff's great. Not worth it for me though. I like to be on land when the snow flies." He shrugged. "We keep telling Nathan if he wants to try it, sign on with another crew for the winter. He's not a fan of planning, so not likely. Snowplowing carries us through winter and works for me."

Luke set his spoon down and looked into the empty bowl. "I think I've finally had enough. You make a mean chicken stew." He stood and carried his dishes to the sink. "Should I rinse these and put them in the dishwasher?"

"Go ahead. Let's head closer to the woodstove." Hannah walked into the living room. Jessie padded quietly behind her and curled up on the rug near the woodstove. Hannah opened the woodstove and added a log to the fire. Latching the door shut, she picked up the wineglass she'd set on the floor and turned as she stood up, only to run right into Luke. Wine sloshed over the edge of the glass onto his shirt.

"Sorry! I didn't hear you coming. Let me get something to clean off your shirt." She hurried back toward the kitchen with Luke following.

"Don't worry about it," he said.

She grabbed a paper towel and started to blot at his shirt. Luke's hands came up and curled around hers. They were warm and steady. She went still and looked up into his green eyes. Her stomach fluttered and her breath became shallow. He released one of her hands and used his free hand to pull the paper towel from her hand and quickly wipe his shirt. He kept a gentle grip on her other hand and didn't move away. Without a word, he pulled her close with one arm, leaned forward, and kissed her. It had been three weeks too many since she'd kissed him, and frightening as it was, it felt like coming home. The persistent worries she had about him evaporated in the heat of their kiss.

He let go of her other hand and cupped her face. Their kiss deepened, and she stepped as close as she could, her body straining toward him. They were flush together. She felt his erection low against her belly and liquid heat building inside of her. In seconds, she felt wild inside. She couldn't get close enough or kiss him deeply enough. Their tongues were slick against each other. He broke their kiss and brought his lips down along her jaw and neck. Shivers rushed through her, his lips leaving a trail of nerves afire. He turned her against the counter, slipped his hands under her bottom, and pulled her against him. She gasped as she felt his erection rub between her legs.

He kept his hands on her bottom and lifted her slowly up onto the edge of the counter. Their breathing was loud and ragged. Hannah's knees fell open; Luke stepped between them. He leaned back for a second and slid his hands under her shirt. As his hands moved up against her body, he pushed her shirt slowly up and over her head. In another moment, her bra fell to the floor. Her hands moving with a sureness she didn't feel, she tore the buttons on his shirt open and gave a sigh of relief at the feel of his chest against her breasts. The feeling was so piercingly good, she could hardly think. They remained locked against each other, Hannah seated on the counter, while Luke's hands roamed over her back and slipped around to her breasts. His touch was featherlight and sure. He cupped one of her breasts and brushed his fingertips back and forth across her nipple. She gasped, only to feel his hand come to a stop and to find him pulling back to look at her. The green of his eyes darkened. He held her gaze with a heated look and slowly brought his head down. His lips closed over her nipple just as he unzipped her jeans and slid a finger past the elastic of her panties, directly into the slick space between her legs.

A deep thrust of his finger and suction just on the edge of pain on her nipple, and she climaxed in a burst of heat. He didn't stop, although he slipped his finger out and caressed her. She felt ripples rise and fall, aftershocks from her climax. Luke lifted his head and looked at her again. Hannah had to work to keep her eyes focused.

"That's it. Either we stop now or soon it will be impossible to stop." He paused for a breath. "Though I would if you asked."

She sat there, her legs dangling around his hips. Her breasts were bare and brushed against his chest. She felt his fingers lingering in her wet heat and his erection against her thigh. She wanted him inside her so bad, she couldn't think straight. For once, she didn't try. She reached to cup his cheek with one hand. "I'm not asking you to stop," she said. She curled her hand around his neck and tugged his lips back to hers. With her other hand, she unbuttoned his jeans and started to slide his zipper down. She paused and pulled back. "Wait."

He leaned back and looked down. "I have protection if that's what you were about to ask."

"That's what I was about to ask. I won't ask if you were planning on this, though," Hannah replied.

He stared at her for a long moment. "Maybe wishful thinking, but planning, no." He leaned forward and captured her lips again.

Hannah resumed sliding his zipper down and slid her hand against his erection. She held still for a moment and then reached past his boxers and caressed him. He was warm and hard in her hand, pulsing velvet skin. Luke went from lazily fingering her to tearing at her jeans. What was left of their clothes came off in a stumbling rush. Next thing she knew, she was bare-naked, and he was lifting her back onto the counter. She took in his muscled body in a quick glance before her head fell back as he kissed along her neck. She heard him tearing at the condom package and reached to help. Her breath came in gushes as he maneuvered into her. She felt the broad head of his shaft slowly ease into her. Her body resisted for a second. She hadn't had sex in over two years, and her body wasn't used to it. She was tight, but the relief of feeling him slide inside was immense. He paused for a moment and then thrust his hips, stroking deep into her. She felt her muscles clench and release. He pulled back and slid with ease into her slick warmth.

"Oh my God. You feel so good," he choked out.

"Don't stop. Whatever you do, don't stop." Hannah brought her knees up and wrapped her legs around his waist. Luke began to move slowly, gradually shifting to a faster pace. As he moved in and out, heat built inside of her, bringing the fire higher and higher. He brought a hand down between their bodies and rubbed just above where they joined. She gasped as another piercing sweet climax rushed through her. He curled both hands around her hips and thrust deep into her. The back of her head hit the cabinet behind her. He threw his head back and came inside her. Lingering pulses ran through her, as he shuddered against her. He lifted his head forward and brought his fore-head to hers. They stayed like that for several moments. Their breathing slowed. She felt boneless. Her legs lost their grip and dangled beside his hips. His arms came around her and held her close. His heart beat against her breasts.

Luke finally pulled back. He took a long look at her, seeming to search her eyes for something. He started to speak and then paused. Finally he said, "I think we need a shower."

Hannah didn't think that was what he meant to say, but she didn't press. "Follow me," she said.

The rest of the night passed seamlessly. They showered together and fell into bed. At some point, Hannah heard Jessie pad softly into the bedroom and curl up on the floor. Luke was spooned behind her, one arm curled loosely around her.

CHAPTER 15

"Toss me that line," Luke called to Jared.

Hannah heard Jared curse and turned to see the mooring line heading in Luke's direction. Jared shook his hand quickly and noticed her glance. "Caught my thumb on the edge of the boat there—no biggie, just a nick," he said.

They had been out for a day of fishing in the bay. The group of customers was from Oregon, a couple and the husband's father and uncle. After a rather speedy morning of reaching everyone's halibut quota, Jared had suggested stopping for lunch in Halibut Cove, a tiny, secluded coastal village across the bay from Homer, a small community at the tip of the Kenai Peninsula and farther south than Diamond Creek. Halibut Cove was off the road system and could only be reached by boat or plane. In the summer, it was an artist enclave. The Saltry restaurant and the town's art gallery were popular destinations for tourists and local Alaskans. They had just finished lunch and were readying the boat to head back toward Diamond Creek.

Hannah had been out fishing with Luke and his brothers

several times over the past few weeks. Aside from the time with Luke, it had further brought her back into the life she'd loved so much before she'd left for graduate school. The brothers handled all the boat work while she was there to help customers with their equipment and getting fish into the boat. Seated on a bench in the center of the boat, she watched the shoreline of Halibut Cove recede as the boat pulled away. The docks gradually became smaller in the distance. She took a breath, taking in the salty scent of the ocean with a hint of spruce from the trees that towered along the shoreline. As they got farther out, she faced forward in the boat and looked ahead at the skyline. It was early afternoon now with the sun high and bright in a clear sky. She felt relaxed and tired.

Luke held the steering wheel comfortably in his hands. He must have sensed her looking at him because he turned, catching her gaze. His eyes locked onto hers, and heat sparked between them. She was flustered by the flare of intensity and looked away. Since the first night he'd spent with her, she was finding it hard to keep any perspective. Part of her wanted him with her as much as possible, while another part of her wanted to push away. For now, lust was winning out over her lingering wariness. He wasn't at her place every night, but every few nights, and she couldn't keep her hands off him. They'd yet to have sex in bed because the attraction between them took over. She found herself thinking the kitchen table was a much better place for sex than a bed, not to mention the living room couch or the floor.

When he wasn't with her, the doubts took over. She hadn't experienced this much chemistry before. She'd thought her feelings for Damon had been strong, but they paled in comparison. *That* alarmed her because she didn't want to want more than the superficial flings she'd had the last few years. She'd promised herself after her parents died that she wouldn't keep living in a way that would have disappointed them the way she had when she'd been running wild. Luke had an almost magnetic pull on her. She couldn't seem to talk herself out of whatever she was walking into. She wanted to find a way to walk the tightrope of not getting in too deep and not making the kind of mistake that would have distressed her parents.

Soft waves rocked the water with enough breeze to stir up the surface in a lazy way. Gulls called as they flew past the boat, likely headed toward Gull Island, a rock outcropping in Kachemak Bay where gulls, puffins, and other birds gathered in large numbers. Hannah turned for a last look back at Gull Island with the boat quickly pulling away. Birds swirled and called around the small island. Facing forward, she felt the momentum of the boat churning toward Diamond Creek. Just as in her life, the past receding into the distance with the future unfurling in front. She only wished she could see ahead in her life the way she could in the water. Mount Augustine stood high in the distance, small clouds arrayed about its peak.

Just over an hour later, Hannah was busy helping the family load their fish in large plastic bins to transport to the Fish Factory to be cleaned, gutted, filleted, and flash frozen in short order. Some visitors chose to do the preparation for flash freezing themselves. Much pride lived among the fishing crowd regarding how well one could gut, clean, and fillet a fish. The docks in the harbor had cleaning stations every few feet for this purpose.

Just as she finished up and was returning to the parking lot with Luke and his brothers, her phone rang. Susie's number flashed on the screen.

"Hey there," she said as she answered.

"Hey, hey," Susie said. "What are you up to?"

"Just finishing up a day of fishing with Luke and his brothers. How about you?" she asked.

"Oh, I'm about brain-dead from trying to sort out the bike shop's finances from last quarter. They just started to use me after years of handling their own books. Let's just say they probably should have gotten some help sooner," Susie said with a soft chuckle. "But that's not why I called. Not to startle you, but Mom's found a good lead and wants to talk to you ASAP."

Hannah felt her stomach drop. "What?"

"Just what I said. She says you can stop by anytime. She's just home doing yard stuff. Are you busy?"

She caught Luke looking at her with a question in his eyes. She ignored him and focused on Susie. "Well, seeing as I've been on the water all day and handling fish, I need a shower."

"Do you want me to swing by your place in maybe an hour and we can go over to my mom's together? I have time."

"That would be great. Can we talk then?" Hannah asked.

At Susie's quick agreement, Hannah slipped her phone back in her pocket. Luke was walking silently alongside Jared and Nathan and looked over at her again. "Should I ask about dinner, or did you just make other plans?" he asked.

"Well...how about I call you later? That was Susie, and she's meeting me in a bit to go see her mom. I don't know how long we'll be, though." She glanced at her watch to see it was still mid-afternoon.

They had reached her truck, parked against the trees in the lot. Jared and Nathan split away from them. Luke lingered beside her for a moment. "A call later would be nice," he said and then leaned over and took her lips.

In less than a second, Hannah thought she might combust. Heat pooled in her center and flared through her from head to toe. They were shielded by the truck cap and the trees to the back. Luke didn't hesitate and brought his body flush against hers. She took a small step with her back coming up against the truck. He pressed against her. Their tongues tangled, and she gasped as she felt his erection cradled against her legs. She couldn't help but part her thighs, inviting him deeper against her. He pressed against her pelvis, spiking sharp, sweet sensations through her.

She brought her hands around his hips and pulled him hard against her. His lips traveled down one side of her neck, nipping gently. His hands slipped underneath her T-shirt and quickly unhooked her bra. A sigh of relief came when his warm hands cupped her breasts. He teased her nipples with one hand while the other made quick work of the button and zipper on her jeans. He cupped her mound for a moment and dipped a finger into her curls, sifting through and sliding into the slippery moisture rapidly building in her core. He was still gently pushing his hips into hers. She could barely stand the sensation of his erection slowly grinding against her in a soft rhythm and his fingers teasing the bud of her clitoris. She heard herself pleading with him as she felt his lips close over a nipple he'd bared with his other busy hand. She distantly heard the sound of voices in the parking lot.

Luke finally sank one finger and then another into her now drenched channel, just as he shifted to her other nipple with a deep suction. Hannah bucked against his hand in seconds, coming apart silently. She felt Luke's hand go still, her flesh pulsing around his fingers. He pulled his lips away from her nipple with a soft nip just as he slowly removed his hand from her warmth, opening his eyes and bringing his gaze to hers. Her head had fallen against the truck. She stood there, feeling limp and still wanting much more than his fingers inside of her.

She met his eyes and smiled ruefully. "It's not fair what you do to me."

He shrugged. "Does this mean you'll be more likely to call me later?"

She rolled her head to one side against the truck. "Oh, is that what this was for? If so, then yes."

Voices from the busy parking lot intruded again. She remembered that while they were protected from view by her truck, they were also in a busy area. She couldn't believe she'd allowed what just happened in such a public place. Luke stepped away and helped her tidy her clothes. Fortunately, after a day fishing, her attire could be sloppy and no one would think anything of it. She told Luke she'd call him later and drove away after a final quick kiss, her body thrumming with the imprint of him against her.

* * *

WITHIN THE HOUR, Hannah was looking at Faye's house as Susie brought her car to a stop in the driveway. She realized on the drive over that she had been working very hard at pretending like she hadn't discovered she had a sister somewhere in the world. Every so often, the thought would rise to the surface of her mind, and each time, she dodged away. Thoughts of Luke were an escape made easy because it was enough for her to struggle with the push and pull of how she felt about him. Following Susie toward the house, she felt a twinge of guilt that she had yet to talk with Luke about this situation. She kept telling herself that she didn't even know if what they had would be more than carefree and skin-deep. Sharing something this personal with him seemed to reflect that she thought he mattered, and she wasn't ready to admit that, even to herself. Faye opened the door, and she pushed thoughts of Luke away.

Faye led them into her kitchen and puttered about getting them coffee and tea.

Hannah sipped at her coffee and looked out toward the

bay. Faye's house offered a different view of the mountains and a closer look at one of the glaciers across the bay. Staring at the icy blue of the glacier, she lost focus.

Faye's voice brought her back. "So Hannah, I'll just get right to it. Here's what I found. I did some digging on forums where adopted children and parents who gave children up for adoption post information. Wait a minute, let me just get my laptop," she said as she quickly got up and walked over to a small desk in the corner of the kitchen.

Faye returned with her laptop, clicked through a few screens and came to a stop. She pointed to a post. "There... this sounds to me like it might be posted by your sister. The details match up. Her name is Emma Neals. Read it and let me know what you think."

LOOKING FOR MY BIRTH PARENTS. *I only have first names, John and Janet. I was born in Raleigh, NC on 2/21/1981. Adopted by Catherine and Franklin Davis and raised in Chapel Hill. My parents told me I was adopted at birth, but they didn't have any other information about my birth parents. Please contact me at..."*

HANNAH READ the brief paragraph three times before looking up at Faye. Susie had stepped out of the kitchen to call Faye's dog, Dante, into the house when he had started barking at a moose that wandered into the neighbor's yard.

"Well, what do you think?" Faye asked. "Enough details fit that I think it's worth contacting her."

Hannah's heart pounded and she felt slightly ill. She read the post once more. "I think so," she said slowly. "I mean, my parents' names are pretty common, but the other details fit from the papers my mom had. How did you find this?" she asked.

"Oh, hours and hours and hours of looking through

different forums like this. There's a lot out there. It's a bit of a funneling process—eventually the search starts to narrow by a process of elimination. I thought about going ahead and contacting Emma, but I wanted to talk to you first. I mean, if you're not ready, well, we have to think about that. Plus, I doubt Emma has any idea she might have a sister. We're going to be dealing with the reality that, if this is your sister, we'll be breaking the news to her that her birth parents passed away and she also has a sister who had no idea she existed until a few weeks ago. That's a lot to throw at someone."

Dante came bounding into the kitchen. He was Faye's latest dog, a large, shaggy mutt who looked to have German shepherd in the mix. He was still young and took a few minutes to settle down. After he attempted to climb on Hannah's lap and then Faye's, Faye distracted him with a chew toy, and he flung himself on the floor by their feet.

Susie returned to the kitchen and poured a cup of coffee. She sat in a chair beside Hannah and captured her gaze. "Well?" she asked.

Faye turned the laptop and pushed it toward Susie, pointing toward the screen. "Read that. I think it's a good chance it might be the Emma we're looking for."

Susie scanned it quickly and looked to Hannah again. "Certainly seems like a good chance it's her. What do you think?"

"I think your mom's right. Now I just have to get up the nerve to send an e-mail. I can't believe this happened so fast. Honestly, I was still trying to figure out how to talk to my relatives about it." She sighed. "I still have to call them. We may not be that close, but if I actually find my sister, I have to tell them somehow."

Susie responded quickly. "First things first. This may or may not be her. And you have time to figure out how to talk to your relatives. For now, I think you should write an e-mail to her, but we could give her my number or Mom's. That way, it's an automatic filter if she calls. You won't be put on the spot. We'll just take a message and go from there. How's that sound?" she asked.

Hannah thought for a moment and found herself nodding. "That's a good idea. If she responds through e-mail, I'll have time to gather my thoughts. If she calls, one of you can take the message."

Faye looked over at them both. "I think you should leave my number, not Susie's."

Susie opened her mouth to respond, and Faye held a hand up. "Susie, I know you, and it will be all but impossible for you to just take a message. I love that you charge through life the way you do, but this is a time when creating a little space might be a good thing. It's not just Hannah we're talking about here, but another person who is doing something that's emotionally challenging even under the best of circumstances."

Susie bit her lip and wrinkled her nose. Hannah turned to Faye. "Faye, you're the only one who can talk to Susie like that and get away with it."

Hannah shook her head and sobered before taking another sip of coffee. "Before I chicken out, I think I should write the e-mail now. I can log into my account online and send it from here, if that's okay. I know myself. If you two hadn't prodded me into letting you start searching for Emma, I'd still be thinking about it, and nothing would have happened. This way, you can read my e-mail before I actually send it."

Susie pushed the laptop over toward Hannah. "I say keep it simple. Don't you think?"

Hannah pulled up her Gmail account and started typing. After having Faye and Susie read the message, she added Faye's number for a contact. Before she could talk herself out of it, she typed in the e-mail address from the forum and hit send. She looked at the clock, and Luke passed through her mind. Faye had gotten up and was washing a few dishes that had been left in the sink. They moved on to less weighty topics and started discussing Hannah's job options. Hannah felt almost numb and was relieved to be with Faye and Susie, both intuitively understanding that she couldn't dwell on this now.

In a short time, Susie was driving her home. Hannah felt strange just going about the rest of her day, wondering if and when she might hear from the woman who may be her sister. Susie asked her about Luke just as she turned onto Hannah's road.

"So was I on target trying to set you up with Luke?" Susie asked slyly.

"Maybe. It's only been a few weeks," Hannah replied.

Susie shook her head with her curls bouncing with each turn of her head. "Of course you'd say that. I know it's only been a few weeks, but you do seem to be spending a lot of time with him. I'm guessing you'll see him tonight."

"What makes you say that?" she asked.

"If you weren't planning on it, you'd have asked me what I was doing, but you haven't said a word. I'm just sayin'..." Susie said with a wink.

"Okay, okay. We haven't confirmed anything yet, but yeah, I was going to call him. And much as it kills me to say it, I have to admit we have chemistry."

Hannah's uneasiness emerged, just talking about him. "There's just a lot happening right now. I mean it was enough to move back on my own. Then I find those damn papers and now I'm searching for a sister I didn't know I had. On top of that, I haven't seriously dated in years and don't know if I want to. I was doing just fine not seeing anyone. And I'm sure as hell not ready to talk to him about this whole sister thing," she said.

Susie came to a stop in the driveway and turned off the engine. She looked over, the teasing look gone from her eyes. "Were you really doing fine? I wouldn't have said so, but I was just as worried about you as your parents were for a bit there. You were running and running hard. After your parents died, it sounds like you went to the other extreme. You don't need to live like a nun, and your parents damn sure wouldn't have wanted that. As for Luke...I had a hunch about you two, but that's it. He's a decent guy. I think you should tell him about your sister. I'm all about just blurting things out."

"The only way I may be able to talk to him about it is to blurt it out. I don't know if I will. As for worrying about me...why didn't you say something?"

"Because I saw how pissed off you got at your parents about it and figured it was better for you to see me as your friend than someone else on your case. Not to mention that you didn't exactly stay still long enough for me to bring it up. If it kept up too long, I probably would have said something."

Hannah didn't want to meet Susie's eyes just yet, so she looked out the car window. She propped the door open for some fresh air and rested her foot on the side. A magpie swooped low and called to another that swiftly followed. The chatter faded as they landed in a tree by the deck. She could see Jessie's silhouette in one of the full-length windows that flanked the side door. Her ears were tilted forward.

Susie continued after a moment, "There's not much you can do other than take everything one step at a time, cliché as that may sound. That's for things with Luke and with whatever happens with finding your sister. Cut yourself some slack."

Hannah took Susie's words in and sat quietly. She gazed into the field by the house. Lupine was blooming in scattered patches, the purple flowers standing out against the tall grasses.

"I know it doesn't help to worry. But I've excelled at it since Mom and Dad died. And maybe I did go to the other extreme after they died, but I was sick and tired of disappointing them. Not to mention that it wasn't like I didn't notice that I wasn't making the best choices," Hannah said. She turned to face Susie and felt tears threaten. "I get why you didn't say anything back then, but I wish you had. Maybe I would have gotten pissed off, but I might have listened."

Another deep breath. "I'll take your advice and have dinner with Luke. Maybe I'll get up the nerve to tell him what's going on."

"And maybe you'll have other things on your mind," Susie said, her sly smile returning with full force. "Time for me to go—gotta swing by the store. Maybe we can get together with Cammi and Dara sometime this week? I ran into Cammi and she wants to see you again."

Hannah nodded. "That'd be great. Thanks for the ride home and for...well, everything else. I'll call you or you'll call me as soon as one of us hears anything. About the e-mail thing, that is."

After Susie left, Hannah let Jessie out and sat on the small bench on the deck for a few minutes in the early evening. Magpies, ever busy, flew among the trees and chattered. Considering what Susie said about those years when she did nothing but flit from one man or place to the next, Hannah experienced a twinge of remorse. She so wished she could have stopped disappointing her parents before they died. On the heels of remorse came that oh-so-familiar feeling of restlessness. Deflecting her thoughts, she slipped her phone out of her pocket and dialed Luke's number.

* * *

LATER THAT NIGHT, Hannah found herself back on the deck, this time with Luke. The magpies were quiet now. The sun had almost fallen below the mountains in the distance. Just an orange sliver was left, the top of the sun curved above the mountains. The heat had disappeared with the sun, and the early night air was cool. Goose bumps rose on her skin, and she wrapped her arms tight against her body. Luke stood with one hip resting against the railing. In the fading light, his profile was outlined against the sky. She was seated on the bench that faced out toward the yard with Jessie curled up beside her.

They had been quiet for several moments, so Luke's voice startled her when he spoke. "You must have been surprised. What are you going to do?" he asked.

"Wait." She shrugged. "Not much else to do. I'm not good at waiting, but I'll have to. I'm sorry I didn't tell you sooner. It was just a lot. A lot, a lot. Between just getting back here and still getting used to my parents being gone, I stalled on this."

"No need to be sorry. We haven't known each other that long. A lot is one way to put it." He looked toward her.

"I just wanted to get it out there. Believe me, it's hard enough to talk about in general. I can only take it in small doses. It started to feel weird seeing you as much as I have and not mentioning it. That's all..." She trailed off and shivered.

He pushed away from the railing. "Let's go in. It's getting chilly."

She led the way into the kitchen. As usual, Jessie ambled in behind her and headed for the dog bed against the wall by the kitchen table. Hannah started to clear off the kitchen counter. Luke silently started loading the dishwasher. She paused when she realized how comfortable she was. Being with Luke doing something as mundane as cleaning up the kitchen felt as comfortable as it would have years back with her parents in the kitchen. Recognizing the feeling for what it was led to a surge of panic. She didn't want to feel this comfortable, it only added to her internal confusion. She focused on pushing the feeling away by methodically rinsing dishes and wiping down the counter.

Luke leaned against the counter. Hannah stood by the sink, which was situated in a small U-shaped area created by the counter, stove, and refrigerator. Her hands curled around the edge of the counter. She turned to face him; he stood directly across from her. Her heart still pounded; she felt like it was trying to beat away the panic. He could easily reach her and did so by simply leaning forward and lifting his hands to rest them on her hips. She allowed her crossed arms to fall. He pulled her to him. In slow motion, she allowed herself to be gently tugged into the haven that was his body. She closed her eyes and felt warmth, comfort, and the now-familiar flickers of heat that built quickly between them. It was as if there were banked coals that were stirred to flame anytime they touched. The panicky feeling faded. Desperate to keep it at bay, along with other thoughts, she lifted her gaze, took a long look into his green eyes, and brought her lips to his. She threw herself into the kiss. The flickers flared into a wild heat. In moments, they were tugging at each other's clothes.

* * *

MORNING SUN SLANTED through the windows that faced the bay, warming the wood on the stairs and floor. Hannah made her way downstairs. She had woken tangled in the sheets with Luke curled behind her, one arm thrown across her hip. It had been early, yet the sun was already brightening the room. She had dozed off to be woken later by his lips on the side of her neck. They had made love yet again. A slow, lazy tangle. She felt fluid and boneless when he had slipped inside her. This morning had felt different than last night. Last night, she had needed to be absorbed into a vortex of heat and brought to the brink in her body. Anything to keep thoughts from intruding. Something had happened in the kitchen, and the feeling of panic that had welled frightened her. But this morning, the panic seemed a distant anomaly. Luke had held her close after she came apart in his arms seconds before he arched into his own climax. They showered together before he left to meet his brothers to do some work on one of their boats.

She walked into the kitchen, seeing a flash of Jessie's tail out of the corner of her eye. Luke must have let her out when he left. Once Hannah opened the door, Jessie trotted in and circled her, tail wagging and tongue flopping. Discovering that Luke had left her with a fresh pot of coffee, she sat down at the table, mug in hand and took a welcome sip. Flipping her laptop open, her e-mail announced with a friendly "bing" that she had new mail. She froze and remembered she might have a message from her possible sister. She hesitated to look, but forced herself. There was a response from the Emma she had e-mailed yesterday. She abruptly got up from the table and unnecessarily topped off her coffee. Standing by the counter, she looked over at her laptop, sitting innocuously on the table.

After a few more sips of coffee to fortify her, Hannah returned to the table and clicked to open the message before she backed out.

Hi,

It sounds like you might be my sister. Wow...I knew when I put this post up that I'd have to figure out how to respond if I heard anything. You left a number. Would it be okay to call? Let me know if and when it's okay to call. I have tons of questions, but

I'm not sure where to start. Thank you for responding to my post. Emma

HANNAH READ the words several times and then sat back. She took a sip of coffee and cradled the mug in her hands. Jessie came over and curled up by her feet. Before she lost her nerve, she replied to the e-mail, typing in her number since she had left Faye's yesterday. She kept it brief and decided on a few times to tell Emma to call. That way, she wouldn't be wondering all day when the call might come. Just as she was about to hit reply, she remembered to tell Emma that Alaskan time was four hours behind North Carolina. After hitting send, she sat still and tried to calm her heart. She was elated and terrified. The thoughts she'd so successfully pushed away through Luke last night came roaring forward. Getting up, she looked around for her cell phone.

She dialed Susie's number, wondering if Susie was up yet. Susie was more of a late sleeper than she'd ever been. It was just past eight now. It didn't surprise her when Susie didn't answer. She left a message, asking her to call back, and walked out onto the deck. Jessie dashed into the yard, sniffing like mad as if she hadn't just been out there. Hannah looked out toward the bay. The sky was dotted with clouds and sunlight shone down on the bay. She abruptly decided to head to the beach for a long run.

* * *

HANNAH RAN ALONG THE SHORELINE. The tide was out, so she could run in the firm sand by the water's edge. Starfish, seaweed, driftwood, and the occasional lava rock dotted the beach. A breeze blew in from the water. She breathed in the scent of saltwater and the earthy scents of tide pool life. A raft of sea otters floated in the distance. Jessie jogged along-side her, frequently stopping to investigate. Hannah pushed herself to run hard, welcoming her pounding heart, the steady pattern of breathing, and the strain and push of her muscles. She grounded herself in the sensations of her body.

After a solid forty-five minutes of running, she slowed to a walk as she approached the area where she'd parked. She was on one of the more remote local beaches. It was accessed by a casual parking area just off the road—really just beat down grass where locals parked when they wanted to get to this stretch of beach. A short, but steep trail down the rocky bluff landed on a lovely stretch of shoreline that offered a view of the water, the mountains across the bay, and Mount Augustine. If you didn't know a town was only a few miles away, you could be convinced you were in a deserted area. The high bluffs shielded views of anything but the ocean and the bluffs themselves. A good six miles or more away, the shoreline turned and the harbor and town came into view.

Hannah was sweaty and tired. Her heart gradually slowed as she and Jessie walked toward her truck. Jessie scrambled ahead of her up the rocky trail and leaped in when she opened the passenger door. When she closed the door beside her and turned the key in the ignition, she felt Jessie nudge her with her nose. She thought back to the day Luke showed up at the house with Jessie and realized how much it meant to have Jessie with her right now. On a morning like this, it meant the world to have Jessie keeping her company in the unconditional way dogs could.

Hannah drove home with one hand on the steering wheel and the other resting on Jessie. She pulled up to the house to find Susie's car parked in the driveway. Susie and Cammi were sitting at the top of the stairs, cups of coffee with the distinctive Misty Mountain label in their hands.

Jessie ran to greet Susie and Cammi while Hannah followed more slowly.

"Hey there," she called.

"Hey yourself," Susie responded. "Got your message. I was in the shower. Since I was already meeting Cammi for coffee, we decided to bring you breakfast and coffee." Susie pointed to a cup sitting on the deck railing. "We thought about breaking in, but decided it was too nice out anyway. Just back from running?"

Hannah nodded and wiped her face on her sleeve. "You mind if I take a quick shower?" she asked as she walked up the stairs.

Susie and Cammi stood as she reached the top of the stairs.

"Of course not. How about you shower and we'll heat these up?" Susie asked, holding up a bag of bakery goods from Misty Mountain. "We grabbed some of the day old stuff, but we can make it seem fresh if we heat it up. Think we have a few ham and cheese savories and some muffins. Your coffee is a shot in the dark. That's what I thought you liked."

Entering the house, Hannah kicked off her shoes, aiming for the coat closet. "Sure. I haven't had anything to eat yet, and coffee from Misty Mountain is perfect any day." She waved toward the stove as they walked into the kitchen. "You know how to use the oven. Check to make sure the pilot light's on though. It's been finicky lately. I may need to have it looked at."

Hannah left Susie and Cammi in the kitchen while she went upstairs to shower. While she stood in the shower, steaming water pouring over her, she realized she hadn't mentioned anything in her message to Susie about the message from Emma. She wondered about bringing it up in front of Cammi and decided she didn't care. She needed to talk. Not to mention that she couldn't spend the rest of her life hiding what she learned, especially if she had found and met her sister.

Susie was talking on the phone when she returned to the kitchen. Cammi sat at the kitchen table, coffee in hand. Hannah sat across from Cammi, who pushed the remaining cup of coffee from Misty Mountain over toward her.

"Haven't seen you in a bit. Thanks for stopping by," Hannah said.

Cammi looked over, absentmindedly toying with the edge of one of the bright red place mats on the table. "I told Susie I wanted to get together soon. She thought this morning was a good time. I need to get your number myself. I have the old one here, but did the phone stay on while you were gone?"

Hannah shook her head. "No, I turned the service off. Don't know who has that number now. Kind of weird. We had it for years. Now I just use my cell. I thought about getting phone service for the house, but I don't really need it. I have the Internet and that's enough with my cell."

She recited her number while Cammi typed it into her phone, and then she put Cammi's in her phone. "I'll probably change it to a local number soon. I have a few friends from back East that I don't want to lose touch with, but I plan on staying here so it makes more sense to switch."

Susie hung up from her call and pulled open the oven just as the timer went off. "I think they need a little more time." She shut the oven and set the timer for a few more minutes. "Sorry about that. That was one of the owners at the brewery. He forgot to send one of the reports over yesterday." Susie pulled out the chair beside Cammi and sat down. "So what's up?" she asked as she brushed her curls back with one hand.

"Just giving Cammi my number."

"Yeah, I told her to make sure to get it. It's not like I need to be your social secretary. But...that's not why you called this morning. Was it just because?"

Hannah took a breath. "Nope, not just because. I got an e-mail back this morning." She looked to Cammi and back at Susie. "Have you mentioned anything?"

"No. That's your call," Susie said.

"Okay, I may be a little slow, but I can tell I'm missing something here. What's going on?" Cammi asked.

Hannah took another breath and plowed forward. "If I seem a little tense, it's because I am. A few weeks ago, I came across some papers of my mother's in a box she'd left with June during the remodeling project. It looks like my parents had a baby girl when my mom was seventeen and gave her up for adoption. I kind of freaked out, but Susie and her mom wanted to help, so Faye started looking online and found a post on a forum. She thought it might be Emma because the details fit, so I e-mailed her yesterday." She ended in a rush and stopped, her breath running out with her words.

Susie turned to Hannah and swiped a curl away as it bounced in front of her eyes. "I'm glad you told her. I honestly had no idea that's why you called this morning, but I don't think it will help for you to keep this to yourself, not from your friends, that is."

Cammi looked toward Hannah and held her gaze. Tears welled for a moment as Hannah took in her warm glance. Softly, Cammi said, "Oh sweetie, I'm glad you're home. Just tell me what you need."

Hannah looked across the table at Cammi with her air of sweetness, her open blue eyes and pixie cut giving her a childlike quality. Hannah had felt a brief rise of the panicky feeling that she experienced last night when she told Cammi what was going on, but it had faded much more quickly today.

"I'm okay, I guess. Since I found the papers, I've alternated between obsessing about it, being angry at my parents for not telling me, and trying damn hard to pretend like nothing's new."

"Do you think your parents wanted to tell you, but just hadn't figured out the how and when?" Cammi asked.

Susie piped up. "My mom told us that Janet had talked to her about it the same year Hannah left for graduate school." Susie caught Hannah's eyes. "Mom thought the whole situation was hard for your mom. I know that doesn't answer all your questions, but...I don't know. Can we see Emma's response?" she asked.

Hannah tugged her laptop over and opened her e-mail. "It's not like she had a ton to say. I wish there were instructions on how to go about this. I mean, what if she's not the right Emma? And how do I tell her, if it's the right her, that our parents are dead?" She pushed the laptop over to Cammi and Susie.

She sipped her coffee while they read. Susie looked over and asked, "Can I pull up the link where her original post was?"

Hannah nodded. "It might take a minute. I sent the e-mail from your mom's computer. I remember the name of the forum though." She recited the name for them while Susie started searching.

Cammi turned away from the screen. "Wow. This is a big deal. Remember how we all used to complain about not having siblings? We were all only children. I hated it when we were little. You might have a sister! That's just crazy to think about," Cammi said.

"You can say that again. Sometimes I'm excited and can't wait to find her. Other times, I just want to pretend I didn't find that paperwork and burn it. If I think about it too long, I start obsessing. I don't doubt that I'd like to find her. But I'm worried about telling her about our parents." Hannah put her coffee down and let her forehead fall into her hands.

"It's just…a lot. This was a giant detail my parents never mentioned to me. Sometimes I'm pissed about that, and then if I think about what it must have been like for them, I feel bad. It's just complicated."

"Found it," Susie said. "Look Cammi, here's the original post my mom found. What do you think?" She tugged on Cammi's sleeve.

Cammi started reading. "You two are forgetting that I haven't heard all the details yet. I'm guessing they fit what she's asking about?"

Susie turned to Hannah. "Go get the papers you found. If you're going to obsess over the details, we might as well have Cammi's opinion too."

"Be right back."

When she returned to the kitchen, Jessie plopped on the floor beside her chair. She handed Cammi the papers and petted Jessie while Cammi read.

Cammi looked back over at the computer, her eyes scanning the screen quickly. "Yup, the details seem to fit. Realistically, it doesn't mean it's her, but I definitely think it was worth e-mailing." She looked back to the papers she'd placed on the kitchen table. "Damn. Can't imagine what you felt like when you came across those."

"Oh, it was weird all right. I need to figure out what to say when she calls. Do I tell her my parents are dead?"

Cammi responded first. "You have to tell her. It'll be awkward if you don't. It sucks to have to tell her, but you have to. Don't you think?" Cammi turned to Susie.

Susie nodded. "I don't see a way around it. Hard way to get started, but it's too important to not tell her as soon as you can."

Cammi and Susie remained there for the next hour or so. They both offered to stop by if and when Emma called if Hannah thought she needed someone there. Hannah thought mostly she'd need someone to talk to afterward. As they got ready to leave, both taking off for errands and work, relief pulsed through her. Despite her worries about finding Emma and the call to come, she didn't feel alone anymore.

She waited on the deck as they pulled away, watching the dust from the road rise and fall behind the car as Susie drove down the hill. Jessie leaned against the railing, her head pushed into the small gap between the railings. It wasn't even noon yet. The sun was high in the sky. The wind was up over the bay, ruffling the surface of the water. Sun glinted against the waves.

CHAPTER 16

"*P*ass me that oil filter," Luke said.

"Right here, dude," Nathan responded.

Luke rolled his head to the side and reached to grab the filter from Nathan's hand. He was on his back on an old skateboard under his truck. He and his brothers tried to handle most basic car maintenance themselves, and his truck was overdue for an oil change. He quickly fitted and tightened the new filter in place. As he wheeled forward on the skateboard, he paused to push the drain pan out of the way. He refitted the plug for the oil pan and wrenched it in place before rolling the rest of the way out.

He slowly stood up from the skateboard and caught the end of it with the toe of his boot to tip it up. He passed it to Nathan who hung it on the wall of the garage where it would stay until the next one of them needed to crawl under one of their trucks. All three brothers drove trucks, the only variations being color and age. Luke's was dark green, Nathan's bright red, and Jared's black. Luke quickly washed his hands in the utility sink.

Nathan had already started to fill the oil and called over,

"Five quarts, right? No matter how many times we do this, I can't remember if it's four or five quarts."

"Yup, it's five," Luke said.

"We're down to two quarts after this. Need to pick up more," Nathan said.

Luke emptied the drain pan into a small barrel and replaced the lid. "Speaking of things to do, whoever does the next run to the recycling center needs to take this up and empty it."

"I'll head over in a bit," Nathan said, giving Luke's truck a pat as he closed the hood.

Luke started another pot of coffee as Nathan headed to shower. He looked out the windows toward the bay. Whitecaps were easily visible and gusts of wind created a misty spray across the top of the water, blurring the view. They had a guiding trip scheduled for tomorrow. He hadn't called Hannah about the trip and wondered how she was doing. It had been a few days since she'd told him that she'd learned her parents gave a baby up for adoption. He knew he was avoiding her, but he didn't like to think about it. Just the fact that he felt the need to avoid her made him uncomfortable. Part of him appreciated that she'd shared something so personal, while another part flinched at that level of closeness. His certainty about keeping relationships casual was faltering, and *that* bothered him.

Jared came through the front door, groceries in one hand and mail in the other. He kicked the door shut with his booted foot.

"Stopped by the post office," Jared said as he tossed a stack of mail on the counter. "Our box was stuffed. We gotta get by there a little more often. Seems like it gets away from us every summer."

Luke started sorting through the mail while Jared put away the groceries. "As usual, more than half of this is junk," he said as he stacked the legitimate mail in a tidy pile and separated the junk mail.

Jared grabbed a coffee mug and filled it. "Damn, I'm tired today. Not sure why."

"Because you work nonstop?" Luke asked.

Jared took a sip of coffee. "Maybe. Don't know. Summer's our busy season. It's not like I'm the only one around here working my ass off." Jared eyed Luke, his gaze pensive.

"What?" Luke asked.

"You're not gonna like it."

"Well, spit it out then."

"Talked to Dad the other day. You know they'll be up next week."

Luke nodded and gestured for Jared to continue.

"Dad mentioned that Mom ran into your old girlfriend, Cristina. Seems Cristina gave Mom some song and dance about how she misses you and wishes things had worked out."

"You're kidding me," Luke said, closing his eyes and shaking his head.

"Wish I was. You never told them why you two broke up?"

"No. Why would I? They don't need a breakdown. She's after any family that she thinks is a ticket for her. My God, was I supposed to tell them about her trying to get Nathan in bed after I wised up and broke it off?"

Jared chuckled, looking sympathetic, which was a rarity. "Well, she must be damn persuasive because I guess Mom's had lunch with her a few times and has it in her head that you didn't give Cristina a chance and that you've been pining after her."

Luke gritted his teeth. "This is such bullshit. It's been almost three years since we were together. Would love to say I can't believe she convinced Mom, but I've seen her in action. She had me hoodwinked right up to the end. I'll just give it to Mom straight. Only way to get Mom to back off."

"Mom won't like it, but that's the quickest way to end Cristina's crap," Jared said.

Nathan was just walking into the room. "Cristina? Are we talking about *that* Cristina?"

"Unfortunately," Luke said with a nod.

Jared quickly filled Nathan in. Nathan grabbed a cup of coffee before speaking. "Dude, she's nuts," he said. "Wait a minute—let me tell Mom about her. Only wish I could do it in person in front of Cristina." Nathan's eyes held a wicked gleam.

"Be my guest," Luke said. "Just promise me you'll talk to Mom soon, like today. I want Mom off this topic before she gets up here next week."

"You got it, man," Nathan replied. "You know though, you got an ace with Mom."

Luke raised his eyebrows in question.

"Hannah," Nathan said simply.

Luke almost choked on his coffee.

"Don't play dumb on this. Mom just wants to think one of us is going to settle down soon. Hannah's awesome. All you have to do is introduce them, and Mom will forget about Cristina," Nathan said. He added, "Hannah really is awesome, by the way. Maybe you should take notice."

"Gotta admit he's right. Hannah will throw Mom off this scent in a minute," Jared said.

Luke bit his lip, shaking his head. "I know he's right. Just not so sure I wanna introduce Hannah to Mom and Dad. I'm not even sure where we're headed. And now Cristina's nosing her way around again. Thought she'd have moved on by now."

"If she did, it didn't last. Probably called her bluff, like you did," Jared added.

Luke rolled his eyes. "Probably so." He looked over to

Nathan. "Cristina won't back off, so either I talk to Mom or you do. No matter what Mom thinks is happening with Hannah, I do *not* want to deal with more of this from Cristina." He shook his head and gritted his teeth. "Damn! Should've known she would find a way to worm her way back in."

Nathan shrugged. "I'll talk to Mom. Better she hears it from me that your old girlfriend tried to jump into bed with me only one day after you two broke up. Gotta say though —watch your back with Cristina. She was *not* pleased when I turned her down. Think she's pretty accustomed to getting her way with men."

"I know, I know..." Luke replied. "Give me a heads-up when you talk to Mom because you know damn well she'll be calling me right after."

Nathan headed out on errands, assuring Luke he'd call. Jared gave Luke a long look.

"What now?" Luke asked.

"So...how are you and Hannah?"

Luke didn't sense Jared was teasing for the moment. "Not so sure where things are headed. Not so sure I want to think about it too much." He shifted in place, restless just thinking about what lay between him and Hannah. The distrust that Cristina left behind was running high at the moment. Thinking about Hannah in that context made him wonder if he'd lost his mind letting himself get so comfortable with her.

"Don't want to think about it, huh? Better be prepared for Mom and Dad. Not sure how you can avoid it with them. They'll be here for a month. Either you pretend she doesn't exist, or you get over it and introduce her," Jared said. He took a swig of coffee. "I'm with Nathan. Hannah's awesome. Don't be stupid." With that, Jared turned on his heel and headed to the office downstairs.

Luke walked to the windows and looked out toward the

harbor entrance. Boats were moving out into the bay at a steady pace. He turned away quickly and called to Jared that he was headed to the harbor. He tucked some snacks and his iPad in his backpack. The sun was bright this morning. As he drove through town, he passed the post office and saw Hannah's truck. He thought about stopping, but hesitated and kept heading toward the harbor. Once he pulled into the parking lot, he made a call to Hannah. Despite his misgivings, he wanted to see her. He left a message about maybe meeting to walk Jessie later in the afternoon before getting together for dinner.

The wind he'd seen from the house was evident as he headed onto the dock toward their boats. Gusts of wind came in bursts with salty spray misting through the air. He tucked his sunglasses away and shook his hair away from his eyes. They kept their two boats docked side by side, so they could access them both easily when they were here. The dock swayed under his feet as he walked. Gulls circled and called above him. He watched an eagle dive low toward the water. He never tired of the wildlife reels that were part of the daily rhythms here. He reached *Iris* first. She was rocking gently in the water. He grabbed one of the mooring lines and pulled her closer to the dock, so he could reach the ladder on the boat's side.

Luke spent the next few hours sorting, cleaning, and organizing gear and making notes in his iPad about gear that needed repair or replacement. By the time he finished, it was late afternoon. The wind had eased. He sat on the bench seat in the guide boat and looked out across the harbor. Summers were busy in the harbor. The harbor had been quieter when he arrived, probably due to the wind, but the flow of people had picked up as the wind died down. He heard the distant chatter of conversations floating across the water and looked past the boats toward the mountains across the bay. He thought about taking Hannah over for a

weekend to a friend's cabin in Tutka Bay and then
wondered what he was thinking. While he was watching a
raft of otters floating close to the shore, he heard someone
call his name and turned to look over his shoulder. A friend
of theirs, Travis Wilkes, was calling to him from the next
dock over as he headed toward Luke.

Luke waved back and called over, "Yeah?"

"Haven't seen you in a bit. Just wondering how you
guys are."

"Busy. Jared's trying to decide if we're gonna make one
more commercial run this season. Otherwise, running
guide trips. You?" Luke asked as Travis approached
their boat.

Travis came to a stop and leaned against one of the
dock pilings. Travis was between Jared and Luke in age.
He was tall and lanky with wavy light brown hair. He
blended in with most of the men who frequented the
harbor, typically attired in well-worn T-shirts, Carhartts,
and XtraTufs, the only variations based on the weather
and how many layers were added. He'd grown up in
Anchorage and moved to Diamond Creek after finishing
college. He had a small guiding business and also worked
for the state Fish and Game. Luke had met him before they
moved up here. Travis used to pick up work doing
commercial fishing runs as a crew member. The year
before they moved here from Seattle, he worked on their
boat for a few weeks. He'd hitched a ride back to Seattle
with them, and they'd become fast friends. Travis was
quick-witted, down-to-earth, and on the quiet side. He
was active with local environmental causes and well read
on various political issues. Luke often turned to him for
the background on the sticky environmental issues that
frequently came up in Alaska, the latest being the contro-
versial Pebble Mine. After talking with Travis and doing
his own reading, Luke firmly planted himself in the camp

of most Alaskans, with the exception of the business crowd, in opposition to the mine.

He and Travis chatted for a few minutes. While they talked, he caught sight of Hannah walking down the dock toward them, her long legs striding and hair swinging. She came to a stop beside Travis.

"Hope I'm not interrupting." She looked at Luke. "I got your message and thought I'd just come find you."

"No worry about interrupting. Travis and I were just catching up." Luke caught Travis's eye and nodded toward Hannah. "Travis, this is Hannah. And Hannah...Travis."

Luke continued, "Travis is a fishing friend. Met the year before we decided to move the business up here." He caught Travis's gaze again. "If you haven't heard of Hannah, she grew up here and moved away for graduate school. Her parents passed away a few years ago." He wondered if Travis had heard about their plane crash. The news was well known around town, but Travis hadn't moved here until after it happened.

Hannah spoke up. "My parents were the ones who died in the plane crash on the way to Barrow about two years ago. Alaska may be geographically big, but it's small in other ways. News like that travels, and it was all over the papers here."

Travis nodded. "Heard about it. Sorry to hear it was your parents. The Grays, right?"

Hannah nodded in response, her expression neutral.

Travis continued, "I've heard about them from plenty of people here. They're certainly missed. Didn't put the pieces together until now, but I've heard about you too. Susie's a good friend, right?"

Luke silently thanked Travis for somehow conveying the right tone with his response and gracefully moving on. He watched Hannah's expression shift from guarded to the inkling of a smile at the mention of Susie's name.

"Yup. Susie's a good friend, one of the best. I would have figured you knew her if you knew Luke. Not to mention that she generally keeps tabs on everyone in town," Hannah said.

They spent the next few minutes talking generally. Luke watched Travis watching Hannah and felt a flicker of possessiveness, but checked it when he didn't sense anything other than general appreciation. He cringed inside when it occurred to him that he felt possessive—he didn't want to consider what that might mean about his feelings for Hannah. She was beautiful with her windblown glossy brown hair and blue eyes. In the time he'd known her, she'd started to lose the sense of grief that she'd seemed to carry with her when he'd first met her. She absentmindedly kicked the heel of her running shoe against the dock piling behind her and kept brushing her hair away from her eyes. Luke checked to make sure everything was locked up on the boat before hopping out to join them on the dock. They started walking toward the harbor parking lot.

Hannah glanced his way and asked, "Did you still want to go for that walk? Jessie's in my truck. I didn't bring her down here because I wasn't sure if you were still working."

Luke saw Travis's eyebrows rise in question and ignored it. "Would love to. Could use a walk with Jessie."

He turned to address Travis. "Susie sent me Hannah's way with Jessie. Remember that dog we found a bit ago?" At Travis's nod, he continued, "Needed to find her a home, and Susie said Hannah was the one. They both lucked out."

"Sweet dog. I met her one time when Nathan brought her down here. Glad you found her a home," Travis said.

They reached the end of the dock where it joined a boardwalk that connected to other branches of the docks in the harbor. Travis said his good-byes and headed back toward where his boat was docked. Before he turned away, he and Luke agreed to meet for coffee over the weekend.

Luke moved along with Hannah. He glanced sideways at her and caught her blue eyes looking back at him. He was getting used to it, but the effect she had on him was disconcerting. Just catching her gaze set a small fire ablaze within him.

Hannah had parked close to the path to the beach. His truck was over against the trees. Without thinking, Luke tucked his hand through her elbow and tugged her in the direction of his truck. In seconds, he pulled her close for a kiss behind the shield of his truck cap. Three days had been three too many. She didn't hesitate and opened her mouth to his. He stroked deeply with his tongue and pulled her flush against his body. He loved that her body aligned with his. Part of his brain reminded him that they were in a parking lot while his body sank into feeling. He slipped his hands under her shirt and felt the soft skin of her abdomen. He kept moving and deftly unhooked her bra so he could hold her breasts. They filled his hands perfectly. His hands couldn't get enough of her. His breathing was rapid and his erection pressed against his zipper. Her hands were traveling up along his back and shifted downward to press his hips against hers.

He felt her gasp into his mouth. He paused when he heard people walking nearby and gentled his kiss until he could pull his lips away. He leaned his forehead against hers and sighed against her lips. When he spoke, their lips were barely touching. "I don't want to stop, but it's busy here. We got lucky last time."

Luke felt her lips move against his, a tease on their own. "I know," she responded in a whisper.

Luke carefully released her breasts with a lingering caress and slid his hands around to hook her bra. He brought his hands up to cup her face and lifted his forehead away. He took a long look into her eyes and leaned forward for a brief kiss before stepping back. Her hands fell away from his hips when he stepped back. She leaned against the truck and sighed. She didn't look away, which was something Luke was growing to love about her. She let herself be in the moment and didn't turn away. He just watched her while she looked back. She reached up and ran her fingers through her hair, twining it into a knot on top of her head and pushing away from the truck.

"So how about that walk with Jessie?" Hannah asked. "She'd let herself out if she could. She loves coming to the beach."

* * *

WITH JESSIE SCAMPERING AHEAD on the beach, Luke reached for Hannah's hand. They spent an hour walking, interspersed with breaks to throw pieces of driftwood for Jessie to fetch in the ocean. Jessie finally started to tire just about the time the wind kicked up again. They turned back, the wind blowing into their faces. When they reached the parking lot, Hannah laughed ruefully at Jessie.

"I forgot to bring a towel for her. She'll soak the seat. Oh well," she said with a shrug. "You mentioned dinner in your phone message..."

"That I did," Luke said. "You need to get Jessie home. Want me to swing by in a bit? I have to drop some things off at the house first."

She nodded and brushed her hair away from her eyes. It had slipped out of the knot she'd tied and fallen in wavy disarray, curling against her neck and down past her shoulders in long waves. He looked into her eyes and pushed away the urge to kiss her. It seemed kisses in the harbor lot led to more than he bargained for with her.

"Sounds good," she said. "That'll give me time to get Jessie fed. We can eat in or out. I'm game either way."

"Let's decide when I get there," he said.

Hannah opened the passenger door and Jessie jumped inside. Luke followed Hannah around to the driver's side. Just before she closed the door, he leaned in for a swift kiss.

Luke walked to his truck and paused to look toward the bay. He kicked at a rock on the ground and tucked his hands in his pockets. Boats were rolling into the harbor. It was close to evening and most would be headed in now, especially with the wind picking up again. Soft quiet enveloped him when he closed the door to his truck. The distant sounds from the harbor were muted. He sat for a moment and thought about Hannah. He wondered about introducing her to his parents. He half couldn't believe it, but he wanted her to meet them. He had no idea what she'd think about it. As he drove out of the lot, he saw Travis entering from the harbor side and slowed to a stop at Travis's wave.

Luke rolled down his window. "What's up?" he asked.

Travis walked over to the truck. "Not much. Just confirming I'll call for coffee this weekend," Travis said and gave him a speculative look. "Rumor has it you've been dating Hannah."

Luke rolled his eyes. "Rumor would be right in that case. What's it to you?"

"Nothing—just thought I'd point out that she's beautiful and seems nice. You might want to give something other than casual a shot."

Luke lifted his eyebrows. "Relationship advice is not your usual gig."

Travis shrugged. "Maybe not. Just saying..." He winked and walked off. He called over his shoulder, "See ya this weekend."

Luke put the truck back in gear and headed toward the road. With the fire that just wouldn't go out between him and Hannah and Travis's comment, he felt restless and out of sorts. He wanted to feel in control of the situation, and he felt anything but. His focus lost, he had to slam on his brakes to avoid missing the turn for the road.

* * *

JUST OVER AN HOUR LATER, Hannah heard Luke's knock on the kitchen door.

"Come in," she called and heard the door open. "In the laundry room. I'll be right out." She entered the kitchen to find Luke seated at the counter petting Jessie, whose tail was wagging madly. Luke had cleaned up since they'd been at the beach. He wore jeans and a blue flannel shirt, but he'd ditched his boots for slip-on leather shoes, and his hair was damp from a shower. She took in his green eyes and slightly rumpled black curls. At his smile, her heart gave a hard thump in her chest. She leaned on the counter opposite him, trying to ignore the way her heart sped almost every time she saw him.

"It's going on six now. I'm not feeling too motivated to cook. How about you?"

He looked over and shrugged. "I'm game to head out for dinner. Do you want to leave right away?"

"I was hoping to wait for the washer to run first. Only takes about a half hour. I wasn't sure just when you'd get here, so I started it before I noticed the time."

Jessie walked over to her dog bed by the wall in the kitchen and curled up. Luke stood and walked around the counter. "In that case..." he said before sliding his arms around her from behind and bringing his lips to the side of her neck.

In seconds, she felt goose bumps rise behind the trail his lips left along her neck. She gasped as his lips traveled down. He pushed the neckline of her shirt out of the way to trace the edge of her collarbone. Hannah twisted around to face him and threaded her fingers through his curls as he tugged at the buttons on her blouse. He made quick work of her bra, while she let her hands fall for a moment to slip her arms out of her blouse. She sighed with relief when she felt his lips close over a nipple. He alternated between gentle sucking and pulling back to breathe on her nipples. She let herself fall into sensation. Her belly tightened inside, and she felt slick moisture build in her center. She pulled back for a moment and gasped one word. "Upstairs."

Luke's gaze held hers, his green eyes burning through her. His rumpled hair made him even sexier. Hannah felt bare and not bare enough. She wanted to be skin to skin.

"Okay...upstairs." He stepped back and followed her. Halfway up the stairs, she felt his hands on her waist and turned to face him. He had unbuttoned his shirt and pulled her close for a kiss. She reveled in the feel of her breasts against his bare chest. They stood on the stairs kissing deeply. He pushed his hips against hers. She gasped into his mouth as the friction of his erection pressing against her center set her nerves alight. She was so ready, she came in a burst against him. He slowly stepped up, holding her close as they gradually navigated up the stairs. His lips left hers only to tug at one nipple and then the other. When they reached the top, he knelt, and she let herself be pulled to the floor. Her back pressed against the cool hardwood, a relief to her hot skin.

They lay close on the floor. Hannah unbuttoned his jeans and slipped her hand inside to force the zipper down. She curled her hand around his erection. He sucked in his breath. She brought her hands away to help him push his jeans down. As he kicked them off his legs, he returned the favor by unbuttoning her jeans and caressing her through her damp underwear. She wiggled her way out of her jeans. They were both naked, save for their underwear. Luke slowed his hand and rolled to the side. He drew one hand slowly up and down the center of her body. She pulsed with readiness when he brought his warm hand down to cup her mound. He leaned forward and licked a nipple again. He rolled on top of her and gently teased her through fabric that was getting damper by the second. She thought she would lose her mind if he didn't touch her where she desperately craved it.

Luke paused for a long moment and held her eyes. "Please..." she said, not even clear what she was begging for.

He rolled off her again and hooked his thumbs on her underwear to slowly slide it down. She pushed at his and sighed when she held his warm erection in her hand, his skin silky in her grasp. He commenced to slowly tease her —long moments of kisses along her neck, soft blowing on her nipples, dragging a trail with his tongue down her belly and to the top of her mound. She was gasping for breath and desperate when she finally felt one finger and then another slip into her channel. He curled a hand around one hip and slowly brought the fingers of his other hand in and out. He paused long enough that she lifted her head to look at him. He leaned up on one elbow and held her gaze as he slowly brought his mouth down to the wet center of her. Her hips bucked against his mouth as he slowly began to lick and suckle; all the while his fingers slowly stroked in and out of her. Her mind clouded and dissolved into nothing beyond sensation. Her climax washed over her in deep pulses.

While she lay dazed, Luke brought his body flush against hers. Her muscles were still convulsing when she felt his large erection pushing into her. It was such a relief to be filled. Hannah sank further into the floor. She was boneless and caught only in sensation. She brought her legs up to clasp his hips, and he rocked into her. Her climax seemed never to end as sensation built from the last aftershocks into another wrenching climax. He threw his head back and pumped fiercely into her, coming into her in a final burst.

He slowly relaxed against her and shifted to the side so his weight wasn't fully on her.

They lay still for long moments, their broken breathing the only sound. Hannah slowly came out of the pool of sensation and turned her head to look at Luke. His eyes were closed, his dark lashes stark against his cheeks. She reached over and pushed a curl away from his forehead.

He opened his green eyes and looked at her. "Do you think the laundry's done?" he asked with a teasing smile.

She couldn't help but laugh. "Were you timing us?"

"No, definitely not. Time is the last thing on my mind when I'm inside you or close to it. Couldn't keep my hands off you, that's all."

* * *

HANNAH WOKE to the feel of the sun on her face and rolled to her side. She'd forgotten to close the curtains last night and sun splashed across the bed. Luke had left about an hour earlier. She had woken to feel his lips on her cheek and a whispered good-bye before he left to make it to the harbor in time to meet his brothers for their trip that day. She rested in the sun and looked out the bedroom windows, which faced the bay. She could see mountaintops and bright sun on the water. While she lay still, she heard Jessie's claws clicking against the floor, gradually coming closer. She felt a cool nose nuzzle her knees and looked down to see a wagging tail. She reached to pet Jessie, sliding her fingers through Jessie's glossy fur.

Hannah pushed herself up and swung her legs off the side of the bed. She remained there for a moment, still petting Jessie. She looked down at her feet and wiggled her toes, smiling at the sight of her purple toenails. Placing her feet into a sun-warmed swath of floor, she stood and headed for the shower. Jessie followed and curled up just outside the bathroom, a habit she'd developed. Hannah stood under the hot water pouring down over her and sighed. She loved a hot, steamy shower. She'd long ago conceded that if she had to choose between lighting and hot water, she'd choose hot water any day. She thought about Luke and last night. After sex on the floor, she had put the laundry in the dryer, and they'd headed into town for dinner. They'd gone to Sally's and run into various friends.

Luke had been his usual friendly, engaging self. Her eyes were drawn to him as if by a magnet. His almost black curls and green eyes made her feel childish in her infatuation. She had to admit that the pull between them wasn't wearing off anytime soon. If anything, the more time she spent with him, the stronger it became. She soaped her hair and tilted her head back. A long rinse later, she reluctantly turned the water off and toweled herself dry. For the moment, she wasn't fighting her attraction to Luke. Recognizing that caused a flash of panic because this just wasn't a place she let herself go, not in years.

Her mind swung to wondering about Emma while she got dressed. About the only thoughts that kept such thoughts at bay were those that included Luke. Emma had responded to her e-mail, but hadn't been able to call at the times Hannah had suggested due to her work schedule. She'd said she'd try to call later in the week. It was now firmly later in the week, and Hannah wished she'd asked for a more specific time. She forced her mind off the topic and went to the kitchen to start a pot of coffee. She had promised herself she'd do the dirty work of job searching today. She spent the next few hours updating her résumé and following up with references. She made calls to the Bay foundation, the Inlet Keeper, and Diamond Creek Conservation and followed up with a contact in Anchorage whom she knew through her parents. He was an old friend of her father's who'd sent her a note some time after their deaths.

199

They kept in sporadic e-mail contact. When he'd heard she was moving back, he'd offered to help her arrange some consulting work in the environmental field.

Hannah was just turning off the computer when her phone rang. Susie's number showed on the screen. Hannah answered, saying, "Hey, what's up?"

"Wondering if I can persuade you to keep me company for a trip to Anchorage."

"When are you going?" Hannah asked.

"Whatever two days work for you next week."

She laughed. "It sounds like you're banking on me going with you."

"I kind of am. It's a long drive alone. Plus, we used to go all the time, and it'll be fun to go together," Susie said, her tone cajoling.

Hannah didn't need to think about it. The trip would be fun with Susie, and she could meet with her father's friend about consulting options. At her assent, Susie promptly moved on. "You haven't mentioned it, but I have to ask...any word from Emma yet?"

"Just what I told you. She couldn't call when I hoped because of her work schedule. She said she'd call later in the week. Now it's later." Hannah sighed. "I'm trying not to think about it. I promise I'll let you know when I actually hear from her."

"I know, I know. I'm almost as impatient as you. What are you up to today?" Susie asked.

"Not much, other than getting stuff ready to seriously look for a job. I can't put it off much longer." They chatted for a few more minutes and agreed on the days for the Anchorage trip. Hannah took Jessie for a walk and headed to town for grocery shopping and a few other errands.

CHAPTER 17

*I*t was late afternoon when Hannah pulled into her driveway to find an unfamiliar car parked in the drive. It looked like one of the rental cars from the airport. Someone was sitting in the driver's seat. After Hannah stepped out and let Jessie out of the truck, a woman opened the door and unfolded long legs before standing. Hannah's heart stopped for a moment. The woman was as tall as Hannah was and had dark, straight hair that fell just past her shoulders, and blue eyes. She was dressed in jeans, slip-on leather clogs, and a bright blue blouse.

Hannah and the woman both stood still for a moment. Hannah felt like she was looking into her own eyes. Jessie broke the silence when she leaped in the air between them.

"Sorry about that. She gets excited," Hannah said and forced herself to continue to speak, extending her hand. "I'm Hannah."

The woman reached out to shake her hand and let go without speaking. She finally cleared her throat. "I'm Emma. I know I should have called, but I got this wild idea that I'd just come out here. When the plane landed, I started to panic because I didn't have your address. I only knew the town because you mentioned it in your first message. So I asked the guy at the rental car place, and he told me where you lived. Seems like Diamond Creek is a pretty small town. I hope it's okay that I just showed up..." Her voice trailed off, and she looked down at Jessie, who was sniffing at her shoes.

Hannah gestured to Jessie. "That's Jessie. She's crazy friendly." She paused and watched while Emma reached to pet Jessie. "Well, would you like to come in?" she asked, not sure what else to say, her manners keeping her afloat while her throat was tight and her stomach in knots.

Emma looked up and nodded. Hannah started walking toward the house and up the stairs, aware of each step and feeling fragile. Jessie and Emma followed her into the kitchen. Hannah busied herself for a moment, filling Jessie's water bowl and looking in the pantry. Her throat remained tight. She had a sense of certainty that Emma was her sister. She knew she needed to tell her right away that her parents were dead. She felt unmoored with no sense of how to navigate this. She walked out of the pantry to see Emma looking out the windows that faced the bay.

Emma turned back toward her. "Wow. It's beautiful here." There was a long pause as Emma just looked at Hannah. "I'm sorry. I've put you on the spot. I just...well... just wanted to meet you and figure out if you're my sister."

Emma shrugged and looked to the floor while she twisted a ring on her right hand. "I got swept up in this idea that I'd just come here and figure it out. Now that I'm here...it seems like it would have been better if we'd talked. I don't even know what your situation is, where your parents, and maybe my parents, are. That kind of thing," she said with another shrug.

Hannah forced herself to speak. "It's okay. I don't think there's a map for us. I promised myself that when you called, I'd tell you something right away. My parents died in a plane crash two years ago. If they were your parents... then it sucks for you to hear it this way. I don't want you to feel misled. I didn't even know I had a sister until a few weeks ago. And here you are...I don't know if it means anything or if I should even say this, but my gut tells me you're probably my sister. I'm sorry you had to hear about my, or maybe our, parents like this. I can't imagine what this is like for you." Hannah ran out of words and waited.

Emma stood before her, still twisting the ring on her hand. Jessie got up and walked over to stand by Hannah. As awkward as this was, she felt steadier now that she'd told Emma about her parents. She let the silence be for a moment and looked out the window. The sun was starting to roll down the sky. It had been bright and clear all day with a brisk breeze coming in off the bay. The sky remained cloudless, offering a clear view of the mountains, which were dark against the backdrop of the sun.

She glanced at Emma again. "Remember the part about no map? How about we sit down?" She gestured to the kitchen table. "Do you want something to eat or drink? I know you had a long day or more of travel. It's not quick to get here from North Carolina." She wondered why she'd offered such a mundane thing, as if nothing were happening, that a person who might be her sister hadn't just shown up at her house. She needed the mundane though.

Emma finally looked up. There was a sheen of tears in her eyes. Emma cleared her throat. "That would be good. I'm starving actually." She walked over to the table and sat down in one of the chairs that Hannah had pulled out.

Hannah quickly pulled out cheese and crackers and offered Emma her choice of drinks. The moments of mundane task chatter cleared some of the tension in the air. Emma nibbled on crackers and petted Jessie who had followed her to the table and sat down beside her.

Hannah pulled a cutting board out. She'd gotten a fresh loaf of bread from Misty Mountain earlier. She sliced it and transferred it to a plate. As she was doing that, she remembered that she'd left her groceries in the car. She glanced over toward Emma who was reaching for a piece of cheese and petting Jessie while she gazed out the window.

"Do you mind if I run out and get the groceries I have in my truck? I forgot they were in there when we came in."

Emma turned toward her. "Oh no. Of course not. Do you need help?"

"No, it's just a few bags. One trip should do it. Be right back."

In a few moments, she was back in the kitchen putting groceries away. She added some sliced deli meats to the plate with the bread. Bringing it to the table, she finally sat down with Emma. Emma appeared calmer. A wobbly smile flashed across her face.

"Thanks for inviting me in. I know it sounds crazy that I just hopped on a plane and came here. You could have freaked out that I asked the guy at the airport where you lived. I'm realizing that the fact you even let me in the door is really nice of you, all things considered," Emma said.

Hannah pulled at a slice of bread and shrugged. "I don't think it's crazy. I can see why somebody would. But… people looking for people do stuff like that. I mean, I think they do sometimes. You have a little more nerve than me. As for asking the guy at the airport where I lived—Diamond Creek is tiny and friendly," she said with a shrug.

A smile flickered again before Emma spoke. "I don't know if it's nerve. I don't know what to say about your parents. I have all these questions, and I realize it's probably not easy for you to have them gone." She paused and twisted at her ring again. "I think you might be right about your gut. Mine says that you're probably my sister too. I don't know what to do. I read all this stuff about people giving people space and some people needing DNA tests done before trying to get to know each other." Emma's voice trailed off, and she looked to Hannah.

Hannah spoke without thinking. "I'm sure we both have a ton of questions. I don't need a DNA test to talk. I'd be curious to do one, but...I don't know. Seems weird to not get to know each other until that happens. I'm not sure what to say about my parents. Do you want to see pictures or something?" she asked.

As soon as those words traveled out, Hannah wished she hadn't spoken. She had rarely looked at pictures of her parents in the years since they died. Every so often she did, but it wasn't easy. She wondered if sharing them with Emma would help in ways she hadn't expected. She stood to go get some from her mother's desk and looked to Emma before she stepped away from the table.

Emma gave a steady look back. "If that's okay, I'd love to see them." Again, she twisted the ring on her finger. "You know, this is just weird. When you said there was no map, that about sums it up."

Hannah nodded. "I'll get some pictures." She caught sight of the clear sky and the waves in the bay as she moved toward the stairs. Her chest tightened as she thought of how much her mother had loved the view here. When she reached the landing, she looked across the familiar room. The time she had been here had eased the feeling of her parents in every room. When she let herself, it was odd to forget they were gone. This room held so many memories, most of them of her mother puttering at her desk or sewing machine. The feeling of her mother's presence washed through her, a stroke to her soul. She pulled out some photos she'd tucked away in her mother's old desk, along with the legal papers about Emma.

Hannah brought the pictures to where Emma sat with Jessie lounging under the table nearby. They were all still in frames. One had sat on her parents' dresser for years. It was of her mother leaning against a dock piling after a morning out on the bay. Her dark hair was windblown, her blue eyes matching the sky. She wore jeans, rubber boots, and a red T-shirt. She looked as if she'd just been laughing. The moment captured her mother's careless beauty and joy. The photo of her father had been on her mother's desk for as long as Hannah could remember. It had been taken in the first year after they moved to Alaska. Her father was taking a break from unloading firewood from the back of a red truck. He was leaning against the tailgate, in jeans and a faded red flannel shirt with battered leather gloves held in hand. The corner of their house was to one side with the fireweed field in bloom on the other. His black hair was already salted with gray, his hazel eyes clear and direct. He looked tired, but happy, a wry smile on his face. The last photo she had brought down was of her and her parents, the summer before she left for graduate school. It had been taken at a dinner party at Faye's house. The three of them were posed on Faye's back deck, Hannah standing between her parents, their arms curved around her. Looking at the photo, she realized that was how she'd usually felt in her childhood, protected, held in the circle of the world her parents created for her.

Hannah laid the photos on the kitchen table. Rather than stumbling over words, she just let herself be quiet. She sat down and laid the envelope with the legal documents in it on the table. She watched while Emma looked, just looked, at the photos. The call of a raven filtered through the open windows, magpies following with their sharp chatter. A soft breeze came in through the kitchen. Jessie had wandered over to her dog bed and fallen asleep; she snorted in her sleep and kicked her legs. The fireweed was close to blooming in the side field. Small mauve buds were visible along the tips of the fireweed. In a week or so, the field would be awash in color. Hannah turned when Emma spoke.

"So these are your parents and perhaps mine. They look kind, lovely actually. You have your mother's eyes."

Hannah responded without thinking. "So do you. It's the first thing I noticed about you."

Emma nodded. "You know, my adoptive parents are wonderful. I had a great childhood. I just wanted to say that. They've been supportive of me trying to find my biological family. It's weird, though...part of me feels like I might be disloyal to them for wanting to know. But..." She shrugged and continued, "I just reached a point where I thought the possibility of regret outweighed anything else."

Hannah took in Emma's words and looked at the photos. "As strange as it was to find out I probably had a sister out in the world somewhere, I can sort of imagine what it was like to know you had other family somewhere." She reached for the envelope of papers and pulled them out. "I brought these down. This is what I found that led me to look for you. I didn't know about you before my parents died. My mom's friend told me she'd been trying to figure out how to tell me about it. But...they died before they did." Her throat felt tight again and she swallowed. "Anyway, I thought you might want to see these." She slid them across the table to Emma.

Emma carefully lifted the papers and read through them. Silence pooled in the room, broken by another raven call that was followed by more aggrieved chattering of magpies. After a few moments, Emma set the papers down.

"So you found these then?" she asked.

Hannah nodded. "Yeah, they were in a file box my mother had stored with a friend during some remodeling they had done here. To say the least, it was startling. Part of me was angry about it, mostly because I guess I thought they would have told me sooner. But...if I've learned anything, I guess it's that we all have complicated lives."

The sound of a car interrupted her. Looking out the window, she saw Susie's blue Subaru come to a stop behind her truck. Susie climbed out and looked toward Emma's rental car. Turning back to the house, Susie caught Hannah's gaze through the window. She waved and walked to the deck.

"Company?" Susie asked as she opened the door.

"It's Emma," Hannah said quietly, meeting her at the door.

Susie looked at her sharply and quirked an eyebrow. Her eyes were concerned and questioning.

"I'm okay," Hannah said, voice still low. "It's a surprise, but it's okay." Susie followed her to the kitchen. Hannah made introductions quickly. "Susie and her mom helped me look for you."

Susie added, "Mostly my mom."

Hannah chuckled. "Mostly her mom. She's the one that found your post on the forum." She looked between Susie and Emma.

Susie, who knew her so well, seemed to sense that Hannah was floundering and jumped in. "Wow, so you just hopped on a plane to Alaska?"

Emma nodded. "Pretty much. I wondered if it was a mistake for a bit, but now it seems okay. Just...weird...and kind of awkward."

Susie, being Susie, didn't hesitate. "Awkward is one way to put it. Long lost family, sister kind of thing. Yup, that's awkward. Not to barge in, but do you want to have dinner at my mom's tonight?" She looked to Hannah. "My mom just called about it, and I was over this way and thought I'd just stop by. We could go over together."

Hannah looked toward Emma and couldn't get a read on what she thought. "Sounds good to me. I need to walk Jessie soon, though. What do you think?" she asked, directing her question to Emma.

Emma looked up. "Okay. I don't want to impose, though. I know you didn't exactly expect to have company."

Hannah and Susie spoke at once.

"Don't worry about that," Hannah said.

Part of Susie's words crossed over hers. "Oh don't worry. My mom loves to smooth things over. She'll be ecstatic that you actually just showed up here."

Emma appeared to find Susie amusing, as a small smile tilted one corner of her mouth up. She looked to Hannah again and asked, "Are you sure it's okay if I go? I meant it when I said I didn't want to impose. I have to figure out where my hotel is and everything."

"You don't need to stay in a hotel. You can stay here," Hannah said and then paused when she realized what had come out. "I mean, it's fine if you want to stay in a hotel. But there's definitely room here. It's just me and Jessie."

Emma waited a beat before speaking. "Well...I don't know. I feel like a broken record, but I don't want to impose. You just met me. Are you sure it's okay to stay here?"

Before Hannah could respond, Susie spoke, gesturing toward Hannah. "If she says it's okay, then it's okay. I've known Hannah for years. I can see why this is weird for both of you. But...this is a small town—it's not unheard of to invite someone to stay, even acquaintances. We don't stand on ceremony around here."

"Susie's right. I wouldn't invite you if it weren't okay," Hannah said. "I won't pretend it isn't strange to be trying to figure this out, but you're welcome to stay here. The house is spacious. It won't be like we're on top of each other. That way, we can have time to get to know each other. I haven't even asked how long you plan to stay—if you planned that is."

Emma looked between Hannah and Susie, the barest of smiles passing across her face. "I hadn't planned much. My ticket is round-trip, but it's one of those where you can pick your return date later. I just have to pick it a week before I plan to leave." She shrugged. "Coming here...I didn't really think it through. I'd love to stay here if that's okay."

Hannah nodded affirmatively. "It's okay. Do you want to get your things from the car? You can do that while I get ready to take Jessie for a walk." She turned to Susie. "You think it's okay if I bring Jessie to your mom's? That way, I can take Emma to the beach with me and then we can meet you at your mom's."

"Of course you can bring Jessie to Mom's," Susie said. "That'll give Dante someone to play with for a bit. You two walk Jessie and do whatever else you need to, then we'll meet at my mom's. Say about six?"

Within a half hour, Hannah was driving to the beach with Emma. Jessie sat happily between them on the bench seat of the truck. Hannah provided brief commentary on the view for Emma, pointing out Mount Augustine and a few of the peaks across the bay. When she brought the truck to a stop in the harbor parking lot, Luke came to mind and she pushed the thought away. She had enough to think about without worrying about what to do about him.

The sky remained mostly clear with a few wispy clouds as the sun slowly made its way down the horizon. Jessie ran out ahead of them and circled back, again and again, joy radiating from her. The walk gave time for Hannah's emotions to settle. The experience of Emma's appearance was so astonishing, Hannah didn't know how to sort out her feelings. The sights and sounds of the shoreline were grounding, tugging her focus away from the confusion she felt about Luke, along with Emma's sudden presence in her life.

She and Emma exchanged questions as they moved

down the beach. Jessie offered breaks of comedy, once fruitlessly swimming after a raft of birds floating close to the shoreline. Emma found the seals that occasionally surfaced amusing, their sleek heads and round eyes curious and watchful. An eagle flew by and swooped down to the water, coming up with a salmon clutched in its talons. The shoreline was giving Emma a show of Alaska—a typical series of events on any given day on the beach here, but more likely seen only in the pages of *National Geographic* by most people.

Jessie eventually tired enough to stay by their sides, at which point they turned back toward the parking lot. Looking toward the harbor and out into the bay, Hannah could see a line of boats stretching into the distance, following the rising tide into the harbor. She caught herself trying to catch sight of Luke's boat and consciously looked away.

In their short walk, she'd learned that Emma was a social worker who worked with adolescents. Emma had gone to college and graduate school at the University of North Carolina, near her hometown of Raleigh. Emma had also shared that she'd recently separated from her husband of two years and started the process of a divorce. She openly acknowledged that the life-shifting process of making those changes had prompted her to finally look for her biological parents. Hannah sensed pain and shame from Emma around her divorce, but she didn't probe.

Emma had a steady stream of questions as Hannah drove toward Faye's house, mostly about Diamond Creek and what it was like to live in Alaska. Once they arrived at Faye's, Faye quickly got them settled at the kitchen table where she'd already laid out a plate of crackers, smoked salmon, and cheeses.

"So what did you think of the beach here?" Susie asked Emma.

"Beautiful. But of course you know that," she said with a smile. "Quite different from the beaches I'm used to in North Carolina. Do you ever get used to seeing eagles and seals?"

After a few moments of talk about the other wildlife Emma might encounter while she was here, Faye jumped right in, staring down the elephant in the room, in this case the fact that Emma had just shown up in Diamond Creek and then had to learn her possible biological parents were no longer alive. Faye turned that elephant into a less intimidating reality. She comfortably shared what she knew from Hannah's mother and drew Emma's story from her. While Hannah had learned some about Emma, she had avoided asking about her adoptive parents. Faye showed where Susie got her directness, although she presented a softer version of it. She simply asked what Emma's childhood had been like. Hannah was relieved to have Faye as a backup. While Faye cared about Hannah and had been close to her parents, she wasn't embroiled in the complicated feelings Hannah was experiencing.

The sun had fallen just above the horizon, becoming a deep red as daylight faded. Dinner passed in a leisurely manner. Hannah found that Emma was someone she'd like as a friend, regardless of the possible biological connection. She came across as reserved, but hints of a brash side showed here and there. Just the fact that she'd come to Alaska unannounced said something about her. She was guarded when discussing her pending divorce, and Hannah again sensed that the story behind it held a lot of power. The presence of Faye and Susie seemed to ease Emma's reserve on questions about Hannah's parents. Between the three of them, they offered as much as they could. To Hannah's surprise, Faye had even looked up the process for DNA testing if Emma and Hannah chose to do it. Hannah's feelings about the DNA testing were complicated. Part of her wanted to do it, just so she would know. With Emma now sitting in front of her, there was also a small fear about how they would handle it if the testing ended up showing that they weren't the sisters that they both had a feeling they were.

With Faye bringing the testing idea up, Hannah learned that she and Emma shared the conflicted feelings. They were able to laugh about it and ended up agreeing to go to the place Faye had located in Anchorage that would do the testing on-site. With Hannah and Susie having already planned a trip to Anchorage the following week, Emma would go with them and be able to see more of Alaska along the way.

The night ended with Hannah driving them home through the soft dusk, realizing that the days were getting shorter. Summer in Alaska had a timeless quality for a period, when the days felt endless and the sun barely set. Energy was high in those days, the light fueling a whirlwind of activity. That feeling shifted when the days began to shorten, and the sense that fall was on its way quickened. The high energy of summer—the long days and short nights —were a stark contrast to the winter, which inevitably came with its truncated days and much longer nights.

The ride back home was quiet. Emma watched the land-scape roll by, commenting only on the moon rising over the bay. After Emma went to bed, Hannah sat on the deck while Jessie explored the yard. The air was cool with a sharp bite to it. The moon and stars were bright in the sky. Ripples on the surface of the bay were visible with the moon casting a soft beam on the water. She wished she could talk to her parents now to ask them about what happened. In some ways, she understood their choice to give Emma up for adoption. She still struggled with not having known sooner that she'd had a sister somewhere and wished they could have met Emma.

Wind ruffled through the spruce trees while the moon rose higher in the sky. It was close to full tonight. Jessie eventually came to her side, jumping lightly onto the bench and turning to face the yard, apparently satisfied with her sniffing for the night. Hannah rested a hand on Jessie's back and stroked her. She wondered about calling Luke tomorrow to ask if he could take them out on the bay for a short trip. She didn't mean to turn Emma's visit into a tourist fiesta, but she did want to show Emma what had mattered to her parents. They had spent as much time as possible out in the bay.

A raven flew by the deck, its flight path low. The sound of wings softly beating the air passed by. Its shadowed form lifted up to land in a tree nearby. Jessie watched intently. Hannah gave her a last stroke and then rose. As she stepped into the house, quiet enveloped her. She walked upstairs, Jessie's furred paws clicking softly behind her.

CHAPTER 18

*L*uke stepped through the kitchen door, entering the house from the garage.

"Luke honey, it's so good to see you!" his mother said, approaching from the living room.

She enveloped him in a hug, stepping back to cup his face. "Look at you, just as handsome as ever."

"Good to see you too, Mom." Luke stepped back when his mother let her hands fall. "How was your trip?" he asked.

His mother, Iris, looked youthful in her midsixties. She was responsible for the black curls all three brothers had. Her black curls were long, glossy, and shot through with silver now. She also had the green eyes that Luke and Jared had inherited. She was tall and willowy, tending to dress in soft, flowing clothes of bright colors. Today, she wore a cream colored blouse paired with a gauzy blue skirt and an emerald green scarf over her shoulders. She loved jewelry and had wide silver bracelets on both arms, a choker with a large blue stone centered at her throat, and silver dangly earrings. She gave off a soft energy that could mask her strong personality. She had been involved in politics for as

215

long as Luke could remember, leaning left with her support of teachers' unions, of which she'd been a member throughout her career, and advocacy for human rights. The polite, sweet woman that came across was just one side of her. She had a steely determination and cared deeply about those she loved and issues that she believed in.

"Our trip was uneventful, which is how I like my plane travel," his mother said. "We're so glad to be here. I'm ecstatic we have a month with you boys."

Nathan stepped to Luke's side and handed him a beer. "Here you go bro," he said with a wink.

Luke knew Nathan figured he needed fortitude for this first evening. He and Nathan had both spoken with their mother after the news about Cristina's meddling. She had been furious that she'd been misled and bothered that Luke hadn't told her what happened sooner. He didn't know if she'd spoken to Cristina since then. He guessed he'd have to get through a few more conversations about it, which would lead right into how much she wanted him and his brothers to find someone. He sighed internally and took a long swig of beer.

His father and Jared entered from the stairs. His father, Matthew, looked just as youthful as his mother, albeit with almost entirely gray hair. His father had the bright blue eyes that Nathan inherited and had once had dark brown hair, which was now mostly white. He was level in height with Jared and Luke, Nathan the tallest by over an inch. His father stayed fit with running and biking. He wore jeans and a flannel shirt, practically a uniform for him.

After greetings with both of his parents, Luke helped get their luggage to the guest room, which was downstairs adjacent to the office with its own bathroom and a small sitting area. The next few hours passed quickly with he and his brothers just catching up with his parents. They broke apart as evening approached before they planned to head out for dinner to the Boathouse Café, his mother's favorite local restaurant.

Luke had gone to the office downstairs to check e-mail when his mother came out of the guest bedroom and sat across the table from him. Looking up, he saw a worried expression.

"What, Mom?"

"Why do you ask like that?" she asked, attempting to look unconcerned.

"Mom...you have that look."

"I have a look?"

Luke shook his head. "The one you get when you have something to talk about that you think I'm not gonna like. We all know the look. Trust me, if you think you've ever had us fooled, forget it. Spit it out."

Iris sighed. "I don't want to have to bring it up, but it's about Cristina."

Luke lifted his eyebrows and waited. His gut told him this was bad news. He'd been prepared for her to bring Cristina up again, but he sensed this wasn't just about his feelings. Rehashing his relationship with Cristina was the last thing he wanted to do because it just reminded him why it was smart to avoid serious entanglements. That train of thought led right to Hannah, and he didn't want to go there now.

"I hate to tell you this, but I made a mistake with Cristina," Iris said.

"So you fell for her song and dance; I already know that. No worries. You didn't know what happened. Now you do. I've let it go, so you can too, Mom."

If anything, his mother looked more worried. "It's not just that. I had this idea that I would surprise you and fly her up here while we were visiting."

Luke's gut clenched. "What?"

His mother's face fell. "Trust me. I know I screwed up. I

just had no idea that she'd behaved the way she did. I thought you'd really cared about her, and then when it ended, I didn't know the details. So…since you haven't been serious with anyone else since then—I mean, it's been over two years, Luke. I somehow thought it must have been because you hadn't gotten over her."

He interrupted her. "Mom, could you get to the point about flying her up here? Please tell me you didn't actually set that up, and that if you did, you canceled it."

She bit her lip. "I canceled the tickets I bought. But I'm worried that she's coming anyway. She knows where you are now, and when I called to cancel the tickets, the airline told me she had called to have them switched to her credit card. They couldn't tell me anything else." She paused and gave him a beseeching look. "I'm so sorry, Luke. I can't believe I fell for the story she gave me. I don't know what else to do. I told her that your father and I knew the whole story. My God, I thought she'd be too mortified to pull anything after that. But I just don't know…"

Luke logged off his computer and slowly closed it. He looked to his mother. As frustrated as he was and flat-out pissed at Cristina, he knew it had been an innocent mistake on his mother's part. "It's okay, Mom." He reached over and placed a hand over hers, which were clasped tightly on the table. "My fault for not telling you why I broke up with her. I just figured you and Dad didn't need the details. And the Nathan thing…we *really* didn't think you needed to know that part. It just confirmed what I eventually figured out about her."

He stood and walked to the windows, stuffing his hands in his jeans pockets. "By the time I broke it off with her, I knew she was pretty manipulative. I just hope she decides it's not worth coming here. Can't imagine she'd think I'd have anything to do with her. I made it pretty damn clear I wanted her out of my life for good after what she pulled with Nathan."

He turned toward his mother who'd joined him by the window. "Let's hope you're worrying about nothing," he said.

One side of her mouth tilted up in a wry smile. "Let's hope. I can't believe how stupid I was. Your father says I was blinded by how much I want grandkids." Her smile broadened at that. "And I still do. So I may have learned my lesson about Cristina, but don't go thinking I'll let you off the hook."

"On that subject...thought you'd want to know I'm seeing someone." Luke heard the words leave his mouth and couldn't believe he'd said them. He had admitted to himself that it would be awkward to avoid introducing Hannah to his parents, but he'd been trying to figure out how to do it and keep the impression that he was only casually interested in her. Funny how it was getting harder by the day to convince himself that was the case. It was too late to take his words back though.

"You are? Oh Luke, that's wonderful! Tell me about her. I would *love* to meet her," his mother said.

"I know, Mom, I know." Luke tucked her hand in his elbow and walked upstairs with her. The short time until dinner was filled with her questions about Hannah. Jared and Nathan enjoyed the rest of the evening immensely while Luke's father was gracious enough to keep his amusement to himself.

CHAPTER 19

"Oh my God," Susie said with a sigh.

"Oh my God, what?" Hannah asked in return.

"I forgot how slow you drive. At this pace, it'll take us an extra half hour to get to Anchorage."

Hannah looked over her shoulder when she heard a snort of laughter from Emma. She turned forward again. "I'm not *that* slow. I'm going almost ten miles over the speed limit."

"Yeah, but you can add another five or ten to that. It's not like the troopers patrol this section of the highway. In fact, I know that between ten a.m. and two p.m., no one's even on duty," Susie said.

"Do you want to drive then? I'm driving because you said you wanted a break to eat."

Emma's efforts to keep a lid on her laughter were to no avail. She finally burst out laughing. "You two are ridiculous! I can tell you've been friends a long time. Only old friends can talk to each other they way y'all do. As for the troopers, how would you know no one's on duty?" she asked Susie.

"Oh, you live here long enough and get to know how few of them there are and how big an area they cover. On this part of the peninsula, no one's on duty for highway patrol then. They have other things to do," Susie said. "I'm still getting used to the 'y'all' thing that you do. Does everyone in North Carolina say that?" she asked.

Emma shrugged. "Mostly. It's just easier."

The conversation throughout the ride continued in that vein with Susie teasing, Emma occasionally losing the lid on her laughter, and Hannah tolerating Susie. As she drove, Hannah again recalled the last drive with her mother on this road and the argument they'd had about her trip to Costa Rica. She wished she could take back some of the things she'd said, but if she'd learned anything since her parents died, it was that only the future was malleable. She glanced in the rearview mirror and saw Emma looking out the window. It had only been a week, and she was still trying to get a sense of who Emma was. Her manners were impeccable, which masked a lot. She was quiet most of the time, but Hannah sensed a determined quality to her. She also had a streak of impulsiveness—her trip to Alaska showed that. Aside from learning about what led her to search for her birth family, Emma had let slip a few clues that her divorce was messy.

Despite Susie's prediction, they made it to Anchorage about when they'd hoped. Just after Hannah drove by Kaladi Brothers, Susie insisted she turn back. Kaladi Brothers was a popular local coffee business in Anchorage and a few other Alaskan communities.

"I'm crashing from my morning dose of caffeine. Kaladi is my favorite, and Emma needs to go too," Susie wheedled.

"I'd love to stop for coffee. I've never heard of Kaladi Brothers though," Emma said.

Hannah changed lanes to turn into a side street to head back toward Kaladi Brothers. "It's a local business. They roast their own coffee beans, sell those, and also have a few coffee shops, only in the larger communities in Alaska."

"They're not quite as good as Misty Mountain, but they're definitely my fave when we're in Anchorage. Plus they have good bakery stuff," Susie said.

Hannah pulled into the parking lot and noticed that Title Wave had relocated near Kaladi Brothers. Title Wave was a massive used and new bookstore.

"Okay, since I turned around to get here, it's only fair that we also stop in at Title Wave. I didn't know they moved here," Hannah said.

Susie sighed dramatically. "Okay, we'll go by there too. We can bring coffee in, right?"

"Think so," Hannah replied.

Susie turned sideways to face Emma in the backseat. "Hannah is a book nut. Always has to go to whatever book-store is nearby."

Kaladi Brothers was much as Hannah remembered it— bright colors, local artwork, and the usual mix of people that made up Alaska: women attired in funky fashion and outdoorsy gear, and businessmen in suits sharing tables with fishermen in jeans and scuffed boots. A smile bloomed in her heart. She'd missed the distinct blend of anything and everything in Alaska. Just like in other areas, there were certainly cliques of people that naturally meshed. But there was more mix and match here. One rarely encountered a street of houses that matched or groups of people that all looked like they came from the same place.

The smell of coffee and bakery goods pervaded the space. There was a low hum of conversation in the coffee shop. They ordered coffees and snagged a table. Hannah looked around the room again, her gaze coming back to rest on Susie and Emma. She still couldn't believe Emma was here. Hannah was glad they'd had some time together before the DNA testing. Her feelings about that were still mixed. Now that she'd met Emma, it would be all the more difficult if it turned out they weren't sisters. Their connection was tenuous and fraught with the complex feelings they each carried.

They had scheduled an appointment for tomorrow morning to go in for the testing. They would have to wait a week for the results. Emma had arranged to stay for a few days past when the results would be in. Hannah was riding waves of memories of her parents some days. She felt comfortable talking with Emma about them and wanted to share, but it brought up so much. In some ways, it was healing, as she'd pushed these memories so far away during the days of her deepest grief. Yet the experience also brought up the confusion, anger, and sadness she felt at never having had a chance to talk with her parents about the daughter they gave up. She was learning that death left many loose ends behind.

Hannah looked across the table again. Susie sat quietly, a rare moment for her. Brown curls framed her face. She caught Hannah's gaze and winked, the corners of her mouth tipping up. Emma was quiet as well, which was not so rare for her, although Hannah didn't know if that was how Emma was when she wasn't in a new place and trying to get to know someone who might be her sister—that on the heels of learning her possible biological parents had died before she had a chance to know them. Despite Hannah's own internal challenges, she realized that Emma's position was just as fraught, if not more so. Emma's blue eyes, so similar to her mother's, were looking toward the artwork hanging on the wall. The monthly display was of local photographs, many of Denali and other popular Alaskan attractions. Emma's dark brown hair hung in straight lines, curling only at the tips along her jaw.

Hannah saw her mother so clearly in Emma. Emma had a graceful sense to the way she carried herself and was almost precisely her mother's height, which was unnerving for Hannah. Aside from her mother, Hannah was accustomed to being much taller than most women. Having Emma around elicited visceral memories of her mother with her similar physical presence.

"This *is* good," Emma said, sipping her coffee.

"Told you," came Susie's quick response.

Susie had spent a lot of time with Hannah and Emma this week. It had gone unspoken, but Hannah guessed that Susie was going out of her way to be around for her sake. Susie's presence smoothed the unfamiliar edges of trying to navigate the situation. They stayed at Kaladi long enough for them to make it most of the way through their coffees and then headed to Title Wave. Hannah breathed deep as they walked into the bookstore. She loved the smell of books that filled the air. On her own, she could spend hours there, absorbed in books. She knew this afternoon wasn't the day for that, but she still managed to leave with an armful of books.

* * *

THE NEXT MORNING, Hannah found herself up much earlier than Emma and Susie. She'd managed to ignore her anxiety about the DNA testing the night before, but woke only to have the feeling sweep through her. She slipped out for a run in the park across the street from the hotel, jogging along a nearby path that circled a lake draped in mist. The sun inched its way up in the sky, piercing the mist in areas, creating soft halos above the lake. A pair of trumpeter swans drifted in unison in the lake. Trumpeter swans were endangered, yet the bird had a strong foothold in areas of Alaska. The pair was beautiful, their white feathers gleaming in shafts of sun as they drifted through. Birds could be heard flitting about the trees. Magpies, of course, announced their presence, chattering loudly. Hannah caught sight of a few, the colors on their wings iridescent in the sun, green and blue flashing through the air. A stellar jay flew past her, its deep blue feathers standing out in the gray light.

She ran through her anxiety, trying to burn it out of her system. When she'd started running cross-country in high school, she'd discovered the power of running to pull her mind off its wheel. Running was a meditation of sorts. She didn't run with an iPod, as many did. She enjoyed the quiet of morning and sank into the sensations of her body, her legs pushing into the ground stride by stride, the heat building the farther she ran. She loved to tire herself to the point that exhilaration flowed through her, the fabled "runner's high." Some insisted the alleged high was a farce. She didn't really care about the biological mechanisms of it; all she knew was that when she ran hard enough and far enough, her body brought her mind to a grounded place, and she was flooded with a soft energy.

Hannah wondered if her experience with running had unconsciously pushed her to figuratively run from relationships the way she had after her breakup with Damon and her parents' death. She was starting to realize running only delayed the emotional reckoning she was facing now. She was relieved she'd returned to Diamond Creek when she did. In her time away, she'd felt unmoored from herself, lost and unable to find an anchor.

The sun had burned the mist off the lake by the time Hannah circled back along the path to run along the other side of the lake. The swans still floated in the center of the lake. Her anxiety had dissipated along with the mist. The pounding of her heart slowed with her steps. She was sweaty and tired, but her mind had ceased its run on the invisible treadmill of anxiety.

* * *

WHEN HANNAH quietly opened the door to the hotel room and stepped inside, she heard the shower running and saw Susie seated on the couch in the sitting room area, still in her pajamas, her curls tousled and her knees tucked against her chest with her chin resting on top. The television was on with the volume low, a local morning news show playing

Susie turned her head to the side, not lifting her head from where it rested on her knees. "Figured you'd gone for a run. I told Emma you usually went even when you weren't home. Don't know how you do it."

Hannah shrugged. "Habit, that's all. Plus, I like it once I get going. How are you this morning?" she asked.

"Still waking up. I'll be better after a shower. Do we need to flip a coin for who gets to shower next?" Susie asked.

Hannah laughed. "No. I can wait. You're quick enough that it won't matter."

"And then we go to Kaladi, right?"

"Of course! You know I need my morning cup of coffee. Emma banks on it too."

* * *

SUSIE ZIPPED through morning traffic to Kaladi. Hannah ordered coffee and a muffin. Next thing she knew, she and Emma were seated in the waiting room of the place Faye had located for them. Susie chattered about her speculation on Hannah's job options. While the testing had become a massive event in Hannah's mind, it was uneventful. She and Emma were swabbed in their cheeks and sent on their way with assurances that results would be in within the week.

Emma glanced to Hannah as they walked out together and spoke. "Well, that was silly to worry about. Now we wait for the hard part." She smiled tentatively.

"I know. I worked myself into a tizzy at points over just getting the damn test done," Hannah said, pushing the swinging door open into the hallway that would take them back to the waiting room.

"You too, huh? I tried not to worry, but it was hard. I'm realizing this next week will probably be worse."

Hannah turned to look at Emma. For a split second, she could have convinced herself Emma's blue eyes were her mother's. It wasn't just the color; it was the shape and something else indefinable. Hannah blinked and batted the feeling away, reminding herself her mother was long gone and Emma might not be her sister. "Yeah, I'm guessing this week will probably be worse. At least for today though, we have a few things to do to keep us busy."

Emma stopped in the hallway and touched her hand to Hannah's elbow. Hannah turned into Emma's gaze. "Thank you. I know this is a weird situation. It means a lot to me that you've included me in your world for a week or so," Emma said. She let her hand fall.

Hannah felt tears well for a moment and then subside. She took a breath. "You don't have to thank me. I'm glad you came, strange as it's been at times." Her eyes took in the hallway around her. The hallway could have been any hallway in hundreds of medical offices. It was tiled with nondescript whitish tiles. The walls were a soft cream color. There was one painting hanging on the wall, a vase of flowers that created a spark of bright color in an otherwise sterile space. There was a poster to one side, listing the signs and symptoms of a stroke.

Hannah looked back into Emma's blue eyes and smiled ruefully. "Let's go. Susie has us booked for the rest of the day."

* * *

ON THE DRIVE back to Diamond Creek, Hannah rode in the back and recalled her solitary drive south when she finally returned home. She no longer felt infused with aloneness. They'd spent the rest of the afternoon shopping, returning with enough groceries for months. Susie kept up sporadic commentary for Emma, pointing out various landmarks. They stopped early in the trip at Portage Glacier for Emma to see a glacier up close—the translucent, almost glowing, blue ice appearing ethereal.

Once they made it to Diamond Creek, they swung by Susie's house first to help her unload her groceries. Susie returned the favor when she dropped them off. The chest freezer in the laundry room was close to full by the time Hannah placed the last item inside. She closed it softly and leaned her hips against the freezer, the quiet in the room enveloping her. The murmur of Susie's and Emma's voices in the yard was distant. She needed to call Luke. He'd kept Jessie for her while they'd gone to Anchorage. His parents had been due to arrive a few days ago. In the week that Emma had been here, as much as she wanted to stop thinking about him, her mind wouldn't obey and her body longed for him. He had come over for dinner one evening and met Emma. She'd wanted to ask him to stay, but she held back.

All three of them tired from the drive, they decided to head to Sally's for dinner. While Susie drove down the hill, Hannah pulled her phone out and called Luke. She got his voice mail, so she left a message letting him know they were back and that they'd be at Sally's. She tucked the phone in her purse and looked out the window at the familiar hillside. Susie was explaining to Emma the different types of salmon in Alaska. For a moment, tears welled. Hannah blinked them back. Being home long enough for a run to Anchorage for errands somehow cemented for her that she was truly back. The sights, sounds, and feelings that she'd only been able to consider in her memory while she was away were once again part of her daily life.

Fireweed was starting to bloom along the lower part of the hill as they approached the road that paralleled the shoreline. In open areas, the weed created swaths of color, a bright fuchsia with a hint of lavender. The seasons were stark in Alaska. In spring and summer, the shoreline was the harbinger of what would come at the higher elevations. The lower elevations brought slightly earlier growth and blossoming. Hannah figured that the fireweed that filled the field by her house would be in full bloom within a week or so. Come winter, the upper elevations led the way. Snow would fall there first. Everyone would keep an eye on the mountains across the bay for the first snows. Termination dust, it was called—the dusting of white on mountaintops, stark against the deep green of the spruce trees and rock that covered the mountains. Once snow coated the mountains and started to creep downward, it wouldn't be long before snow fell elsewhere.

She looked across the bay at the mountains and saw boats dotting the water, most headed toward the harbor. Glancing over at the post office parking lot to see who might be there, she saw Frank's truck and thought she should give him and June a call to see how they were doing. In minutes, Susie was pulling up at Sally's. It was early for Sally's to fill up, so they were able to snag a booth without waiting. Not long after they sat down, Cammi came over, her short honey-colored hair shiny and her eyes lighting up as she reached their booth.

"Hi! Can I sit for a minute?" Cammi asked.

Hannah slid over to make room. "Of course you can. What's up?"

Cammi sat beside Hannah and slipped an arm over her shoulders. "Not much. Just saw Susie's car, so I stopped in to say hi. How was Anchorage?"

Hannah shrugged. "The usual. We did errands. I met with my dad's old friend about some consulting work. I've got two places lined up to talk with. I think I'll actually be able to start working soon, other than just odd jobs. How have you been?"

"You know, staying busy making coffee. Summer's my money time. You know what that means...work every day." Cammi shrugged and turned to Emma. "How are you enjoying Alaska?"

Hannah had introduced them last week when they'd run into Cammi at the grocery store. She had taken Emma to Cammi's coffee truck the following day.

While Cammi and Emma were talking, a waitress had walked over to the booth. After they ordered drinks, Cammi turned to Hannah. "So what's up with your father's friend and work stuff?"

"He gave me some contacts and has two consulting jobs lined up for me. It'll take me a bit, but he thinks I can probably end up doing full-time consulting work, especially if I'm willing to travel now and then," she said.

"Explain to me what you'll be doing," Cammi asked. "I know you have your degree in environmental science, but I don't quite know what you'd be doing for consultation."

"It varies. Usually I could consult on projects, maybe building or something, when they need to assess the environmental impact in an area. I also might be able to help with assessing how to set aside areas to be protected, like when they set up the conservation heritage project here. If there are problems, say runoff affecting a nearby river, I can help with support on how to ensure they mitigate the effects. Are you bored yet?"

Cammi shook her head. Emma spoke up. "I'm not. I haven't heard much about your work yet, so I'm curious."

"Well, it's not quite yet my work—it's what I'm trying to make happen. Before I moved back, I worked for a wetlands conservation organization. It was a small nonprofit. They did a lot of educational stuff, provided consultation on building projects that were near wetlands, and helped identify areas that needed to be protected. That's the kind of thing someone does with a degree in environmental science," she explained.

Their waitress approached the booth with their drinks and took their order. Cammi decided to join them for dinner. Conversation moved on to local gossip. Cammi was usually privy to what was happening in town with her coffee truck being a popular stop when it was open in the summer months. Hannah looked around Sally's while they talked. The knot of tension that she'd held inside for so long was slowly unraveling since she'd been back in Diamond Creek. The pared-down décor of Sally's with its wooden booths and the low hum of conversation created a sense of familiar comfort for her.

Hannah took a sip of her wine and glanced toward the door. She wondered if Luke had gotten her message yet. She knew his parents were here, so she wasn't sure he'd be able to meet her tonight. As the thought passed through her mind, the door swung open, and Jared, Nathan, and Luke pushed through. All three looked as if they'd come straight off the water, still wearing rubber boots and sporting wind-blown hair. Her heart gave a thump and her belly fluttered. With Emma here, she hadn't seen as much of him as usual. If there was a usual in a new relationship, that is. He glanced around the room and lifted his chin with a smile when he saw her, dimples flashing. He tapped Jared on the shoulder and turned him in the direction of their booth.

Jared reached them first. "Hey there," he said with a brief nod. Hannah watched his eyes travel to Susie who merely took a sip of wine and nodded. She wondered if Jared ever relaxed. Of the three brothers, he came across as the most serious, rarely letting down his guard.

Luke and Nathan had stopped the waitress on their way and appeared to be ordering drinks. When they came over, they stopped at a nearby empty table and lifted it to place beside the booth.

"We're joining you all, in case you hadn't noticed," Nathan said with a wink. "Luke seems to think we've been invited, or I guess he has."

Susie piped up. "Luke was invited, and we'll say you and Jared are too, now that you're here."

Cammi got up and helped them situate the table and three chairs and gestured for Luke to take the spot she'd vacated by Hannah in the booth. He slid in beside her.

"So, how was Anchorage?" he asked.

"Good. The usual errands. How are your parents?"

She had to focus to think with the heat of Luke's thigh resting against hers. She looked over at Emma who was telling the others how much she'd enjoyed seeing the Portage Glacier up close.

"Parents are good. They're at the Boathouse tonight. Mom loves it there and wanted a date with Dad, so we took off on a short fishing trip this afternoon." He gave her a long look. "What are the chances I could have a few hours alone with you tonight?"

Her heart sang, and she ignored the voice inside that told her not to get so excited.

"Pretty good. You probably can't stay with your parents here, huh?"

Luke shook his head. "It's not like I can't. Just that you don't even want to know how far my mother would run with that. Okay with Emma here?

"I'm pretty sure she knows we're grown-ups," Hannah said with a smile.

"I know, I know. Just didn't want to take away from your time with her," he said. He changed topic. "Jessie did great this week; she's had even more fun since my parents got here—more hands to pet her."

"Thanks for taking care of her," Hannah said.

"Anytime. Although I'd rather not have you gone for too many days." Luke paused and looked away before glancing back to her quickly. "Not easy for me to admit, but I missed you."

Hannah's heart kicked up, and she looked at his profile. "I missed you too." She was startled that Luke had said what he did and just as startled that she'd responded as she did. The feeling was true, but she had honed the skill of not letting any man matter this way. Vulnerability spiked through her.

The moment passed, and they were drawn into the conversation with the others. The rest of the evening passed quickly, filled with food, drinks, and company. Hannah looked around Sally's while they were eating. She could picture her father talking with friends at one of the tables in the center of the dining area. He'd often met with friends after work here a few times a week. Sometimes he would play music with his band of friends on the small stage in the bar area. Her mother didn't go to Sally's as often as he did, but she often came when he played. Hannah recalled evenings when she was much younger. Her mother would bring her along when her father played music. They usually sat in one of the booths along the wall in the bar area with a friend or two of her mother's. Hannah would manage to stay awake for maybe the first hour or so and then doze off, allowed to lie down on the booth seats with a blanket draped on top of her or balled up into a makeshift pillow.

The visceral experience of those memories felt simultaneously distant and near; the years between then and now felt outside of time. Her mind returned to the present, Luke's thigh still warm against hers. He'd rested one hand on her leg, his thumb absentmindedly stroking her leg.

Catching Susie's gaze, she flushed when Susie winked. She wasn't quite ready to admit it, but Susie's hunch might have been right. The group broke up not long after. Susie agreed to take Emma home while she and Luke went to get Jessie to bring her home.

CHAPTER 20

*H*annah leaned against the deck railing at the house. Jessie was running wildly around the yard in the dark. Night was coming earlier every day now with the long summer days fading fast. Time seemed to race in Alaska as summer wound to a close; endless days rapidly became shorter. One sensed the quickening of winter, as fall was a blink here, not a true season. Snow would fall as early as October, nights coming early and slow summer sunsets a distant memory. Hannah thought back to Jessie's reaction when she'd arrived at Luke's house with his brothers. Jessie had leaped in the air and circled her excitedly. She'd tried to kneel down to greet her, only to have Jessie almost knock her over in excitement. His parents hadn't returned from dinner yet, so she hadn't met them.

She felt Luke's arms slip around her from behind. His body lined up behind her, and heat radiated through her from head to toe. She sighed and leaned her head against his shoulder.

"Did I mention it was good to see you?" he asked.

J.H. CROIX

"Maybe, but you can say it again if you'd like," she replied, her lips curving into a smile.

"It's good to see you," he said with a small laugh.

She felt his laugh through to her toes. After they'd let Jessie out, she'd hollered a greeting to Emma who was already on her way to bed. Emma had waved from the upstairs landing before turning toward the guest bedroom.

"How were the past few days?" she asked.

His shrug lifted her head slightly, and she brought it up and turned in his arms to face him. He stepped back just enough for her to turn and kept his arms looped around her waist. "Busy with work, and then our parents got here. I should warn you—they want to meet you."

She experienced a moment of hesitation. She had considered that she'd likely meet them, but it represented something more concrete than she was ready for with Luke. "I'd like to meet them," she heard herself saying, not so sure how she felt about it.

"I guess we hadn't really talked about that. If it's not okay, you can say so."

Hannah thought for a moment about what it would mean to meet Luke's parents. Despite her mixed feelings, she wanted to meet them and that surprised her. "It's okay. I want to meet them." Her answer was bittersweet because it also reminded her that she'd never have the chance to introduce him to her parents. Her thoughts were interrupted by a growl from Jessie, accompanied by a loud rustle in the yard. Luke looked over her shoulder toward the yard. Turning in his arms, she could make out the shape of a moose on the edge of the yard, just where the lawn met the field of fireweed. It was a young male, its antlers outlined in the dark. Jessie ran onto the deck and stood beside them. They heard the moose snort and paw the ground and then saw his large shadow turn away and amble into the fireweed. The moose made a soft swishing sound as he walked

238

into the field, the fireweed and other greenery brushing against his sides.

Hannah looked down to Jessie who stood at attention beside them, staring into the dark field. "Well, Jessie seems to know how to handle herself with moose. If she ran into any before, it hasn't been since she's been with me. It can get dicey when dogs chase moose."

Luke followed her gaze to Jessie. "Good thing. Doesn't surprise me though; she's a smart girl."

Hannah reached down to stroke Jessie, who was still staring into the yard but had relaxed enough to sit down. She leaned her hips against the deck railing. "Back to your parents...I won't pretend it doesn't make me nervous to meet them. But I'll get over it," she said with a shrug.

"They won't bite. But just be aware that my mom's been on the hunt for one of us to produce grandkids. No matter what we say, she can't get off it."

"I see," she said. "You can't be their only target...there's three of you."

She felt more than saw his smile in the dark. "Well, no... but Jared insists he's never getting married, or even having a serious relationship. And Nathan...well...he's Nathan. Focused on having a good time for now. That leaves me. Probably wouldn't matter all that much except that I'm actually seeing someone—you, that is."

Luke leaned one hand on the railing. He was still standing close to her and tilted his head sideways. "Sorry to say, pressure's on me unless Jared changes his mind or Nathan settles down a bit. Not sure what my chances are on those fronts."

She laughed. "Probably not great. What's the deal with Jared insisting relationships are too messy? I get it with Nathan. He's still young, or living like he is."

One of his hands unconsciously worried at a loose nail on the railing. She loved his hands. They were strong and nimble—roughened from his life on the water, but sensitive.

Luke shrugged. "Jared's...well...orderly. Old story. He got burned pretty bad by a woman he took seriously; she ended up being involved with someone else on the side. Since then...He's a good guy, heart of gold. Thought maybe moving away would shake him out of this. Not yet...but all I can do is be his brother. He doesn't take well to being analyzed."

Hannah pictured Jared, so often serious, keeping to himself. The darkness thickened around them. A mist was blowing in from the bay, soft and cool against her skin. She shivered. Luke's hands cupped her arms and stroked up and down.

"We should get inside," he said.

* * *

As Hannah slipped between the sheets, weary from the trip, she was chilled in the way that being tired only exacerbates. It would take too many minutes for the heat to seep through her body. Luke's weight dipped into the other side of the bed. He rolled into her and enveloped her in a warm embrace. He shifted them so that he was spooned behind her, his heat radiating against her. She sighed into his warmth and felt her body begin to relax.

"You have to go home," she mumbled.

"In a bit," Luke said softly. He stroked her hair away from her cheek and let his arm relax against her side, his palm resting on her abdomen. The last thing she remembered was feeling safe and falling swiftly into a deep sleep. Sometime later, she woke to feel Luke's hand stroking along her hip. Heat pooled in her abdomen and down between her legs. Between slow strokes, he slipped the tank top she slept in over her head and pushed her underwear off. She dragged his boxers off with her feet. They made slow, sleepy love. Without words, they traced each other in the dark. He entered her in a slow slide, pushing into her from behind while they remained in the curled embrace that had lulled her to sleep. She pushed her hips against his and arched her neck as he nipped her gently. She came seconds after he entered her and felt him pulse inside of her and relax.

Hannah fell into an even deeper sleep, awakening to bright sun shining through the bedroom windows. She came slowly awake, recalling that Luke had whispered good-bye just before she'd fallen asleep again. The curtains were open. While the sun was warm, she could see that the wind was high—trees swaying and whitecaps visible on the bay.

She lay still for another moment, relishing the sensation of being home and being able to look out across the bay while she still lay in bed. She was naked in the sheets, the flannel soft on her skin. She heard the bedroom door push open. Jessie padded into the bedroom, her claws softly clicking against the wooden floor. Jessie rested her chin on the edge of the bed, her tail swinging slowly back and forth. With a few strokes for Jessie, Hannah pushed herself up and swung her feet to the floor. Jessie gave a quick lick to one of her feet and then moved to curl up by the bathroom door.

After breakfast and coffee with Emma, Hannah wandered onto the deck, Jessie racing into the yard. Fireweed blooms were starting to show in the field by the house. The patches of purple from lupine were almost gone now. Summer was waning as rapidly as it arrived in Alaska. Within a week or so, the field would be bright with fireweed, the last blooms of summer coming and going in a burst of wild color. Fall here was subtle in its show of color. Rather than swaths of color decorating the sky, the reds and yellows coated the ground. Alaska was heavily covered in evergreen, primarily spruce trees, which didn't turn colors like the hardwoods covering the East Coast. The ever in the green was a gift in the longer, darker days of winter and snowy white.

The sense of relief at being home, back in Alaska, was acute. The relief was followed by a wave of longing to be able to talk with her parents. She missed their presence. She thought of Emma being here, in the home and place they'd loved so. Although they'd never talked with her about Emma, she knew it would have meant a lot to them that Emma came to find them. The anger she'd felt at finding out about Emma had dissipated. What remained was a sense of sadness and loss at what her parents had missed.

Jessie meandered into the spruce woods behind the house. Hannah looked down the road toward the bay, the road appearing as if it tumbled into the water in the distance once it curved over the hill and down, disappearing out of sight. The wind was higher yet again. The day was clear, the sky empty of clouds. Whitecaps roiled the surface of the bay. Her mind traveled back to last night. Her feelings for Luke were sharpening, and she wasn't sure how to handle that.

She considered meeting his parents and decided she was just going to have to take it a day at a time. She also wondered what Luke felt about her. He'd told her he'd missed her, but she didn't know what that meant to him. As loving and attentive as he was to her physical needs, she didn't yet know how to interpret his feelings. He tended toward keeping things light, but she was so accustomed to looking for that, she didn't know if it was accurate. She laughed to herself. She didn't know how to interpret her own feelings, so it wasn't likely she'd know how to interpret his. A wave of anxiety crested inside her, her chest became tight, and her heart beat rapidly. She forced herself to take deep breaths, and the wave subsided. The more she tried to analyze her relationship with Luke and what it meant, the harder it was to just let it be. She pushed a loose tendril of hair away from her eyes.

A burst of magpie chatter brought her head around to the back of the house. Jessie came racing out of the trees, her tongue hanging out and her tail flying high as she ran toward the deck. A lone magpie flew above her and dove down. Jessie galloped up the steps and came to a sliding stop beside her. Hannah reached to pet her and watched as the magpie that had been chasing Jessie swooped up again, the sun catching the color on its wings, a flash of iridescent green and blue. The chattering quieted. Jessie's panting gradually slowed. Hannah finally stood and walked back into the house with Jessie following her.

CHAPTER 21

*A*lmost a week later, it was late afternoon when Hannah brought the truck to a stop near the mailboxes at the base of Emerald Road. Shifting into neutral, she rolled down the window to get the mail. Her mind was cluttered with thoughts about Emma and the fact that Emma was scheduled to leave in three more days, along with a pending dinner tonight with Luke's parents. Her mind skipped from one source of anxiety to the next.

Parking in the driveway, she sifted through the mail, her eyes landing on the name of the testing lab on the return address of one envelope. Her heart began to pound and her breath became short. She looked away, tucked the mail in her purse, and went into action, grabbing bags of groceries. As she came up to the deck, Emma opened the kitchen door. Jessie raced out and circled Hannah in greeting.

"Hey, let me help with those," Emma said, reaching to take some grocery bags from her.

Hannah set the pile of mail on the counter. Jessie curled up on the floor, smack in the center of the kitchen. As she emptied the grocery bags, she kept tripping over Jessie.

She shut the fridge and looked over at the mail, an innocuous pile of envelopes. Emma came out of the pantry. Hannah let her breath out. "Well...I think our results are here."

Emma looked up quickly. "Really?"

She gestured to the mail on the counter. "Take a look. Do you want to do the honors?" she asked.

Emma looked pensive and shrugged. "I don't know."

They stood there, looking at the mail for what felt like an endless minute.

Hannah shook her head abruptly. "Well, let's get it over with. This is one of those moments when Susie would be helpful. She'd have torn it open the second she saw it."

Emma chuckled. "That she would. Okay, let's do it."

Emma stepped to the counter and slid the pile of envelopes apart. Hannah stepped to her side as Emma opened the letter. Her throat tightened and tears welled as she quickly scanned the letter. For the gravity of the news, it was presented as simply as any lab results. She and Emma were a match. She took a step and leaned against the counter.

Emma folded the letter and put it back in its envelope. "Wow. That simple. Ever since I found out I was adopted, I wondered who I was related to." Silence fell between them. Hannah heard only the sound of Jessie's breathing and the muted sound of the wind blowing in the trees outside.

Emma's voice broke through the quiet. "Now I know. God, this is weird." She looked to Hannah. Her eyes were moist as she brought a hand up to wipe away a tear.

There was a tremor in Emma's hand. Hannah thought about the last two years, of feeling alone and disconnected, and about her mother's file box with the papers that led her down the path to finding Emma. She imagined thirty-three years ago when her mother gave birth to Emma and gave her up. She wished her parents were alive to know that

Emma's life had been good, from what Hannah could gather —and alive to know that Emma had wanted to find them.

Her gaze returned to Emma. She took in the blue eyes that reminded her of her mother and the straight dark hair that fell in clean lines to frame her face.

Hannah finally spoke. "I don't know what to say or do either. It's strange to have an answer. I realized the other day that I never asked you how long you were looking for my parents. I mean...our parents. We can say that now and know it's not a guess." Her heart and breath had slowed again. She felt funny, an odd relief washing through her.

"I looked for about a year," Emma said. "My parents were supportive; they always were. They gave me what information they had—not much. Back then, adoptions were different. Records were sealed and all that. My mom was a little worried when I decided to hop on a plane and come out here." Emma took a long breath. "It's still sinking in that my biological parents died before I had a chance to find them. You're the sister I never knew about—the bonus."

Hannah thought about what it would be like to wonder about another family, to start to look only to learn that the parents one wondered about were gone, gone in a way that they couldn't be found. The grief that she was still sorting out pierced through her. The secret that her parents carried must have been a heavy weight.

"You're the bonus for me too. It is weird..." She waved her hand around. "That I found out I had a sister, that Faye found your post, all of it...Aside from my own stuff around my parents dying, I'm sorry—I really am—that you didn't get the chance to know them."

Emma wiped another falling tear away. "I know...it's enough that I found you."

Hannah's cell phone rang. She looked around the kitchen to find where she'd set her purse. Another ring, and she found it on the table by the door.

Susie's voice came through. "Hey, what are you doing today? I need help getting an old desk out of my office. Sorry for the short notice, but the new one I ordered showed up early."

Susie's mundane request and familiar voice grounded her. She looked toward Emma who was pouring a cup of coffee and answered, "Not much really. I was just unloading groceries. I'm having dinner with Luke and his parents later. Plenty of time between now and then to help with your desk."

"You sound funny. What's up?" Susie asked.

Leave it to Susie to sense that something might be off. Hannah caught Emma's eyes and put her hand over the mouthpiece. She quietly asked, "Can I tell her?"

Emma nodded. "Of course!" She appeared puzzled that Hannah felt the need to ask.

"If I sound funny it's because we just got the DNA results. We're a match."

There was a long pause and then Susie's voice burst back through the phone. "Wow! I mean I thought you would be, but...it's official. Can I call my mom?"

"Oh yeah. Your mom deserves to know, seeing as she did most of the work."

"The hard part's over. How are you?" Susie asked.

"Feels weird. It's wearing off, though. Now we just carry on. Speaking of carrying on, when could you use help with the desk?" she asked.

"Sometime between now and when you have dinner with Luke and his parents, which I expect an update on by the way."

Hannah felt the smile in Susie's voice. "How about an hour? I'll see if Emma won't mind coming too."

"Works for me. I'm here all afternoon."

She hung up and looked toward Emma who was sipping coffee at the kitchen table. Hannah looked around the kitchen and into the living room. The home that had felt strange without her parents in it felt like home again, albeit in an altered way. The expectation of having her parents here had dissolved with the reality that they wouldn't and couldn't be here. She walked into the living room. Her hand brushed across the top of the woodstove, the soapstone cool and smooth against her palm. Stopping by the window that faced the bay, she counted the peaks across the water, softly mouthing the numbers. Jessie came to her side and sat down by her feet.

* * *

HANNAH'S SHOULDER was jammed against the wall in Susie's office. She craned her neck around the edge of the desk and saw Susie's curls bounce. She appeared to be shifting around to get out from between the wall and the desk. Emma was holding the other end of the desk, opposite from her.

"So, Susie, was the plan to get Emma and me to move this while you watched?" Hannah asked.

Susie shimmied out from her spot by the wall and grinned. "That wasn't the plan, but it only makes sense. The two of you have longer arms than me. I can barely reach around the edges."

Emma laughed and hoisted the end of the desk. Hannah pushed her shoulder away from the wall and followed suit. The desk felt like picking up a boulder. It was an old style office desk, constructed almost entirely of metal. With Susie giving verbal guidance, they maneuvered the desk out of her office, through the waiting area, and into the parking lot.

"Okay, where now?" Emma asked.

Susie pointed to the dumpster. "There. Just leave it over there. Do you need to rest for a sec?"

Hannah and Emma shook their heads in unison and kept moving. "Harder to pick it back up," Hannah said.

"If you say so," Susie said with a shrug.

Setting the desk down, Hannah gave her arms a shake and glanced at Emma.

"You're a good sport. We've got you running around town moving furniture," she said.

Emma dusted her hands on her jeans. "Don't mind," she said.

Susie arched an eyebrow at Hannah. "See. She doesn't mind helping."

"If I minded, I wouldn't be here. I should have known we'd do the hard labor," Hannah retorted.

Susie beamed at her and threw her arms around her. Hannah reflexively hugged her back. When she stepped away, Susie's eyes were glistening.

"You okay?" Hannah asked.

"Just glad you're home." Susie turned to Emma. "If you haven't figured it out, you've got a pretty awesome sister."

Hannah felt tears push behind her eyes.

Emma looked between them. "I've noticed."

Susie looked back and forth between them. "What gives? Is she coming back to visit more now?" she said, gesturing to Emma. "I mean, it's official. Maybe you should move here."

Emma looked startled. "I was actually thinking about it."

Just as Hannah opened her mouth to respond, a black truck pulled into the parking lot. Jared stepped out of the truck. Susie wrinkled her nose and waved in his direction.

Jared gave a return wave, walking toward them. "What's got all three of you here today?" he asked.

"They came to help me move that old desk." Susie gestured to the desk. "I got a new one. Maybe you can help set it up."

Jared appeared to be fighting off a smile and gave it up.

His white teeth flashed while he shook his head. "You know how to rally the troops, huh? Don't have much time, but I can help. Just came by to drop off the paperwork you wanted." He held up a manila envelope and handed it to Susie.

"Excellent," Susie said, taking the envelope. "The new desk is in the waiting room. I took the packaging off, but it's too much to move myself. I promise it won't be as heavy as the old one."

Jared shook his head, again trying and failing to keep his smile hidden. When he smiled, he reminded Hannah of Luke. They shared the same coloring, dark wavy hair, and green eyes. They returned to the office, Jared talking with Susie about accounting details for their business.

With Jared's help, they had Susie's new desk situated where the old one had been within a few minutes. Susie jumped and clapped her hands when the desk was in place. Hannah watched Jared, yet again, fight off a smile. He gave in to it, threw back his head, and laughed.

Jared caught Hannah's eyes when he finished laughing. "So...hear you're meeting us for dinner tonight."

She nodded. "Yup. To meet your parents." She tried to sound nonchalant.

Jared winked. "They'll love you. Don't worry."

That wasn't what worried Hannah. Rather, it was the fact that she'd gotten involved enough with someone that meeting his parents made sense.

Jared turned to Susie and Emma. "You're both welcome to come as well." He held Susie's gaze. "If you're not too busy rearranging, or did we take care of all that for you?"

That got him a roll of the eyes from Susie. "I really appreciate your help. As for dinner, I'd love to. What time and should I bring anything?" she asked.

"Six or so. Bring whatever you'd like—but no salmon. Need room for halibut in the freezer." He glanced at his watch. "Gotta go."

After Jared drove off, Hannah stood still in the gravel lot for a moment and looked around. Susie's office was smack in the middle of downtown Diamond Creek on Main Street. The street wasn't crowded by most standards, but it was lined with various businesses. Almost everywhere in town, a view of the bay anchored the area. Main Street ran parallel to the base of the hill where most of the residential part of town was situated. The back of Susie's office was against a wall of spruce trees that marched upward along a steep incline.

Hannah tilted her head back, her eyes tracking to the top of the hill. She heard Susie's voice and turned away from the hill. Susie and Emma were standing beside her truck. Hannah walked over to them.

"I was just saying to Emma that I didn't forget what she said right before Jared showed up. The part about thinking about moving out here." Susie looked to Hannah as she spoke.

Hannah thought about what it would be like to have Emma here for more than a few weeks. The whole situation was so new that her feelings had yet to settle. Yet she knew she'd love a chance to get to know Emma beyond a few weeks' time. Looking at Emma, she saw shades of her parents—her mother in Emma's eyes and her father in her smile. Considering how they would have felt to know that Emma would even consider living in Diamond Creek brought a hitch to her breath.

"What about that? Living here, that is?" Hannah asked.

Emma looked between them. She waited a beat, appearing to gather her thoughts. "Just that I thought about moving out here. It's so beautiful here. I..." She looked hesitantly to Hannah. "It'd be nice to get to know you more. I don't know how else to find a way to understand my biological parents. I can't meet them, so..." Her voice became small. "Maybe that sounds strange."

"It's not strange. Diamond Creek was really important to them. They were a big part of the community," Hannah said.

Susie nodded. "They were. Practically everyone knew them. I can't guess how to go about getting to know them, but…it's not crazy to spend time where they spent so much of their lives. Plus, we'd love to have you around more." Susie hooked her arm in Emma's.

"Well…I'm thinking about it. But I didn't know how you'd feel," Emma said, turning to Hannah.

Hannah spoke without thinking. "I'm with Susie on this one. I'd love for you to be here. How would your family feel about it?"

Emma didn't hesitate. "Oh, my mom and dad would be supportive. They'd like to come visit too. I've talked to them almost every other day since I've been here. They've always been supportive about me finding my bio family. I'm not saying they wouldn't miss having me nearby. Other than my parents…I'm not tied down. My divorce should be finalized soon."

"Well, just let us know when you'll be back," Hannah said. "Even if it's just for a long visit."

Susie, thinking the subject was settled, moved on to needling Hannah about meeting Luke's parents. Susie knew her well and likely noticed Hannah was nervous, but Hannah wasn't in the mood to talk much about it. She didn't bite at Susie's jokes, but was relieved Jared had invited Susie and Emma to dinner. Their presence would diffuse the attention on her.

CHAPTER 22

A few days into his parents' visit, Luke had invited Hannah to join them for dinner at the house. He'd spent hours obsessing over the best setting to introduce Hannah to his parents, the repetitive thoughts about it annoying him because it wasn't like him. Against the lingering annoyance about Cristina's meddling, he was mentally and emotionally caught in a tug-of-war over how he felt about Hannah. On the one hand, his preference for avoiding serious entanglements held sway, yet another part of him wanted to let go of that with Hannah. The fire between them was so strong, it overcame his common sense. If it was nothing more than lust, Luke didn't think he'd feel torn. But he genuinely liked Hannah. He couldn't even consider that his feelings might be stronger.

He leaned his head through the open sliding glass door onto the deck. Jared was readying the grill to start the salmon.

"When did Nathan say he'd be back with Mom and Dad?" Luke asked.

"Six," Jared replied, leaning to turn on the propane. "By the way, I invited Susie and Emma too. Saw them with Hannah when I went by Susie's office. Figured they would keep Mom a little distracted."

Luke snorted. "Maybe. Good idea though." He looked at his watch. "I'll head out to pick up Hannah—be back in a few."

* * *

LUKE HADN'T SEEN Hannah for a few days. When he walked into her house and realized she was alone, he took one look at her and pulled her close for a long kiss. Coming up for air, he tugged her into the living room. Clothes came off in seconds as they tumbled onto the couch. Thought returned only after Hannah was languid in his arms, both of them sated. He glanced around the room to see a trail of their clothes leading from the kitchen into the living room. Losing control like that was a first for him.

"Where's Emma?" he asked, in an effort to distract and gather himself.

Hannah lifted her head from where it rested on his shoulder to glance up at him. "I left her at Susie's office. We helped move a desk for Susie, and Emma offered to help rearrange more furniture. Jared invited them up for dinner too."

Luke nodded, a sense of comfort stealing over him as he lay with Hannah in his arms. It took a moment for him to realize he hadn't responded to her. "Oh yeah, Jared mentioned they were coming. Hope that's okay."

"I figure they'll take the pressure off of me," Hannah replied with a wry smile as she slipped out of his arms and stood.

Luke looked up at Hannah from where he lay on the couch. Sun filtered through the hair around her face, her blue eyes bright. His chest tightened just watching her, he longed to tug her back into his arms and lose himself in her. Abruptly, he pushed himself up, the activity of getting dressed breaking through his fevered thoughts. He pulled himself together, but was shaken on the drive back to the house.

The moment his mother laid eyes on Hannah, Luke knew he had a problem on his hands. Iris immediately took Hannah's arm and walked her over to the couch. Luke looked toward Nathan, who grinned at his discomfort. "Better you than me," Nathan said.

"Trying to decide if it's better to join them and fend Mom off, or if it'll only be worse with me," Luke said.

"Worse with you. If you're sitting right there, Mom's more likely to have visions of your wedding," Nathan replied with a chuckle.

Within a few minutes, Susie and Emma arrived together. Iris broke away from Hannah to greet them. Luke breathed a sigh of relief. His father was out on the deck helping Jared with the salmon grilling. He wandered out there, only to have his mother follow him out.

Iris came right to his side. "Luke, Hannah is lovely."

"That she is," Luke said, trying to keep it brief. He gritted his teeth, questioning his choice to introduce Hannah to his parents. After experiencing those moments with Hannah earlier—when he just couldn't seem to hold the reins of his feelings—he was irritable and out of sorts. The pressure of his mother's hopes was a tad more than he could handle tonight.

Iris gave him a pointed look. "You may be frustrated with me about Cristina, but Hannah had nothing to do with that. You *are* dating her, are you not?"

"Yeah, I am. Just don't want the third degree during dinner."

Iris waved a hand. "Your mother telling you Hannah is

lovely is *not* the third degree. But...I can take a hint. I'll leave you alone on this for tonight."

Iris stepped over to Susie and Emma, just as Hannah came through the door onto the deck. She was beautiful, and all Luke wanted to do was pull her into his arms again and forget about everything else. That thought was followed immediately with him wondering if he'd lost his mind. The pressure from his mother wasn't helping his already muddled feelings about Hannah.

"How you holding up?" Luke asked, stepping to Hannah's side.

"Just fine. Your parents are nice, not that I expected them to be anything but. I know you warned me about your mom, but she's not laying it on too thick. Not yet at least."

"Let's hope it stays that way."

The next hour or so passed uneventfully. Luke thought he was going to get through the night without his mother trying to marry him to Hannah on the spot. Then the fun began. Just as they were getting up from the table, the doorbell rang. Nathan strode to answer it. Luke had his back to the door as he rinsed plates at the sink.

"Uh...Luke, think we have a problem," Jared said.

He whipped around to see Cristina standing at the door. Nathan was clearly thrown as he just stood there, frozen in place. Cristina looked just as Luke recalled. Shoulder-length shiny brown hair, in a perfectly coiffed bob. She had dark brown eyes, shaded with a silvery color, and bright red lipstick. Her outfit was way out of place in Alaska. She wore a fitted black miniskirt over stockings with high-heeled black leather boots. She was tall, but not as tall as Hannah. Luke didn't feel even a spark of attraction for her and wondered how he hadn't always seen her for what she was —shallow and calculating.

Cristina stepped through the door without being invited

and strode into the kitchen, her heels clicking on the floor. Luke sensed he was about to witness a debacle and wished he knew how to stop it. Hannah stood by the table with Emma and Susie. They had all paused in the middle of picking up plates. His mother had gone to the bathroom. His father was just coming in from the deck.

Cristina, bold as ever, spoke first. "Luke, so good to see you. Don't know if you heard, but I ran into your mother recently. She invited me up here."

Nathan had shifted into gear finally and followed her into the room. "What the hell are you doing here?" he asked.

Cristina gave Nathan a cursory glance before bringing her eyes back to Luke. "I'm here for a visit. Iris seemed to think Luke might miss me," she said.

Luke felt sick to his stomach. He didn't want Hannah witness to Cristina's games, but he had no choice.

"You know damn well I didn't miss you. You also know that once my mom realized that you'd manipulated her, she uninvited you," Luke said forcefully.

Just as he finished speaking, Iris returned to the room. Gasping, her mouth dropped when she saw Cristina. "What are you doing here?" Iris demanded, stalking to face Cristina.

His father and Jared came to stand near Luke. Looking around, Luke realized his family had literally circled behind him with the exception of his mother who was facing down Cristina. Hannah and Emma were hanging back by the table, but Susie quickly moved to stand by Iris. Luke wanted a chance to pull Hannah aside and explain, but there was no time for that. He had to get Cristina out fast.

Cristina lifted her chin. "I'm here for that visit, Iris. The one you said might be a nice surprise for Luke."

Iris narrowed her eyes. "You lied. I had no idea that you were just a girl after our family's money. Luke had the decency not to bad-mouth you when he broke up with you. He also didn't bother to mention that you tried to seduce Nathan after that. And before you blame him for that, Nathan's the one that told me."

Cristina looked shocked at how direct Iris was with her. Luke knew she'd been fooled by his mother's polite exterior. He would have laughed were it not for the fact that he was more worried about what Hannah thought. Hannah looked guarded, her eyes shuttered.

"That was a misunderstanding on Nathan's part. He's the one that tried to seduce me," Cristina retorted, trying to spin the story to her advantage.

Luke thought his mother might implode. "You need to get out," Iris said, her voice raised. "You are not welcome here. And before you go thinking you can stay in town and try to weasel your way back into Luke's life, we will make sure everyone in town knows exactly who you are. This isn't Seattle—Diamond Creek's way too small for you to get away with how you treat people."

Luke groaned at what his mother said next. "I didn't know it when you tried to go through me to get to Luke, but he's with someone else," Iris said, waving in Hannah's direction. "Just like any mother, I just want my boys to be happy, so I made the wrong assumption when I didn't know he was seeing anyone. You leave him alone. He's happy with Hannah, and I won't let you interfere." Iris ended with an emphatic nod, her face flushed.

Susie stepped past Iris. She had to look up at Cristina and did so without hesitation. "I don't know all the details, but one look at you and I know you're full of it. She's right," Susie said, gesturing to Iris. "If you think you can hang around and try to find some other way to manipulate people here, forget it. Take my word for it, everyone in town will know you're bad news. I'll personally guarantee it."

Cristina seemed taken aback, but Luke knew her. Cristina wouldn't back down. The only reason he hadn't seen this ugly side of her sooner than he did was because she was getting what she wanted. The second that stopped, her brittle façade collapsed.

"Please leave, Cristina. Forget about this. We were over when I ended it. That's not gonna change," Luke said. He walked to the door that Nathan had left open and held it, waving his hand for her to walk through.

Cristina sauntered toward him and stopped in front of him. "So, that's how it's gonna be? You're pretending we never had something special."

"Because we never did. Now go."

Cristina took a long look around the room, her eyes lingering on Hannah in a measuring way. She narrowed her eyes when they returned to him. "We'll see if this is over."

"Just go," Luke said.

He didn't realize he'd been holding his breath until Cristina finally walked back out the door. He kept it open to watch her rental car leave the driveway.

* * *

A MERE FIVE MINUTES LATER, Luke saw yet another drama unfolding. After Cristina had left, just when Luke wanted to have a few private minutes with Hannah to explain the mess, it was impossible to get a moment alone. Iris had publicly apologized to everyone for the fiasco with Cristina, Jared and Nathan confirming the details. Susie was in the thick of the conversation, announcing she'd make sure the whole town would blackball Cristina if she tried to stay around. While Luke knew she was right to be concerned about that, he kept his eyes on Hannah. When he managed to catch her eyes, they were distant.

Just when he thought things were winding down, Iris sat

beside Hannah on the couch. Iris clasped her hands together. "Hannah, I'm so sorry. You have to know that this was my fault. I had no idea Luke was seeing you. Just like I told Cristina, he was nice enough not to tell his father and me what happened with her. I honestly didn't know what she was like. All I knew was she was the last girl that he seemed serious about. I meddled where I shouldn't. Please don't hold this against Luke," Iris said.

Hannah responded politely, but Luke couldn't really tell what she was thinking. He went to move to her side, but didn't get there before his mother spoke again.

"It's so nice to see Luke with someone like you. I just know you two are going to last. I can see it. I can't wait for the wedding," Iris proclaimed, her hand coming to her throat and her eyes getting misty.

Luke's father finally intervened. "Iris, honey, let this rest for now," Matthew said, attempting to get Iris off track.

Iris turned to Matthew. "I just need to make sure Hannah understands. I don't want her to blame this on Luke."

Hannah stood abruptly. "Don't worry. I understand," she said, a little too brightly. She strode toward the front door. "Susie, can you take me home?" she asked over her shoulder, not even turning to look.

Susie looked to Luke quickly and nodded in Hannah's direction. Hannah hadn't waited for Susie's response and was already out the door. Luke followed her. He found her standing by Susie's car, her arms folded tightly and her back to the house.

"Hannah," he began.

"Where's Susie?" she asked, spinning to face him.

"She's still inside," he said, thinking quickly, trying to figure out what to say. "Look...I had no idea my mom had talked to Cristina until last week. *No* idea. We broke up over two years ago, before we moved up here. My mom just… she's a little too excited about getting us settled and fell for Cristina's BS. Don't turn this into something it's not."

Hannah didn't respond at first. He wanted to keep explaining, but sensed that wouldn't help. She finally looked up.

"I can't do this. I can't. Between this mess with Cristina and meeting your parents," she said, waving her hands toward the house, "I don't even know what I want right now, and your mom is convinced we're getting married. I need a break."

She stepped back from him, her back against Susie's car. "Go back inside and let me leave. I'm not sure when I'll call you."

Her voice was high and strained. Luke wanted to pull her into his arms and tell her she didn't need a break, that this was just a giant misunderstanding. She had turned to look at the bay, her eyes unfocused and shuttered.

"Hannah…can we talk about this?" he asked.

Silence ticked by for a long moment. "Please go ask Susie to come take me home," Hannah said, refusing to look his direction.

Luke waited, hoping she'd at least look at him. When she didn't, he finally turned away and went inside, relaying her request to Susie. He hated that he had an audience for this fiasco. Susie and Emma left within moments, and there he was with both of his brothers and parents witness to the aftermath of mayhem.

His head ached and he just wanted to be left alone, but that didn't seem likely. He ignored them all and remained in the kitchen on the pretext of cleaning up. For a minute, he thought he might be allowed to have some peace. Just as that thought entered his mind, his mother got up and came to his side in the kitchen.

"Luke…" she said.

"Let it go, Mom."

"Honey, I can't tell you how sorry I am about this mess. If you want me to, I'll call Hannah and try to talk to her."

Luke could not believe she was proposing that, after everything that had happened. He wasn't prone to blowing up, but he did now.

"No. That's the last damn thing that I want you to do! I get that Cristina pulled your chain and you fell for it. But… my God, Mom! What the hell were you thinking telling her where I live and getting her a plane ticket? And on top of it, you just *had* to go and start spouting off about how Hannah and I were gonna last! You're talking about a wedding, and I've only known her for a little while!"

Luke tossed the dish towel on the counter and stalked into the living room. He grabbed the remote and turned the TV on. Not to be deterred, his mother followed him in there and sat beside him.

"Luke…That just came out. I know I shouldn't have said it."

"Iris, you might want to drop this now," his father said. Matthew stood and picked up her hand, moving to tug her away.

"But I just want him to know I'm sorry," she said, her gaze turned up to Matthew, eyes pleading.

"Think he knows that, hon. No need to rehash," Matthew replied.

Luke gritted his teeth, ignoring them both.

Iris wasn't to be dissuaded though. She put her hand on Luke's arm. Luke shrugged it off and stood.

"Listen to Dad, Mom. Back the hell off. Leave me alone, and for God's sake, leave Hannah alone. I haven't even known Hannah that long, and here you are pretending like we'll be together forever. And Cristina…your meddling brought her here. Just drop it."

Luke stalked out of the room, flinging the door to his bedroom open and slamming it shut. For good measure, he locked the door. Leaning his back against the door, he slid to the floor, the picture of Hannah's stony eyes running through his thoughts again and again.

CHAPTER 23

*H*annah walked along the beach returning to her truck, Jessie running ahead of her. The tide was coming in; waves had washed away her footprints from the start of her walk. Gulls circled above, calling loudly. A seal followed their trek along the shore. Its sleek head surfaced again. The seal held still in the water, round dark eyes curiously watching her and Jessie. After a moment, the seal lifted higher in the water and then dove under, its body curling against the waves.

A small stream came down from the highway, and a path followed alongside the stream, leading to a small parking area. The path was a short but steep climb up the bluff that hugged the shoreline. The sand gave way to grass and then fireweed, the bright blooms now fading, the ground nearby scattered with blanched fuchsia petals. As Hannah passed a small field, a bull moose stood on the far side. He watched her silently, standing tall in the grass, antlers silhouetted against the blue sky.

There was a bite to the air and had been for the past few weeks. Fall had taken hold, the faded fireweed a harbinger.

Fall would be brief with winter nipping at its heels. At the truck, Jessie promptly leaped in and curled up on the seat. Hannah leaned down and put her forehead against Jessie's soft furred face. Jessie rubbed against her and licked her hand.

Hannah drove the route home. What had felt peculiarly new for a while had resumed its familiarity. The landscape of Diamond Creek was tattooed in her memory. With her parents gone, the memory had altered. She saw the same sights through a different lens, a lens of loss and reconnection. The loss of her parents was an echo now. She hadn't stopped missing them and figured she never would. It was just that it was no longer a pain she ran from, but a lesson in how love morphs with loss and what you remember of those you loved. She thought of Emma who had returned to North Carolina last week.

Her thoughts traveled to Luke and the last time she'd seen him—last week at the dinner with his parents. The restless feeling she'd been so accustomed to before her parents died had been flickering since that night. She figured Luke thought she was upset about Cristina. Oddly enough, after she'd had a little time to think, it was clear to her that he'd had nothing to do with that. It was his mother proclaiming that they were destined to last that propelled Hannah into asking Luke for a break. While she didn't dwell on it much, she had taken one look at Cristina and thought she came up short if that were the kind of woman that attracted Luke. Cristina had been polished and crackling with charisma, all that Hannah wasn't. Hannah shook those thoughts away.

Hannah walked onto the deck, Jessie meandering through the yard. The sun was setting; dusk falling softly in its wake. The already crisp air was getting colder. Fall brought rich lavender streaks to the orange and red of sunsets. As winter set in, the sky would often reflect purple against the snowy mountains. Alpenglow, it was called. She looked to see if termination dust had fallen yet. The mountains remained free of snow, but she expected to see it creep downward any day now. She took a breath and caught a hint of woodsmoke. The distinct scent brought to mind the sensation of warmth and a fire in the woodstove, a haven in the cold, dark nights with the orange glimmer an anchor in the darkness. The night temperatures were already approaching freezing. With winter coming, she found herself missing Luke and wishing she didn't. She tried to push him out of her mind, failing completely.

Entering the house, Hannah looked around, quiet surrounding her. Jessie licked her hand and patiently looked up at her. She gave Jessie a stroke on the head and went to fill her water bowl. She considered building a fire in the woodstove, but the idea made her lonely. After demanding a break from Luke, she berated herself now, wishing she'd kept her mouth shut and hadn't overreacted.

Reconsidering that fire, she quickly tossed the last few pieces of wood from the wood rack into the stove and started a fire. The sky was darkening outside, only a few remaining streaks of color were left from the sun, which had made its bow not long after she came inside, sliding gracefully behind the mountains. A crescent moon rose behind those same mountains, a curved sliver of silver in the sky.

She ordered pizza for dinner and ate by herself in the living room. Firelight flickered against the hardwood floor, reflecting through the glass in the stove door. She curled up on the sofa, sipping wine and flipping through television channels, loneliness arcing through her. Jessie's presence eased the teeth of loneliness, but Hannah couldn't shake the fear that she might have just blown something good with Luke. That sense was at war with the restlessness that had protected her heart for so long.

She considered calling Susie, but Susie had already made it clear that she thought Hannah had overreacted. Her next thought was that she should call Luke, but she wasn't ready yet.

*   *   *

HANNAH STOOD in line at Misty Mountain, checking her watch. Susie was supposed to meet her, but she was a few minutes early. She ordered coffee and snagged a table, aimlessly flipping through the newspaper while she waited. Boots clicked across the floor and came to a stop by Hannah's table. Her eyes landed on a pair of shiny leather boots before she looked up, finding Cristina. Cristina was just as put-together today as she'd been the evening last week. Not a hair out of place, subtle makeup that enhanced her dark eyes, and bright red lipstick. She wore fitted black jeans and a quilted vest over a red silk blouse. Hannah felt mediocre in her jeans and fleece jacket. She brushed her hair back and waited.

Cristina arched an eyebrow when Hannah didn't greet her. A smirk followed. "So, this is how it's gonna be? As promised, your friend has made sure everyone in town knows me and thinks I'm a bitch. I won't be around much longer, but just thought I'd let you know that Luke's no angel."

Hannah remained silent, refusing to engage. Just as Cristina started to speak again, the door to the coffee shop opened, and Susie walked in. She quickly saw Hannah and Cristina and almost sprinted to their table.

"Heard you were still around," Susie said without preamble. "You obviously don't have enough sense to realize you're not wanted here."

"It's a free country," Cristina replied. "What's it to you, anyway?"

"You're messing with my friends," Susie said, her eyes dark with anger.

Hannah stood up by Susie. Every so often, she took pleasure towering over other women and now happened to be one of those times. She looked down at Cristina. "I'm not sure what your point is, but you're wasting your time."

Cristina looked up at her. "Woman to woman...just trying to do you a favor. I dated Luke for over a year. He dumped me after Nathan tried to come on to me. Before and since then, all he's known for is being a player."

Hannah felt flushed. As mixed as her feelings were about Luke, she knew he wasn't what this woman wanted her to think. Susie started to respond, her finger almost on Cristina's nose.

"What the hell are you still doing here?" a male voice asked.

Hannah turned and saw Nathan and Luke approaching, Nathan a few steps ahead. He stopped beside Susie, facing Cristina.

"This is bullshit. You know damn well Luke doesn't want you around," Nathan said, cutting Susie off.

Hannah almost laughed aloud when Susie high-fived Nathan. Luke came to stand beside her. "Leave her out of this," Luke said, gesturing to Hannah. "You played your games with my mom and you're pissed because you can't get your way with me, but you're not gonna drag her into this."

Cristina glared at Luke. "Believe what you want. I just thought she should know what kind of man you are."

Nathan cut in. "The kind who has enough sense to dump you when he finally saw you for who you were."

"If you think this is going to work, it took me about two seconds to see you for what you are," Susie said, her words coming out sharply. "A shallow, superficial bitch. It's none of your business what Hannah thinks of Luke, and she's

271

smart enough to see through you." Susie moved closer to
Hannah.

Hannah looked at Luke finally, having avoided doing so
at first. He looked angry, but distant. She knew the anger
was directed at Cristina, but she wasn't sure about the
distance. She turned to Cristina. "Why don't you just go? No
one wants you here."

Cristina lifted her chin, her shiny hair falling in perfect
lines as she moved. She shrugged. "Whatever. Just remember, I'm the one in this situation who has nothing to lose.
What reason would I have to lie?" She shifted her gaze to
Luke, her eyes cold. "Just doing a girl a favor." She turned on
her heel and walked out.

Hannah looked around and saw plenty of eyes on them.
She sat down and took a gulp of coffee.

"What is her deal? Why the hell is she still in town?"
Susie asked, directing her questions to Nathan and Luke.

"Because she likes to play games," Nathan said. "No other
reason."

"And she can't stand it when she doesn't get what she
wants," Luke said. "She doesn't really want me; she just
wants to be the one calling the shots on that." He grabbed
the closest chair and sat down abruptly.

Hannah felt him looking at her. Susie was still talking to
Nathan, venting her annoyance with Cristina. Hannah
finally lifted her eyes to Luke's. Just seeing his deep green
eyes brought a pang to her heart. His eyes were wary, but he
didn't look away.

"Sorry she dragged you into this. You okay?" he asked.

"I'm fine. If you're worried that I believe her—don't be."

A look of relief flashed across his face. "Does that mean I
can see you again soon?"

That old familiar feeling flared inside Hannah, the one
that made her want to run, literally and figuratively. On the
heels of that came the thought that Luke mattered to her—a

lot. She looked into his eyes again, but found she just wasn't ready yet.

She shrugged. "I don't know…"

The wary look returned to Luke's eyes. He turned away. "Okay…if you don't believe her, what's the problem?"

Hannah looked around the coffee shop, seeing they were surrounded by people. Susie and Nathan had walked over to order coffee. She wanted to explain to Luke that she hadn't asked for a break because of Cristina, but because the idea that his mother saw them as a couple that could last terrified her. She just wasn't ready to explain that now and certainly not here with an audience.

"Can you give me a little more time?" she asked.

He nodded; his lips tightened, a muscle in his jaw twitching. "Of course," he said tightly. "Call me when you're ready." He stood abruptly and walked to Nathan's side. She watched while they got their coffee and left, a sinking feeling inside.

Susie sat back down and gave her a long look. "So you sent him packing again, huh?"

"Susie, cut me some slack. I can't even think straight. I don't need you on my back."

Susie didn't back down, but then she never did. "Okay… you want me to cut you some slack. I will, but that doesn't mean I'll lie to you about it. It's plain as day that Luke's crazy for you. You won't admit it, but you're crazy for him too. I'll let it rest for now, but I'm not going to watch you throw this away over something stupid."

* * *

LUKE STRODE down the dock at the harbor. A brisk breeze blew in from the bay. Stepping onto the boat deck, he walked to the bow and looked out over the harbor. The sun had fallen behind the mountains, streaks of light reaching in its wake, pink and lavender swirling in the sky. He shivered and walked into the cabin. With a sigh, he sat down in a booth. He'd been in a crappy mood ever since the encounter with Hannah at Misty Mountain. Funny thing was he wasn't dwelling on Cristina's part, but that he wasn't sure why Hannah wanted a break. He reminded himself that he'd been back and forth about her, so it shouldn't matter to him so much that she wanted a break. He tried to resurrect the old lines he told himself about why he liked relationships to stay casual, but it wasn't working. He just kept thinking that he wanted her back.

He absentmindedly traced the grooves in the table's wood surface. Just as he was convincing himself he needed to pull himself together and leave, he felt the boat shift and heard someone stepping onto the deck. In another moment, Nathan opened the cabin door, looking in with a questioning gaze.

"Uh...what are you doing here? Just came by to get my rain jacket. Left it the other day." Nathan tucked the lone rain jacket hanging on the wall under his arm. At Luke's silence, he sat down, facing him on the opposite side of the booth.

"What's that look?" Luke asked.

"Just wondering what you're doing here."

Luke shrugged. "Hell if I know."

Nathan nodded, his eyes considering. "I got a hunch."

"Oh really?"

"Hannah. You've been a bear since she asked for a break," Nathan said.

Luke started to deny it and then gave up. "This whole thing's gotten under my skin. Between Cristina's crap and Mom putting pressure on me...and now I don't know what going on with Hannah."

Nathan gave him a thoughtful look. "So just admit she matters."

Luke rolled his eyes. "Dude...would I be saying anything about her if she didn't matter?"

Nathan shook his head. "Doesn't look like it to me. Forget Cristina's bullshit and Mom pressuring you. Forget your usual routine with women. Forget how pissed you are that Hannah asked for a break. Dude, she needs to know you're in love with her."

Luke took his words in and couldn't believe it was Nathan, of all people, telling him this. "You think I'm in love with her?" he asked incredulously. He recoiled at the thought.

Nathan nodded emphatically. "Yup. You are—even though you keep trying to pretend you're not. Maybe you should use our business name as your motto for Hannah – let her be the one that didn't get away."

Luke sat silently. His initial reaction was to tell Nathan he was full of it. But...a small part of him knew Nathan might be right. He just couldn't believe he was now in the position of figuring out how to persuade Hannah to give him a chance, and he sure as hell couldn't believe he was entertaining the idea that he might have fallen in love with anyone.

He looked over at Nathan, who looked amused. "Not funny, dude," Luke said.

"Oh, it's funny all right—me being the one to give you relationship advice."

Luke smiled wryly. "Yeah...wouldn't have predicted that." He sobered. "You might be right—about how I feel about Hannah. Just have to figure out what to do."

Nathan lifted his eyebrows. "You will. But don't think too much...just do." He glanced out the windows. "Getting dark. Takeout? Your choice: pizza or Chinese."

Luke looked toward the cabin windows; the sky was barely light now. His chest was tight, and he didn't want to think. "Pizza sounds good." He stood quickly and looked to

Nathan. Nathan stood and slipped his cell phone out of his pocket.

"I'll order. One veggie and one loaded with meat. Mom can think we're trying to be healthy with the veggie," he said with a wink.

Sometimes Nathan's willingness to let heavy topics lie was just what was needed, and now was definitely one of those moments. "Sounds good to me."

They climbed off the boat. It was close to dark with early stars winking in the sky. The sliver of moon visible shone against the water, the light rippling with the breeze that stirred the water. Nathan headed for the pizza place, and Luke headed home ahead of him.

If his parents or Jared sensed his inner turmoil later while they were eating, they elected to leave him be for now. He lay in bed that night, his mind revisiting his conversation with Nathan. He couldn't believe he might have stumbled into falling in love with Hannah. He had to find a way to talk to her. Sleep was slow to come.

CHAPTER 24

A few days later, Hannah finished a morning run, deliberately running until she was exhausted. She tried to scald her thoughts away with a shower so hot she could barely tolerate it. She was just coming downstairs when she heard tires on gravel. Susie's car came to a stop in the drive.

Susie came bearing coffee and savories. She didn't waste time once Hannah took a sip of coffee. "Okay, I told you I'd cut you some slack, but I'm backing out. You look miserable. Call Luke and cut the crap."

Hannah wanted to avoid this conversation. She felt tears well. "I'm not ready for a relationship. Why isn't that okay?"

Susie's brown eyes held her gaze, warmth showing through her frustration. "It would be okay if it wasn't obvious to me you're avoiding. I watched you do nothing but hook up with losers after you caught Damon cheating on you. You made damn sure not to date anyone that mattered. Whatever...I got it. Then you went the other direction after your parents died...dating no one. You finally find someone worth it, who's obviously into you, and you're on the verge of letting it slip away. That's just dumb. This, this break thing, whatever the hell that means, is pointless."

Hannah couldn't help but chuckle at Susie's earnest concern. She sobered quickly. "I'm confused. I really am. I just need a break to catch my breath and my thoughts. Is that okay?"

Susie gave an elaborate sigh. "No! After worrying about you almost every day since your parents died, I was finally starting to think you made it through and had someone for you and maybe Luke would help me not worry so much about you being alone." Susie teared up for a second and quickly shook her head.

Hannah reached a hand out to Susie's shoulder. "I know you've worried. And you have no idea how much that means to me. I got spooked by how great it was with Luke. Meeting his parents pushed me over the edge."

Susie placed her hand over Hannah's, which still rested on her shoulder. "You sure it's not that Cristina thing? 'Cause if it's that…"

Hannah shook her head emphatically. "No, it's not that. I mean the whole drama didn't help when we were at dinner, but I can see her for who she is. It's just…"

"Just that Luke's really great and you're freaked out. Get over it."

Hannah laughed against the tight feeling in her throat. "Give me a few days. Can we agree not to talk about it just for a few days? I need a minute to think."

Susie gave her another long look and then shrugged. "A few days. But that's it. Then we're talking again. For now, let's eat."

Susie was true to her word and let the subject of Luke and Hannah lie quiet. By the time Susie left, the sun was high in the sky. The fall sky was bright blue with wispy clouds high above, a brisk breeze blowing in from the bay. Hannah felt the bite of loneliness again. She held her cell phone in her hand for long minutes, thinking about calling Luke, trying to find a way to explain the confusion she felt.

CHAPTER 25

*L*uke came back from a run to find Jared leaning against the counter, cup of coffee in hand.

"Morning. Still some coffee for me?" Luke asked, leaning against the counter as his breath slowed.

"Plenty of coffee," Jared said, grabbing a mug and filling it for Luke.

Luke took a welcome swallow and looked around. "No one else up yet?"

Jared shook his head. "Dude, it's not even six yet. We're the early birds in the family. Dad'll probably show his face in a few." Jared gave him an appraising look before continuing. "Not that you mind. Mom's been beside herself since Cristina showed up last week and blew a hole between you and Hannah. Heard that Cristina booked her return flight finally. If she bothers you again, I'll make sure she gets a clue and butts out."

Luke took a long look at his older brother. Jared held his cards so close and was so private about personal matters that it was easy to forget that those who mattered to him mattered a lot. He could be ferociously protective of his family, and despite his avowed avoidance of relationships, his feelings ran deep.

"Appreciate that. No worry though. I'll deal with Cristina. Can't imagine she'll stick around much longer. Shouldn't have surprised me that she pulled this stunt...but it did. I'm just pissed that she dragged Mom and Hannah into it."

Jared waited a beat. "What's up with Hannah?"

Luke raked a hand through his hair. "Not much. She asked for a break the same night Cristina showed up. Saw her the other day...she says it wasn't because of Cristina. Just asked for more time. Hell if I know."

Jared remained quiet long enough that Luke looked over. "What?"

"Weren't even sure about introducing her to Mom and Dad...now you're cranky about a break. Just sayin'...thought you didn't want to get tied down."

Luke battled back at the bite of frustration that kept nipping at him. He was frustrated with Cristina for getting tangled up in his life again, annoyed with his mother for her well-intended interference, and irked at himself for not realizing how important Hannah was before this mess happened.

"Maybe I didn't for a while there. Wouldn't be so bad now," Luke said, looking to Jared. "Don't know if I can deal with trying to get Hannah back and get Mom to keep her nose out of it while she's here. I'd better not hear you blabbing to Mom about this."

Jared tilted his head, eyebrows lifted. "You think I'd do that? Dude, I'll owe you big-time if you tie yourself down first. Mom just might back off me and Nathan for a bit. Trust me, not a word from me." He lobbed a balled-up napkin at Luke's shoulder. It bounced off him and onto the floor.

Luke grabbed it off the floor and tossed it in the trash. "Okay, play interference for me when I need it then."

"Say the word, and I'll distract Mom and Dad for hours." Jared turned to go downstairs. "Off to do some work for a bit."

Luke took another sip of coffee and headed for the shower. He hadn't yet allowed himself to think too often about how much Hannah mattered, but saying it aloud to Jared made it real. He considered Nathan's point that he needed to *do* something about it and pondered where to start.

* * *

A FEW DAYS LATER, Hannah sat staring at her computer screen. She was supposed to be working on a project for a consulting job. Instead, she was ruminating over Luke. Despite her hope that a break would help resolve her confusion, she just missed him. She gave up and turned off her computer. As she stood, Jessie got up from where she'd been napping by Hannah's feet and followed her down the stairs.

Hannah looked out to the bay for a long moment. She wondered what her parents would say if she asked right now. She'd tried so hard to stop disappointing them after they died. Her poor judgment with men had haunted her. She couldn't seem to find the balance between letting go into something good and the careless choices she'd made. Her cell phone rang. She strode to the kitchen counter, hoping it was Luke. Susie's number flashed at her.

"Well, don't sound too excited to hear from me," Susie said in response to Hannah's lackluster greeting.

"It's not that. I just kind of hoped you were Luke."

"The ball's in your court. You already know what I think —call him," Susie said.

"I know, I know. I'm afraid he's pissed off."

"Oh my God, just call him!"

"Just give me a minute—I will. That's not why you called. What's up?"

"I'm taking the rest of the day off. Let's have lunch."

"You got it. Want me to meet you in town?" Hannah asked.

"I have to swing by the store. How about you meet me at my place in about an hour?"

Hannah quickly agreed, and they got off the phone. The call with Susie shook her off the treadmill of thoughts about Luke. She took the next half hour to actually work on the consulting project. Susie was waiting on her deck when Hannah pulled up.

"Made that call yet?" Susie asked while they drove to town.

At Hannah's slight shake of her head, Susie rolled her eyes. "Next week is the limit."

As soon as they walked into the Boathouse Café, Hannah was reminded of Luke. Just as she managed to stop thinking about him, he walked into the café with Jared.

"Well, well," Susie said. "Couldn't avoid him forever. It'll be more awkward if you don't say hi, you know."

Hannah glared at Susie. "I know that. It's not like I don't want to say hi."

Jared led the way to their table. "Hey there, didn't expect to see you two here in the middle of the week."

Hannah looked to Luke. He caught her eyes, but his gaze was guarded. She couldn't read what he might be thinking. She wanted to rewind back a couple of weeks and get a kiss from him, instead of the distant, subdued feeling she got now.

Susie had quickly jumped in and was chatting with Jared. They seemed comfortable pretending like Luke and Hannah weren't there. Hannah took a breath. "Hey there. How's it going?" she asked.

Luke held her eyes for a moment. She saw a flash of hurt and anger, but it disappeared as quickly as she glimpsed it. He nodded. "Fine. How are you?"

"I'm okay," was all she could manage. She wanted to tell him she was ready to end this stupid break, but she couldn't bring herself to talk about that here. She caught Susie's eye in a moment of desperation. Susie started asking questions that included Luke and Jared, moving the general conversation onto getting ready for winter and how the fishing season went. Hannah fell quiet and wished she had the nerve to ask Luke to talk outside. A few minutes more, and she watched Luke and Jared walk over to another booth. She tamped down the tight feeling in her chest and throat.

Susie looked over at her and shook her head with a soft laugh. "Call that man and stop this stupid break. You don't want a break and neither does he."

Hannah groaned and put her head in her hands. "Ugh. I need...oh I don't know." She lifted her head and swiftly brushed her hair away from her face.

Susie picked up one of the menus. "Get over yourself and call him." She started reading the menu and then looked back at Hannah. "Just remember that I'm only giving you a hard time because you're my best friend."

Hannah couldn't help but smile. "I know. I'm getting there." She glanced around, wishing there wasn't an audience here. "I forgot that it's impossible to hide in this town."

Susie laughed. "That it is. Order some food, and let's get on with the day."

* * *

LUKE SLID into the booth on the far side of the restaurant from Hannah and Susie. Jared sat across from him, gave him a wry grin, and shook his head. "So...still haven't called her yet? Maybe I will sic Mom on you after all."

J.H. CROIX

Luke rolled his eyes and grabbed a sip of water that the waitress had just brought over to the table. She took their drink order and left menus on the table.

"Could we just let this go for now?" Luke asked.

Jared laughed softly. "Sure. Just get over yourself and call her."

"Not so simple. Last thing I want to do is pressure her."

Jared gave him a long look. "Sure, that oughta work out well for you. Ignore her. You barely looked at her over there —not gonna help."

Luke glared at him.

Jared shrugged. "You got nothin' to lose except maybe she'll know that you give a shit."

Luke casually looked in Hannah's direction. He had line of sight to her side, so she couldn't see that he was watching. Her hair fell in loose waves. He missed the feel of her hair in his hands. He sensed that she was tired. The anger he felt a few minutes ago faded quickly. He wasn't ready to admit it to Jared, but he got his point. He looked away from Hannah and flipped through the menu, hoping to shake loose the tightness in his chest and throat.

* * *

LATER THAT AFTERNOON, Luke turned into the parking lot at the harbor. Stepping out of his truck, he heard the hum of activity coming from the docks. While the flow of tourists was slowing down as they entered into fall, activity in the harbor remained steady as some fishermen got their boats ready for winter trips and others were battening down for winter. He started walking toward the docks and took in the view of the water. Gulls called and flew along the shore. A few eagles were resting on dock pilings, looking regal and immense compared to the gulls.

Before he reached the docks, he heard his name.

Turning to look around, he saw Cristina walking in his direction. He closed his eyes and gathered himself. Just the sight of her infuriated him. She stalked to him, her booted heels striking the pavement. She stopped a little too close for his comfort. He stepped back, and she stepped closer again. He crossed his arms and waited. In the moment before she spoke, he took a long look. Her hair was perfectly done, even in the wind. Straight, glossy brown locks curved along the line of her jaw. He'd once thought her dark brown eyes were beautiful. He saw that they were objectively so now, but that they held a calculated edge. She lifted her chin.

"So, this is how it ends with us? You just ignore me and let your family run me out of town."

"It ended with us over two years ago," Luke said.

"You loved me. I know you did. I think you still do, or you'd be serious with Hannah. Your mom didn't even know about her. That's not someone you're planning on keeping around."

Luke held still, anger flaring. He waited a beat to get his thoughts in hand. "I loved the idea of you. That's *not* who you are. Leave Hannah out of this."

Cristina smirked. "Too late for that."

"Don't you have a plane ticket out of here yet?" he asked, his anger a hot simmer.

She held his eyes for a long moment. "Of course. I can only handle being in the middle of nowhere for so long. I just wanted to give you one last look at what you're giving up." She turned and looked toward the water. "Plus—it's always fun to make somebody wonder."

Luke followed her gaze and saw Hannah on the beach, Jessie at her side sniffing the ground. Hannah stood in place, looking in their direction. He couldn't see her expression, which meant she couldn't see his. All she saw was that he was talking to Cristina. He hated that Cristina had manufactured yet another moment like this and he'd walked right into it.

"Get the hell out of here," he said. He didn't even look at her, and turned to walk away. Seconds later, he heard the sound of a vehicle abruptly stopping. Glancing back, he saw Jared's truck stopped beside Cristina. Jared climbed out and walked around to Cristina. He couldn't hear the words they exchanged, but next thing he knew, Cristina climbed into Jared's truck. Jared's expression was grim. Jared gave him a wave and drove away quickly.

His cell phone rang, Jared's number flashing. "What the hell is going on?" he said by way of greeting.

"Here's the deal—I'm escorting Cristina to the airport. I won't leave until I see the plane fly away. And don't worry... she's going. I'll explain later," Jared said, his voice clipped.

The line went dead. Jared's truck sped toward the highway. "I'll be damned," Luke said to himself.

He scanned the beach for Hannah. She was nowhere to be seen. He quickly glanced around the parking lot, but saw no sign of her. Her truck was still there though, so he leaned against it, ready to wait her out.

Within a few minutes, Jessie barreled toward him, greeting him with yips. He knelt to pet her, looking up when Hannah reached the truck.

"Hey there," he said.

She didn't respond—just opened the truck and tossed her jacket inside.

Luke pushed away from the truck and walked to her side. "Look, if you saw that, you saw me walk off."

He put a hand on her arm. She shook it off.

"Here's the thing," Hannah began. "I don't know what to think. Just when I'm about ready to call you, I look over and see you talking to Cristina. I believe you when you say you had no idea she was coming here. It's all over your face. What's messing me up is that she must have meant something to you once…and I'm *nothing* like her. So what the hell do you see in me?"

Between Cristina's games, trying to come to terms with the fact that Hannah meant a hell of a lot more to him than he'd planned on, and now this, the anger that had started when he saw Cristina bubbled over.

"Seriously? Right now, all I know is that this is a shit-storm I didn't see coming. Yeah…I was stupid enough to fall for Cristina once. Learned my lesson. Thought I learned it well until you came along. Now it seems like you like to play games too. Forget it." Luke stalked away. Jessie tried to follow him, and he heard Hannah call his name. He ignored them both.

* * *

LUKE SAT in the boat cabin, leaning his head against the back of the booth. The sun cast long shadows through the cabin. He soaked in the silence. His heart rate finally slowed. He wondered if Cristina had flown away yet. A wave of bitterness washed through him. She'd screwed his life up before and managed to do it again. The events of the last few weeks had reminded him why his plan to keep relationships light had been a good idea. He shied away from thinking about Hannah. A shadow fell across the booth. Luke looked up to see Nathan entering the cabin.

Nathan winked. "See you're hard at work already."

Luke couldn't muster a response.

"Dude, what's wrong?" Nathan asked. He slid into the opposite side of the booth. "You don't look good."

Luke eyed him and shrugged.

"Is this about Cristina? Jared called to tell me he'd just made sure she was on a plane out of town. Thought that would be good news."

"That part is. But before that, she managed to set me up for Hannah to see me talking with her."

"And?" Nathan asked.

"And now Hannah wants to know what the hell I see in her. So I told her to forget it." Just saying the words out loud made Luke cringe inside.

"Luke—don't tell me you're gonna let Cristina get exactly what she wanted if she couldn't have you."

"What am I gonna do? Honestly, it's not worth the trouble," Luke said.

Nathan slapped his work gloves on the table. "Bullshit. Mope around—that's all you've done since Hannah asked for a break. Don't be stupid. Mom feels so bad about what happened that even she's backed off. For God's sake, dude, if she can do that, you can get over yourself."

Luke rolled his head side to side against the back of the booth. "I don't know, man."

Nathan held quiet and just looked at him until Luke started to get uncomfortable.

"What?" Luke asked.

"Already went over this with you. Before this mess started, it was obvious Hannah was special to you. Even with Cristina, you weren't like that. Don't be stupid. Go find her and set it straight," Nathan said.

Luke sat up straighter. "Damn, you're just spouting relationship advice. Maybe you should start a column."

"Fine. Be cranky with me. Hannah matters to you...*a lot*. Don't usually bother, but you're my brother and you matter to me. Remember what I said last week? Get over yourself and make it right with her. No guarantees, but...the way you're headed, you're guaranteed to keep feeling the way you do now."

Luke felt the tightness in his chest ease. He wasn't ready to admit it, but he just might have heard Nathan's point. He looked to Nathan, one side of his mouth curling up. "Okay, man. Maybe I'll take your advice. For now...can we get some work done?"

Nathan gave him a considering look and nodded. "Yup."

A few hours later, Luke walked back up the dock. *Iris* was ready to be pulled from the harbor and stored for winter. Nathan had already taken off. Luke headed toward the beach and walked onto the rock-strewn shoreline. The tide was out, revealing a few starfish scattered in tide pools. He absentmindedly kicked at rocks. The endless days of summer were past, and time was quickening as they headed into winter. Streaks of faded purple, yellow, and red radiated out from the sun as it fell low in the sky, about to roll below the horizon. He looked out to the mountains; the termination dust ended in a bright white line against the green flanks of the mountains. There was a bite to the air. He made his way back to his truck, thinking about Hannah every step of the way.

CHAPTER 26

*H*annah looked over at Susie who was glaring at her. "Why am I the one getting a hard time? Luke is the one that said to forget it. Go bother him," Hannah said. They were seated at the counter in Susie's kitchen. Hannah had stopped by for dinner and drinks with Susie, Cammi, Dara, and Maggie. The others were in the living room watching *Deadliest Catch*, a pastime for Alaskans who enjoyed assessing the "reality" of the show.

Susie brushed a curl out of her eyes. "The way I see it— you're just using this as another way to keep avoiding Luke."

Now Hannah was the one glaring. "Avoiding what?"

"That you might have a shot with Luke. Finding a halfway decent guy is something you went *waaay* out of your way to avoid once Damon screwed you over. Luke sure as hell isn't perfect, but neither are you. So he had the hots for Cristina once upon a time? Whatever," Susie said with a shrug. "Most of us have people in our past that we wouldn't be caught dead with now. I'm not saying Cristina's little stunt wouldn't have messed with my head. Just saying that you shouldn't use it as another excuse. Plus—she's long gone."

"How do you know?"

"Kinda funny. Jared's buddies with Officer Thomas— Darren Thomas, remember him? He was a few years ahead of us in school. Anyway, he's a cop now. Jared got him to agree to issue a trespassing summons if she showed up at my office because we figured she would. He'd have had to if I called anyway, but Jared greased the wheel so it happened fast. She showed up at my place before she went to the harbor that day when you saw her with Luke. She was out of there like lightning when I called the cops. So, when Jared found her at the harbor, he let her know she had two choices: leave with him, or he'd let Darren know exactly where she was. Not like trespassing's a big deal, but she'd have to deal with it. He even got Darren to follow them to the airport." Susie smiled slyly.

Hannah was incredulous. "I can't believe you two did that!"

"Oh, yes you can...you know me. I do what needs to be done. So does Jared. We weren't about to sit around and let her keep messin' with you and Luke," Susie replied with a chuckle.

Hannah sat back and shook her head. "Should have known. Guess I should thank you," she said.

"Won't really matter if you keep finding one reason after another to avoid Luke."

Hannah closed her eyes and took a breath. "Okay...so what if I've been avoiding him? He told me to forget it."

"Oh my God! So you're just gonna let it go? You had enough nerve to ask for that stupid break. Maybe you can summon the old Hannah, who used to chase off moose and dive in the cove, and ask her to pick up the phone and call him. You'll never know what he might say if you don't bother," Susie said. She sipped her wine and gave Hannah an assessing glance.

Cammi entered the kitchen and refilled her wineglass. She looked between Hannah and Susie. "What's up?"

Susie waved in Hannah's direction. "Just trying to convince Hannah to remember that she used to be a lot more daring than she is now."

Cammi turned to Hannah, nodding emphatically. "You were always the one we could count on to do something crazy, and you never backed down. What's got you on her case?" she asked, directing her question to Susie.

"Luke. She's avoiding him, and I think it's dumb," Susie said.

Cammi looked back to Hannah and sipped her wine. "I think I'm missing a ton of details, but Luke's a good guy. And you two were so cute together! Not sure I know why Susie's on your case, but give Luke a shot," Cammi said sweetly. She patted Hannah on the shoulder. "And Susie's right...you seem a lot more...subdued, I guess. I know you've had a lot to deal with the last few years, but it wouldn't hurt to channel that wild part of yourself." Another smile, and Cammi headed back to the living room, her long gauzy skirt swishing with each step and the scent of flowers trailing in her wake.

"Does she ever not smell like flowers?" Hannah asked.

Susie giggled. "Always does. It's that scented oil stuff she wears. She loves it." She paused and looked at Hannah, holding her gaze. "It's not just me that noticed how you've been. Subdued is a good way to put it. You don't have to be so wild that your parents would freak out if they were still here. I just hate seeing you let something good pass by because you're too afraid to try."

Tears pressed against Hannah's eyelids. She tried to hold them back, but one tear slid down her cheek. She quickly wiped it away. Susie reached over and squeezed her hand. "I'll shut up for now. Just think about what I said."

* * *

THE NEXT DAY, Hannah did nothing but think about what Susie and Cammi had said. She finally cleaned out the shed, her mind whirring over thoughts about Luke as she organized garden tools and sorted fishing equipment, getting filthy in the process. Later that night, she flipped aimlessly through television channels and petted Jessie who curled up beside her on the couch.

The restless feeling that had prodded her into those years of wild, careless relationships and far-flung journeys was just a small flicker. She'd pushed so hard against it after her parents died that she had become almost obsessed with not doing anything risky. And her heart had become brittle behind the walls she'd built around it. Luke had caused some fissures in that wall, and that scared her. Cammi had offered to perform a cleansing ceremony for her to help her get back in touch with herself. Just recalling Cammi's earnest offer, Hannah started laughing to herself. Maybe a ceremony would help, but she had an idea of what she needed to do. It was the doing that she had to work up to.

* * *

HANNAH KICKED at a rock in the sand. Jessie ran ahead as usual, tail wagging, and nose to the sand. The breeze off the bay came in brisk gusts. She loved this time of year. Winter wasn't here yet, but one could feel it coming. The air held a sense of urgency. As a child, she'd loved cozy fall nights by the woodstove, the precursor to much longer winter evenings of quiet and warmth, the cold held at bay. The last few days, she'd almost called Luke about a hundred times.

She wanted to apologize for what she'd said at the truck. She'd seen the hurt in his eyes when she'd asked him what he saw in her. She wanted to explain that she'd just reacted to the sight of Cristina—so polished and beautiful, so *not* how Hannah felt. She also knew Susie and Cammi were on to something. She was avoiding Luke because her feelings for him scared her. She needed to get back in touch with the Hannah that chased moose, dove into the cove in the winter, and had a lot more fun.

Just as Luke crossed her mind, she heard a sharp squeal from Jessie and glanced in her direction. Jessie was running back toward Hannah, her tail flying high behind her. Hannah turned around. Luke was striding in their direction. Her heart kicked up as she walked to meet him.

When he reached them, he knelt down to greet Jessie, looking up with a tentative smile. Hannah smiled back, her heart in her throat.

"Saw your truck and figured you were out here with Jessie. Hope it's okay that I came over to say hi," he said as he stood. He dusted sand from Jessie off his hands and jeans. His green eyes held hers for a long moment. She saw uncertainty flash there, but he didn't close up with that guarded gaze she'd seen the last few times they saw each other. They stood silently for a moment.

Hannah realized she should respond. "I've been meaning to call you. Just kept losing my nerve."

Luke smiled ruefully. "Been meaning to call you too. Took my chance when I saw your truck."

Hannah started to tell him she was sorry, but stumbled on her words. Luke put a hand on her shoulder. "Hang on."

She stopped and looked back at him. His hand stayed on her shoulder, sliding down to her elbow. Warmth seeped through her fleece jacket.

Luke took a breath before speaking. "I screwed up the

other day. I was pissed off at the whole situation with Cristina and blew up at you instead."

He appeared to gather himself. "Here's the thing...didn't plan on it, but you matter to me...*a lot.*" He looked away, his throat moving in a swallow. "I'm not so good at this kind of conversation. But...I love you. There--said it." He chuckled softly.

He looked to her, his eyes wary. He forged on. "I just... just wanted to make sure you knew where I stood. With the things that have happened the last few weeks...thought maybe you should know how I felt."

A wash of relief poured through Hannah, followed by her eyes filling with tears. She looked to Luke and saw the vulnerability in his eyes and what it must have cost him to tell her this when he didn't know where she stood. "I'm sorry too. But all I've done is miss you and worry that I overreacted to meeting your parents, Cristina showing up, and..." She choked on her words. Luke pulled her close into his arms. She held tight and just breathed him in. She stepped back after a few moments.

She looked to him through her tears. "I love you too. I just hadn't quite figured that out yet when all that drama with your parents and Cristina happened." She knuckled away her tears. "I got overwhelmed..." She paused, struggling to explain. "Susie's been on me about all this. But...you know...I just didn't expect *this* to happen so fast," she said, gesturing between them.

Luke grinned. "Wanna bet if Susie plotted with Jared and Nathan? Don't want to admit it, but they pushed me in the right direction. You don't have to be sorry for asking for a break. Between my mom's pressure and Cristina's games— don't blame you for needing a minute." He tugged her back into his embrace. She felt Jessie rub against her legs. They pulled back, looking down to see Jessie's wagging tail, her tongue lolling out as she circled them both.

"I should get her home. Do you want to stay for dinner?"
Luke's smile was wide. "Absolutely."

The evening passed with pizza, beer, wine, and relaxing in front of the fire. They were seated on the couch, Hannah's legs resting across Luke's lap when he turned to look at her. She looked back into his eyes, trying to gauge his green assessing look.

"What?" she asked.

He shrugged and started to turn away, but looked back. "Just wondering."

"Wondering what?" she asked.

Silence fell between them, a charge pulsing through it. He gave his head a small shake and leaned in for a kiss. She fell into his kiss, the feel of his lips against hers anchoring her as sensation washed through her. She opened her mouth on a sigh. He pulled back and looked at her. He cupped her face in his palms, his thumbs brushing errant locks of hair back. She wanted to ask what he was thinking, but sensed he wasn't ready to talk. He brought his lips to hers again. Thought was wiped from her mind. Pure feeling took over, and she dove straight into it.

Heat built between them in seconds. She tugged at the buttons of his shirt, baring his chest and running her hands across it. Luke's lips traveled down the side of her neck. He traced her collarbone with his tongue and followed his way back up her neck, nipping lightly at her ear. She shivered. He started to pull her soft cotton shirt up and paused. He pulled back and glanced at Jessie.

"Feels strange to do this in front of her," he said.

Hannah followed his eyes to Jessie, who lay still but her dark eyes were open and watching them curiously. "Upstairs," was all she could force out.

After they stood, Luke briefly checked the fire. Jessie sighed and closed her eyes again when they walked up the stairs. Hannah's skin felt on fire. Her throat was raspy. She was lost in need for him. He followed her into the bedroom, which was cool. Goose bumps rose on her skin. She heard the door close behind him and felt his hands on her shoulders. He whirled her around to face him and turned them both until her back hit the door. He pressed full length against her and kissed her deeply. She slid one hand up his bare chest and brought the other around behind his neck, her fingers slipping into his curls. Their tongues tangled in a slow dance.

She pulled away to gasp for air. Liquid fire pooled in her abdomen and between her legs. She felt his erection pressing into the center of her. His lips trailed down her neck. He swiftly pulled her shirt up, unhooked her bra, and tossed them to the floor. He moved to the center of her breastbone and left a trail of soft kisses and puffs of air down her chest and belly. His tongue circled her navel. Her breath came in short gasps. She grabbed his hair and pulled him up for another kiss. She pushed against him. He stepped back. What clothes were left came off in a rush. The cool air hit her flushed skin, heightening the sensations flaring through her. Luke pulled her to the bed. He must have felt her slight shiver against the shock of the air and flipped the covers back, only to roll them underneath and cocoon them in the bed.

She sighed into his mouth, reveling in the feel of his bare body, skin to skin with hers. His fingers trailed up her thigh, finding their way into her slick folds. He slid one finger inside of her and brought his thumb across the top. She came in a rush, surprised by the force of it. Luke pulled back, his hand remaining in the moist heat of her. She opened her eyes to find his green gaze steadily watching her. She brought a hand up to caress his cheek. "Don't stop on account of that."

She felt his breath against her lips, a small laugh escaping him. "Oh no, not stopping."

He proceeded to bring her back to the brink, time and again. His hands and lips left a map of sensation across her body. She was desperate by the time he finally came into her. The sheer relief of having him enter her almost brought her to another instantaneous orgasm. He paused for a long moment when he came fully against her. She was stretched tight around him. He brought his forehead to hers. Their eyes met, a mere inch apart. He began to move, barely shifting his hips, rocking slowly into her. She began to come in waves of feeling that crested with each rock. She felt him finally let go. He threw his head back with a final push against her. She pulsed around him. He relaxed against her, their skin damp.

CHAPTER 27

*L*uke fell against Hannah and shifted to the side so he didn't crush her. She murmured something incoherent. They were still joined. She hooked one of her long legs around his hip. He brought a hand up and caressed her hip. He felt boneless, almost weak. Hannah did that to him. Every time. He opened his eyes to look at her. He could see the pulse beating in her neck. Her eyes were closed. A tear slipped down her cheek. He thought to ask and thought better of it. Instead, he lifted his hand from her hip and pushed her hair away from her face. The long waves of her hair were in wild disarray, tangled about her neck and face, and fanned out across the pillows. She opened her eyes at his touch and turned her head to look at him. Her blue gaze pierced him.

"Hello again," he rasped. He cleared his throat, holding her gaze.

"Hello to you," she said, her eyes crinkled at the corners. She brought her hand to his cheek, held it for a moment, and then let it fall. The lone tear had dissolved.

He continued to sift through her hair. He thought back to the moment downstairs when she asked him what he was wondering. He'd been wondering when to ask her to marry him. Ever since Nathan mentioned it, the thought had been on his mind. But he held back for now, thinking it was enough that the break was over.

He'd been staring at the ceiling, caught in his thoughts. He turned to look at Hannah. Her eyes had fallen closed again, although her face was still turned toward him. The bedroom was cool. The covers he'd thrown over them created a small cocoon of warmth. He watched her for a few moments, her chest rising and falling. She fell into sleep, her hand resting on his chest, legs tangled with his. He followed her into slumber.

* * *

LUKE LOOKED out across Hannah's yard. They'd woken to a frost-covered landscape. The mountains across the bay were snow-tipped. Thick hoarfrost was draped upon the greenery. Sunlight reflected again and again through the tiny prisms of frost. The field of fireweed was muted; furred icy spikes stood out on the tall weeds. It was early yet. He'd made his way downstairs before Hannah and started a pot of coffee. The smell of coffee filled the kitchen.

At the sound of Hannah's footsteps coming down the stairs, Jessie ran to greet her. Luke took in the sight of Hannah. She carried herself with her usual unself-consciousness. She had a fresh-scrubbed look; her hair fell in damp waves past her shoulders. Her feet were bare, bright red toenails peeking out from under the edges of her jeans. He recalled that he'd loved her feet that day he'd found her at the house, that unexpected morning months ago. Her blue eyes were bright even from across the room.

"Thanks for starting coffee," she said, walking toward the counter.

"My pleasure," he said.

They sat at the kitchen table in the quiet dawn, mist rising off the field, the frost dissolving where the sun struck. Luke thought he'd like to wake up to this every day —a quiet morning, coffee, and most of all, Hannah. He appreciated that there wasn't a need to talk. That was something he loved about her. She didn't tend to try to fill silence. She just let it sit, comfortable with its presence.

Before long, the mist that rose off the field dissipated along with the frost. Bright sun shone through the kitchen windows. Hannah finally stood and stretched. She turned to look at him. "What's on your schedule for the day?" she asked.

He thought for a moment. "Meeting Nathan at the harbor to get our boats pulled out for storage. That'll take a few hours. Aside from that...not much. You?" he asked.

"A little work on one of my consulting jobs. Then some more cleanup in the shed outside," she said, nodding her head in the direction of the shed. "I finally got started on it yesterday and want to finish before winter. Fall here is so quick. After that...well...maybe you could stay again."

Luke stood and reached out to tug Hannah toward him. He held her in a loose embrace. "Oh, I'll stay again," he said, dropping a kiss on her nose.

She gave him a heated glance—her blue eyes almost level with his. He again appreciated that she was a tall woman. With barely a dip of his head, he leaned in for a kiss. Their lips touched for a second, and then Jessie barked loudly and ran to the door. Hannah stepped away and looked into the yard. "Moose," was all she said.

He walked over and followed her gaze out the window. A female moose with two young calves stood at the edge of the field. Jessie's bark had drawn the moose's attention to the house. She stood calmly in the field, tall, gangly, and brown. The two young calves stood at her side, waiting to follow her lead. Hannah shushed Jessie whose barks subsided to soft whines. The moose finally looked away from the house and turned back into the field. She appeared to be moving slowly, but Luke knew better. Moose had such long legs, they tricked you into thinking they weren't moving fast. They covered ground rapidly with their rambling stride. The calves followed at varying distances, as if connected by an invisible tug line. The soft fuzzy brown of their fur caught seeds from the fireweed, which had fluffy seedpods that floated about in the wind. In moments, the threesome had crossed the field and disappeared into the spruce forest on the far side. Jessie quieted and lost interest, walking back to her bed and lying down with a sigh.

They made plans to meet for a beach walk by the harbor in late afternoon. Luke thought about his parents as he drove down the hill heading toward the harbor. Just yesterday, they'd flown back to Seattle. His mother had apologized yet again at the airport for getting drawn into Cristina's games. She'd done her best not to pressure him anymore about Hannah, but the undercurrent was there. His mother's fervent wish for him and his brothers to settle down had only been intensified by meeting Hannah. He was relieved for the moment that they weren't there to ask questions about him and Hannah. It was enough to face down his own feelings for her, much less try to juggle how to talk with his parents about it.

He couldn't believe he was thinking about marriage. He'd pretty much convinced himself that he'd be content to live as a bachelor with casual flings on the side. Seeing Cristina reminded him why he'd come to that conclusion, but Hannah had blown his resolve to pieces. Without a doubt, he knew he wanted to come home to nights like last night every day.

* * *

HANNAH CLOSED her laptop and looked around the room. Jessie lay by her feet, sound asleep. She sat in her mother's old office chair and swiveled around to face the stairs. She'd cleaned her mother's items out of the desk and organized it for work last week. She was finding it easier to rearrange the house as she needed and not cling to the memories of her parents. She'd been busy since Luke left this morning. It felt good to start working on what she wanted. It cemented the feeling that she was here to stay.

The sound of tires on gravel caught her attention. Jessie lifted her head, turning in the direction of the drive. Hannah walked to the edge of the stairs where she could see through the windows on the side. Seeing the front of Susie's car, she walked downstairs and stepped out to the deck with Jessie following. Susie was rummaging in the backseat of her car.

"Hey there," Hannah called to Susie. She heard a muffled reply, and then Susie straightened and looked over the top of the car.

"Hey, just came by to bring you some zucchini from my mom's garden. She's clearing out what's left of her vegetable garden before the snow flies." Susie pulled a tote from the backseat of her car and walked toward the deck. Her brown curls were in wild disarray.

"That looks like a lot of zucchini," Hannah commented, eyeing the size of the tote.

"You have no idea how much zucchini my mom has. Ever since she retired, gardening is one of her big things in the summer," Susie said. "I get roped into finding takers when it's time for her to get the garden cleared out before winter. So here you are...lots of zucchini." Susie set the tote down and opened it to show Hannah a bag—full of giant zucchini.

Hannah looked to Susie. "What am I going to do with all this?"

"Oh, I have that down pat. I'll help you get it ready to freeze. Then you'll start making zucchini bread for every potluck in town and giving it away for the holidays. I have a great recipe," Susie said with a wink.

Hannah laughed. "Okay then. How long will it take to get it ready to freeze?"

"Not long. You have a food processor, right?" she asked.

Hannah nodded, and Susie picked up the tote, heading for the kitchen door. Susie spoke over her shoulder. "Now, where's that food processor?"

Hannah realized she was either going to bear witness to the whirlwind that Susie could be, or help her out. Within the hour, the zucchini was tidily packed in freezer bags, and Susie had produced a bottle of wine she'd brought.

Susie held the wine aloft. "Where's your corkscrew?"

Hannah went to get it and returned to the table with two wineglasses. Susie filled both glasses. She looked to Hannah with a question in her eyes.

"What?" Hannah asked.

"Just wondering when you were going to mention Luke. Ran into Nathan at Misty Mountain this morning. He's convinced you two are meant for each other. He also mentioned that Luke didn't make it home last night," she said slyly.

Hannah shook her head. She wanted to avoid answering, but Susie was waiting expectantly. "Sooo...Luke found me on the beach yesterday. I'm sure you have an opinion on how it should have happened, but the break is over." She grinned widely just saying it out loud.

Susie looked at her thoughtfully and set down her wineglass. "I'm getting skid marks on my tongue here, but I'll keep my opinions to myself. I'm just damn glad you didn't let this slip by."

"Skid marks, huh? Guess I don't give you enough credit for trying to keep your mouth shut," Hannah said.

Susie grinned. "I'm with Nathan on this one. I think you two are good together. Plus—I saw the possibilities for you two. Luke's good for you, and it's plain as day he adores you. If there's anything I want for you, I want someone who does that. At the least. Wouldn't mind if he got you to loosen up either."

Hannah took a sip of wine. "I can admit that Luke and I have a good thing going. I'll try to stay out of my own way."

"Keep me posted if I have to head you off at the pass before you want another break," Susie said. "As for other topics, have you heard from Emma?"

Hannah nodded and filled Susie in on their e-mails and calls. The distance of having Emma away was giving her time to come to terms with knowing she had a sister. Emma was busy with work and figuring out what she was going to do as far as whether to stay in North Carolina for now or consider a move to Diamond Creek. Now that the shock of Emma's existence was past, she was glad Emma had impulsively flown out here. It was the quickest route through an awkward situation.

After Susie left, the house felt quiet and still. Susie tended to do that. She was a whirling dervish of energy. Her absence created a contrast. Hannah looked around the kitchen. The sun was low in the sky; fading rays of light shone across the hardwood floor. Jessie was curled up in a patch of sunlight, her black fur tipped a dusky gold from the sun.

* * *

HANNAH ARRIVED at the harbor parking lot to find it half-empty. She didn't see Luke's truck, so she headed toward the beach, Jessie galloping ahead of her. The wind was coming in lazy gusts off the water. The mountain range across the bay stood tall and quiet against the sky. Snow had fallen last night, the peaks bright white now. The deep green of spruce that lined the mountainside gave way to a line of white with rocky areas jutting out. She checked her watch and wondered where Luke was.

She quickly called him. He answered on the first ring. "Hey there. Forgot to stay at the harbor and wait for you. Can you give me a few minutes? Just finishing up at the boatyard."

"No problem. I wondered where your truck was when I got here. Figured you were tied up. I'm just walking with Jessie. We'll stay close to the parking lot."

She walked along the water with Jessie scampering from scent to scent and back to Hannah. A small flock of cormorants landed in the water nearby. A loon that had been floating in solitary until their landing lifted from the water and resettled farther away. A few gulls called in the distance. She heard the distinct sound of an eagle's high-pitched screech. Tracking the sound, she caught sight of an eagle landing on a piece of driftwood down the beach.

If she'd tried to say what she'd missed most of Alaska when she'd lived in the East, it probably would have been walks on the beach. The cool air, the earthy scents of saltwater and tide pool life, and the majestic views across the water anchored her. The sun was setting with the moon rising nearby. She looked ahead at Jessie whose pure joy lifted her heart every time they came to the beach.

The sound of footsteps approached. Turning, she saw Luke jogging up to her. His dark curls were in disarray. He was wearing faded jeans, a blue fleece jacket, and boots. Her heart quickened and her breath followed suit. He stopped in front of her. The green of his eyes stood out against his flushed face.

Luke was winded. "Not the best idea to run on the beach in boots. Not too efficient."

Hannah bit her lip, her heart dancing just at the sight of him and the relief that she wasn't trying to push him away. "No, probably not." She nodded in Jessie's direction. "As you can see, Jessie's walking herself. I'm just following her." She tucked her hands deeper into the pockets of her red down vest.

Luke gave a whistle in Jessie's direction. Upon catching sight of him, Jessie raced toward them and circled him with yips and leaps. He knelt down and petted her, his large hands stroking across Jessie's back. Hannah loved his hands, strong, sure, and gentle all at once. He gave Jessie another stroke and straightened to standing.

"In case you think I forgot—I didn't. Just wasn't paying attention to the time," Luke said, turning to walk alongside her.

Hannah enjoyed the easiness of being with him. She entertained him with her unexpected afternoon of zucchini and heard about his afternoon. Somewhere along the way, her hand found his. She absorbed the warm embrace of his palm cupped around hers. Their strides were close to matching. The wind picked up, and they turned back toward the parking lot. The sun disappeared below the horizon, appearing to slip into the water. Mount Augustine sat alone in the distance, a volcano in the middle of the bay. The sun had left a halo of color around Mount Augustine. The moon was half-full in the early evening sky, sitting low above the mountains.

Hannah turned in the direction of her truck, seeing that Luke had parked beside her. Their hands were still clasped when they reached the trucks. She didn't want to let go. He didn't seem any more inclined than she did to let their hands come apart. She looked to the path from the beach to see when Jessie would come through. In seconds, she heard the rustle of grass, and Jesse bounded into the parking lot, making a straight line to them. She finally let go of Luke's hand and went to open the passenger side door for Jessie.

Her cheeks were red from the cold, and her hands were freezing. As she came around the front of the truck, Luke rubbed his hands up and down her arms.

"You're cold. Winter's moving in fast this year. Feels like only a week ago that evenings were still warm."

He tilted his head, just the slightest bit, and brought his lips to hers. She felt the warm point of contact where their lips joined straight through her body, a piercing jolt. He deepened the kiss for just a moment, his tongue gliding in with a deep stroke. Then he pulled back and looked at her without speaking. Hannah could hear the waves rolling into the shore. Salty air stung her cheeks. A gust of wind caught her hair and blew it in a swirl around her head. Luke brushed her hair back from her face and loosely cupped her cheeks with his hands. The moment hung between them; their gazes held. She felt her throat tighten and wanted to cry, but not for sadness.

A rustle sounded in the trees. They turned in unison. A moose stepped out through the trees, followed by a lone calf. The mother moose lifted her head high and appeared to sniff the air. The calf mimicked the mother. Hannah and Luke stood quietly, along with the moose and her calf. Luke's hands had slipped from her cheeks when they turned and were resting on her arms. The moose finally snorted, seemed to decide they weren't a threat, and began to amble through the parking lot, the calf following her at a slow trot. It was late enough into the season that the calf reached her mother's shoulder, a far cry from the tiny size that moose calves were when they were born in the spring.

There was a good distance between them and the pair,

so they remained still until the moose and her calf made it to the far side of the parking lot. Luke turned to look at Hannah again through the gloaming. She saw the white of his teeth flash.

"One question. Just for you to think about." He paused for a long moment and took a breath. "What if we thought about something more serious?" he asked.

Hannah felt her heart race, and tears again threatened.

"Such as?"

Rare as it was, she saw uncertainty in his eyes. He seemed to gather himself before he spoke.

"Well...to be blunt...what about something more serious like a commitment?"

She wanted to laugh. As skittish as she was, she realized he was as well, in his own way. She didn't want to push, but she felt like she had to.

"A commitment?"

Luke rolled his eyes. "You're not making this easy. Maybe we could think about marriage." He took a quick breath. "There. I said it."

Her heart unfurled. All the hesitations and doubts with which she was so familiar dissolved in the face of certainty.

"We could think about that," she said.

She was rewarded with another bright flash of white in the deepening dusk.

"That's all I wanted, just for us to think about it."

She started to move closer to him, but Luke held her arms steady. "Give me a minute. All I know is this—when you asked for that break, I missed you like crazy. Won't pretend I was looking for something like this. But...I've never missed anyone the way I did you those few weeks."

The tears that had been threatening rolled down her cheeks. She wiped them away with her hands and looked through the haze at Luke. She nodded and started to speak, only to find that she didn't know what to say.

So she said that. "I don't know what to say. Other than…yes."

She saw Luke smiling back at her. He gave her arms another brisk rub. "You're shivering and I'm kinda cold, which tells me it must be freezing. Get in your truck. I'll follow you home."

She simply nodded.

An hour or so later, they were at Hannah's house with a fire in the woodstove, the heat starting to radiate through the house. Jessie had gobbled up her food within minutes of their arrival and promptly curled up on the chair in the living room. Hannah had set aside some zucchini and baked it with a rice, mushroom, and cheese filling. They'd eaten in front of the fire using the coffee table. The television rumbled in the background while they rested on the couch, her legs thrown across his lap.

Luke turned away from the television and looked at her. She quirked an eyebrow in question. He held her gaze for a long moment and leaned over for a kiss, his head resting against the sofa. Their lips met in a leisurely exploration. He lifted a hand and brushed some stray hairs away from her face. She must have dozed off because she woke to find herself being carried upstairs, her legs draped over Luke's arm while he held her close to his chest.

"You don't have to do that," was her automatic comment.

"On no, we're getting all the way up. No easy feat to get you in my arms without waking you up."

She smiled against his shoulder. "Okay, you don't have to put me down."

He reached the top of the stairs and turned down the hall to the bedroom. The air was much cooler up here away from the heat of the woodstove. Tugging her clothes off, Hannah fell into bed. Luke rolled in beside her, tucking the down comforter around them. The sheets were cool and slick against her skin. His body was a warm furnace. She snuggled close, resting her cheek against his shoulder. A sense of comfort and rightness washed through her. Jessie padded into the bedroom behind them, her claws clicking softly against the floor, and then curled up by the foot of the bed with a deep sigh. That was the last thing Hannah remembered before falling into a deep sleep.

CHAPTER 28

A few weeks later, Hannah drove up the hill to her house and saw an unfamiliar car in the driveway. As she pulled into the drive, she saw Emma step out of the car and laughed aloud. Visit or more, it felt right that Emma decided to just show up again.

Jessie leaped out of the truck, racing to greet Emma with yips and circles. Hannah followed Jessie and opened her arms for a hug. "I can't quite do Jessie's greeting justice, but it's good to see you."

Emma returned the quick hug. "Good to see you too. I decided a surprise stop at your house was the way to go." Emma stepped back and took a long look around the yard and out toward the bay. "Wow—nice to see this view again."

Hannah gave her a questioning look. "Well, what's with the visit? Not that you needed to, but you didn't mention you were coming. It's a bit more than a hop, skip, and jump from North Carolina to here."

A flash of uncertainty passed through Emma's eyes. "I wanted a little more time here. Thought another surprise visit would bring good luck. Although I'm not imposing on you this time. I went behind your back and had Faye find me a small rental for a few months. I knew Susie couldn't keep it from you, so I got ahold of Faye." She shrugged sheepishly.

"You can stay here!" Hannah exclaimed. "There's plenty of room. And the surprise is perfect, just how it should be."

Emma gave her an assessing look. "I figured you'd say I should stay here. But...rumor has it you and Luke are all but officially shacked up. I don't want to get in the way," she said with a sly smile.

Hannah rolled her eyes and looked away. She figured it was either Susie or Faye who'd told Emma how often Luke was here. She minded and simultaneously didn't mind. It was nice to have friends who had their noses in her business because it meant they cared even when they were annoying.

"So, where will you be staying?" Hannah asked.

Emma gestured toward the back of the house. "Faye found me an off-season rental on the road on the back side of the trees—Alpine Lane. I have to go by the realty place to pick up the keys. Thought I'd chance it and see if you were home first."

Jessie had left to do her usual perimeter run of the yard and returned to Hannah's side, nosing her hand. She absent-mindedly stroked her. "Why don't I go to town with you? We can catch up. Give me a few minutes to put away some groceries."

Emma smiled. "I was hoping you'd say that. I'd like the company."

The afternoon passed in an idiosyncratic blur. Being with Emma felt oddly comforting and familiar. This feeling existed alongside the still unsettling awareness of the fact that she had a sister and the attendant novelty of their relationship. They took Hannah's truck to town, Jessie seated between them. Along with picking up the rental keys, they visited Susie at work. Susie had been ecstatic to see Emma and incredulous that her mother had kept the secret about Emma's planning. Hannah called Luke and left him a message while they were in town. He had left for Anchorage with Jared yesterday and was due to return that evening.

As the afternoon rolled along, Hannah sensed that Emma was still sorting out where she wanted to be and what she wanted to do. There was still much she didn't know about the path that had led Emma here to begin with, but she avoided pushing. Hannah drove up the hill past fields of faded fireweed. The day was overcast and damp, as fall so often was. The air felt raw. The pavement was slick from the rain that had been spitting off and on throughout the day. Alpine Lane was a tad higher on the hill than her road with the scenery largely the same—clusters of spruce trees giving way to fields of fireweed. Emma directed her to a driveway almost hidden by alder trees. A small cabin sat back from the road. It was a basic A-frame design with a whimsical touch. The roof was deep green metal, the siding stained with a light finish, and the trim a bright purple. A purple star was mounted toward the top of the A-frame, where the sides of the roof met in a point.

"This is cute. What's the deal with it? Just a winter rental?" Hannah asked.

Emma shrugged. "The realtor said the owners used to live in the area and they moved away about a year ago. I guess they don't have a firm plan on whether it's just a winter rental, but they let me sign a three-month lease, which is all I wanted for now. They agreed to let me reconsider if I decide to stay longer."

"Did the realtor mention who the owner was? I wonder if it's someone I know."

Emma shrugged again. "Don't know, but I'm sure that between you, Susie, and Faye, one of you will find out."

They walked together to the front door, which was situated in the center on a small porch. The inside of the cabin was open and airy. The downstairs was comprised of an open living room and kitchen area with a bathroom to the back. A spiral staircase led upstairs, which included a loft area that was furnished with a desk, two reading chairs, and built-in bookshelves lining the walls. A door upstairs led to the single bedroom, which had a balcony off the back. It was perfect for one person and came fully furnished.

After a brief exploration, Hannah drove Emma back to the house for her to pick up her rental car. Watching Emma drive away, she stood on the deck as a misty rain fell softly around her. The mountains across the water were shrouded in fog, their outlines blurred. The bay was slate gray. Wind skidded across, stirring up whitecaps. The green of the spruce trees surrounding the field was bright among the shades of gray and faded fireweed. A path had been beaten down by the moose that often wandered through the field.

Calling for Jessie, she waited until she heard her rustling her way through the trees. It occurred to her that she could probably walk to Emma's cabin if she cut through her backyard to the road behind. After toweling Jessie dry, she took a long look around the house. Her gaze paused on a book of Luke's left on an end table by the couch. One of his sweatshirts was thrown on the back of the chair that Jessie loved. Jessie jumped onto the same chair and curled up. A wave of emotion rocked Hannah. She had a sister nearby, and her parents would never walk into this house again. To experience that and see the markers of the new life she was shaping drove the point home that she was letting her parents go. The house felt like hers now, not an echo chamber for memories of her parents.

EPILOGUE

he morning of winter solstice had dawned cold and clear. Snow blanketed the landscape of Diamond Creek. Hannah and Luke were married late that afternoon, almost exactly six months to the day that they'd met on that cool summer morning. The ceremony was simple, and they were married in front of the local judge, who'd been a friend of her father's. Susie, Emma, Faye, and Luke's family, parents and all, were witnesses. Hannah had kept her wedding dress simple—a cream colored silk sheath. She paired it with a string of her mother's pearls and matching earrings. Luke had worn a dark navy suit that brought out the green of his eyes. After a wink and a promise that she'd behave, the judge had allowed them to bring Jessie in the courtroom since Jessie's wandering had brought Luke to Hannah's doorstep those many months prior.

Jared and Nathan threw a large party at the Boathouse Café. The café was filled with friends who had watched Hannah grow up and old friends of her parents. During the party, Hannah observed Jared once again trying to hold back his smiles when he was around Susie. She had the effect of alternately irritating and amusing him. Hannah briefly wondered what that might mean and decided to leave well enough alone for now. She had enough to worry about with Luke's parents, Iris in particular, abandoning any tact about their desire for grandchildren.

Looking out the windows while she sipped wine, she took in the view. The mountains stood tall and silent across the bay. The setting sun gave the snow-coated mountain-tops a lavender hue—alpenglow. By the time the party broke up, the sun was long gone and the moon high in the sky. Luke's hand in hers, she felt a rush of adrenaline—an old, familiar feeling, but this time not tinged with anxiety and fear. Instead of tamping it down, Hannah let go of Luke's hand and ran ahead to the edge of the dock. The water in Otter Cove was bright from the moon. She tore off her coat and whipped her dress over her head, kicking her shoes off. Her wedding attire lay in a rumpled heap on the dock. Clad only in her underwear, she glanced to Luke who had stopped at the edge of the dock just beside her. His gaze was bemused. She grabbed his hands and pulled him close for a quick kiss. Turning away from Luke, Hannah bounced on her heels and dove into Otter Cove. Plunging into the icy water, her lungs seized for a moment. Breaking the surface, she looked up at Luke, whose head was thrown back in a laugh. Shivering, she swam for the ladder at the end of the dock, exhilaration arcing through her. She climbed the ladder and stepped into Luke's warm embrace.

* * *

Thank you for reading When Love Comes - I hope you loved Hannah & Luke's story!

For more steamy, small town romance, Tess & Nathan's

story is next in Follow Love. Tess takes a vacation to Alaska, colliding with the oh-so-sexy Nathan Winters. Nathan's never met a challenge he didn't win, but Tess tests him to the limit. Don't miss Nathan's story!

Keep reading for a sneak peek!

Be sure to sign up for my newsletter for the latest news, teasers & more! Click here to sign up: http://jhcroixauthor.com/subscribe/

SNEAK PEEK: FOLLOW LOVE BY J.H. CROIX; ALL RIGHTS RESERVED

Chapter 1

*N*athan leaned over the side of the guide boat and tugged on the fishing line. While he didn't know what was on the other end, it was definitely live because he could feel the sense of vibration. Still tugging on the line, he looked over his shoulder to call to his oldest brother, Jared. Just as Nathan turned away, water splashed his shoulder. Turning back, he glimpsed a king salmon, now fighting madly against his grip on the line. King salmon were called king for a reason; even average ones weighed in at fifty plus pounds with some topping one hundred and more. He guessed this one to be medium sized, roughly two feet long and had to wrestle to keep hold of the line.

"Damn!" he said as the salmon bumped against the side of the boat. "Could use a little help here," he called. Wrestling a slippery salmon wasn't easy.

Michael, the man who caught the king salmon, started to move towards Nathan, fishing pole in hand.

"Stay put, I don't want the line to loosen at this point,"

Nathan directed. His other older brother, Luke was coming his way from the front of the boat.

Nathan and his brothers ran a commercial fish and guiding business, The One That Didn't Get Away, in Diamond Creek, Alaska, a small town on the shores of Kachemak Bay. Kachemak Bay was one of Alaska's coastal jewels, straight out of a postcard. A large bay off of Cook Inlet in South central Alaska, Kachemak Bay was home to several tourist hubs in Alaska. Though small, Diamond Creek was busy and catered to its tourists with world-class restaurants, shops and art galleries. Mountains encircled Kachemak Bay, eerie translucent blue glaciers were tucked between a few mountains, and Mount Augustine, a lone volcano, sat sentry in the bay. Along with the natural beauty, the bay was famous for its salmon and halibut fishing, drawing hordes of tourists from spring until the snow fell.

Today, they were hosting a family - Michael, Tess, Simon and Jordan - for a full day of fishing. Michael was father to Tess and Simon, both adults, and grandfather to Jordan. Nathan had to tamp the impulse to flirt with Tess. He couldn't keep his eyes off of her. She had short honey-colored hair that curled in a tousled bob around her face. She had a soft, rounded figure, curves in all the right places. Her ginger colored eyes and luscious mouth, bow shaped and bright pink, kept drawing Nathan's gaze. Though quiet, she had a sly sense of humor in the company of her family.

"So Dad, I thought the plan was to catch a record size halibut," Tess commented sardonically.

"I'll take a king salmon," Michael replied with a wide grin.

Nathan looked to Tess. "Oh don't worry, we'll make sure he gets that halibut," he said with a wink. For a flash, he saw a spark of interest, a tease, in her eyes and he almost lost his hold on the fishing line. *Focus on the fish, stupid.* He had to force his eyes away from her—she was distractingly delectable.

Luke reached Nathan's side and leaned over with a net as the king salmon continued to thrash against the side of the boat. With Nathan maneuvering the feisty salmon into the net, he and Luke lifted it over the side together. Just as they set the net down, Luke lost his grip, and the salmon flung itself free from the net and slapped Nathan in the face with a slimy tail. He lost his footing and slipped onto the boat deck, landing just beside the salmon.

"Really?!" he said, looking to the salmon who ignored him and gave another flick of its tail.

Luke shook his head, trying and failing to hold back a grin. "Sorry about that, couldn't keep a hold of the net."

Nathan rolled his eyes. "Noticed that. Only wish you'd been the one whacked in the face."

A towel landed in his lap. He turned to see Jared grinning at the wheel of the boat. "Thought you could use that."

Nathan snatched the towel up and wiped the slime off his cheek. Standing, he tucked the towel over his belt and looked to Michael. "Your call on whether you keep this one or release it. You have a king tag, so you can keep it if you want."

Michael came to stand at his side. He looked admiringly down at the salmon. "Let's release it. My goal is halibut and if I'm gonna keep a king, I want it to be record size. Let me get a picture though." He quickly snapped a photo with his phone.

Nathan nodded and turned back to Luke. "Let's get this back in the water. Think you can manage to keep me from getting knocked down again?" he asked Luke.

"Oh I'll do my best. Salmon love a fight though. He seems to have settled down now," Luke replied.

Nathan looked down at the king salmon, which lay still on the deck, its gills laboring. "Good size one, at least fifty pounds," he said. With efficiency, he and Luke went into motion. Luke held the salmon's mouth open while Nathan grabbed the hook and carefully worked it out. In short order, he picked the salmon up and lifted it over the side of the boat, holding it steady in the water for a moment before gently letting go.

* * *

THE SILVER of the salmon flashed briefly in the water before disappearing under the waves. Tess stared out over the water for a moment to see if it would reappear, but all she saw was the sun's reflection against the water. She lifted her gaze to look at the volcano sitting in the distance. She'd read plenty of tourist materials on the flight to Alaska from North Carolina and learned that she was looking at Mount Augustine, which sat alone in this area of Kachemak Bay. It rose starkly from the water, wispy clouds floating around the top. It had erupted twice in recent decades, once spewing ash for days at a time. The latest eruption had been subtler, if there was such a thing as a subtle volcanic eruption, but ash had still disrupted flights in and out of Alaska. The volcano seemed lonely to her, but then she wondered if she thought practically everything seemed lonely since most of the time she felt that way. With a mental shake, she turned to look towards her father.

He was getting ready to drop his line back in the water, listening patiently to one of the guides about the best way to prep his line. His smile was wide. This fishing trip to Diamond Creek, Alaska was a dream for him. He'd planned to go for years. Her mother, Celine, had come on the trip with them, but was prone to seasickness, so she'd stayed ashore to visit the many tourist shops in town. Tess had joined them for this trip in addition to her brother, Simon, and his son, nine-year old Jordan. While Tess might not be the fishing connoisseur that her father was, she loved the outdoors and enjoyed fishing.

Tess shifted her gaze to Nathan who was talking to her father. The three Winters brothers ran the guiding business, The One that Didn't Get Away. Tess guessed Nathan to be the youngest. All three had almost identical black wavy hair. The only difference in how unruly it was. Nathan's was the shaggiest, his black curls almost touching his shoulders. He had dark blue eyes while the other two brothers had green eyes. Tess had to keep dragging her eyes away from Nathan, which annoyed the hell out of her. He was the quintessential outdoorsman—handsome with a rugged, sexy edge—so sexy that a mere glance sent her pulse wild.

He and his brothers had been nothing but kind and funny. They happily regaled her father with fishing stories and earnestly shared his love of all things fish. She could tell they'd let him talk all day and that earned major points with her. They were also kind to Jordan who was so excited about this trip he was practically vibrating. He was a relentless font of questions, filled with a sense of curiosity and wonder.

Her father caught her absentminded stare and waved her over. She stepped around a cooler and dodged a fishing pole with the few steps it took to get to him.

"Tess, honey, I was just telling Nathan here that I used to take you and Simon fishing when we went out to Cape Hatteras in the summers. It made me remember that time you caught a giant grouper," her father said, curling an arm across her shoulders.

Her father looked towards Nathan again. "She was around Jordan's age, eight or nine, and had a blast tugging that fish into the boat. Grouper's good to eat. Not quite as famous as Alaskan salmon and halibut, but cooked right, it's delicious."

Nathan turned his bright blue eyes to her. They crinkled

at the corners when he smiled. "So have you inherited your father's love of fishing? Or you're just a good sport and tag along because you know he loves it?" he asked with a wink.

Tess felt her lips curling in a smile, almost in spite of herself. Butterflies swirled in her center, rattling her composure. Nathan's smile was sparks to tinder—hers, that is. She forced her attention to the moment, tilting her head to the side and glancing to her father. "It's a bit of both. I almost always go fishing with my dad, so you could say I tag along. But then, I love it whenever I go. Hoping to take my turn at a halibut in a bit here. I was just waiting to give dad a chance to be the first to catch one."

Her father smiled even wider, if that was possible. He was so damn happy since they'd stepped off the plane here, just about everything elicited a smile.

Nathan glanced back and forth between them. "That makes your dad happy," he said with a chuckle. "Whenever you're ready, let me know. May not have known your dad long, but I doubt he cares who catches the first halibut."

Tess didn't try to avoid smiling this time. "You're right about my dad, which is why I want him to catch the first halibut. As much as he loves to fish, this is his to take." She looked to her father again. "Get that line back in the water before Jordan or Simon beats you to it. You love talking about fishing as much as actually fishing, but you can talk and fish at the same time." She leaned her shoulder into him with a soft push. "I'll sit with you." She turned back to Nathan. "If he doesn't bring a halibut up in the next half hour, how about helping me get going?"

Nathan nodded. "Of course. That's my job."

"How about you help me get set up this time?" her father asked Nathan. "I thought I knew how far to let the line go, but I'm not sure."

Her father's arm slid off her shoulders as he turned to step to the side of the boat. Nathan gave her a long look before he followed her father. Her heart fluttered and she felt a flash of heat in her core. It had been so long since she'd felt that way towards any man, it was unsettling. She distracted herself by looking around the boat. Jared appeared to be the assigned boat driver. He stood at the helm, holding the steering wheel in a relaxed grip. Of the three brothers, he was the most reserved, but still friendly with a wry sense of humor. Luke, the other brother, was busy talking with Jordan. He knelt beside Jordan and appeared to be explaining something related to nautical knots as he held a length of boat line in his hands and gestured to one of the knots. Jordan nodded along. While Tess couldn't hear what they were saying over the wind on the water, she could hear the tone of their voices, Jordan's lilting in the way it did when he was asking question upon question. The fluttering in her heart had stopped and the heat subsided inside. She shook her head. The last thing she needed was to get worked up over some fishing guide from Alaska.

The pace of the day picked up with her father catching the first halibut of the day, Jordan following with another catch and finally her brother. With Nathan's help, Tess got a line in and felt a tug on the line within minutes. Luke was nearby with Nathan, both helping get fish situated in the cooler. Luke looked over when Tess exclaimed, "That was fast!"

"Sometimes it's all timing—seems to be on your side. Hold steady and reel in at a slow, even speed," Luke said.

Before she knew it, Tess was looking at the flat eye on one side of the halibut. A few fish later, Jared had turned the boat towards Otter Cove, the boat harbor for Diamond Creek. Tess sat on a bench at the back of the boat. The salty wind blew through her curls as the boat bounced in a rocking rhythm on the waves. Turning back towards the ocean, she took a long look at Mount Augustine. The cushion shifted under her legs. She turned forward again to find Nathan sitting down beside her.

"So how was your first day on the water here? In love with Alaska yet?" he asked.

Despite her usual reserve, Tess felt herself smiling without thinking. She was disconcerted by how easily charmed she was by Nathan. His nearness flushed her, just *melted* her reserve. Nathan waited patiently for her to respond. Little did he know she was just trying to get her bearings. His presence was potent, her body humming while her mind reminded her not to be silly.

"My first day on the water here was pretty good. Dad has wanted to fish in Alaska forever. I'm glad he's finally here," Tess said politely.

Nathan's eyes took on a mischievous glimmer. "Your dad was an easy mark to love it. But...I meant how was *your* day?" Nathan asked.

Tess looked back at Nathan, his dark blue eyes crinkled at the corners, his shaggy curls in disarray. Paired with those amazing eyes, Nathan had chiseled features with a perfectly proportioned nose sitting between sculpted cheekbones and a strong chin. Much as she resisted it, just looking at him raised the heat inside her. She looked away, not comfortable with how much she wanted to keep looking into the deep blue of his eyes. That inconvenient melting sensation flared.

"Didn't realize you'd need to think so hard to answer," Nathan commented wryly, his words bringing her attention back.

Tess looked back into his eyes for just a moment, giving in to the temptation to tumble into that mesmerizing blue. Since the way her last relationship had splintered about a year ago, she rarely let herself think much about how she felt. It was easier. But she was in Alaska for a three-week stay. Allowing herself to indulge the intense yearning

Nathan elicited wouldn't matter in the long run. After they left, she'd likely never see or hear from Nathan or anyone in Alaska again.

"Okay, how was my day? My day was good. It's beautiful here, no doubt about that. I love being on the ocean anywhere and Alaska's no different. Except for getting a view of mountains, glaciers and a volcano. That's an amazing sight to witness. Plus, catching a halibut in under fifteen minutes was fun," she finally said.

Nathan's quick grin only raised the heat inside. "I'd like to take the credit for how fast you hooked that halibut, but it's clear you've had some experience with fishing. And the view here is pretty phenomenal. We love it. That's one of the reasons we moved here."

Her heart racing—dear god she practically needed to fan herself—Tess found herself asking a question before she had a chance to stop herself. "Where did you move from?"

"Seattle. Like your dad, our dad loves to fish, so we grew up fishing in Washington waters. We decided to start a commercial fishing business down there together and eventually came up here to fish a few times. Liked it so much that we relocated the business and ourselves up here. Can't imagine living anywhere else now."

"Diamond Creek is a bit of a change from Seattle," she said.

"Up here, we live somewhere we love instead of planning to travel here. Kind of like your dad really. Sounds like he spends a lot of time visiting places he might rather live."

"You can say that," Tess said, relieved that polite conversation seemed to slow her heart rate. "Where he lives in North Carolina, he's right on a river, so he gets to fish pretty often. But he likes to try different places. Alaska's been on his fishing bucket list for years."

The wind had started to pick up. The boat rode into a large swell, followed by a smaller choppy wave that threw

Tess against Nathan's side. He reflexively put his arm around her waist. Just when Tess thought she'd gotten a hold of herself, her heart was off to the races, her stomach fluttering. His arm was warm and strong against her back. She wanted to lean into him and stay that way. She glanced up at Nathan and found him looking down toward her intently. Her heart gave a quiver and the simmering heat in her center turned up a notch. Nathan's hand rested just against her hip. He flexed against the soft curve, a subtle caress. She gasped and tore her eyes away, the water a blur of whitecaps in her muddled gaze. Nathan's loosened his grip and let go, his hand curling the bottom of the bench again. Her body immediately missed his touch, sighing at its absence.

Whether he meant it or not, Tess wondered if he was reacting to her confusion. His gaze had been direct...ardent. Yet she'd looked away...the moment passed. Relief and disappointment tinged with sadness clashed. If she imagined herself to be someone else, someone that could just let go and enjoy this attraction, it would be so much simpler.

Nathan called out to Jared. "Looks like the wind is kicking in. Want me to take over steering for a bit? You've been at it all day."

Jared called back without turning. "No worry. Be to the harbor inside of a half hour."

Nathan shook his head. "That's Jared. Can hardly stand it if we offer to help for something he thinks is his job."

Curiosity rose in Tess. She wanted to know more about his family. While Nathan could have sounded critical, his comment had a loving tone to it.

"So I guess he usually drives?" she asked.

"Almost always. But it's okay. We may be brothers, but we get along better than most. Luke and I take care of whatever Jared doesn't," he said. 'Speaking of that, nice chatting for a few, but I have to take care of a few things before we get to the harbor." He stood from the bench and looked down at her, another easy grin gracing his face. "Don't suppose I could persuade you to go to dinner with me sometime in the few weeks you're here?"

Tess flushed head to toe, her heart danced and those magnetic eyes of his stoked the smoldering heat in her center. She wanted to jump up and say yes, and *that* annoyed the hell out of her. Her cautious side was dominant, oh-so-practical. She could recite by heart all the reasons any romantic entanglement wasn't worth it. Though practical and safe, it was a lonely place to be. A tattered corner of her heart wanted more. Before she knew it, she was answering honestly. "I'm not sure. I don't know what our plans are for the next few days."

His grin didn't waver. "Think about it. Diamond Creek may seem like it's the middle of nowhere, but we have some good restaurants here. You'll be seeing me again either way. Your dad booked us for four more trips."

Tess nodded. "Okay, maybe. I'll think about it." As soon as the words slipped out, Tess couldn't believe she'd said them. The last thing she needed was this way too handsome Alaskan fishing guide to take her on a date.

Nathan winked and turned away, striding to the boat's small cabin. His back muscles flexed as his arms swung. She could only imagine what kind of shape he was in, given the active life he and his brothers led. He was tall, easily over six feet, with broad, strong shoulders and a rangy build. He seemed far too handsome to consider her worthy of a date. While Tess didn't consider herself unattractive, her last boyfriend had often made passive comments about her being a little too curvy. Her breasts were prone to spilling out of blouses. She was on the short side and could rarely find tops that fit right as they seemed to be designed for thinner women. She absentmindedly tucked her hair behind her ears, her honey-colored curls getting wild in the wind.

She spent the remainder of the ride watching the shore get closer, trying and failing to keep her mind and eyes off of Nathan. The shoreline here was nothing like the ocean shore in North Carolina, which was bright sand, patches of tall grass and swaths of flat beaches with the occasional sand dune. In Alaska, the ocean splashed against glaciers, mountainsides and rocky beaches. The shore in Diamond Creek included steep cliffs, leveling off into lush green spruce forests, and beaches of gray sand covered in colorful rocks. Otter Cove was the name of the tiny cove in which the boat harbor was tucked, protected somewhat from winds and cold. Jared deftly steered the boat into its slip at the harbor docks. Nathan and Luke were ready the minute they pulled in, tossing lines over the dock pilings. Tess's eyes were glued to Nathan. He was tall and lanky, his sinewy muscles rippling under his cotton shirt. Jared cut the engine and quickly went into motion, getting the two full coolers ready to pass over to Nathan and Luke on the docks.

After stepping off the boat, Tess, her father, brother and nephew entered a whirl of activity. Within an hour, she was waving goodbye to Nathan and his brothers as Simon drove their car rental way from the Fish Factory, the local business that would be flash freezing and mailing their halibut back to North Carolina on overnight delivery. A friend of her father's would be picking up the packages and depositing them in the chest freezer in her parents' garage.

Tess looked out the car window and saw Nathan give a wave. Her hand lifted in return. He flashed a wide grin. She couldn't believe he had her even considering a date with him. Just as she started to turn away, Nathan turned to look towards Jared and stepped into one of the small boulders lining the parking lot. He stumbled into Luke who was beside him and then onto the ground. Before she looked away, she saw him look in their direction again and couldn't help but laugh. As handsome as he was, he seemed to have a knack for falling, at least today.

Read Tess & Nathan's story!

Follow Love

Go HERE to sign up for information on new releases: http://jhcroixauthor.com/subscribe/

TO CHECK out my next series, please enjoy the following excerpt from Take Me Home, the first book in the Last Frontier Lodge Series!

SNEAK PEEK: TAKE ME HOME

*M*arley Adams walked up the old ski trail, taking in the view around her. The air held a bite of winter though fall had yet to entirely pass. Cresting the top of the trail where an abandoned ski lift sat, she turned and looked behind her. Her breath caught in her throat. Kachemak Bay lay sparkling in the sun. Mountains rose behind it on the far shore, snow-tipped and bright. She was home. Home was Diamond Creek, Alaska, a fishing village and tourist mecca in Southcentral Alaska. Breathtaking views, wildlife galore, and a tight-knit community of independent, hardy souls. The place she couldn't wait to get away from once she graduated high school. Today, she let her heart soak it in, the one and only place that ever felt like home.

She breathed in the bracing autumn air, scented with spruce and the hint of snow to come. The ground danced with color. Most of fall in Alaska happened underfoot as the landscape was heavily forested with evergreens. She turned around and eyed the ski lift. The lift swayed and creaked in the breeze. It felt like a lifetime ago when her parents had brought her up here with her sister to ski when they were little girls. The exhilaration of rushing down the bunny slope and tumbling into the soft net at the bottom was vivid in her memory. Sometime during her childhood, the ski lodge had closed and stayed empty all the years since.

Curiosity drew her to walk up to the tiny building by the lift. She wiped her arm over the smudged window and peered inside. A woodstove sat in the corner and a bench along one wall. A first aid kit was on the floor and a discarded jacket on the bench.

"Excuse me, are you aware you're trespassing?"

Marley leapt away from the window with a squeak, whirling around to find a man leaning against the corner of the building. The man in question had short brown hair, gray eyes, sharp features, and a body that looked as if it had been sculpted in stone. Even though it was chilly enough for her to wear a lightweight jacket, he wore nothing over the t-shirt that hugged his muscled chest and arms. His legs were rock-hard and encased in sleek running pants. He looked as if he was out for a run. His gray eyes held hers. They were bright gray, as if they held lightning inside. His energy was potent masculinity. He didn't seem unfriendly, but neither did he appear welcoming. Against all reason, her body hummed at the sight of him. He was just...pure man.

"You startled me," she finally replied.

The man arched a brow and remained silent.

"Um, I hiked up the old ski trail. I didn't know that was a problem. We used to do it all the time when I was growing up."

The man nodded slowly. His gray eyes left her and traveled around the view, landing back on the small building he leaned against. "Right. Should have guessed that," he finally said.

Marley had never seen this man and though she'd lived away from Diamond Creek for over a decade, she came home for visits every year and knew most of the locals. If she didn't know them, her parents did. As far as she knew, no one had lived at Last Frontier Lodge for years. Residents still lamented its closure.

"Are you from around here?" she finally asked.

The man's mouth tightened. If she'd known him, she might have thought sadness flashed through his eyes.

"Depends on how you define that."

"I grew up in Diamond Creek. I used to ski here when I was a little girl. I haven't lived in town for a while, but last I knew, this place was closed and empty." She took a breath, gathering her courage. Her heart raced wildly, and she struggled to keep her composure. Whoever this man was, he had a hell of an effect on her. She couldn't even think clearly enough to introduce herself. "I'm Marley Adams. I live down the road from here," she finally said, gesturing vaguely in the direction of the little cabin on her parents' property where she'd recently moved.

Those gray eyes landed on her again. For a minute, she thought he wasn't going to respond. He cleared his throat. "I'm Gage Hamilton. My grandparents used to own this place. I was born in Diamond Creek, but my parents moved away when I was little. My, uh..." He paused and closed his eyes, grimacing slightly. When he opened his eyes again, she knew for sure what she saw was sadness. "...grandmother died recently and left the lodge to me and my younger siblings. I always loved it here when we came to visit, so I moved here. I'm planning to fix the place up and reopen, hopefully this winter."

"Oh. I'm so sorry about your grandmother," Marley said, uncertain what else to offer.

Gage nodded tightly. "Thanks. I was pretty close to her. Still getting used to the fact that she's gone."

Marley nodded, curiosity swirling inside, but she sensed now wasn't the time to ask the many questions as she had.

"It's great you're planning to reopen the ski lodge. People still talk about it back when it was open. Aside from staying busy with locals, this place was hopping all winter long with tourists."

"That's what I'm hoping for." He paused and glanced at her again, his eyes softer. "I didn't mean to sound harsh when I asked about the trespassing thing. I came up for a run and didn't know who you were, so…"

"Oh, it's okay. You should know plenty of locals hike up here and use the old trails for cross-country skiing. It's not like people don't know someone else owns it, it's just no one's been here for so long, people figure it's okay."

Gage nodded slowly. "I was thinking maybe I should make some kind of announcement, but I haven't quite sorted out the details yet."

"Oh. Well, as soon as word travels that you're here and plan to reopen, you might want to be ready for lots of people showing up to say hi," she said wryly. "Diamond Creek's a small town. This is big news."

Gage smiled, and Marley thought she might swoon. Dear God, he had a dangerous smile. When he wasn't smiling, he had that whole, smoldering sexy and kind of intimidating vibe—just enough to keep her body in check. When he smiled, her body spun like a top inside—heat and electricity swirling. His eyes crinkled at the corners, the gray brightening and his mouth softening.

Get a grip, Marley. You've known this man for less than five minutes. If she let her body talk, all she could think about was what it would feel like to run her hands over his body, which was nothing short of a miracle. Though if she touched him, she'd likely melt on the spot.

Gage cleared his throat. "So, how far away do you live from here?"

"About a quarter mile down the road from the entrance to the lodge. My parents own about ten acres adjacent to the lodge. Their house is further down the road. I moved into a small cabin they used to rent out to tourists in the summer. It's tiny, but it's got everything I need."

Gage nodded. "Well, feel free to walk around here as much as you want. I suppose I'd better come up with some kind of plan to handle the locals hikers, huh?"

Marley shrugged. "People won't expect to be able to do whatever they want once you get this place up and running. So you needn't worry. You might want to notify the town hall and maybe put a notice up in the paper. Otherwise, someone being helpful might call the police if they don't know who you are and see you around the property."

Gage threw his head back with a laugh. Her stomach burst full of butterflies. She shook her head and forced herself to look away.

"I'll take it as a good sign that I have to worry about that." Gage followed her gaze out over the bay. "Well, I'm gonna keep running. Sounds like I'll see you around."

She nodded. "I'm sure you will. If you need anything, just stop by. You can see my place from the entrance to the lodge. It's the little cabin with a red roof sitting on the hill nearby."

Gage grinned. "I've seen it. Well, I'm off. Enjoy your walk," he said with a quick wave before he took off running. He went around the ski lift and turned up onto the next trail nearby—a much steeper and more advanced trail—and proceeded to run up at a steady pace. Marley had never run up that trail, but she knew without a doubt it would be grueling. He ran without his pace changing. No wonder he was in such good shape. She finally turned away and began her descent, the view stretching before her.

For the first time in months, she obsessed about something other than the crash and burn of her grand plans to make something of herself. Gage filled her mind—his rock hard body, his sensual mouth…and whoever he was behind his guarded nature.

* * *

GAGE PUSHED himself up the trail, his legs finally beginning to tire when he reached the top and paused beside another ski lift. He turned and looked behind him. He could see Marley walking down the trail below. He'd seen her long before she paused at the small building between trails. He'd only been at the ski lodge for a week, but he'd already memorized the pattern of trails and had been cutting across between two trails when he heard her walking. He'd paused in the edge of the woods and watched her. Her auburn hair glinted in the sun. Curiosity drew him to approach her. Why he felt the need to start off by confronting her about trespassing was beyond him. He shook his head. Not exactly the best way to introduce himself to his new neighbor.

From a distance, he'd thought she was beautiful. Up close, she took his breath away. Her wavy auburn hair was paired with forest green eyes, a pert nose, and a sensual mobile mouth—so kissable, he'd had to restrain himself. To make his body tread the edge of embarrassing himself, her body was flat out beautiful—curvy and athletic at once. She'd worn a green fleece jacket zipped halfway, which revealed a thin cotton shirt pulled tight across her breasts, her nipples peaked in the chilly air. From there, her waist dipped then curved into lush hips and strong legs hugged by her fitted leggings. She'd seemed entirely oblivious to the effect she had on him. Wearing his form-fitting running clothes had forced him to rein his body in and required so much attention, he knew he'd come across as a little too brusque. As he watched her walk down the trail, her auburn hair caught in the wind, flying wild behind her.

Marley. He turned the name over in his mind. It suited

her though he couldn't say why since he barely knew her. He watched her until she rounded a curve in the trail and vanished from sight. With a sigh, he glanced around. The building beside this stopping point for the ski lift was also in dire need of a new coat of paint. He turned in a circle. The vantage point up here offered a three hundred and sixty degree view. Kachemak Bay lay glittering under the sun in one direction, Cook Inlet could be seen beyond that with Mount Augustine, a volcano, rising in the waters. In the other direction lay Mount Illiamna, another volcano. Southcentral Alaska lay within the Ring of Fire, an area within the Pacific basin where over seventy-five percent of the world's active and dormant volcanoes lay. As a little boy, Gage had loved this detail about his birthplace.

Returning to Alaska and his grandparent's ski lodge was a childhood dream. His parents had moved away when he and his four younger siblings were little. They went to visit Last Frontier Lodge every summer until his grandmother had closed down the lodge after his grandfather passed away. She'd moved to Bellingham, Washington to live with his parents until she passed away. Gage had long ago let go of his childhood dream to return to Alaska because life... happened. Dreams turned into fragments of hope and hope was hard to find for him anymore. He'd recently retired from the Navy after years of active duty as a Navy SEAL and had been struggling to find a way for life to make sense.

Gage had been surprised to learn his grandmother had left the lodge to him and his siblings since he hadn't even known it was still in the family. He'd inherited the largest share of the lodge with her will stipulating the lodge must be reopened within one year, or they would be required to sell it and divide the profits. He'd assumed she'd sold it as she rarely spoke of it. At loose ends and searching for something to give his life meaning again, he hadn't hesitated for a minute to move to Alaska. The neglected state of the ski lodge would give him something to focus on beyond what he'd stared down on one of his last missions.

He took a last look around and began jogging slowly down the trail. An eagle flew across the trail ahead of him, its wings casting a wide shadow on the ground. Magpies chattered in the trees. When he reached the lodge again, he jogged down the drive to the road and looked toward the cabin he now knew to be Marley's. It was hard to miss with its bright red roof practically glowing amongst the deep green spruce trees surrounding it. He turned and looked at the sign for the lodge. It hung at a drunken angle, one of the chains holding it up broken. The lettering on the sign was faded—something else to replace. He looked at Marley's cabin again, sitting on a small rise, a cheery picturesque home. Her auburn hair, green eyes, and sensual mouth flashed in his mind. The mere flicker of her and his body reacted.

READ MARLEY & Gage's story!
Take Me Home

GO HERE to sign up for information on new releases: http://jhcroixauthor.com/subscribe/

FIND MY BOOKS

Thank you for reading When Love Comes! I hope you enjoyed the story. If so, you can help other readers find my books in a variety of ways.

1) Write a review!

2) Sign up for my newsletter, so you can receive information about upcoming new releases & receive a FREE copy of one of my books: http://jhcroixauthor.com/subscribe/

3) Like and follow my Amazon Author page at https://amazon.com/author/jhcroix

4) Follow me on Bookbub at https://www.bookbub.com/authors/j-h-croix

5) Follow me on Twitter at https://twitter.com/JHCroix

6) Like my Facebook page at https://www.facebook.com/jhcroix

* * *

Diamond Creek Alaska Novels

When Love Comes
Follow Love
Love Unbroken
Love Untamed
Tumble Into Love
Christmas Nights

Last Frontier Lodge Novels

Take Me Home
Love at Last
Just This Once
Falling Fast
Stay With Me
When We Fall
Hold Me Close
Crazy For You

Into The Fire Series

Burn For Me
Slow Burn
Burn So Bad
Hot Mess
Burn So Good

Brit Boys Sports Romance

The Play
Big Win
Out Of Bounds
Play Me
Naughty Wish

Shameless Southern Nights (with Ali Parker)

Down & Dirty #1
Down & Dirty #2
Down & Dirty #3

Catamount Lion Shifters

Protected Mate
Chosen Mate
Fated Mate

Destined Mate
A Catamount Christmas
Ghost Cat Shifters
The Lion Within
Lion Lost & Found

ABOUT THE AUTHOR

USA Today Bestselling Author J. H. Croix lives in a small town in the historical farmlands of Maine with her husband and two spoiled dogs. Croix writes steamy contemporary romance with sassy independent women and rugged alpha men who aren't afraid to show some emotion. Her love for quirky small-towns and the characters that inhabit them shines through in her writing. Take a walk on the wild side of romance with her bestselling novels!

Places you can find me:
jhcroixauthor.com
jhcroix@jhcroix.com

Made in the USA
Las Vegas, NV
19 March 2021